THEY WISHED HER
A HAPPY BIRTHDAY . . .

Lady Balaclava stood up. "And now, I shall drink to you . . . but as our guest of honor, Henry shall have first go at everything."
Feeling very foolish, Henry took a bite of the cake. It was delicious.
"Now the champagne . . . from *my* glass."
Henry took a sip. It, too, was excellent.
"And now the roses." He buried his nose among the blooms and smiled with pleasure.
"Ah," said Lady Balaclava. Laughing gaily, she took a bite from the marzipan cake, a sip from her glass, and a long, luxuriant sniff at the roses.
She got no further. Suddenly with a bewildered expression, she gasped and fell. Henry caught her in his arms as she collapsed like a rag doll.
"For God's sake," he cried. "Get a doctor! Quick!"

. . . AND MANY DEADLY RETURNS

MURDER INK.® MYSTERIES

SCENE OF THE CRIME™ MYSTERIES

A Murder Ink.® Mystery

MANY DEADLY RETURNS

Patricia Moyes

A DELL BOOK

Published by
Dell Publishing Co., Inc.
1 Dag Hammarskjold Plaza
New York, New York 10017

This book has been published in England under
the title of *Who Saw Her Die?*

Dell ® TM 681510, Dell Publishing Co., Inc.

ISBN: 0-440-16172-X

Reprinted by arrangement with Holt, Rinehart and Winston

Printed in the United States of America
First Dell printing—April 1981

FOR PIERRE DOROLLE

1

It was not a large apartment, but it was full of sunshine and furnished with slightly austere good taste, and its big picture window looked out over a sweeping view across Lake Geneva to the mountains beyond. In the small room that was furnished as an office, the telephone on the white-wood desk began to ring.

It was answered almost at once by a dark, stocky man who came into the office through the connecting door from the living room.

"Dr. Duval speaking." His French was tinged with the rich, rough edge of a Valaisan accent, which had survived his move from the mountains to the gentler lakeside landscape of the canton of Vaud. "Oh, it's you, Pierre. Nice to hear from you. . . . Yes, just got home yesterday. . . . The answer? What do *you* think? 'No,' of course . . . the Institute is politely interested, but when it comes to hard cash for a research project . . . no, no, I'm not too depressed . . . getting used to it by now. . . ." The dark man lit a cigarette deftly with his free hand, and laughed. "Certainly there's a way, my friend. Beg, borrow, or steal a fortune, and finance the laboratory myself. . . . Well, a man can dream, can't he?" Duval's eyes were on the distant mountain peaks. "That's very kind of you . . . when? Saturday next? That's . . ." He glanced at a big calendar on the wall. "That's the fifteenth of June, isn't it? I think we'd love to . . . around eight . . . splendid . . . I'll just have to check with Primrose . . . she's out shopping right now, but unless I ring back . . . thanks a lot, Pierre . . . love to Simone. . . ."

It was only a minute or so after Dr. Duval had rung off that he heard the front door opening. He called out, in English, "Is that you, dear?"

"Of course it is, Edouard. What a silly question." Primrose Duval came into the living room, her arms full of parcels. She was a thin, blond woman in her forties, who could only have been English. She looked as though a puff of wind would blow her away—cotton frock, cardigan, string of pearls, and all—and as though she would not venture to say "Boo" to a sparrow, let alone a goose. This appearance of fragility was utterly misleading, as her husband knew well. Primrose had a will not so much of iron as of flexible steel. Like the proverbial reed, she would bend but not break.

"Pierre Rey just rang," said Edouard Duval.

"I've asked you a thousand times, Edouard, to use *one* ashtray, not ten." Primrose laid a stack of parcels on the dining table by the window. "Look. Four separate ashtrays, each with one small speck of ash in it. Now they'll all have to be washed."

"I'm sorry, dear."

"You always say that, but you go on doing it. It's not as if I had a full-time *femme de ménage* to do the housework. What did Pierre want?"

"To ask if I'd had any luck with the Institute in Paris. I told him the bad news. Oh—and he and Simone want us to go to dinner next Saturday. I said we'd go."

"Oh, really, Edouard—you can be maddening."

"What have I done now?"

Primrose was studying her pale face in a wall mirror. She ran her long fingers through her dust-blond hair. "It's time I went into Lausanne for another perm. Another sixty francs to scrape out of the housekeeping. You know perfectly well we can't go to dinner on Saturday."

"Why not?"

Primrose turned to face her husband, and spoke quietly and deliberately, as though to a backward child. "Because it's the fifteenth. Mother's birthday. We shall be in England."

"Merde!"

"Edouard! Just because you have forgotten—"

"It's not just because I'd forgotten, although of course I had. But you know exactly my opinion of your mother and her birthday. Why on earth we have to submit to this pantomime every year—"

"Please, Edouard. We've been into all this before. It's a family tradition, and we can't break it."

"I shall be very busy at the hospital next week. Why don't you go to England alone? You can take the cake, which is all your mother cares about." Dr. Duval sounded like a sulky schoolboy.

Primrose said, "Don't be childish, Edouard. I'll call Simone and tell her we can't dine."

"The sooner your mother dies, the better it will be for everybody," said Edouard Duval.

"Well, she's as strong as a horse and as fit as a fiddle, so you can put *that* idea out of your head," said Primrose tartly. "Besides," she added, "I'm really very fond of her. . . ."

"You are a liar, my Primrose," said the doctor. He seemed to have recovered his good humor. "She embarrasses you dreadfully, and if you had to see her more than once a year, it would kill you. You remember what happened the one time she came here?"

Primrose smiled at him in the mirror. "I'd better telephone Bonnet's about the cake," she said.

In the mirror Dr. Edouard Duval smiled back at his wife. They understood each other very well.

The little Dutch house stood on its own small island, in the crisscross of canals which make a sort of archipelago of that part of South Holland. Behind the house, the island was precisely cultivated into row after row of carefully tended plants, and a plank bridge connected it with the neighboring island, which was entirely covered in glasshouses. For this was Aalsmeer, and it is in Aalsmeer, clustered around the famous auction building, that the greater part of Holland's cut flowers are grown. A neat wooden notice on the lawn in front of the small house announced that P. van der Hoven was a grower of first-class blooms for the wholesale market. It was superfluous to add that he specialized in roses, for this was self-evident.

Piet van der Hoven himself was in the largest of the greenhouses, inspecting the big, beautiful Baccarat roses, which grew in obedient abundance, each dark scarlet head as symmetrically perfect as a guardsman's busby in a military parade. Piet himself was neither symmetrical nor military in appearance. He was large and untidy, with a lock of fair hair perpetually falling over his broad forehead and obscuring one of his candid blue eyes.

His wife, as she walked down the warm, scented aisle of the glasshouse, thought that he looked like a clumsy Labrador puppy; touching, in a way—but puppies can be irritating, too. Especially when they fawn at one's feet all day, tripping one up, smothering one with untidy affection. Violet van der Hoven was dark and neat, with small features and finely shaped hands and feet. At thirty-eight she was five years older than her husband—a state of affairs which had provoked dire forebodings of disaster from her elder sister at the time of the wedding; but despite Primrose's gloomy prophecies, the van der Hovens had been married for seven years already, and Piet appeared to be more in love with his wife than ever.

Now, hearing Violet's light step on the concrete floor, he looked up from his work, and his amiable face split into a huge smile of welcome.

"Darling," he said. "What are you doing here? Is it time for lunch already? Am I late?"

Violet could not help smiling back. The puppy was very endearing.

"No," she said. "It's not twelve yet."

"How pretty you look." Piet pushed the perpetual lock of hair out of his left eye. "Is that a new dress?"

"This?" Violet laughed, a little bitterly. "What a

memory you have! I bought this two years ago at C. & A. for twenty-five guilders."

"Well, it looks charming."

"I had a letter from Daffy this morning," said Violet, not changing the subject. She caressed a rose bloom in her slim fingers.

"Oh, yes?" Piet had returned to his work. "What did she say?"

"Just that she's in Paris, restocking her wardrobe before she and Chuck go back to the States. She says Cardin's collection is a dream."

Piet grinned at her from behind the plant he was tending. "All right, all right. I get the point. Unfortunately, my dear, even the best rose-grower in Aalsmeer doesn't make a fortune these days. If you wanted to buy clothes at Cardin instead of C. & A., you should have done like your sister, and married an American millionaire."

"Perhaps I should," said Violet. But she said it quietly, and Piet did not hear. Louder, she added, "You haven't forgotten the roses for Mother's birthday, have you?"

"My Violet, have I ever? I am keeping two dozen of my finest Baccarats—these here. I shall cut them on Friday evening, just before we leave for the Hook."

"As a matter of fact," said Violet, "I think this birthday-tradition business is a lot of nonsense."

"That is because you are English. Here in Holland, we respect birthdays."

"God, you don't have to remind me of *that*. Spending the whole day sitting around a table, smiling and making small talk, while the entire family and all one's friends and acquaintances drop in and out, each of them bringing a present worth a guilder and eating and drinking a good five guilders' worth—"

"At least," said Piet, with unruffled good humor, "your mother's birthday isn't like that."

"No, thank heaven," said Violet. After a pause she added, "I hope to goodness she hasn't invited any of her terrible friends this year. It's bad enough with just the family and Dolly—but when she drags out those gargoyles

. . . 'Tiny' This and 'Tubby' That and 'Babsie' Something Else, all in their sprightly sixties, all reminiscing about the gay old days at the Kit-Kat and the Embassy and Quags . . ."

"I have always found your mother's friends charming," said Piet.

"Piet," said Violet, "you're too good to live. I'll go and get lunch."

Daffodil Swasheimer stood in front of the full-length triple mirror in her suite at the Hotel Crillon, regarding herself with narrowed, critical eyes. Several large packages with Cardin labels had just been carried reverently upstairs by the hotel staff. Now Daffodil was trying on her purchases and gauging their effect.

She could find little to criticize, either in the clothes or in herself. She was thirty-three years old, with the figure of a fashion model, coppery-blond hair, a creamy complexion, regular features, and dark blue eyes. In fact, she had been working as a mannequin when, five years ago, she had met and married Charles Z. Swasheimer. As one of a team of six model girls, she had been in the United States on a "Boost British Fashion" tour, and she had been introduced to Chuck Swasheimer at a New York cocktail party.

"Be nice to him, darling," one of the other girls had whispered. "Millionaire. Kitchen sinks."

Daffodil had eyed Mr. Swasheimer coolly and appraisingly. She had judged him to be about sixty, gray-haired and not bad-looking in a rugged sort of way. It was hard to see the man, really, through the thick veneer of his wealth—the impeccable suit, the expensive after-shave aura, the touches of gold everywhere: cufflinks, tie pin, cigarette lighter, the occasional tooth.

Daffodil had said, without preamble, "I believe you make kitchen sinks, Mr. Swasheimer."

Chuck had been surprised. As a rule nobody mentioned the source of his wealth on social occasions. "Why, yes. So I do."

"Then we have a lot in common," said Daffodil. "My great-grandfather invented the first self-flushing water closet in England."

"You don't say!" exclaimed Swasheimer, enchanted. "My grandfather patented the Swasheimer U-bend evacuation pipe in 1906. Say, Miss—er—"

"Codworthy. Daffodil Codworthy."

"Well, Miss—er—Miss Daffodil . . . if you're not busy later, why not let's you and I go get ourselves a bite to eat someplace. . . ."

Six months later Charles Z. Swasheimer was divorced by the third Mrs. Charles Z. Swasheimer on the grounds of intolerable mental cruelty, and the Hon. Daffodil Codworthy became Mrs. Charles Z. Swasheimer the fourth. At last, Chuck told his friends, at last he had found a woman who took an intelligent interest in his work. He used to talk to Daffodil earnestly and for hours on end about waste-filterage systems and grease traps, and frequently remarked what a shame it was that Daffodil's father was dead, and therefore unable to swap drainage yarns with him. Daffodil agreed.

Primrose thought the whole idea of the marriage disgusting, and said so on every possible occasion. Violet was quietly jealous. It gave her some satisfaction, however, to remark that, on the rare occasions when the sisters and their husbands met, Daffodil would from time to time gaze at Piet with a distinct wistfulness. Piet never appeared to notice. He admired Mr. Swasheimer immensely, but considered Daffodil a pretty but pampered doll, who would never make a good housewife. This, for a Dutchman, is a terrible condemnation.

Daffodil struck a final attitude, straightened the back of her collar, and came out into the sitting room of the suite, where Chuck was immersed in the financial columns of *The New York Times.*

"Like it?" she asked.

He looked up, blinking through his gold-rimmed spectacles. "What? Oh, the outfit. Sure. Sure. Just dandy."

"What it really *needs*," said Daffodil thoughtfully, "is a great chunky brooch—just *here*."

"Well, why don't you wear one?"

"Because it must obviously be green, honey, and I don't have my emeralds in Europe with me."

"You can buy one, can't you?" Chuck seemed unable to understand his wife's obtuseness. "Cartier's isn't that far off. Call them and have them send some along for you to look at right away."

"Honey, you're so clever." Daffodil dropped a kiss on her husband's gray head. "I'll do that. I want to look rather special for tonight."

"Tonight? Why for tonight?"

"Because we're dining at Maxim's with Warren, remember?"

"Oh." Chuck lowered his paper. "Sorry, honey, I clean forgot to tell you. The dinner's off. Warren called while you were out shopping. Seems he has to go to Milan in a hurry—some trouble over the Italian deliveries. He sent his regrets and love to his beautiful stepmother." Swasheimer chuckled. "Between you and me, Daffy, I'm not at all that sure he has to go to Milan at all. I'd not be surprised to find him out in the Latin Quarter with a blond tonight. However—" He picked up his newspaper again.

"Well, I call it pretty inconsiderate," said Daffodil. "Ruining our evening. What shall we do now?"

"Do? Why, I thought we'd just dine here at the hotel. I've got work to do."

"Then you won't want me in your way. I'll go and have a duty dinner with Kitty Prestwether. She's been pestering me ever since we got here."

"Kitty Who?"

"You know. The Cyrus K. Prestwethers. It'll be a bore, but . . ." Daffodil picked up the house telephone. "Get me Cartier's, will you? Yes, call me back. By the way, Chuck, I suppose you've forgotten the champagne for Mother's birthday on Saturday?"

"Land sakes, so I had. Make a note of it in my diary

for me, honey, and I'll have the office fix it tomorrow. I'll have them arrange for it to be waiting for us at Dover."

Three hours later Daffodil Swasheimer—wearing her new Cardin dress with a huge diamond-and-emerald brooch—alighted from her taxi outside Maxim's Restaurant. The *maître d'hôtel* hurried to welcome her.

"I believe Mr. Swasheimer has booked a table—Mr. Warren Swasheimer . . ."

"Why, yes, Madame . . . Mr. Swasheimer is already here . . . this way. . . ."

Warren C. Swasheimer, eldest son of the first Mrs. Charles Z. Swasheimer, was thirty years old, and had recently taken charge of the Paris office of his father's firm. He was very dark—the first Mrs. Swasheimer had been a Mexican film actress—and everybody remarked on his great charm. He stood up politely as Daffodil came over to the corner table.

"How nice to see you," he said, smiling, as the waiter slid Daffodil's chair into position. "I'm so sorry Father couldn't make it."

"He's very busy," said Daffodil. "He has so little time in Europe."

"Of course. I quite understand."

The waiter produced an acreage of menu cards and withdrew. Behind the screen of listed delicacies *à la carte*, Warren took Daffodil's hand in his.

Softly he said, "Difficult, darling?"

She smiled. "Easy."

"He doesn't suspect?"

"Not a thing."

"When can I see you again?"

Daffodil laughed. "Darling, we've only just met."

"I know, but we've so little time. How long are you in Paris?"

"Until Friday evening."

"Can't you stay longer?"

"Not a hope. It's Mother's birthday. We have to go to England."

Warren looked suddenly serious. "Ah, yes. Your mother's birthday. You wouldn't want to miss that."

Daffodil looked straight at him out of her dark blue eyes. "I certainly wouldn't," she said.

"Now, look," said Warren. "I've an idea. . . ."

Two airline tickets from Geneva. A reservation for a Rolls-Royce on the Dunquerque-Dover night boat. A double cabin on the Hook-Harwich ferry. Six packed suitcases. An elaborately iced cake. Two dozen dark red roses. A case of vintage champagne. All converging on the house known as Foxes' Trot, near the village of Plumley Green in the county of Surrey.

2

"You wanted to see me, sir?" Detective Chief Superintendent Henry Tibbett closed the door of the assistant commissioner's office carefully behind him and waited respectfully for whatever might be in store.

He had a good, flexible working relationship with his superior officer at Scotland Yard, and, as far as he could think, he had done nothing to blot his copybook or rouse the wrath of the powers that were. Nevertheless, a summons to the Old Man's office was always a little unnerving. At best, it usually meant an uprooting from comfortable routine. At worst, it could be anything.

"At least, I'll know in a moment," thought Henry. One of the A.C.'s many virtues was his directness, his total lack of beating about the bush.

"Oh. Ah. Yes. Tibbett. Sit down, old man."

Henry sat down. The assistant commissioner polished his already gleaming spectacles. "Settling down well in your new office?" he asked.

"Very well, thank you, sir."

"No complaints about the general upgrading in rank, I trust?"

"Most certainly not, sir. We're all delighted."

"Good. Good. Cigarette? Mind if I smoke a pipe?"

Henry accepted a cigarette with growing bewilderment. This prevarication was completely out of character.

The A.C. lit his pipe, with a certain amount of fuss, and then said, "And your wife? Keeping fit, I trust?"

"Emmy's fine, thank you, sir."

"I . . . er . . ." A couple more energetic puffs. "I was wondering Tibbett, whether . . . that is . . . are you doing anything special at the weekend?"

"Naturally, if there's a job, sir—"

"You and your wife. You're both invited."

"Invited?"

"Yes. If you're free, of course." The assistant commissioner cleared his throat, in deep embarrassment. "Crystal—that is, Lady Balaclava—would be delighted if you and Mrs. Tibbett would be her guests for the weekend. At her place in Surrey. Plumley Green."

Henry said nothing, because he could think of nothing to say. The name Crystal Balaclava rang a bell somewhere in the back of his mind—not only because of the bizarre juxtaposition of the words, but connected with gossip columns, glossy magazines, lavish parties . . . but surely that had been long ago. Henry Tibbett, who was in his middle forties, had taken no interest in gossip columns before the Second World War, and very little after it; but he seemed to remember that even in the nineteen-fifties Lady Balaclava was referred to in a faintly surprised manner, as if the reporters were astonished to find her still in circulation. That's right. He remembered now. She had been one of the Bright Young Things of the twenties, one of the dazzling hostesses of the thirties. Now she must be rising seventy. What on earth . . . ?

The assistant commissioner had turned a becoming shade of tomato pink under Henry's baffled and silent stare. He said, "You probably think it rather strange, Tibbett. I don't believe you have met Lady Balaclava."

"No, sir. I haven't."

"Well—it's like this. Lady Balaclava has approached the Home Secretary personally. She . . . she has asked for police protection."

Henry relaxed. The situation was still puzzling, but at least it could be dealt with. "In that case, sir," he said, "it's surely a matter for the Surrey police—if the protection is warranted, that is. What is it that the lady is afraid of?"

The assistant commissioner looked unhappy. "It is rather complicated, I fear, Tibbett," he said. "The fact of the matter is—Lady Balaclava is convinced that an attempt will be made on her life."

"Good heavens. What makes her think that?"

"That's just it. She won't say. There seems to be no good reason to suspect any such thing. Of course, she is nearly seventy, and a widow, living in a large country house with just one woman companion, but—"

"If I may say so, sir—"

The assistant commissioner held up his hand. "Just a moment, Tibbett. I know what you are going to say. That here at the Yard we get half a dozen crackpot old ladies every week, all convinced that assassins are lurking under their beds. We deal with them politely and sympathetically, but firmly. We reassure them, we ask the local police patrol to keep an eye on the house—and we send them packing."

"Exactly, sir."

"Well, in this case we can't do that." The A.C. spoke almost defiantly, with some return to his usual downright manner. "The circumstances are exceptional. Is that clear?"

"Yes, sir."

"The fact is . . ." Diffidence was creeping in again. "You know who Lady Balaclava is?"

"I was just trying to recollect, sir. I seem to remember seeing her name in society magazines some years ago—"

"That's right. She was Crystal Maltravers, daughter of old Sir Giles Maltravers, and one of the brightest sparks of the twenties. You wouldn't remember, of course. Before your time. Somewhat before mine, too, but my father . . ." The A.C. smiled reminiscently. "Yes, they cut a wide swathe in London society, did Crystal and her set. Then she surprised everybody by marrying Charlie Codworthy. He was a rough diamond—immensely rich, of course. North Country. Made a fortune out of . . . em

. . . domestic appliances. A lot older than Crystal. Soon after they married, he was created Baron Balaclava. That was in the thirties. Crystal made him buy a huge house in London, as well as this place in Surrey, and they entertained like . . . well . . ." Words failed the assistant commissioner. Nobody, in his experience, had ever entertained like the Balaclavas. "Or rather, she did. My father took me along to some of their parties when I was a very young man. Lord Balaclava was never in evidence. Hardly surprising."

"No, sir," said Henry, feeling that something was expected of him.

"Well, Charlie—Lord Balaclava—was killed during the blitz, when the London house was bombed. Crystal went to live permanently at Plumley Green. After the war she tried to revive the old social atmosphere—but of course, things weren't the same. The gay old crowd had dispersed. Some had been killed during the war, some had gone abroad, others had become . . ." He hesitated.

"Respectable?" Henry suggested with a smile.

The assistant commissioner smiled back, relieved. "I was going to say 'responsible,' he said, "but I can see that we mean the same thing. Yes, the wild youngsters of the twenties were the solid, married, rapidly climbing Establishment figures of the fifties. Crystal lost touch with most of her old friends. Became something of a recluse, in fact. But now she has come up with this extraordinary request, and . . ."

"And she still has influential friends?" said Henry.

"That's just it, Tibbett." The assistant commissioner seemed more relaxed. "I'm glad you understand the position. "I myself never knew her really well—I was too young for her," he added, with simple regret. "But many men in public life today . . . the present Bishop of Battersea was engaged to her, if you can call it that, for a short time in 1923—before he entered the ministry, of course. . . . Sir Basil Uttwater of the Home Office—well, there was quite a scandal . . . forgotten now, of course, but . . . then at least two of our High Court judges were

involved in the famous bathyscope party in the Serpentine
. . . the young naval lieutenant who smuggled her out to
the Mediterranean in his battleship in 1929 is now an admiral . . . you do see what I mean?"

"I think I do, sir."

"Good. Good. Well . . . there you have it." The assistant commissioner sat back in his chair and blew his
nose loudly.

"I understand the position, sir," said Henry, "but I still
don't see why the Surrey police can't—"

"Don't be obtuse, Tibbett. Of course they can't."

"You said that she had asked for police protection."

"A figure of speech. She asked for you personally."

"But she doesn't know me from Adam!"

"She knows of you. Personally, I have always been
against the mention of officers by name in the press, but
. . . there it is. Lady Balaclava has read about you, and
she is impressed. Nobody else will do. She has therefore
invited you and your wife down to Plumley Green for the
weekend, and there is no question of taking no for an answer. You are expected on Friday evening, in time for
dinner. My secretary will give you details of the address.
Any questions?"

"Yes," said Henry.

The assistant commissioner, who had obviously decided
that the interview was over, looked surprised and not
pleased. "Well?"

"If the lady wants police protection—"

"I have already told you—"

"If she wants to be protected by me in person," Henry
amended, "I really can't see the use of my visiting her for
the weekend, with or without Emmy. Is there anything to
stop her from being murdered on Monday, after I have
left? Or are we to move into the house on a permanent
basis?"

"Ah. Yes." The A.C. shuffled some papers on his desk.
"I'm glad you raised that point. The fact is that it is Lady
Balaclava's birthday on Saturday. She is expecting . . .

that is, members of her family will be visiting her for the weekend."

"You mean," said Henry, "that she expects to be murdered by a relative."

"She didn't say that." The A.C. spoke hurriedly and with emphasis. "No, no. There is no reason to jump to that conclusion. She has merely requested protection for this weekend."

"And she gave no reason for these curious suspicions?"

"None at all. None at all. The wayward fancies of an elderly woman, if you ask me. If it were anybody except Crystal Balaclava . . . but there it is. And so the commissioner and I would take it as a personal favor, Tibbett, if you and your wife could see your way to accepting the invitation. The whole thing is purely unofficial, you understand. I hope you will enjoy yourselves."

"I'm sure we shall," said Henry.

"Foxes' Trot?" said Emmy. "I don't believe it."

"That's what it says here," Henry replied. "Foxes' Trot, Plumley Green, Surrey."

"I mean, it can't be a real old country name. It must be a ghastly twentieth-century pun. I wonder what on earth the house looks like."

"We'll soon know." Henry swung the car to the left as the traffic lights turned green. It was half-past five on Friday evening, and they were in the center of the little country town of Hindhurst. The wide, tree-lined main street, with its rows of graceful Georgian houses, terminated in a T-junction controlled by traffic signals. A signpost indicated that the main road to the southwest bent around to the right, pointing the way to Petersfield and Portsmouth; to the left, a very much smaller road, little more than a lane, led to Trimble Wells, Bunstead, the Plumley Green.

Within a few minutes the last council housing estate had been left behind, and the scattered country cottages in their bright gardens had given way to woodland—spinneys of silver birch, clumps of sturdy oaks, and an occasional heathery knoll surmounted by a circle of pines. It was at a point where bracken grew thickly under the oaks that Henry spotted a small track leading off to the right, and a battered wrought-iron sign, swinging from an overhead bough, indicating that this was Foxes' Trot.

The drive—if such it could be called, for the gravel was overgrown with vetch and clover, and the original iron gates had long since disappeared—wound upward and away from the road for several hundred yards, through woodlands which promised to burgeon with bluebells in the spring. Then the trees thinned out, the drive took a final upward twist, and Henry's car swung around to the last bend into the graveled forecourt of Foxes' Trot.

"Good God," said Henry. And Emmy said, "I told you so."

The house, which had been built in a clearing in the woods, appeared to date from the late twenties. During the first months of its life, Henry thought, it might even have been impressive—a conglomeration of cubic blocks in dazzling white concrete, like a child's castle of building bricks on a nursery floor, pierced by big metal-framed plate-glass windows. The concrete had probably not remained white for more than a year or so; now, more than forty years later, it was dingy gray, streaked with brownish rivulets where the rust from the window frames had been rain-washed down the walls. It looked like a pile of cardboard shoeboxes which had been left out in a thunderstorm.

In contrast, however, to the shabbiness of the house and the overgrown drive, the half-acre or so of garden immediately surrounding Foxes' Trot was beautifully kept. There was a velvet-smooth, closely mown green lawn; a sunken pool with a small fountain in the shape of a saxophone, from whose stone trumpet a thin jet of water played upon floating pink and white water lilies; and neatly weeded flowerbeds blooming with delphiniums and lupins, asters and aquilegia. Henry made a mental note that somebody cared a lot about this garden and must be putting in a lot of work on it.

The front door of the house stood ajar, and as Henry and Emmy climbed out of their car the strains of "Anything Goes" came wafting out to greet them. The only other car in the driveway was an open Bentley of early-thirties vintage, lovingly preserved. Henry pressed the doorbell, which responded with a complicated chime. He looked at Emmy and grinned.

"This is going to be amusing," he said.

"It's certainly going to be *something*," said Emmy with a touch of gloom.

They waited. The gramophone declaimed the Cole Porter lyrics jauntily from the interior. Otherwise, the house seemed deserted.

Henry rang the bell again. After a moment a high, clear, well-bred female voice called, "Dolly!" Only the gramophone answered. The voice called again, "Dolly, darling! Front door!" Then, after a moment, "Oh, blast the girl!"

There was a clatter of heels on the parquet inside, and the door was flung open with an extravagant gesture by Crystal, relict of the late Baron Balaclava. She cried, "My dears! How too divine of you to come!"

It took Henry a moment to register the fact that she was still a beautiful woman, because the overwhelming first impression was so bizarre. The henna-dyed bobbed hair, the bandeau, the short, unwaisted dress of drooping yellow crepe, the bright red cupid's bow painted on wrinkled lips, the pearly-white stockings, the foot-long jade cigarette holder—they all added up not to a parody of the fashion of forty years ago but to the thing itself. One glance at Crystal Balaclava was enough to point up how essentially modern were the so-called "looks" of the twenties and thirties in the current fashion magazines. This was the real thing, and it looked every year of its age.

"It is Henry Tibbett, isn't it?" Henry detected a faint undertone of disbelief. People who knew him only by reputation often expected rather more than a mild-looking, sandy-haired middle-aged man. "And Mrs. Tibbett?" Lady Balaclava's bright eyes flickered over Emmy's plumpish figure, her short dark hair, her face with its peach-bloom skin almost innocent of cosmetics. "Basil said you'd been angelic enough to give up a whole weekend to poor little me. Too divine of you. Come in and have a cocktail."

Before Henry had time to answer, Lady Balaclava's gaze shifted, and Henry realized that she was looking over his left shoulder, at something behind him. Turning instinctively, he saw a massive and somewhat formidable figure making its way across the lawn from the direction of the greenhouse, which could just be glimpsed among the camouflage of shrubbery. It was impossible at this distance to tell if the newcomer was male or female—the cropped gray hair, the weatherbeaten features, the corduroy knee breeches and open-necked shirt were appropriate to either sex. Even the voice was ambiguous.

"Did I hear you shouting, Crys? What's up?"

Lady Balaclava looked annoyed. "So there you are, Dolly," she said. "Mr. and Mrs. Tibbett have arrived."

"So I see." At close quarters Henry was surprised to see that the mannish face was coated with a thick layer of Pancake makeup, in a grotesque parody of femininity. Dolly, for her part, looked the Tibbetts over critically. Then she scratched her head with a pair of secateurs and said, "Well, you'd better take them in and give them a drink."

"I did think you might have been here to answer the door, darling," said Crystal Balaclava a little peevishly.

"I was spraying the azaleas," said Dolly. To Henry and Emmy she added brusquely, "I'm Dorothy Underwood-Threep. Commonly known as Dolly. I'm Crystal's lady companion." She bared her teeth in a savage grin, presumably to indicate that this was a pleasantry. "Pleased to meet you. Must get back to my azaleas. See you at the dinner trough."

Whereupon she turned on the heel of her stout brogue and strode away across the garden.

Lady Balaclava said, with a sigh, "Isn't Dolly divine? We are *very* old friends. She'll be in that gruesome greenhouse for a couple of hours at least, so we can have a talk."

She ushered the Tibbetts into a large hall, which was

made entirely of black and white marble. A chromium-plated staircase spiraled down into the center of it. The only furniture was a white-marble table, on which two spineless and elongated dolls, representing Pierrot and Pierrette, lounged beside a telephone.

Lady Balaclava led the way through the hall to a door at the far side, beyond which the gramophone was now playing "A Room was a View." She said casually, "Just leave your cases in the hall. Dolly will take them upstairs later."

The drawing room was perfectly in period, but at least comfortable. Chrome and concrete were replaced by Knole sofas, unpolished weathered oak, wrought-iron tables, and leather poufs. The largest piece of pale oak furniture was the cocktail cabinet. Lady Balaclava swung open its large doors, to reveal that the inside was lined with pink mirror, reflecting and re-reflecting apparently endless ranks of bottles.

Henry and Emmy, with some misgivings, accepted a White Lady apiece. Crystal mixed them with great élan in a chromium shaker, dancing the Charleston as she did so, setting her ropes of beads swinging. Then she poured the icy white liquid into two flat glasses, which at once misted on the outside. Henry and Emmy sipped cautiously. It tasted absolutely delicious.

Lady Balaclava said, "Well—you're a pretty silent couple of chaps, aren't you?" She gave Emmy a critical look. "You should wear black, darling. It's so slimming." She glanced complacently down at her own flat chest and skeletal torso. Clearly, it had not occurred to her that a figure which had been boyish and appealing in the twenties might be grotesque in the seventies.

Emmy, who did not take offense easily, smiled and said that she did, indeed, frequently wear black, but that it had seemed inappropriate for a sunny summer's day in the country. "After all," she added, "I'm not in mourning."

"Not yet, darling," said Crystal Balaclava dryly. She drained her drink and refilled the glass. "Well, sit down and I'll explain. First of all, don't forget that Dolly has no idea who you are. She's divine, of course, but frankly rather stupid. She thinks you are friends of Basil's. I presume you do know him?"

"I'd hardly describe myself as a friend of Sir Basil's, Lady Balaclava," said Henry.

"I thought he was in charge of Scotland Yard and all that."

"Well, of course, the Home Office has overriding responsibility for all police forces, but the day-to-day administration—"

"Oh, for God's sake, don't get technical," said Lady Balaclava. "And remember to drop the 'Sir' if Basil's name comes up in front of Dolly. She may be slow, but she's not mentally deficient."

"My assistant commissioner told me," said Henry, "that you had asked for me by name, Lady Balaclava. If you had heard of me, isn't it likely that Miss . . . Miss Underwood-Threep may have, too?"

"Not a chance. Dolly never reads the papers, on principle. And less of the Balaclava and Underwood-Threep, if you please. We are Crystal and Dolly, while you are Henry and . . . ?"

"Emmy."

"Emmy. How quaint. Now, Basil must have told you why I asked you to come here."

"Not personally," said Henry. "The message filtered through the usual channels. You think that somebody is planning to kill you."

"I know it," said Crystal calmly.

"But why on earth—?" Henry began.

"Let me get you another drink, and I'll tell you." As she picked up the shaker, the automatic turntable changed the disc, and Sir Nöel's astringent voice began to commiserate with the poor little rich girl. "Rather appropriate," said Crystal as she refilled the glasses. She sat down on a leather pouf and lit a cigarette. "You know who I am, of course?"

Henry said, "Mrs. Charles Codworthy, *née* Maltravers,

more recently Baroness Balaclava. Widowed during the war."

Crystal nodded approvingly. "You've done your homework," she said. "Yes. Poor Charlie. You never knew him, I suppose?"

"I'm afraid not."

"Everybody said that I married him for his money. That was quite correct, of course. I did. Don't look at me like that, Emmy. You young people are so easily shocked. Nobody in their senses would have married Charlie for anything else. But he did have an awful lot of lovely lucre, and I was sick to death of amusing aristocratic poverty. The funny thing is that I got quite fond of the old boy in the end."

"He was an industrialist, I believe," said Henry.

"His grandfather," said Lady Balaclava, "was the only begetter of Codworthy's Little Marvel—the first self-flushing water closet, which broke upon an astounded world in the eighteen-fifties or thereabouts. Don't expect me to get the details right, because I don't have that sort of a mind, thank God. All I know is that the Little Marvel founded the Codworthy family fortunes. By the time Charlie took over the business in 1900, Codworthy's were the largest suppliers of loos in Europe. But Charlie had bigger ideas, bless him. He branched out into baths, wash basins, tiling, and so on. Then more companies were bought up, and Codworthy's moved into furniture and textiles and . . . well, by the time I met Charlie, it was an empire. What I'm driving at is that Charlie was very, very rich."

"I have gathered that," said Henry.

"You're brilliant, darling," said Crystal. "So was Charlie, in his own infuriating way. People have said, you know, that one of the conditions on which I married him was that he should buy himself a peerage—you could in those days, of course."

"What a vile thing for people to say," said Emmy.

"But it was absolutely true. Absolutely. I promise you." Crystal laughed ripplingly. "I adore you, Emmy. You look so *utterly* scandalized. Well, Charlie agreed—and then he

got his own back. He insisted on becoming Lord Balaclava."

"But why?"

"Because—according to him—his grandfather had
conceived the Little Marvel in a house in Balaclava Terrace, Wigan. I happen to know that's not true. It was Balmoral Terrace, but Charlie wasn't allowed to call himself
Lord Balmoral, for obvious reasons. No, he chose Balaclava just to score off me—I could be a baroness, all right,
but he made sure I'd have Balaclava Terrace on my back
for the rest of my life. Dear Charlie. He had quite a sense
of humor." Crystal sighed reminiscently. Then she went
on, "I dare say you're wondering why I'm telling you all
this ancient history. Well, it's quite relevant. I want you to
understand just how . . . just how well Charlie knew me.
That's why he deliberately drew up his will in the way that
he did. Another White Lady?"

Henry said, "No, thank you," at the exact moment
when Emmy said, "Yes, please." He looked at her and
grinned inwardly. Emmy was cross.

Crystal said nothing, but poured another drink into
Emmy's glass with a sweetly bitchy smile. Then she went
on, "Charlie and I had three daughters. The fact that they
were christened Primrose, Violet, and Daffodil had nothing, but *nothing*, to do with me. Charlie was very sentimental about his mother, whose name was Daisy. Thank
God she died before I even met him. But he had this
quaint idea of flower names for the girls and anytime I
tried to protest he threatened to cut us all out of his will.
So of course I gave in. And then poor old Charlie literally
flew up to join the angels, propelled by one of Hitler's
bombs. We never found enough of him for a funeral. We
just had a rather divine memorial service, and then we all
went out and got as tight as ticks. Emmy, darling, you
look positively outraged. We can't have that, can we,
Henry? Let me get you both another minuscule drink."

This time Emmy said, "No, thank you," at the exact
moment when Henry said, "Yes, please." As Lady Balaclava turned toward the cocktail cabinet, with her back to

them, Henry stuck his tongue out at Emmy, and she grinned reluctantly. Too late, they remembered the pink mirror. Crystal Balaclava had seen them, and was amused.

Turning back with Henry's recharged glass, she said, "I really should have been an author of cliff-hangers. Here you are, all agog to hear about the will, and I intend to go off at a tangent, or whatever it is that one goes off at. About this house. We found this bit of land in 1925. There had once been a farm on it, called Foxes' Hide. It was Tubby Blenkinsop who had the divine idea of calling it Foxes' Trot. How we all laughed! Well, I got little Davy Arbuthnot-Jones to do the design, and his friend Hubert Smithers did the interior, and the whole thing cost the earth, and Charlie was furious, but . . . it was a rather special house. Still is, don't you agree? Of course, Dolly and I live here very quietly now, but time was . . ." Crystal waved her cigarette holder nostalgically. "Anyhow, after poor Charlie went to join the morning stars, I moved down here permanently. No choice, of course. Nothing left of 197 Barkman Square except a large hole in the ground. So un-chic. Actually, of course, I was down here when it happened. We both were, but Charlie had insisted on going up to town for some board meeting or other. Quite mad of him, of course, but nobody could ever talk sense to Charlie where business was concerned. Anyhow . . . where was I?"

"You were going to tell us about Lord Balaclava's will," said Henry.

"So I was. What a bright little detective it is. Well, I can't hope to explain Charlie's will, because I'm a bird-brain—but the effect of it was to prevent me from laying hands on more than a teeny-weeny income for all of my life. Everything is what they call 'in trust' for the girls, and there is *no way* anybody can do anything about it until I die. Each of the girls has the same monthly pittance that I do, the capital grows fatter by the moment—and there we are. *But*—and here comes the interesting part, Henry darling—as soon as I die, the very *instant*, the entire capital will be split into three and handed over, utterly sans strings, to Prim, Vi, and Daffy in equal shares. And that," added Lady Balaclava, "in a nutshell, is why somebody is going to kill me."

Henry leaned forward. "What I'd like to know, Lady Balaclava, is—"

From the hall, a stentorian voice called, "Crys!"

"In the drawing room, darling!" fluted Crystal. To Henry she said, "Go on."

"Are any or all of your daughters—?"

The door opened, and Dorothy Underwood-Threep strode in. She flopped down on the velvet-covered settee, her legs asprawl, and said, "Let's have a drink, then. Those azaleas have been killing me."

Crystal smiled at Henry. "I'll tell you later, Henry darling," she said. Then, to Dolly, "You'd better fix yourself a cocktail. We've finished the White Ladies."

"Lazy bitch," said Dolly. "I mixed that shaker for myself at lunchtime."

"How divinely inhospitable you are, Dolly," said Crystal. "By the way, Henry and Emmy have left their bags in the hall."

"I've already carried them up," said Dolly, apparently without rancor.

"Angel," said Crystal. Dolly went over to the cabinet and began mixing herself a drink. Crystal added, "Henry has been dishing me all the latest dirt about Basil. Riveting, darling. Wait till you hear."

Dolly snorted. "Basil was always a fool," she said. "What's he been up to now?"

Crystal smiled angelically at Henry. "Tell her, Henry darling," she said. And then leaned back luxuriously to savor his embarrassment.

3

As it turned out, it was Dolly who got Henry neatly off the hook. Still with her back to the others, she said, "Really, Crys, you are prehistoric. Basil is thoroughly respectable these days. You could take him anywhere. In fact, I gather that people do. I suppose Henry's thinking of that old story about the Bolivian ambassador's wife and the diamond earring."

"What's your version of it?" Henry asked quickly. Dolly turned to face him. "There never was a word of truth in it," she said. "That little cat Tiny Mainwaring invented the whole thing from start to finish. In any case, it was years ago." She sat down heavily and swallowed her cocktail in a single gulp. "So, tomorrow is the great day. When do the hordes arrive?"

"There won't be any hordes," said Crystal. "Just the girls and their husbands. And the Tibbetts, of course."

"Well, let's be thankful for small mercies," said Dolly. She turned to Emmy. "Have you been allotted a present?"

"A present?" Emmy was bewildered.

Crystal said, "Oh, don't be a bigger idiot than you need, Dolly." To Emmy she added, "There's a foolish sort of tradition in the family. Each of the girls brings me the same birthday present every year. I needn't bother to mention that it was never my idea. Charlie's little whim. Sentimental old fool. Anyhow, it seems to amuse the girls, and it saves them the problem of what to give Mamma."

"And what are these presents?" Henry asked.

"I was about to tell you," said Crystal with a certain strange emphasis. "Primrose—she's the eldest, and married to a French-Swiss doctor called Duval—Primrose brings my birthday cake from Switzerland. Vi and Piet bring me flowers—rather obviously, since Piet grows them for a living. He's Dutch—such a quaint fellow. And of course, Daffy and Chuck bring the champagne."

"Why 'of course'?"

"Because Chuck just happens to be a millionaire—the genuine homespun variety from Texas. Daffy has been a very clever girl."

"So all your daughters married foreigners, did they?" said Emmy.

Crystal laughed. "The result of expensive European finishing schools," she said. "Except in Daffy's case, of course. She's the beauty of the family as well as the babe. She doesn't look one little bit like Charlie. Did you say something, Dolly darling?"

"I snorted," said Dolly accurately.

"I can't imagine why. Daffy doesn't look like me, either. She must be a throwback."

"I'm going up to change," announced Dolly. She stood up. "Come along you two. You're in the Black Room."

Crystal Balaclava gave Henry a long, slow wink as he and Emmy obediently followed Dolly out of the room and up the spiral stairs.

The room which had been allotted to the Tibbetts was a little surprising. The walls, washbasin, curtains, furniture, and sheets were black, the carpet, satin bed cover, and bedside telephone were white; the ceiling was made entirely of pearl-gray mirror.

"One of Hubert's little follies," remarked Dolly. "I suppose one might grow to love it in time, but nobody has yet been able to stand it for long enough to find out. At any rate, you can be thankful you're not in the Dali Room. Your cases are in the cupboard."

"Thank you very much," said Henry.

"Your bathroom's through there," said Dolly. "Black too, of course. Does it make you feel sick?"

"I beg your pardon?"

"The ceiling. It turns some people's stomachs. Like being on shipboard."

"I think we'll survive," said Henry. "We're both good sailors."

"First rate," said Dolly. "You'll need to be." She sat down on the white satin bed and lit a small cigar. "Well, Chief Superintendent, welcome to Foxes' Trot. I sure am glad to see you, as they say in the movies." She glanced at Henry's face. "Oh, I suppose Crys has told you I don't know who you are. I never cease to wonder what a fool she is. It was mean of her to make that remark about Basil. I don't suppose you've ever even met him."

"Only once or twice," said Henry cautiously.

"Well, I got you out of it very prettily, you must admit," said Dolly. "And Crys didn't suspect a thing. It's important to let her go on thinking I don't know. Has she told you why she sent for you?"

"She was beginning to, when you came in."

"Well, I'll save her the trouble. She's got this crazy idea that one of the girls wants to murder her. That is, one of the girls and/or her husband."

"You say it's crazy?"

"Of course."

"The money motive seems pretty strong."

"Fiddlesticks. Daffy is married to a millionaire. Vi and Piet don't have any ambitions as far as money goes. Even Crys admits that. Prim and Edouard are comfortably off—and Prim is devoted to Crystal. Always has been. The whole idea is ludicrous."

"What interests me," said Henry, "is where Lady Balaclava got this ludicrous idea."

Dolly snorted again. "She's the one to tell you that, not me. It's all ridiculous."

"If it's so ridiculous," said Henry, "why did you say that you were pleased to see me here?"

"Simply because it'll reassure Crys, and we can get this gruesome birthday ceremony over without too much horror. You heard about the presents? Well, Crys is convinced that one of them will be designed to poison her."

"I've never heard of anybody being poisoned by a bunch of roses," said Emmy.

"Then you haven't been reading the same fanciful fiction as our Crys," said Dolly. "According to her favorite penny-dreadful author, it's possible to impregnate flowers with some lethal substance which causes instant death to any fool who takes a good sniff at them. The cake is obvious, of course—cyanide in the almond paste. As for the champagne—"

"That presents problems," said Henry. "With ordinary wine, you might be able to uncork it and slip in poison. But champagne—"

"You're perfectly right, of course," said Dolly, "and in fact even Crys doesn't take the idea seriously. Apart from anything else, she admits that neither Daffy nor Chuck has the faintest reason for wanting to kill her. However, it seems to amuse her to make out a case for the champagne. No pun intended. She says it would be possible to inject poison through the cork. And then, of course, there's the old trick of cyanide in her glass before the bubbly is poured in."

"Just supposing," said Emmy, "that the champagne or the cake or the roses *are* poisoned—no, don't interrupt me, darling—if something is poisoned, what on earth is Henry supposed to do about it?"

Dolly laughed raucously. "A very good question, duckie," she said. "I'll tell you. Crys is going to arrange for Henry to smell and taste everything before she does."

"Well, I'll be damned," said Henry. And Emmy said, "She doesn't want a detective. She wants a . . . a . . . what were those people called who had to taste things before Roman emperors ate them?"

"Roman emperors had their faults," said Henry, "but I don't think they actually ate people."

"Oh, don't be idiotic."

"Crys imagines," said Dolly, "that if there is anything wrong, Henry will spot it at once."

"You bet he will," said Emmy. "After he's dead, I dare say we may all notice that something is slightly wrong."

"Now, don't carry on so, love," said Dolly comfortably. "The very fact that Henry is here at all will nip any incipient murderer in the bud."

"But I understood—" Henry began.

"—that nobody was to know your identity?" Dolly laughed again. "Quite right. I am supposed to think that you are an innocent outsider, roped in to play the part of taster-in-chief. The girls are supposed to think you're a friend of Basil's. We'll all keep up an amusing charade—but, believe me, *everybody* will know who you are. And when I say everybody, I mean the entire village. It would take a bold man to commit a murder under the very nose of the CID. Or a bold woman, come to that."

Henry said, "But you don't take Lady Balaclava's suspicions seriously?"

"On the face of it, they're ridiculous," said Dolly. "On the other hand, I've known Crys long enough not to underestimate her. *Something* may happen. So keep your eyes skinned, Chief Superintendent." She stood up and ground out her cigar stub in the black-marble urn by the bed. "See you downstairs later." She strode out of the room.

By the time that Henry and Emmy had unpacked and experimented with the facilities of the black-marble bathroom, it was after seven. Emmy, mindful of her hostess's advice, changed into a black silk jersey dress, which was undeniably slimming. Henry put on a clean white shirt, gray flannels, and a blazer. Feeling like minor characters in a prewar musical comedy, the Tibbetts went downstairs.

The record player was at it again, this time surprisingly up-to-date with a selection from *Pal Joey*. To the strains of "Bewitched, Bothered, and Bewildered," Henry and Emmy walked into the drawing room.

Crystal was perched on the arm of a sofa, facing the door, and making great play with her cocktail glass and her yard-long cigarette holder. She had changed into a bright orange shift, with a beaded fringe which reached just to her bony knees. Facing her, with their backs to the door, were two masculine backviews, both wearing dinner jackets. As they turned to greet the newcomers, Henry was not at all surprised to see that one of them was Dolly, nattily dressed in evening wear, complete with taped-seam trousers, a frilled white shirt, and a black bow tie. The other was a good-looking young man, with very fair hair and a slightly harassed expression.

Crystal cried, "Ah, there you are, darlings! You know Dolly, of course. This is Dr. Griffiths, who keeps our bodies and souls together with maddening efficiency, don't you, Tony? Tony—meet Henry and Emmy Tibbett, old friends of Basil's from London. You remember Basil? Dolly, get the shaker moving. Henry is dying of thirst—I can always tell when a man needs a drink. Tony is dining with us—if there's anything to eat, that is. *Is* there anything to eat, Dolly?"

"Of course there is," said Dolly gruffly. She was busy with the cocktail shaker.

"Dolly is a miracle," remarked Lady Balaclava rather smugly. "She simply spirits food out of thin air. I don't know *how* she does it."

"No, you don't, do you?" said Dolly. "Another snort for you, Tony? Hand over your glass. We're having shrimp cocktail, if you're interested, followed by osso buco. I made it this morning, and it's been cooking all afternoon."

Crystal beamed. "You see? Miraculous. I don't know what I'd do without you, Dolly darling."

To Henry's surprise, Dolly blushed under her greasepaint. "I do what I can," she muttered. "I've always tried . . ." There was the suspicion of a break in her voice. The shrilling of the telephone provided a welcome release from an inexplicably embarrassing moment. Dolly said, "I'll take it," and marched out into the hall.

Dr. Griffiths sipped his drink and said shyly to Henry, "So you're a friend of Sir Basil's? I've only met him once myself, but Crystal—Lady Balaclava—often talks of him. . . ."

"I hardly know him myself," said Henry hastily. This topic of conversation having been exhausted, an uneasy silence descended.

Crystal said to Emmy, "How clever of you to wear black, Emmy darling. So slimming."

Emmy decided that this had gone far enough. Sweetly she said, "And how clever of you to pick orange, Crystal. So fattening."

To her surprise, Crystal was delighted. "My dears, you really must visit us more often. You bring quite a breath of Mayfair into our country retreat."

"Chelsea, actually," said Emmy.

"Of course. Silly of me. Poor old Mayfair has become desperately unchic these days."

"It's nearly all business now," said Emmy. "Of course, some people do still live there—"

"*Not*," said Crystal, "the sort of people that you and I would find amusing, I am sure." She smiled at Emmy with genuine affinity.

Dolly came in from the hall. She said, "That was the post office. Phoning through a telegram."

"A telegram?" Crystal looked suddenly alarmed. "Not—?"

"From Lausanne," said Dolly. She seemed unaccountably cheerful. "Edouard is sorry, but he has been called away to an unexpected conference. Primrose will be coming over alone."

Crystal seemed to relax. "Oh, that tiresome man. How can a conference be unexpected?" She appealed to Henry. "Have you ever been called to an unexpected conference? Of course you haven't. Edouard is *very* naughty, and I shall write and tell him so." She turned to Dr. Griffiths. "My son-in-law is a doctor, too," she said, "but Swiss, alas. Hates England. So provincial, but there it is. Poor Edouard, I'm afraid he is a very boring character, and quite rightly feels inferior when he comes here. Never mind. So long as Primrose brings the birthday cake, nobody will be missing anything." It seemed to Henry that she gave a slightly sinister emphasis to the last sentence.

"Ah, well, we shall be quite a small party tomorrow—such a shame you can't make it, Tony. Still, we'll make up in quality what we lack in quantity—shan't we, Emmy darling?"

"We'll try," said Emmy without much conviction.

Dinner was a surprisingly gay meal, chiefly due to Dolly's restored high spirits. In the intervals of serving excellent food, she cracked bluff jokes with young Dr. Griffiths—who seemed to find this a relief from the full blast of Crystal's charm, which was turned onto him from the other side of the table. Henry and Emmy contributed little to the conversation, but enjoyed their food. Afterward, when Dolly had served coffee, Crystal suddenly stood up and said, "Dolly, be an angel and entertain Emmy and Tony. I've something in the library I want to show Henry."

Dolly looked up, alarmed. "Now, Crys, you're not going to—?"

"A new game that I have invented," said Crystal to Henry. "Only two can play."

"Crys," said Dolly, "you promised—"

"Oh, fiddle-dee-dee," said Crystal. "I did no such thing. Come along, Henry."

For a moment it looked as though Dolly might try to prevent Lady Balaclava from leaving the room by force. She jumped to her feet and was halfway to the door when Crystal swept past her, shooting her such a look of steely command that it stopped Dolly in her tracks. Rather sheepishly, Henry followed his hostess.

The so-called library was a small room at the back of the house, and it was quite out of key with the rest of the establishment. It was shabby, suburban, and cozy. The books which gave it its pretentious title were a motley lot, ranging from tattered paperback thrillers to tomes on sanitary engineering. Between these extremes, Henry noticed the complete works of Charles Dickens, most of Kipling, and a representative selection of Arnold Bennett and early Priestley. One thing all the books had in common: they had been read and reread, as their worn covers testified, but some time ago, for all were covered with a film of fine dust. The furnishings consisted of a large mahogany desk, a swivel chair, and a large armchair upholstered in well-worn leather. It took no great powers of detection to deduce that this room had been the late Lord Balaclava's retreat from the febrile racket of Foxes' Trot.

Crystal Balaclava closed the door carefully behind Henry and then went over to the desk—which, Henry noticed, had been carefully dusted, unlike the books. She perched on the edge of it, swinging a thin leg provocatively, and said, "Now I'll show you the game that only two can play." Seeing Henry's apprehensive expression, she broke into a peal of laughter. "Don't worry, darling. Not *that* game. This one."

She flicked open one of the desk drawers and produced what appeared to be a pack of cards and an ordinary glass tumbler; but as Crystal arranged the cards in a circle, face upward on the desk, Henry saw that they were not playing cards, but that each was boldly printed with a letter of the alphabet.

Crystal put the tumbler upside down in the center of the circle and said, "Table-turning. Ouija. Spiritualism. Whatever you like to call it. I suppose you think it's all nonsense."

"I really know nothing about it," said Henry.

"Then come and learn. Sit there." She motioned him to the swivel chair. "Now, rest your fingertips lightly on the top of the glass. Both hands. Touching mine. The circle must be unbroken."

Henry did as he was told. "What happens now?" he asked.

"Ssh." Crystal was leaning back, her eyes closed, an expression of extreme concentration on her face. Henry sat quite still. Nothing happened. A full minute passed, dragging its feet so that it felt like half an hour. Henry was about to lose patience when the glass moved.

It began to rock from side to side on its rim, like a living animal trying to escape from a tether. Without opening her eyes, Crystal whispered, "Don't press on it. You're holding it back."

Henry had not been aware of the fact until then, but it was true that he had been exerting a certain downward pressure. He took the weight off his fingers, so that they were barely resting on the base of the glass—and at once, as if liberated, it started darting about the circle of letters. At first it seemed to be playing, delighted to be free, but certainly making no sense. Henry found it difficult to follow the cavorting of the glass without breaking the contact between his fingers and Crystal's—but each time that he momentarily lost touch, the glass stoppped abruptly, as if an electric current had been switched off.

After a minute or so of this frolicking, Crystal said softly and reprovingly, "That's enough. That's enough." The glass hesitated, came to rest, then gave a playful little rock. Crystal laughed gently and said, "All right, all right. Now. Who is there?"

The glass began to race again. Crystal said, "Yes, I know who you are, but Henry doesn't. Spell your name for Henry."

The glass sulked for a moment, but then began, deliberately yet delicately, to slide over the polished surface of the desk, lightly touching one letter card after another. C-H-A-R-L-I-E.

Henry said, "Your late husband?"

Crystal nodded. Then she addressed the glass. "Now tell Henry what you have told me."

The glass hesitated. Henry, while not actually identifying it with the late Baron Balaclava, was forced to admit that he was by now thinking of it as an animate object. Its moods were as recognizable as those of a dog or cat.

"Please, Charlie," said Crystal seriously. And it did not sound ridiculous.

Slowly, with obvious reluctance, the glass began to spell out its message. D-A-N-G-E-R. The glass rocked uneasily. M-U-R-D-E-R. It stopped.

"Who is going to be murdered?" Crystal asked calmly.

C-R-Y-S.

"And by whom?"

D-O-N-T . . . A-S-K . . . D-A-N-G-E-R . . .

"Now, don't be silly, Charlie," said Crystal briskly. "Who is going to murder me?"

DO-N-T . . . A-S-K . . .

"I am asking, Charlie. Tell us at once." Crystal spoke with impatience—exactly, Henry guessed, as she had spoken to her husband when he was alive.

Once again the glass rocked sulkily. Then it seemed to make up its mind. Very slowly and deliberately it made its way across the desk to the letter D.

It was at this moment that the door of the library was flung open, and Dolly said furiously, "Crystal!"

Afterward Henry could never be sure of the exact sequence of subsequent events. His fingers left the glass, and so did Lady Balaclava's. The glass itself leaped—or did it; how could one be sure?—up from the table and toward the ceiling. Then it crashed down again and splintered into a thousand fragments, scattering the letter cards. Then Dolly switched on the powerful overhead electric light, and all illusion vanished.

Dolly said, "Tony is just leaving. He wants to say good night to you, Crys."

Crystal Balaclava was leaning back in her chair—not lounging, but poised to spring, like a panther. She said, "There was no need for that, Dolly."

"There was." Dolly stood in the doorway, lumpish and unhappy in her ridiculous dinner jacket, but stubborn. "Go and say good-bye to Tony."

"God damn your eyes," said Crystal, but her voice was better-tempered. "All right." She stood up slowly and glanced at the desk. "Clear up that mess, Dolly. And get some sticking plaster for Henry. I'm afraid Charlie bit him."

Henry glanced down at his hands. Sure enough, a trickle of blood was running from one of his fingers, staining the card marked D. By the time he looked up again, Crystal had gone.

Dolly took a packet of adhesive-plaster dressings from a drawer in the desk and stanched Henry's finger. Then, from the same drawer, she produced a yellow duster, swept up the pieces of broken glass, and deposited them in the wastepaper basket.

Henry said, "So this is where Lady Balaclava gets her information."

Dolly, her back to him, said, "Apparently."

"Why didn't you tell me?"

"Because you wouldn't have believed me. Anyhow, it's nothing to do with me."

"Lord Balaclava," said Henry, "didn't have time to tell me who was planning to murder his—widow."

"That's just as well." Dolly still kept her back to him.

"Oh? Why do you say that?"

"Because he's a liar."

"He has told Crystal a name, has he?"

"No. He won't—or so she says."

"So when you say he's a liar, you mean that the whole thing is a fraud, do you?"

Dolly turned at that, her face flushed, her black tie awry. "I never said that." She picked up the wastepaper basket and marched angrily out of the room.

When Henry followed her, there was no sign of anybody in the hall, and in the drawing room Emmy was sitting by herself, nursing an empty coffee cup. Henry said, "Let's go up to bed."

"To bed? But where is—?"

"The doctor has gone," said Henry, "and there's no sign of our hostess or her friend. I presume that they have gone to bed, too."

"I call that a bit rude," said Emmy.

"It is very rude," said Henry, "but the aristocracy of forty years ago was very rude. And we seem to be involved with it. So let's just go quietly to bed."

"Quietly? In *that* room?"

"The room may be loud," said Henry, "but we needn't be. Besides, I think we should get our beauty sleep. Tomorrow may be strenuous."

In spite of the decor, they both slept very well.

4

Henry woke early. The summer sunshine was probing inquisitive fingers through the gaps between the black curtains and tracing geometric patterns on the white carpet. Beside Henry in the huge bed, Emmy slept face downward—the black silk sheets heightening the whiteness of her bare shoulders, the frilly white pillow contrasting with the blackness of her hair.

All this, together with his own sandy-haired head and blue-pajamaed torso, was reflected to Henry from the pearly mirror ceiling, as he lay on his back and contemplated this strange case which was not a case. The letter D spun in his head. D for Dolly. D for Daffodil. D for Dr. Duval. D for Danger. D for DON'T ASK. The glass had moved—no doubt about that. Henry was sure that he had not pushed it, so Crystal must have done so. He remembered how the glass had leaped into the air like a living thing, and for a moment his determined skepticism wavered; but the thought of the spirit of the late Baron Balaclava propelling a tooth mug around his erstwhile desk too preposterous to entertain seriously.

So, it seemed, Crystal Balaclava had chosen this bizarre way to communicate her suspicions to Henry. Why? At a guess, because they were so flimsily founded that a straightforward exposition would have invited disbelief or even mockery. And Crystal had been foiled by Dolly Underwood-Threep, who had literally upset the applecart and sent the tumbler flying before it could spell out its message. Somebody in this house, Henry decided, was very frightened; but he was not convinced that it was Lady Balaclava. ·

Emmy woke at eight, and she and Henry were up, dressed, and downstairs soon after nine. The house was silent, and seemed deserted. Emmy, after a short search, located the kitchen. Its door, which led from the white-marble hallway, was disguised behind a *trompe l'oeil* panel representing a checkerboard with cubist chessmen.

The kitchen itself was spick and span. All traces of last night's dinner had been washed, dried, and neatly put away. Breakfast trays were laid with fresh linen, china, and cutlery. All that was needed was to boil the eggs, make the toast, and fill the teapots. The timer was just ringing to indicate that the eggs were cooked, when the back door opened, and Dolly came in. She was once more wearing the corduroy breeches and khaki shirt in which Henry and Emmy had first seen her. She nodded approvingly at Emmy.

"Got everything you need? Good show. Up early, I see. Earlier than most of Crys's friends. But then you're not real friends, are you? Silly of me. Help yourself to anything you want. I'll be in the greenhouse if you need me." Giving Emmy no time to reply, she strode out into the garden again, slamming the door behind her.

Henry and Emmy were just finishing breakfast when they heard the crunching of wheels on the gravel drive. They did not hear the roar of an engine, for Charles Z. Swasheimer's Rolls-Royce had an engine which whispered; nor did they hear the slamming of car doors, because the doors of Rolls-Royces click discreetly shut, with a small sound like a mouse nibbling a nut. What Henry and Emmy did hear, a minute or so after the car had stopped, was Daffodil's clear voice calling, "Hi, there! Anyone at home?"

Emmy put down her egg spoon and looked at Henry. "Do you think we should—?"

"Yes, I reckon we'd better," said Henry. "Dolly is in the

greenhouse, and I doubt if Crystal will appear before noon."

"I wonder which—?" Emmy began. But her question was answered.

The flutelike voice, with its faintly American intonation, called again. "Mother! It's Daffy and Chuck. Where are you, darling?"

"Come on," said Henry to Emmy. "We'd better do the honors." They went out into the hall.

Daffodil was standing in the middle of the marble foyer, striking an attitude in her new Cardin number. She obviously felt—as Henry did—that it was a pity there was no fashion photographer handy, because the rankest snapshot of Daffodil in that setting and those clothes would have found a place in any trendy magazine, and no questions asked. As it was, Daffodil abandoned her attitude, focused her sapphire eyes unenthusiastically on Henry, and said, "Well, hello. Who are *you?*"

Henry said, "My name is Tibbett. Henry Tibbett. This is my wife, Emmy. We're . . ." He hesitated, then remembered the Americanism. "We're house guests of your mother's for the weekend. You must be Mrs. Swasheimer."

"You never said a truer word," said Daffodil, and Henry wondered why she seemed to regard this statement as an exquisite private joke. "And call me Daffy. Everybody does. Where's Mother?"

"In bed and asleep, as far as I know," said Henry. "Dolly's in the greenhouse."

"She would be," said Daffy. "Ah, here's Chuck. My husband. Honey, meet Henry and Emmy Tibbett. House guests of Mother's."

Daffy flung an expansive hand toward the front door, and Henry and Emmy found themselves being introduced to a stolid musculine backview, which was entering the hallway rear-first, pushing the front door open with sturdy buttocks in the process. A moment later Mr. Swasheimer's unorthodox method of entry was explained. Both his arms were fully occupied in carrying a large and heavy cardboard carton, which had the name of a world-famous champagne house printed on every available surface. Denied the use of his hands, Mr. Swasheimer had no alternative but to open the door with his seat.

"Hi, there," he remarked genially, to nobody in particular. "Say, Daffy, where can I park this baby? It weighs a ton."

"Just dump it on the floor, hon. Dolly will see to it."

With a certain amount of difficulty Charles Swasheimer lowered his burden to the ground. Then he straightened, mopped his brow with a white silk handkerchief, and turned to Henry and Emmy with a friendly grin, his right hand outstretched.

"Well, I sure am glad to meet you folks," he said. "Sure am glad that you're here to celebrate with us. Daffy's mom's birthday," he went on, with a vocal gear change to reverential, "is a kind of sacred festival to us, isn't it, baby? Just a simple family gathering—that's why I always drive myself down here. Yes, sir—I give the chauffeur the weekend off, and Daffy and I take the night ferry from Dunkirk like everyone else, and we drive ourselves through this lovely little old country of yours—"

Daffy interrupted him with a sharp little sigh of impatience. "I suppose we're the first, as usual?"

"Yes, you are," said Emmy. "Have you had breakfast, by the way? It's all prepared—"

"I know, I know. In the kitchen. Do-it-yourself cookery—except that poor bloody Dolly's done all the hard work last night, and all we have to do is to boil the eggs. Still, it makes Chuck feel like a real live tough independent lumberjack. Isn't that so, honey?" Daffodil said the last four words with such a warm, teasing, affectionate smile at her husband that the latter—whose face had drooped into the uneasy expression of a man whose wife is being deliberately awkward—now beamed, embraced her briefly, and said, "Daff's a great little kidder. She knows how much I look forward to a weekend like this. Come on, honey. Let's go boil an egg. Be seeing you, folks."

The Swasheimers disappeared into the kitchen, and Emmy said, "What a nice man."

"What a pretty girl," said Henry.

There was a short silence. Then Emmy said, "We may as well finish our breakfast, I suppose."

A couple of minutes later they heard the front door opening again, and then Dolly's voice from the hall remarked, "What the—? Oh, champers. So you've arrived."

"Dolly, *darling*. How divine to see you!" caroled Daffodil, who must have emerged from the kitchen. "Why, I declare you grow younger every year. I just don't know how you do it. Chuck, come and say hello to Dolly."

"Why, Miss Dolly . . . excuse the apron . . . I was just boiling the eggs for Daffy and me . . . well, well, it's sure good to see you. . . ." Chuck Swasheimer rumbled on, like a good-natured St. Bernard dog greeting an old friend.

Dolly said curtly, "If you'll let me get into the kitchen, I'll put a couple of bottles on ice. No, no, I can't shake hands. Got to wash this poisonous stuff off first . . . go on into the dining room. I'll bring your breakfast in when it's ready."

After a few halfhearted protests the Swasheimers joined the Tibbetts in the dining room. Chuck, regretfully untying the waistbands of an unsuitably frilly hostess apron, said, "She's a good sort, Miss Dolly. Daffy and I have often said we don't know what Lady Crystal would do without her—haven't we, Daffy?"

"For the umpteenth time," said Daffy, subsiding gracefully into a chair, "Mother is *not* Lady Crystal, she's either Lady Balaclava, or plain Crystal. To be Lady Crystal, she'd have to be the daughter of an earl or a duke, and have the title in her own right."

Swasheimer grinned and shook his head. "It's all beyond me, you Britishers and your titles. I can't for the life of me see that it matters—"

"Well, it does," said Daffy. She closed her pretty mouth like a steel trap. After a moment she added, "It annoys Mother very much when you call her Lady Crystal."

"Well, now, honey, I sure wouldn't want to upset Lady . . . your mother. I guess now that I'm one of the family, I'll just call her Mom."

"Good God," said Daffy, and closed her eyes. Henry and Emmy were relieved when Dolly arrived from the kitchen bearing a tray of eggs, coffee, and toast. She dumped the tray unceremoniously in front of Daffy, saying, "You can be Mother, Daffodil," accompanying this remark with a hoot of laughter. Then she sat down on a chromium chair, her sturdy legs in their corduroy breeches planted firmly apart, like trees, and went on. "I'll take a quick cuppa with you, and then get back to my azaleas. Got a bit of bad news for you, my lad," she added to Chuck. "The Bentley's out of action. Blown a gasket, poor old girl, and Willy Trumper at the garage says it'll be weeks before he can get a spare. So you'll have to do taxi duty."

"Why, that'll be a pleasure," said Chuck.

Simultaneously Daffy said, "Oh, God. What a bloody bore."

Dolly, who was buttering a piece of toast, ignored both remarks. She went on, "Your first assignment will be Vi and Piet. They came over on the night ferry from the Hook and should have reached Harwich about an hour ago. They'll be in Liverpool Street by eleven, cab to Waterloo, and hope to catch the eleven-forty to Hindhurst, getting in at twelve-forty-three. If they're not on it, you'll just have to wait for the next train—the ten-past-one."

"Oh, honestly, Dolly," protested Daffodil. "I do call that a bit thick. You mean we may have to sit around in that ghastly stationyard for half an hour—?"

"*You* won't have to," said Dolly crisply, "but Chuck may."

"But Dolly—"

"Vi can't possibly be sure of catching that train. You know what London traffic can be like."

"Well, she could telephone if she misses it."

"Yes, and probably miss the next one as a result. Do stop complaining, Daffodil. It's very unattractive. Thanks—three lumps and plenty of milk. Primrose won't be arriving till later. Her plane touches down at London Airport at ten to two. Say half-past three at the Kensington Terminal. She should catch the five-to-four from Waterloo, getting to Hindhurst at a quarter to five. It's the fast train."

"And I suppose we're expected to meet it, too?" inquired Daffodil. Henry noticed that she seemed to be making an effort to appear better-tempered.

"You suppose correctly," said Dolly, taking a noisy gulp of coffee.

"Well, now, Miss Dolly," said Chuck, "I guess I'd better make a note of all this. I'm an idiot about appointments without my secretary," he added with an apologetic smile. He took a gold propelling pencil out of his pocket and applied it to a slim, crocodile-bound notebook. "Vi and Piet, twelve-forty-three at Hindhurst Station. If necessary, wait for the extra train. Primrose and Edward—"

"Just Primrose," said Dolly. She put her cup down and wiped her mouth with the back of her hand.

"What?" Daffodil sat up straight. "You mean Edward's not coming?"

"We had a telegram last night," said Dolly. "Dr. Duval has been called to an unexpected conference, and very much regrets—"

"Golly," said Daffodil. "I bet Mother's hopping mad."

"On the contrary," said Dolly, "I think she is relieved."

"Gee, that's tough on Ed, missing the party," said Chuck.

Daffodil gave her husband, who was still making notes, a look of chilling contempt. Then she turned back to Dolly. "Any more jobs for us?"

Dolly seemed quite unaware of any irony in this remark. She simply said, "Only to open the champagne, as usual. Primrose will be bringing the cake, of course."

"No other gruesome house guests this year?"

"Only Mr. and Mrs. Tibbett," said Dolly dryly.

Daffodil had the grace to color slightly. She said, "Why, yes. We've met. I didn't mean—"

Dolly drained her cup. "We all know exactly what you meant, Daffodil." She stood up. "Well, back to the grindstone. Or, to be accurate, the insecticide spray. See you for lunch."

Chuck Swasheimer said tentatively, "Miss Dolly, when do you think that Lady Crystal——?"

"Not before noon," said Dolly. She stumped out, slamming the door behind her.

But Dolly was wrong. Within a few minutes the uneasy silence which had fallen on the dining room was broken by a brisk clatter of high heels on the steel staircase; and the next moment, Lady Balaclava made her entrance, preceded by a pungent wave of expensive scent. She wore bell-bottomed pink silk pajamas, trimmed lavishly with a pink-dyed boa, and her jet cigarette holder was much in evidence.

"Darlings!" she cried.

"Lady Crystal!" Chuck Swasheimer choked slightly over a mouthful of egg and hastily wiped his mouth on his napkin as he struggled to his feet.

"Hello, Mamma," said Daffodil. She sounded bored. "You're looking well."

"If I am, it's a miracle," said Crystal peevishly. "I haven't slept properly for weeks. How are you, Charles? Have you met the Tibbetts? Great friends of Basil's. Pour me a cup of that disgusting coffee, Daffy darling." She surveyed her youngest daughter critically. "That's a new brooch."

"Got it a few days ago in Paris," said Daffodil casually. "The design's not too bad, considering it's off the peg."

"Daffy felt that her new outfit needed something green," Chuck explained, almost apologetically. "There was no time to get one designed and made specially."

"Well, *I* wouldn't wear that thing," said Crystal.

Chuck's face fell. "You mean, you find the design that bad, Lady . . . that is . . . Mom?"

Crystal flickered a glance at her son-in-law. Then she said, "Emeralds are unlucky. Everybody knows that. You are simply tempting fate, Daffy."

"I'm not superstitious," said Daffodil, "and I adore tempting. Here's your coffee, Mamma."

Lady Balaclava dropped into a chair, helped herself liberally to sugar, and began to stir her coffee. She said, "Has Dolly told you about the Bentley?"

"She has, and honestly, I think it's a bit much—"

"We couldn't be sorrier, Daffy darling, but there's really nothing for it. I can hardly ask Mr. Winkfield and his taxi to hang around at the station, waiting for—"

"Exactly!" Daffy was triumphant. "You can hardly ask Mr. Bloody Winkfield, but you don't mind asking us."

Lady Balaclava was unimpressed. "Of course I don't, darling," she said. "You're family. Aren't you, sonny," she added to Chuck.

Daffodil laughed merrily, as Swasheimer's look of shocked surprise gave way slowly to a raspberry-rich blush. "Mamma, I love you," she said.

Lady Balaclava addressed herself to Chuck. "My name is Crystal," she said very clearly, "and I am younger than you are." Before the big American could distill an answer out of his confusion, Crystal had turned to Daffodil with a diamond-bright smile. "And now, darling, I want to hear *everything* you've been doing—New York, Paris, Rio—every tiny little thing. Did you run across Fatty Belmont in Florence? He lives in a miserable little *pensione,* I believe—so sad, when you think of the Porchester Square days. . . ."

"I guess I'll go and see to our bags," said Chuck. He stood up, with a certain injured dignity, and marched out of the dining room. Neither his wife nor his mother-in-law gave any sign of seeing him go; nor did they react when, a couple of minutes later, Henry and Emmy also made a tactful withdrawal. Daffodil was by then giving her mother a blow-by-blow account of the Paris collections, which Crystal interspersed with memories of Schap and Worth and Molyneux in the old days. Both were entirely absorbed by the subject in hand.

Henry and Emmy went out into the garden. For once, in a way, the English summer was living up to its image on the "Come to Britain" posters—although a slight heaviness in the air, a tendency to darkness around the horizon, might have made a meteorologist think a bit. For the moment, however, the sun shone from a dark blue sky and the heat was beginning to rise, shimmering, above the well-groomed flowerbeds of Foxes' Trot.

Emmy sat down on the stone steps which led down to the lily pond, and said, "This must be the most peculiar job you've ever had, darling."

"I don't regard it as a job." Henry squatted beside her, filling his pipe from his leather tobacco pouch. "I regard it as a lunatic but amusing weekend."

"That's all very well, Henry, but . . . supposing something should happen to Lady Balaclava . . . ?"

"I shall apply for Dutch nationality," said Henry firmly. He lit his pipe and puffed noisily, without any noticeable effect.

"They're a curious lot," said Emmy, "but endearing. Most of them. Chuck Swasheimer, for instance. And Dolly."

"Dolly," said Henry, "is the center of this whole odd business. Shall we pay her a visit? The greenhouse, I think she said."

The greenhouse stood in the middle of a neatly laid-out vegetable garden, which extended from the kitchen door of Foxes' Trot up to the boundary with the surrounding woods. The first thing Henry noticed was that all its windows were open, giving it the air of a flight of butterflies; as he approached, he could see Dolly Underwood-Threep moving around inside. In addition to her corduroys and leggings, her stout shoes and leather jacket, she had put on gauntlet gloves and a strange sort of Australian bush hat. She was carrying a large metal spray can.

Henry put his hand to the greenhouse door handle, but before he had time to turn it, there was an indignant bellow from inside. "You, there! Tibbett! Get back, you fool!"

Surprised, Henry stepped back. Dolly thrust her head out of one of the open windows. "What in hell do you two think you're doing here?" she demanded.

"Hoping to have a word with you," said Henry.

"Oh. Well, no harm in that. But get out of here first."

"Can't we come in and—?"

"You *can* come in, I have no doubt, Mr. Tibbett, but you *may* not." Dolly withdrew her head from the open window, like a retreating snail. A moment later she was outside the greenhouse, peeling off her rubber gauntlets. "Sorry if I appeared rude, chaps. I'm used to it, you see, but it's dangerous stuff. Don't want anybody going sick before Crystal's party, do we?"

Henry had become aware of a disinfectant smell, not unpleasant drifting out from the greenhouse windows. He said, "You mean, the insecticide—?"

"Flyaway," said Dolly. "A pretty, proprietary name for a very nasty poison. Ten percent of an organic phosphorus called parathion, permitted for use in greenhouses. Ha!"

"Why do you use it, if it's so dangerous?" Emmy asked.

Dolly gave her a withering look. "Because it's effective, duckie," she said. "It's also safe, if you use it right. Protective clothing, a good washdown with pure water after handling the spray, all windows open. But, as you see, I take great care not to allow any unauthorized people within a mile of it. No matter *who* they may be," she added with a look at Henry.

"But surely," Emmy said, "unless one actually swallows the stuff—"

Dolly laughed, without amusement. "That's what people think," she said. "In fact, fatal doses have been absorbed through the skin, over a long period—or just breathed in if the air is full of the stuff in the form of dust."

"If it's so dangerous, it shouldn't be legal," said Emmy.

"I am in complete agreement with you, duckie," said Dolly, "but it's not up to me. Well—what did you want to talk to me about?"

"Spiritualism," said Henry. "Table turning."

"This nonsense of Crys's? You didn't take it seriously?"

"It hardly matters how I took it," said Henry. "The point is that Lady Balaclava apparently takes it seriously."

"More fool her," said Dolly.

"She also explained to me," Henry went on, "that it is a game to be played by two. Two living people, that is. The late Lord Balaclava makes three."

"Poppycock."

"If you have such a poor opinion of the game," said Henry, "why do you play it?"

Dolly gave him a blank stare. "Me?"

"I deduced that you were the second person in these sessions."

"Then you deduced wrong, my friend. I wouldn't touch that muck with a barge pole. As deadly as parathion, in its own way."

"Then you must surely know," said Henry, "who *is* Lady Balaclava's usual playmate."

For a moment Dolly said nothing. Then she said, "I know nothing about it. Crys knows I disapprove. She takes good care not to mess about with that sort of thing when I'm around. Well, have a good morning. I'm off back to my own particular poison. Why don't you take a walk in Plumley Woods? They're very pretty at this time of year." She turned on her heel and went back into the greenhouse, pulling on her gloves as she went. Once inside, she hesitated, and seemed to come to a decision. Once again she stuck her head out through an open window. She said, "I have noticed that Crys is particularly vocal about this nonsense on Wednesday mornings."

"What does that mean?" Henry asked.

"Just that I often go to the cinema in Hindhurst on Tuesdays," said Dolly, "and Tony Griffiths generally drops in to have dinner with Crys."

5

Daffodil's fears proved groundless. Violet and Piet van der Hoven arrived at Hindhurst on the 12:43 train, and by one o'clock the Rolls was whispering up the drive again with its four passengers—for Daffodil had decided to meet her sister and brother-in-law at the station after all.

Henry and Emmy had taken Dolly's advice, and a walk in the woods, arriving back at the house at half-past twelve. They had found Crystal, now wearing a becoming Chanel-type suit, alone in the drawing room. Henry had asked if she had any particular instructions for him concerning the imminent birthday party, and had been told simply to "Stick closer than a brother and do *just* what I tell you, Henry darling."

When Henry asked point-blank who was Crystal's partner in the table-turning game, she had looked at him with raised pencil-thin eyebrows and replied, "Surely you can deduce that, Chief Superintendent?" using his rank with insulting emphasis.

"Dr. Griffiths, perhaps?"

This suggestion provoked peals of laughter, a positive refusal to discuss morbid topics any longer, and instant recourse to the cocktail cabinet. It was then that the Rolls had appeared in the drive.

Dolly, who had come in from the greenhouse at midday and was currently busy in the kitchen, came hurrying out into the hall to greet the new arrivals. Her manner was noticeably more enthusiastic than it had been for Daffy and Chuck earlier in the day.

"Vi . . . Piet . . . good to see you, chaps. . . . Good journey? Not too rough? Splendid. . . . Got the roses . . . ? As if I didn't know. Give them here. I'll get them out of their box and into water. . . . Just dump your bags, I'll take them up later. You're in the Dali Room, I'm afraid. Bad luck, but you all have to take your turn at it. . . . You'll find Crys in the drawing room with the Tibbetts . . . oh, friends of Basil's, I believe . . . quite harmless, a bit nondescript. . . ."

Dolly's stentorian voice floated effortlessly through the closed drawing-room door. Crystal winked at Henry. "That's what *she* thinks," she remarked in a stage whisper. "So brilliant, darling, to appear so utterly *nothing*. No one will *ever* guess who you are."

Henry was still mulling over this backhanded compliment when the van der Hovens came in, followed by the Swasheimers. Emmy was struck at once by the contrast between the two couples. The Swasheimers were highly polished, sophisticated, exuding wealth as an atomizer exudes scent—the elderly, portly husband, his lack of physical charm disguised by superlative tailoring and grooming; the young, pretty, lacquered wife, setting a high price on herself. A happy couple.

The van der Hovens were not exactly shabby, but they showed signs of the determinedly bright neatness which characterizes the badly-off when dressed in their best. Piet was big-boned, tall, and handsome, and seemed on the point of bursting out of his inexpensive gray suit—not because it was too small for him, but because his sheer physical energy seemed to overflow it. Violet wore a trim navy-blue suit, made of good material but not fashionable—because fashions change, and this suit would have to do for years. Her hair, which normally she set simply but attractively at home, had been "styled" by an inexpert hairdresser into a hard and unflattering shape. Her makeup was rudimentary, and it occurred to Emmy that with her fine, pale skin and excellent features, Violet would have looked far prettier with a clean-scrubbed face than with this overpowdered, red-lipped mask. As it was, she looked more than the statistical five years older than her husband, and she also looked worried. Not a happy couple.

"Violet, *darling*, how well and pretty you look. I don't know how you always manage to be so clever with your clothes." Crystal's voice was as bright and insincere as a shower of tin pennies. She regarded her second daughter with a dazzling smile which failed to hide both contempt and dislike. "And dear Piet. Handsome as ever. May your raddled old mum-in-law claim a kiss?"

"The pleasure shall be entirely mine, Crystal." Piet van der Hoven spoke slowly and correctly in his too perfect English. Henry noticed a faint hesitation before he pronounced Lady Balaclava's name. He guessed that this was a stumbling block for all Crystal's sons-in-law presumed that they were under orders to use her Christian name. Anything smacking of the maternal would be firmly vetoed. Piet then took Crystal in his huge arms and kissed her soundly, with no suggestion of cheek-pecking. Crystal emerged from the bear hug looking faintly surprised and said, a little breathlessly, "Now, you must meet Henry and Emmy Tibbett. Great friends of Basil's. I don't think you know Basil. Henry and Emmy are spending the weekend with us. . . ."

Henry and Emmy were shaking hands and exchanging polite greetings with the van der Hovens when Dolly came in, carrying a silver bowl in which she had arranged the twenty-four magnificent dark red roses. Her nose was buried in the blooms, and she said, "The smell of them, Piet! Divine. You are a genius!"

Crystal threw up her hands in mock alarm and covered her eyes. "Naughty, naughty!" she cried. "Take them away, Dolly! You know I'm not supposed to see *any* of my presents until this evening! I'm not looking! I won't look! Henry, make her take them away!"

"Oh, very well," said Dolly. "All a bit childish if you ask me."

"Now, don't be a spoilsport, Miss Dolly." Chuck Swasheimer loomed up in the doorway behind Dolly. "Give the roses here. I'll take them out to the kitchen till this evening. You go right in and join the party."

And a party it soon became, even if slightly uneasy and full of unexplained tensions. Daffy, as if by unconscious reflex, flirted with Piet van der Hoven. Violet, who seemed to be indulging in school-girlish hero-worship of her mother, played yes-woman to Crystal, laughing exaggeratedly at her jokes and confining her conversation to such remarks as, "Oh, *Mother!* How marvelous! Did you *really?*" Chuck Swasheimer found a sympathetic listener in Emmy and was soon off on his hobbyhorse of domestic plumbing systems. Emmy had taken a great fancy to Chuck, and as a housewife was genuinely interested in sinks and waste-disposal units, so the conversation was mutually satisfying. Henry took his drink over to the windowseat, where Dolly Underwood-Threep was sitting by herself, gazing out over the sunlit lawn.

She greeted him cryptically. "I wish to God I knew how he does it."

"How who does what?" Henry sat down beside her.

"Piet. Those roses. Bloody marvelous. Here I am, call myself a gardener, and my best blooms look like bachelor's buttons beside his Baccarats."

"He's a professional rose-grower, isn't he?" said Henry. "Surely that must—"

"Makes no difference. Shouldn't, anyhow. Of course, in Holland he may be able to get hold of chemical preparations that I can't, but—"

"Talking of chemicals," said Henry, "I've been wondering just where you keep this lethal parathion of yours."

Dolly gave him an amused look. "The great detective at work? Sorry, shouldn't have said that, but nobody can hear us. If it interests you, it's kept in the greenhouse, which is locked. I carry the key myself." She patted the pocket of her corduroy breeches.

"But the windows are open?"

"You don't think I'd leave the stuff within arm's reach

of a window, do you? No, no, you needn't lose any sleep over that. There's nobody but me who can get at that tin. And even if they could, I don't suppose any of this lot would appreciate how dangerous it is."

"Except Piet van der Hoven."

"Oh. Yes, to be sure. Except Piet." Dolly gave one of her loud, abrupt laughs and repeated, "Except Piet, of course."

Henry could not understand the curious emphasis of her last words, and said as much, but received no illuminating reply. Dolly merely drained her drink and said that she must be getting on with lunch. She went off into the kitchen and soon returned to say that the meal was ready. It consisted of an excellent cold buffet. With it Dolly served—in a perfunctory manner—a couple of bottles of very good Meursault Charmes, whose only fault was that the vintage label (an excellent year) indicated that it had been kept rather longer than advisable for a delicate white Burgundy.

When Henry and Emmy both accepted the offer of wine with enthusiasm, Dolly looked thoroughly taken aback and began searching for a corkscrew. It suddenly dawned on Henry that this was not a wine-drinking household and that these bottles were mere symbols, to be trotted out on social occasions, politely refused, and returned to the cellar. Doggedly, however, he persisted in his acceptance. Eventually a corkscrew was found, and Henry opened the wine himself. As he had suspected, it was delicious, but threatening to go "over the top." It would have been a sin to leave it undrunk any longer.

As for the other members of the party, Crystal and Dolly continued to knock back gin-based cocktails; Chuck and Daffy made good headway through a bottle of Scotch, which they had brought with them; Piet drank bottled beer, and Violet stuck to orange juice.

After lunch Crystal announced her intention of going back to bed, so as to be bright-eyed and bushy-tailed for the evening's celebrations. The Swasheimers went up to their room to unpack before driving to the station to collect Primrose. The van der Hovens set out for a walk. Henry and Emmy followed Dolly into the kitchen and offered to wash up. To their surprise, their offer was quickly and graciously accepted.

"Very kind. Can tell you're not any of Crys's normal friends—if 'normal' is the word for most of them, which I doubt." Dolly hooted with laughter. "Matter of fact, I'd be most grateful. Got a few things to do."

Like the garden, the kitchen showed evidence of Dolly's efficiency, neatness, and love of order. Built-in cupboards housed plates, cups, and saucers, ranged with military precision; the enameled container marked TEA really did have tea in it; knives, forks, and spoons were carefully segregated; the gas oven was as shiningly spotless inside as out. Emmy felt a little daunted as she turned on the tap and started on the piles of dirty dishes.

Henry had selected a clean tea towel from the cupboard, but Emmy was not at all surprised that the stack of clean, wet plates mounted untouched on the draining board. She turned around, to see Henry, the tea towel slung over his shoulder, squatting on his haunches to examine the contents of a low cupboard.

"Found something interesting?" she asked.

"Possibly." He put a hand into the cupboard and moved something, then peered in for a better view. "This is where Lady Balaclava's birthday presents are being stored, by the look of it. The roses are here—and they do smell good, as Dolly said. Ten bottles of vintage champagne—the other two must be in the refrigerator. And a small parcel done up in flowered paper and red ribbon, with a card addressed to darling Crys from her silly old Dolly. The cake will presumably come later, with Madame Duval."

Emmy said, "And nothing from us. How awful, Henry. Let's walk to the village as soon as the washing up is done, and get a box of chocolates or something. We can't appear empty-handed this evening."

"That's a good idea," said Henry, "but you'd better go alone. I think I should stay here."

So it was that Emmy set out for Plumley Green, while

Henry stationed himself with a newspaper in the drawing room, near a window from which he could observe the comings and goings of the household.

Nothing sensational happened. Dolly came downstairs from her room and went into the garden, where she started weeding the herbaceous border on the far side of the lawn. Soon afterward the Swasheimers came downstairs and also went out onto the lawn. Henry saw them talking to Dolly for a moment or so. Then they both got into the Rolls and drove off—much too early, Henry noted, for meeting Primrose. After that nothing happened for some twenty minutes, when Dolly completed her weeding and made her way up to the greenhouse. Some half-hour later the van der Hovens arrived back from their walk. That is to say, Violet arrived back. Henry saw her come across the garden toward the house, and a few moments later he heard her light step in the hall and on the stairs, as she went up to the Dali Room, at whose insomniac horrors Henry could only dimly guess. Some ten minutes later Henry saw Piet van der Hoven come into the garden from the woods. He did not come into the house, however, but instead made his way to the greenhouse, where Henry could see him deep in conversation with Dolly.

The Swasheimers arrived back in the Rolls just before five, bringing with them Primrose Duval and the birthday cake from *Maison Bonnet* of Lausanne. As the trio came in through the front door, Henry heard Daffodil say to Primrose, "Mama's in bed, of course. Vi and the Flying Dutchman have gone for a jolly tramp, equally of course. Dolly is up to her eyes in the azaleas. There's nobody else except a rather curious couple called Tibbett."

"Friends of Mother?"

"I . . . I suppose so." Daffodil sounded thoughtful. "Not the usual sort, though. Quiet and madly refined. Mamma keeps on saying they're friends of Basil's—you know, her old beau—but I don't believe it. I think she's up to something."

"I expect they're just some sad little people that Mother picked up somewhere and felt sorry for," said Primrose penetratingly. "It wouldn't be the first time. You know how she gets about people who look as though they need a square meal. Rather sweet, really."

"Anyhow," said Daffodil, "they appeared to be house-trained. You'd better come straight up. Chuck'll bring your case, won't you, honey? You're next to us. We're in the Syrie Maugham Room. Vi and Piet have drawn the short straw this year, poor things."

"I'd better do something with this," said Primrose.

At once Charles Swasheimer said, "Just you give the cake to me, Primrose, and I'll put it with the rest of the gifts before I carry your bag up."

As the two sisters climbed the stairs, Henry heard Daffodil say, "Edouard has a cheek, I must say. Mamma is *not* amused."

To which Primrose replied, "Don't be mean, Daffy. He really does have a conference, and there was nothing he could do. . . ."

Upstairs a door opened and closed, and the voices were lost. A moment later Chuck Swasheimer's heavy tread sounded on the stairs, and then was silent. A few minutes later Emmy came back from the village, with the best box of assorted chocolates available from the Plumley Green General Stores.

"It's marvelous country," she said. "Pine woods and sandy paths and harebells and fantastic views. That's why I stayed out so long. Well, we'd better put these in the cupboard."

She handed Henry the chocolates, together with the heavily floral birthday card which was all that the local newsagent could provide. Inside it bore the legend:

> Once more the happy day is here,
> The one I long for all the year,
> When I can say, with heart so true,
> "A Happy Birthday," dear, to You.

* * *

Well, it couldn't be helped. Henry took out his fountain pen and added the words, "With all good wishes from Henry and Emmy Tibbett." Then he and Emmy went into the kitchen to add their offering to the store in the cupboard.

The first and most noticeable thing about the cupboard was the new addition—a large, square box of white cardboard, luxuriously embellished with the words *Maison Bonnet, Pâtisserie, Confiserie. Lausanne.* Gently Henry lifted the lid. Inside was an iced cake of fantastic elaboration. In the center of the cake, among the golden scrolls and pink sugar roses, stood a miniature Swiss chalet made of marzipan, with a chocolate roof and shutters, and a crystallized rose petal for its red front door. Around this masterpiece of the cakemaker's art, the words *Happy Birthday, Crystal* were traced in pistachio-green icing. Henry replaced the lid of the box and added his humble box of chocolates to the hoard. He was about to shut the cupboard door again when he suddenly noticed something. He reached in, over the assembled gifts, to the back of the cupboard. When he turned to face Emmy, he had something in his hand.

It was a red, cylindrical tin, with an aerosol spray on the top of it, and the word *FLYAWAY* printed around it in white letters. Small print underneath recommended the contents as an insecticide suitable for greenhouse use, and even smaller print advised the user to wear gloves, to keep the preparation away from the skin and eyes, and to wash well in clean water after use. Above all, added the proprietors, in print so small as to be almost invisible to the naked eye, Flyaway should not be ingested, as even a very small dose could prove fatal. It contained, whispered the final line, ten percent parathion.

"That must be the stuff Dolly uses on the azaleas," said Emmy.

"Exactly," said Henry. "And it's supposed to be kept in the greenhouse under lock and key. Above all, it shouldn't be in the kitchen."

"Perhaps Dolly made a mistake . . ." Emmy's voice trailed off into silence. In this kitchen, it was unthinkable that Dolly should have misplaced anything by accident.

"What's more," said Henry, "I'm ninety-percent certain that it wasn't in the cupboard earlier on. Well, it's certainly not going to stay here. I'll take it up to our room and lock it in the bathroom. And now, we'd better go and change, or we'll be late for the party."

Henry and Emmy came downstairs on the stroke of six, to find that everything had been prepared in their absence by the indefatigable Dolly. The drawing room was transformed. A circle of chairs had been arranged around a low marble table, on which the gifts were laid out. The cake formed the centerpiece, flanked by the roses in their silver bowl, the Tibbetts' chocolates, and Dolly's small package. Two bottles of champagne, their flanks misted and steaming, stood in ice buckets, ready to fill the nine tulip-shaped glasses which were grouped around them. All was ready but so far Henry and Emmy were alone in the room. Quickly Henry took a clean handkerchief from his pocket and polished the already gleaming glasses. He did not intend to leave anything to chance.

As the party assembled, Dolly—almost unrecognizable in a short but droopy dress of lilac crepe—marshaled its members, like a sheepdog coping with an errant herd. The big armchair facing the table was for Crystal, of course. Henry was to sit on her right, with Emmy beside him. Dolly would be on Crystal's left. Then Primrose. The other two couples were to occupy the four chairs which faced Crystal across the table.

At exactly five past six, when everybody had been drilled into position, the door from the hall was flung open, and Lady Balaclava made her entrance. It was impressive. She was wearing a creation in gold lamé, stitched all over with sequins and pearls, and embellished with quantities of white ostrich feather. Its hem was cut in a series of points, like golden icicles, and fringed with gilt beads. Crystal's short, hennaed hair was encircled by a diamanté bandeau, slightly tarnished, and her cigarette holder—ebony, with diamond chips—was longer than ever. She posed dramatically on the threshold and cried, "Darlings!"

Right on cue, the first champagne cork flew out between Chuck's fingers with a satisfying pop. Glasses were filled and raised, Crystal was surrounded and kissed, and her health drunk. Henry noticed that she herself left her champagne untouched—correct procedure, of course, for the subject of the toast—but brought the full glass to the table with her. She sat down, and with a tiny wink at Henry patted the seat of the chair on her right, indicating that he should sit there.

Next came the ceremony of cutting the cake, which was accomplished amidst much laughter. Slices were distributed, but Henry noticed that Crystal had cut only eight.

"What about you, Lady Balaclava? You've forgotten yourself."

"Indeed I haven't! What a suggestion, Henry darling!" A gale of laughter. "No, no. Primmy knows how I adore marzipan. That dreamy chalet on the top is for me." Lady Balaclava bent over the cake, knife in hand, and deftly detached the little almond-paste house. A moment of some sort had evidently been reached, because everyone fell silent.

Crystal stood up, her glass in one hand and the marzipan chalet in the other. "And now, my dear darlings," she said, "*I* shall drink to *you*. And I shall eat your gorgeous cake and smell your beautiful roses, and open these two intriguing parcels, and we shall all *wallow* in this dreamlike bubbly, because I don't want a *drop* left in that case tomorrow. But first . . ."

She turned to Henry. "As our guest or honor, Henry shall have first go at everything."

Crystal thrust the marzipan chalet toward Henry's mouth. Feeling very foolish, he took a bite. It was delicious. Everybody applauded.

"Now the champagne!"

"But I've already—" Henry protested.

"From my glass," said Crystal quietly but firmly. Henry took a sip. It, too, was excellent.

"And now the roses." Crystal picked up the silver bowl and presented it to Henry, who buried his nose among the blooms and inhaled their scent with pleasure.

"Ah!" said Lady Balaclava with what sounded like deep satisfaction, and perhaps some relief. "Now . . . darlings. A very happy my birthday to you all!"

Everybody sprang to their feet and raised their glasses. Crystal, laughing gaily, took a bite from the marzipan chalet, a sip from her glass, and a long luxuriant sniff at the roses. "Blissful," she murmured. "Divine . . ."

She got no further. Suddenly, with a bewildered expression, she put a hand to her face and began rubbing it nervously. Then she gasped and clutched her throat. As Henry sprang to help her, she staggered, her face now suffused to a ghastly purple, her breath coming in noisy, agonized gulps. Henry caught her in his arms as she collapsed, like a rag doll.

"For God's sake," he cried. "Call a doctor! Quick!"

Dolly, her face green, rushed out into the hall.

"And get away from her, the rest of you. Give her a chance. I'm going to try artificial respiration."

Primrose was sobbing. Violet seemed turned to stone, her face rigid with horror. Daffodil was screaming, while Chuck tried to calm her. Piet stood behind Henry, like a willing but clumsy dog, anxious to please but unsure what to do.

A few moments later Dolly came back into the room. "The doctor will be here in a few minutes," she said faintly. She swayed and put a hand to the door jamb to steady herself.

Henry looked up at her. "Her heart seems to have stopped beating," he said. "I'll go on with artificial respiration, but—"

Suddenly Dolly screamed. "She's dead! Crys is dead!"

And she was perfectly right.

6

It was Emmy who quietly but efficiently cleared the room,
leaving Henry to continue in peace with his ineffectual attempt at resuscitation. Nobody seemed reluctant to go.
Lady Balaclava was not a pretty sight, and, from the moment of Dolly's scream, everybody seemed to take it for
granted that she was, in fact, dead. Her daughters and
sons-in-law readily accepted Emmy's assurance that they
really could not help, and might even hinder if they
stayed. Dolly needed even less urging. Immediately after
her outburst, she had turned and raced upstairs.

Emmy escorted the others up to their rooms and suggested that they should stay there for the time being, until
Henry and the doctor had done their work. Nobody
queried that Henry should take charge, with Emmy as his
ADC. Daffodil was quiet now, and all of them seemed
dazed. Emmy came downstairs again, and into the
drawing room.

Henry, looking up from his labors, said, "I'm afraid it's
no good, but I'll keep going till the doctor arrives. Nobody must leave the house."

"They're all in their rooms," said Emmy. She was
feeling sick and tried not to look at Crystal and her terrible, discolored face.

"All the same, you'd better keep an eye open. There are
only the front and back doors, as far as I know. You'd

better go out and keep watch—after you've rung the police."

"The police?"

"Of course."

"But you—"

"I'm here purely unofficially," said Henry. "And a bloody mess I've made of it. Go and ring the local station. Tell them it's suspected poisoning."

Emmy said nothing, but went out into the hall. Henry returned to his exhausting and useless task. When he heard the door open a minute or so later he said, without looking up, "What did they say?"

"I beg your pardon?"

The voice was young, deep, and feminine. Henry looked up abruptly, to see a young woman standing in the doorway. She was brown-haired, with a gently pretty face and very large eyes. Henry had never seen her before.

Seeing his bewildered expression, the newcomer said quickly, "I'm the doctor. May I see her, please?"

"The doctor? But Dr. Griffiths—"

"He went on holiday this morning. I am his locum. Now, if you'd just let me—"

With relief Henry handed over to the girl. She dropped down on her knees beside Crystal Balaclava, opened the small brown suitcase which she carried, and began her examination. It was not long before she sat back on her heels and said, "She's dead. I'm afraid. Must have been practically instantaneous." There was a little pause, while she repacked instruments into her suitcase. "I haven't introduced myself. My name's Massingham."

"Mine is Tibbett," said Henry. "I—my wife and I—are weekend guests here."

"I see." Dr. Massingham stood up. "Well, I'm afraid I have bad news for you. The police will have to be informed."

"My wife is telephoning them at this moment," said Henry.

Dr. Massingham raised her eyebrows slightly but made

no other comment. She said, "Who else is in the house? Was it your wife who called me?"

"No. No, that was Miss Underwood-Threep. Lady Balaclava's . . . er . . . lady companion. Her three daughters are here—Lady Balaclava's, I mean—and two sons-in-law. They're all up in their rooms. It was her birthday, you see. A family gathering."

"Can you tell me exactly what happened?"

Henry described the birthday celebrations, and Crystal's collapse. Dr. Massingham nodded slowly. "It looks like acute poisoning," she said. "Possibly one of these pernicious modern insecticides. The P.M. will show if I've guessed right. Better not touch anything. The police will want to see things just as they are—including the poor lady, I'm afraid. They'll be sending their own doctor, of course. A very unpleasant business for the family—and for your wife and yourself, I fear. You're probably not familiar with police work, but—"

"I am very familiar with it," said Henry.

Dr. Massingham gave him a long look. Then, suddenly, recognition dawned. "Good lord," she said. "Tibbett. Inspector Tibbett of Scotland Yard. I've seen your picture in the papers. Am I right?"

"Except in one small detail," said Henry. "I was promoted last year. It's Chief Superintendent now." He smiled at her. He liked this girl.

"Well, well, well. And you just happen to be a weekend guest in a house where the hostess drops dead, obviously poisoned. I didn't think that sort of coincidence happened outside the pages of—"

"It doesn't," said Henry. "That is to say, it wasn't entirely a coincidence."

"I see. So you are not altogether surprised."

"I'm sorry, Dr. Massingham," said Henry, "but I really can't discuss . . ."

"No, no. Of course you can't." Dr. Massingham walked over to the sofa and sat down. "I'm afraid I shall have to stay here until the police arrive."

"Naturally." There was a pause. Then Henry said, "You mentioned insecticides."

"That's right."

"Just what did you have in mind?"

Dr. Massingham looked at him quizzically. "I'm sorry, Chief Superintendent. I really can't discuss—"

"No, no. Of course you can't." There was another pause, less uneasy. Then they looked at each other, and both laughed. Henry said, "All right. I'm here, absolutely unofficially, because Lady Balaclava had an idea that somebody was going to murder her."

"She was right, it seems. Somebody in her own family?"

"Why do you say that?"

"Well, you said that the other people in the house were her daughters and sons-in-law, didn't you? Oh, except for the lady companion, of course."

"Exactly," said Henry. "Now, what were you saying about insecticides?"

Before Dr. Massingham could reply, Emmy came in. "I've just—" she began, and then stopped, surprised, as she saw the other woman.

"This is Dr. Massingham, darling. Doctor—my wife, Emmy. I'm afraid Lady Balaclava is dead."

"I spoke to the local sergeant," said Emmy. Her voice was not quite steady. She was trying to avoid looking at Crystal's body, and finding it difficult "He'll be along in a few minutes, with the police doctor."

Dr. Massingham said, "In that case, I think we should get out of this room, and leave it just as it is for the police to see. Don't you agree, Chief Superintendent?"

"I do," said Henry. "And I think you might take a look at Miss Underwood-Threep, Doctor, if you don't mind. She was in a hysterical state just now. Emmy will take you upstairs. . . ."

Sitting alone in the kitchen, Henry tried to fight against a feeling of profound depression and failure. He had been sent here specifically to prevent just this tragedy from happening—and what good had he done? Despite his vigilance, somebody had succeeded in getting at the tin of

Flyaway, had extracted some of it and placed a fatal dose . . . where? He himself had drunk from Crystal's glass a moment before she did, had smelled the roses, had eaten the marzipan. That must have been it. The marzipan. It must have been sheer good fortune for Henry that not he but Crystal had bitten into the poisoned part of that innocent-looking little candy house. The remains of it were still clutched in Crystal's convulsed hand. The police would analyze it. They would find the traces of parathion.

The Swiss chalet. That led directly to Primrose. To Primrose, and to her husband, the absent Dr. Duval, so suspiciously prevented from joining the party by an unexpected conference. Surely he could not be so naïve as to imagine that his mere physical absence would divert suspicion from him? Henry wished that the local police would arrive. He was anxious to get things moving.

In fact, they arrived within minutes. With much roaring of engines and squealing of tires on loose gravel, two black police cars and an ambulance organized themselves into the space left by Henry's car, the Rolls, and the immobile Bentley in the drive, and then disgorged a stream of people. There was Detective Inspector Sandport from Hindhurst, aided and abetted by Detective Sergeant Arrowsmith and also by Sergeant Merryfield of the Plumley Green uniformed branch. There was Dr. Bartlett, the police surgeon—elderly, slightly fussy, but clearly competent. There were photographers and fingerprint experts, ambulance men and drivers. Foxes' Trot buzzed with activity, in a grim parody of a weekend party of the good old days. And as in the good old days, Crystal was the center of attraction, but with one important difference.

Dr. Massingham came downstairs, having administered a sedative to Dolly, and conferred professionally with Dr. Bartlett. In a surprisingly short time the formalities were completed, Crystal's body was removed in the ambulance, the experts packed up their gear and departed in one of the black cars. Henry found himself alone in the drawing room with Inspector Sandport and Sergeant Arrowsmith. The inquiry had begun.

The detective inspector stood up very well to the shock of learning that he was interviewing a chief superintendent from Scotland Yard. He accepted with calm amounting to stodginess Henry's assurance that he and Emmy happened to be weekending purely by chance. He cracked a few leaden jokes about it being a bit of luck to have a trained observer on the spot. He then proceeded with a series of textbook questions. Henry told him all that he knew, excepting only his interview with the assistant commissioner at Scotland Yard.

When Henry had finished, Sandport said, "I see. So you surmise that some person had administered weedkiller to the deceased?"

"Not weedkiller," said Henry. "Insecticide. A ten-percent-parathion solution, as used in greenhouses. And I'm surmising nothing for the moment, Inspector. I've simply told you what happened and what I observed."

"Of course, Chief Superintendent. Quite correct." Sandport sounded like a *viva voce* examiner giving a candidate credit for having sidestepped a trap. "Now, re the members of the family, who I shall soon have the pleasure of meeting. . . ."

"Whom," said Henry under his breath. The stilted idiom of police phraseology annoyed him enough, without glaring grammatical errors thrown in. Louder, he said, "I can't help you much, I'm afraid. I only met them myself for the first time today."

Sandport gave him a quizzical look. "I appreciate your attitude, Chief Superintendent," he said. Henry wondered what on earth he meant. "Am I right in assuming that the members of the family are unaware of your status as a police officer?"

"Miss Underwood-Threep knows who I am," said Henry. "I don't think it was mentioned to any of the others. There was hardly time."

"No, there wouldn't have been, would there?" said Sandport with no expression whatsoever. "Well, I think that's all for the moment. I will now conduct my interviews with the local doctor and the inmates of the house. I'm not suggesting that you should be present . . ."

"Of course not," said Henry quickly. "This is your investigation, Inspector, and I'm a mere member of the public. Perhaps a suspect—who knows?"

"You will have your little joke, Chief Superintendent," said Inspector Sandport lugubriously. "Nevertheless, I thought we might have a chat later on, after I've seen the other people. Two heads are better than one," he added with the air of one composing a brilliant epigram.

"If you wish it," said Henry. "By the way, I hope you don't mind if I make a phone call—to my assistant commissioner. I feel I should let him know what has—"

"Yes, you would want to do that, wouldn't you, sir?" said Sandport.

Henry thought, "He's rumbled me, all right. Not nearly as slow as he looks."

"If you'd be kind enough to ask the local doctor— what's his name?"

"Massingham," said Henry. "And it's 'her.' The girl who was talking to the police surgeon."

"A lady doctor." Inspector Sandport sounded full of gloom. "Well, I'll have to see her just the same. If you'd ask her to step in here . . ."

Henry found Dr. Massingham with Emmy in the kitchen, drinking a cup of tea. He sent her in to talk to the inspector, and then went upstairs. He had decided to call the assistant commissioner from the privacy of his room.

It was funereal and a little eerie in the Black Room. Somebody had drawn the black curtains, leaving only chinks through which the light of the setting sun could squeeze its way. Henry sat down on the bed and picked up the white telephone, which crouched like a small albino animal in the artificial dusk.

He should not have been startled to hear a voice. He should have realized that this was but one extension of the single telephone line which linked Foxes' Trot with the outside world. All the same, it was with a sense of shock that he heard an agonized feminine voice saying, "Crystal is dead." For a split second, a rushing wind of superstition invaded his mind, irrational and therefore horribly convincing. Then a distant masculine voice said, *"Quoi? Qu'est-ce tu dis?"*—and Henry knew that he was listening to Primrose telephoning the news to her husband.

Primrose, who had been pale but self-possessed after her outburst of weeping downstairs, now sounded overwrought. "Edouard, it's horrible . . . the cake . . . everyone will say . . . everyone is saying . . . they're such bitches, you know them. . . ."

"Primrose, my Primrose. Calm yourself. I am desolated to hear of your mother's death, but I don't see what I can—"

"You can come over here, now, this minute!" Primrose's voice rose dangerously. "You can't leave me to face this alone, Edouard! It's not fair! The cake—"

"Now, Primrose, you know that this conference—"

"Oh, to hell with your conference! You don't understand, Edouard. You *must* come. You *must*. I . . . I won't say any more. The whole family is probably listening in. Edouard, *you must come*."

There was a pause at the other end of the line, so that for a moment Henry thought that the call had been disconnected. Primrose evidently had the same doubt, because she said anxiously, "Edouard? Are you still there? Can you hear me?"

"I can hear you, my Primrose." Dr. Duval sighed, a mixture of resignation and exasperation that came clear across the five hundred miles between Lausanne and Plumley Green. "Very well. I shall come. Now, tell me just what has happened. . . ."

Henry decided not, after all, to make his phone call from Foxes' Trot. He replaced the receiver quietly, leaving the Duvals to continue their conversation, and went downstairs. Having interrupted Inspector Sandport's interview with Dr. Massingham for long enough to establish leave of absence, he followed the path that Emmy had taken earlier, over the hill and down into the hamlet of Plumley Green. There he found a telephone box.

The assistant commissioner was not in his office, of course. It was Saturday. However, Henry had no difficulty in finding out his private telephone number—and was unpleasantly surprised to be told that it was Trimble Wells 482. Bad enough to have to explain matters to the old man, without his being within spitting distance of the scene of the crime. Still, it had to be done. Henry dialed the number.

For some time the telephone rang unanswered. Then the A.C. himself, panting slightly, came on to the line. "Tibbett? Ah . . . forgive me . . . was working in the garden . . . all going well, I hope. . . . What's that? . . . What are you trying to say, man? . . . Yes, I heard you, but . . . Dead? . . . Poisoned? . . . But, good God, you were there specifically to prevent . . . no, no, I realize that, but . . . heaven knows what Sir Basil will say . . . let alone the commissioner . . . What's that? . . . Of course you must remain in charge . . . Inspector Who? . . . No, no, no, out of the question . . . you should never have allowed . . . well, yes, I agree, proper procedure and so forth . . . yes, yes, yes, of course I know . . . fortunately, the chief constable is a neighbor of mine . . . leave it to me, I'll have a word with him . . . I must warn you, Tibbett, I take a very serious view of this . . . under your very nose . . . the reputation of the Yard . . . the very least you can do now is to clear the matter up quickly and efficiently. . . . I shall ring the chief constable now, and I expect results from you. Fast. Keep in touch."

Henry, feeling like a schoolboy after a sticky ten minutes in the headmaster's study, made his way slowly back to Foxes' Trot. Emmy had been right. The countryside was very beautiful in the soft evening light, which touched the tall, straight pine trunks with pink and gold, echoing the purple haze of the wild heather. Henry, however, was in no mood to appreciate the beauties of nature. Sensibly, he had stopped lashing himself mentally for having allowed Crystal's death to happen, and he was now wholly absorbed in analyzing the problem, reducing the random mass of information in his mind to a rational scheme, from which, he hoped, a pattern would emerge.

Thus it was that, by the time he reached the house, the wheels of authority were already turning. The assistant commissioner had telephoned to the chief constable. The chief constable had telephoned the head of the local CID, who in turn had contacted Inspector Sandport at Foxes' Trot. Sergeant Arrowsmith met Henry in the hall with the news that the inspector would be grateful if the chief superintendent would spare him a few minutes right away.

Inspector Sandport was sitting on the drawing-room sofa making notes in a bulky looseleaf book, and looking far from happy.

"Well, sir," he said, "I've had my chief on the blower." Henry felt that the "sir" had cost him a painful effort. "Seems the chief constable has been on. He thinks that, since you so fortunately happened to be on the spot . . ." There was a wealth of irony in the slightly stressed word "happened." ". . . and since it's possible that, after I've made my report, he *may* decide to ask for assistance from the Yard . . . well . . ." Sandport stopped, having lost the thread of his sentence a couple of clauses back. "Well, the long and short of it is that you are to sit in with me while I interview these people. Tomorrow, when the pathologist's report comes in, we'll know better where we stand, and if the chief constable *should* decide . . ."

"It's very kind of you, Inspector," said Henry. "I'll try to be as unobtrusive as possible. After all, it's your case."

"For the time being," said Sandport a little bitterly. He sighed and then went on in a businesslike voice, "Well, so far I've spoken to nobody but the doctor. Seems quite intelligent, for a woman." He ruffled through the pages of his notebook. "Her snap diagnosis is poison, quite probably by an organic phosphorus insecticide, such as this Flyaway stuff. Naturally, she can't be sure till we get the p.m. results, but our Dr. Bartlett agrees entirely with Dr. Massingham. No doubt about it, I should say. Now, as I understand it from Dr. Massingham, it's possible for poisoning to occur by what she calls repeated small exposures to organic phosphorus compounds, which needn't necessarily be swallowed—they can be breathed in, or even absorbed through the skin."

"That's what Dolly said—I mean, Miss Underwood-Threep. I told you how she refused to let us into the greenhouse while she was using the spray," Henry said.

"Exactly," said Sandport. "My first reaction was that this sad business was probably an accident. I mean to say, Lady Balaclava may well have picked up small doses in her own greenhouse. I put the idea to Dr. Massingham."

"And what did she say?"

"Knocked it right on the head, I'm afraid."

"She did? Why?"

"Well, it seems that in cases of repeated small doses, you don't get a dramatic collapse and death like this. The person becomes ill gradually, over a period of hours or even days. Dr. Massingham says—and Dr. Bartlett agrees—that what happened this evening could only be caused one way."

"And what is that?"

"What the doctors call a massive dose, taken orally. In plain terms, the poor lady had just swallowed a ruddy great mouthful of the stuff. Well—when I say a mouthful—a whacking great dose in medical terms, although it seems little enough to a layman like myself. Seems that around a hundred and fifty milligrams is a fatal dose . . . that's about two-hundredths of an ounce. And that's what they call 'massive,' if you please."

"If it was taken orally," said Henry slowly, "it must have been either in the champagne or the cake."

"Precisely. Well, we'll soon know. Both have gone off to be analyzed in the labs. I've even sent the roses along for good measure."

Henry said, "If the poison turns up in the marzipan, Madame Duval and her husband are bound to come under very grave suspicion. As far as we know, the cake was taken straight to the kitchen cupboard and stayed there in its box until Miss Underwood-Threep brought it out for the party. If the champagne was poisoned—well, we must have an accomplished conjurer in the party. It couldn't have been in the wine itself, because nobody else was affected."

"Ah, but what about the glass? Two or three grains—"

"It just happens," said Henry, "that I polished all the glasses myself just before they were used. And don't forget that I actually drank out of Lady Balaclava's glass a moment before she did. If anything was slipped into her glass, it must have been done while I was smelling the roses—at which time Lady Balaclava was actually holding the glass in her hand. Quite a conjuring trick."

"My money's on the cake," said Sandport, "and I guess yours is, too. Let's see . . ." He consulted his notes again. "Madame Duval brought it into the house. Mr. Swasheimer took it from her and put it away in the kitchen. Miss Underwood-Threep brought it out again. and . . . em . . ." He stopped, embarrassed.

"Well?"

"Well, sir . . . I understand that you and Mrs. Tibbett were in the kitchen after lunch. You did the washing up, I believe."

"But that was before Madame Duval arrived."

"Ah, yes. But you went back later on, to put your own gift in the cupboard. You saw the cake, and you noticed the Flyaway and removed it, as you told me. Now, don't get the idea that I'm suspicious of *you*—dear me, no. All I'm saying is, if you had access to the cake, then other people may have had, too. That's all I'm saying."

"This is all highly speculative," said Henry. "Until the lab report comes in, we've no proof that it was the cake."

"No *proof*," agreed Sandport. He was a master of sinister stresses in his speech. "Well, now, sir . . . with your permission, I suggest we get on with interviewing these people. Just to get acquainted, as it were, and hear what they have to say."

"It's your case, Inspector," said Henry again. "Pay no attention to me. With any luck, nobody will even notice I am here."

Inspector Sandport grunted. Then he asked Sergeant Arrowsmith to go upstairs and ask Miss Underwood-Threep if she would step down to the drawing room for a few minutes.

Henry walked over to the window and looked out into the deepening dusk. He felt sorry for Dolly, sorry for poor Crystal, sorry for Sandport, and sorry for himself. He wished he could have poured himself one of Dolly's White Ladies from the cocktail cabinet. His morale was at a very low ebb indeed.

7

Dr. Massingham's sedative seemed to have had the desired
effect on Dolly. She came striding into the room with her
usual no-nonsense panache, sat down squarely in front of
Inspector Sandport, lit a cigar, and said to Henry's back,
"Well, Chief Superintendent, you might introduce us."

"I beg your pardon?" Sandport had gone very red.
Henry turned around to face the others.

"I presume," said Dolly, waving her cigar at Sandport,
"that this little man is your junior. Is he to take a note of
our conversation? Is that why he needs three ball-point
pens and two notebooks?"

Henry said, "I shall be delighted to introduce you. Miss
Underwood-Threep, this is Detective Inspector Sandport
of the Hindhurst CID, who is in charge of the case. Inspector—Miss Dorothy Underwood-Threep, lady companion to the late Lady Balaclava."

Dolly was not interested in Sandport. She said to Henry,
"In charge? What d'you mean, in charge? You're in
charge."

"No," said Henry. "At this stage, I'm only an observer.
The inspector will ask the questions, and I hope you will
answer them fully."

"I'll answer them as I think fit—at this stage," said
Dolly. She blew a smoke ring just above the inspector's
head, stopping only just short of the impudence of blowing
it into his face, and winked at Henry.

Sandport, falling back on officialese in his discomfort, said, "You are Miss Dorothy Underwood-Threep?"

"Are you deaf or something? Mr. Tibbett has just introduced us."

"Your age, please?"

"None of your bloody business."

"A matter of routine, madam."

"Over twenty-one," said Dolly blandly.

"I must ask you to be more precise, madam."

"Very well." Dolly winked again at Henry. "I am three years and four months younger than the Duke of Windsor. Work that one out."

Sandport sighed. "We'll leave it at 'over twenty-one' for the moment, madam," he said. "Now, you live here at Foxes' Trot permanently, I understand."

"I have lived here," said Dolly, "from 1941 until today. I'm afraid I can't say more than that."

"And what does that mean?" The inspector was wary, on the lookout for traps.

Dolly shrugged. "I was employed by Lady Balaclava—"

"Employed?"

"Oh, in the most genteel way, like all lady companions. Nevertheless, employed. Now that my employer is dead, there seems no reason why I should continue to live here."

"You don't imagine that Lady Balaclava will have provided for you in her will? After so many years—"

Dolly laughed bitterly. "Poor Crys. Her will doesn't amount to a row of beans. Hasn't the chief superintendent told you?"

Sandport glanced at Henry, who said, "We haven't discussed that aspect of the case."

"Oh, well, then—I'll tell you myself. Crystal didn't have two half-pennies of her own to rub together. All the money was Charlie's—that's her late husband—and he left it tied up in so many knots that all the king's horses and all the king's men couldn't unravel them. Crystal had this house, for her lifetime. And the income from a smallish block of capital, for her lifetime. Each of the girls also had a small income from untouchable capital, for Crystal's lifetime. Now that she's dead, the trust ends. The capital will be divided among the girls." Dolly's smile was savage. "You are under the same roof as three very rich women this evening, Inspector."

"You're suggesting that any of the three daughters would have had a motive—?"

"I'm suggesting nothing. I'm telling you the facts."

"Hm." Sandport cleared his throat. "I believe you are a keen gardener, Miss Underwood-Threep."

"I am."

"And you use a considerable amount of insecticide in your greenhouse—notably the brand known as Flyaway."

"Oh, really," said Dolly impatiently. "There's no need to hedge. You think Crys was killed by a dose of Flyaway, don't you?"

"I never said so, madam."

"You didn't have to. Well, the answer is—yes, I do use the stuff. I know exactly how dangerous it is. I use thick protective gloves, and leave all the windows of the greenhouse open when I'm spraying. Nobody else is allowed in there, and no Flyaway is ever allowed in this house—"

"Never?"

"Never," Dolly repeated firmly. Then, after a tiny pause, she said, "Oh, my God. You mean, some has been found in the house?"

"I didn't—"

"No, you didn't say so, and you are asking the questions. Point taken. Go on."

"The greenhouse is kept locked, I believe. Who has the key?"

"I do." Dolly produced an old-fashioned key from her pocket. "Here it is. And there's not a second one, I assure you."

"If you don't mind, madam, I'd like to borrow that key for a while."

Dolly hesitated, then said, "Oh, very well. But be careful."

"I will, madam. Now, how many tins of Flyaway are there in the greenhouse at the moment?"

Promptly Dolly replied, "Two. One open and the other not."

"Thank you, madam." Sandport made a note. "Now, you took the various birthday presents as they arrived and put them into the kitchen cupboard, didn't you?"

Dolly frowned, thinking. "I took in the champers from Chuck and Daffy," she said. "They were the first arrivals, this morning. I put two bottles in the fridge, and the rest in the cupboard. Then . . . yes, I took the roses from Piet in the hall. That was later, just before lunch. I put them in water, and brought the vase into the drawing room—it seemed so childish to hide them away. But Crys was a child in some ways. Ever since . . . what was I saying? Oh, yes . . . Crys insisted that they must be kept for the evening, and I think . . . wasn't it Chuck who took them out to the kitchen?" Dolly appealed to Henry.

"Yes, it was Mr. Swasheimer," said Henry.

"And the cake, Miss Underwood-Threep?"

"The cake was already in the cupboard when I came down to get things ready." Dolly's voice was tense and nervous. "I've no idea who put it there. Primrose, I suppose."

"And your own present to Lady Balaclava?"

Surprisingly, Dolly blushed. "I put it in the cupboard this morning."

"May I ask what it was?"

"You may. And I shall tell you, because you only have to unwrap it to find out. It was a game."

"A game?"

"A card game. Crys loved games. I told you, she's . . . she was a child in many ways."

"And the box of chocolates from Mr. and Mrs. Tibbett?"

"The first I saw of them," said Dolly, "was when I went to the cupboard to fetch the things for the party."

Sandport had been making notes. After a moment he looked up and said, "So, you went to that cupboard first when the Swasheimers arrived, later to put in your own gift, and finally to get the things out in the evening?"

"That's right."

"And you never saw . . . anything else . . . in there?"

Dolly looked puzzled. "Anything else? Well, there are a couple of odd plates and some flower vases which we don't often use—"

"I mean—you didn't see anything unusual?"

Dolly suddenly became angry. "If you mean a tin of Flyaway," she said, "no—certainly not."

"So anybody who said they'd seen Flyaway in that cupboard would be lying?"

"In my opinion, yes," said Dolly. She lit another cigar, and her hands were trembling. "If there was a tin of the filthy stuff in there, it could only have been planted by somebody who . . . who wanted to make trouble for me. And after all, Inspector—you must admit that of all the people in this house today, I had the least motive for killing Crys. Good God, don't you understand . . ." Her self-control suddenly crumbled, flaking away like old paint. "Don't you see . . . Crys was all I had . . . Crys . . . and this house . . . what'll happen to me now? What'll become of me? What am I going to do . . . ?"

Dolly's tears were unbearably embarrassing. Inspector Sandport was only too happy to let her go back to her room. Henry escorted the sobbing woman upstairs and persuaded her to take another of the pills which Dr. Massingham had prescribed.

When Henry returned he found Inspector Sandport putting the finishing touches to his notes. He looked up and said, "Poor lady. One can't help but feel sorry for her."

Henry said, "You feel sorry for her, do you?"

"Certainly. Of all the people here—yourself excepted, of course—she had the least to gain and the most to lose by Lady Balaclava's death. Everybody knew she was in charge of the Flyaway. . . ." He paused. Then he said, "I've just been up to the greenhouse. There's one full tin there, and one opened one, just as she said."

Henry said, "I checked in my room just now. The third tin is still there."

"Well, there you are," said Sandport. "It does look as

though somebody was trying to throw suspicion on her. And yet, when you come to think of it, there's more Flyaway in this world than the tins of it in this house. I dare say it is obtainable in other countries. In Switzerland, for instance." Sandport paused impressively. Henry did not react. Sandport rapped his ball-point pen against the cover of his notebook. "You admit the possibility, at all events, Superintendent?"

"Of course I admit the possibility."

"Then I suggest we talk to Madame Duval."

Primrose was very distressed. Her faded blond beauty seemed to have dimmed and shriveled under a gray veil of anxiety and tears. She twisted a small lace handkerchief nervously between her fingers throughout the interview and spoke in a whisper.

Her husband had been planning to come over with her, she said, but he had been prevented at the last moment by a conference. What was the last moment? Oh . . . it must have been . . . yesterday afternoon. Henry had the impression that, for Primrose, yesterday afternoon was ten thousand years away, across an unbridgeable abyss. She screwed up her pale blue eyes as if making a vast effort to peer through the mists of time. Yes . . . yesterday afternoon . . . a call from the Institute of Immunology . . . a request to present a paper on Monday, which would have to be prepared over the weekend . . . poor Edouard . . . he hadn't wanted to do it, but a man's career must come first, mustn't it? . . .

Inspector Sandport gave a grunt which might or might not imply assent, and proceeded to ask about the cake.

Primrose was on the brink of tears. "That dreadful cake . . . I wish I'd never set eyes on it. . . ."

Ponderously Sandport said, "Do you mean, Madame Duval, that you have reason to believe that poison was administered to your mother in the marzipan ornament—?"

"Of course not." Suddenly Primrose's voice was sharp. "Of course not. But that's what people are saying. And . . . well . . ." Her voice faltered again. "There is a certain sort of . . . I mean to say, Mr. Tibbett drank from

Mother's glass, and we all smelled the roses, but only Mother ate that particular piece of marzipan, so . . ." She buried her nose in the tiny handkerchief. "Oh, it's all so horrible. . . ."

With some difficulty Sandport led her back to facts. She had telephoned to Bonnet's, she said, the previous week . . . Thursday, she thought . . . to order the cake. Bonnet's were a famous firm. Her mother adored their cakes, so it was traditional that the Duvals should bring one each year for her birthday. Yes, the mixture was always the same—a light sponge with cream filling and a lot of almond paste. Only the decoration varied from year to year.

"I picked up the cake from the shop yesterday, only just before I caught the train to Geneva. Edouard dropped me off at Bonnet's and went on to his hospital by car. I collected the cake and took a taxi from Bonnet's to the railway station—and from there to Geneva and the airport. Nobody could possibly have tampered with the cake. I carried the box on my lap all the time . . . in the airplane, too. . . . I was afraid the icing might get spoiled. . . ."

The mention of the word "Flyaway" provoked fresh tears. "I've never heard of the stuff . . . well, of course I've heard of it *now*, everyone has been talking about it. ever since . . . ever since . . . I've absolutely no idea if you can buy it in Switzerland . . . how should I know? We live on the sixth floor of an apartment block . . . yes, I have a couple of window boxes, everyone does, but I've never used any sort of . . . yes, of course I knew that Dolly was keen on gardening, she always has been . . . no, I *didn't* know she kept that stuff in her greenhouse. . . . I tell you, I haven't been near the greenhouse in years . . . it just simply doesn't interest me, is there anything wrong in that? . . . Well, you make everything I say sound so . . . so . . . I don't know . . . you twist things and put words into my mouth. . . ."

From his quiet vantage point on the window seat Henry listened with interest. Sandport was certainly being singularly ham-handed with Madame Duval. Nevertheless, he wondered just how much of her rising distress was natural, and how much self-induced or even contrived. Whatever the cause, Primrose was now sobbing bitterly into her inadequate scrap of embroidery, and it was clear that no more useful information would be forthcoming for the time being. Sandport told her she might go, and asked if she wished to be helped upstairs. Primrose shook her head violently and ran out of the room.

Daffodil Swasheimer, by contrast, was entirely in control of herself. The only emotion that Henry could discern in her was anger. No, anger was too strong a word. Irritation. Impatience.

She sat down facing Inspector Sandport, and before he could open his mouth she said, "Now, Inspector, let's get this over as quickly as possible. My name is Daffodil Swasheimer. I'm Lady Balaclava's youngest daughter. I know that I stand to inherit a lot of money on her death. We all know it. The thing is that in my case, it couldn't matter less. My husband is a millionaire several times over. We arrived this morning from Paris, having crossed with the car on the night ferry from Dunkirk to Dover. Have you got all that, or am I going too fast?"

"Not at all, Mrs. Swasheimer." Sandport sounded positively deferential. He seemed fascinated by Daffodil's emerald-and-diamond brooch, which glittered wickedly in the light of the table lamp. Outside, it was beginning to grow dark.

Daffodil went on. "We brought a case of champagne for Mother's birthday. We always do. Actually, we nearly forgot it this time—I remembered just in time to remind Chuck. He had his secretary order it from the firm in Reims, and they shipped it to Dover, where we picked it up. Dolly can confirm that the case was sealed up when we arrived here—so if you think we doctored a bottle, you can think again."

"I think nothing of the sort, Mrs. Swasheimer. In fact, it's no secret that the champagne is in the clear. And as for Lady Balaclava's glass—well, Mr. Tibbett drank from it just before she did."

"Tell me," remarked Daffodil dryly, with a glance at

Henry, "is it usual to have a layman present at interviews of this sort? I merely ask."

Sandport hesitated and looked unhappy. Henry said, "No, Mrs. Swasheimer, it is not usual."

Daffy raised her eyebrows. "So——?"

"You merely asked. I have answered your question."

"Oh, well." Daffodil lit a cigarette. "It doesn't matter a row of beans to me, one way or the other. My main concern, Inspector, is that I . . . my husband and I . . . have to get back to Paris tomorrow. There's no question to our staying here. You understand that?"

"I understand what you mean, of course, Mrs. Swasheimer," said Sandport, "and I sincerely hope that . . . well . . ." He cleared his throat and tried again. "You weren't thinking of staying for the funeral, then?"

"I was not."

"Ah. Well, now . . . we'll have to see what we can do. Now, to get back to this morning. I believe Miss Underwood-Threep took the champagne in for you?"

"You believe rightly. Chuck brought the case in from the car and left it in the hall. Dolly humped it into the kitchen, and I never set eyes on it again until the party."

"But you and your husband did go into the kitchen to prepare breakfast for yourselves?"

"We started to—but Dolly came in, bustling and bullying as usual, and turned us out."

"You didn't notice a tin of Flyaway in the kitchen?"

"No. Was there one?" Daffy sounded intrigued. "So *that's* why Dolly was so keen to get us out of there. Didn't want us to see it, I suppose."

Sandport put on a grave expression, which made him look like a bad-tempered fox terrier. "Are you implying, Mrs. Swasheimer, that Miss Underwood-Threep—?"

"If the cap fits," said Daffy carelessly. "Actually, though, it hadn't occurred to me that Dolly bumped Mother off. Why should she, I mean? She was onto a soft berth with Mother, and she knew it. No—I only meant that there was this rigid rule about no Flyaway coming into the house. If she'd carelessly left a tin of it in the kitchen, she wouldn't want Mother to hear of it."

"You all knew about the Flyaway, then?"

"Of course."

"And yet," said Sandport, "Madame Duval told us she had never heard of Flyaway before today."

"Then she's lying," said Daffy calmly. "She's hysterical, of course. You won't get any sense out of her until Edouard arrives."

Daffodil then described briefly the events of the day— meeting the van der Hovens at the station, the lunch party, collecting Primrose from Hindhurst, and finally the birthday party itself. "In between times," Daffy added, "Chuck and I retreated to the chamber of horrors laughingly known as our room, and drank Scotch out of tooth mugs. Neither of us can stomach Mother's grisly cocktails. That's about all I can tell you."

"Well, I don't think I need trouble you any more for the time being, Mrs. Swasheimer," said Sandport.

"You won't trouble me any more at all, Inspector," said Daffy with a calm and pleasant smile. "I told you, we're leaving in the morning."

"Well, now, Mrs. Swasheimer, it may not be quite as simple as that . . . we are waiting for the pathologist's report, and until—"

Daffy stood up. "We are leaving in the morning," she said. "I'll give you our Paris address. If you want to stop us, you'll have to arrest us. I do hope I've made myself clear."

She smiled again, stubbed out her cigarette, and walked out of the room, leaving a lingering aura of expensive scent behind her.

Sandport said, "Very awkward. That is to say—well, Mr. Swasheimer is an influential man. I wouldn't want to upset him. Still, I don't see how we can let them go."

"Leave that young woman to me," said Henry. "I know how to deal with her sort."

Sandport looked immensely relieved. "Well, sir, if you

would . . . it would certainly be a weight off my mind. I suppose we had better see Mr. Swasheimer now."

The interview with Chuck was short and uninformative. Not that he was helpful—on the contrary—but he had nothing to add to what Daffodil had said, and he appeared to be affected by such a sense of reverence that he found it difficult to express himself at all.

"Dear, dear Lady Crystal . . . Mom, I used to call her . . . a very great lady, Inspector . . . an ornament of this mighty old country of yours . . . honored to have known her . . . to have been one of the family, in fact . . . irreparable loss . . . consider it a privilege to undertake all the funeral arrangements . . . can't be here myself for the sad occasion, but would wish no expense to be spared . . . everything done the way *she* would have liked it. . . ." Chuck's voice was hushed, as in a cathedral. Sandport thanked him and terminated the interview.

Violet, of all Lady Balaclava's daughters, was the only one who appeared genuinely affected by grief. She had been weeping, and there were dark circles under her gray eyes. Henry thought, irrelevantly, that Violet was a figure made for tragedy. The fine bone structure of her face was beautiful under her chalk-white, tightly drawn skin. In a trivial situation Violet had been ill at ease, even gauche. In tragedy she achieved nobility. With her calmly dignified grief, she might have been a character from Sophocles. The unfashionable suit and unbecoming hair style were forgotten, unimportant.

She sat down silently and waited for Sandport to begin. He, too, seemed moved by Violet's grief, because he began, rather clumsily, by offering his condolences. Violet bowed her head and whispered, "Thank you."

"I know this must be very distressing for you, Mrs. van der Hoven," Sandport went on, sounding distressed himself, "but you realize that we have to make inquiries. And that means questions."

"Of course."

"Well, now—I understand you and your husband brought a bunch of roses as a present for your mother?"

"Yes." Violet's voice was barely audible. "Two dozen Baccarats. We bring them every year. They are . . . were . . . her favorites."

"Your husband is a professional rose-grower?"

"Yes. At Aalsmeer. It's the biggest center in Holland for cut flowers."

"So . . ." Sandport hesitated, embarrassed. "Forgive me for mentioning this, Mrs. van der Hoven—but I presume you are familiar with the various insecticides used in greenhouses."

Violet shook her head slowly. "Not really," she said. "Piet is the expert. I have very little to do with the glass-houses."

"You know Flyaway?"

"I've heard of it. Dolly uses it here, and Mother makes—used to make—a great fuss about not allowing it indoors. Piet won't touch it, of course."

"He won't? You mean, he never uses it?"

"Never. He says it's too dangerous."

"But he must use insecticides?"

"Yes, of course. But never the parathion type."

"So the roses you brought could not have been sprayed with—?"

Violet gave a little gasp. "Oh! *Of course* not. Surely you didn't think . . . ?"

"No, no, madam. It's just that we have to ask these questions. Pure routine, of course."

"Then you know for certain that Mother was poisoned by a parathion insecticide." Violet spoke quite calmly. It was, Henry thought, the voice of somebody whose worst fears have been confirmed, so that the confirmation comes almost as a relief.

Sandport cleared his throat. "Well . . . strictly speaking, madam . . . no. We don't know for sure. But all the indications point that way, so we are, as you might say, proceeding on the assumption. The pathologist's report will make it definite, one way or the other."

"I understand." Violet inclined her head slightly, like a monarch giving the royal assent. "Then of course I will tell you all I can. Piet—my husband—has been keeping these particular roses under his personal care. He is very fond of my mother and takes a great pride in bringing her the finest specimens from his glasshouses. Dutchmen take pride in their work, and the fruits of their work." It said a lot for Violet's new-found dignity that this did not sound pompous. She went on, "He cut the roses yesterday evening and packed them in one of the special ventilated boxes which we always use for export."

"You traveled by the night ferry from the Hook to Harwich?"

"Yes. We arrived at Hindhurst about a quarter to one. Daffy and Chuck met us, because the Bentley is out of action. Dolly positively snatched the box of roses out of Piet's hands as we came in through the front door—she always does. Then she brought them into the drawing room in a vase, but Mother made her take them away again. She has . . . had . . . this superstition about not seeing her presents before the party. Poor Mother." Violet paused and then added, "She believed in fate, you know."

"Yes. Very sad. So you didn't see the roses again?"

"Not until . . . until Mother died." Violet's voice, although barely audible, was quite steady.

"Quite so, madam. So . . . you arrived just before lunch, and lunched with the family. Then what did you do?"

"I went up to our room to unpack. Piet went out into the garden. When I was ready, I came down and we went for a walk in the woods. We got back about five—just in time to bathe and change before . . ."

"Did you know, madam, that your husband spent some time in the greenhouse during the afternoon?" Sandport spoke quickly, and with a sharp edge to his voice, but Violet did not react.

"He may have done. Now you come to mention it, I came back to the house before he did after our walk. Piet was messing about with some wild heather on the heath. He may easily have gone into the greenhouse to talk to Dolly. He has a great admiration for her. He's often told me what a wonderful job she makes of these gardens, single-handed. They always have a long horticultural session as soon as we arrive here."

Piet van der Hoven was obviously more worried about his wife than anything else. Violet idolized her mother, he explained earnestly to Sandport in his fractured English. She was extremely distressed—not hysterical, no, no, but perhaps too calm. He feared she might break down completely. He thought he should take her home to Holland as soon as possible. It would be a great mistake to stay for the funeral, which would only upset her. He was planning to arrange for their return . . .

With difficulty Sandport steered the conversation back to the matter in hand. Piet confirmed, indignantly, that he would never allow Flyaway or any other parathion insecticide in his greenhouses. He knew that Dolly used them, and he could understand it. Such sprays were quick and efficient, "Miss Dolly must snip the hooks," he added.

"Eh?" said Sandport.

Henry said, "Cut the corners."

Piet beamed. "My English is not so hot," he agreed. "I discuss this precise matter in the glasshouse with Miss Dolly today. This Flyaway is dangerous, I say her; but she say Flyaway is never at home. Always in the glasshouse. You mind yourself, Miss Dolly, I say. You too always in glasshouse. She laugh."

"You saw the Flyaway in the greenhouse, did you?"

"Yes, I see the blick—the tin, as you say. And then I go in to my Violet. So happy is she to be in England with her lovely mother. And now . . ."

Piet was off again, and could only be stopped by Sandport's suggestion that he should go back to the Dali Room to be reunited with his wife. He went, at a shambling run.

More as a matter of form than anything, Sandport then took a statement from Emmy. Then he finished making his notes, sat back in his chair, and said to Henry, "Well, there we are, Chief Superintendent. Nothing more I can do here until tomorrow, when the reports come in. But assuming that the lady was killed by an oral dose of

Flyaway—and I think you'll agree we have to assume that much—well, the cake is the culprit. Can't get away from it."

"Given all your assumptions," said Henry cautiously, "I agree with your conclusion. But—"

"Madame Duval," went on Sandport, "collected the cake from the shop. Her husband never even saw it. The box wasn't opened until it arrived here. The most reasonable hypothesis is that the Flyaway was injected into the marzipan ornament after the cake was put into the kitchen cupboard. Miss Dolly could have done it. Mrs. van der Hoven could have done it while her husband was in the greenhouse. If you'll forgive me for saying so, you or your wife could have done it." He laughed uneasily.

"What about the Swasheimers?" said Henry.

"Oh, I think we may disregard them."

"During the afternoon—"

"They had no possible motive for killing Lady Balaclava."

"You're assuming," said Henry, "that this was murder for money?"

"What else could it have been?"

"I don't know. I asked if that was your assumption."

"Well—yes, it is." Sandport sounded defiant. "In my humble opinion, Chief Superintendent, we should concentrate on Miss Underwood-Threep and Mrs. van der Hoven. One had the opportunity, the other the motive. Perhaps when Lady Balaclava's will is read . . ." He began to gather up his papers. "I'll see you in the morning," he said. "Things should be clearer then."

In fact, in the morning things were very much less clear. Henry's day began with an impatiently ringing telephone soon after seven o'clock. It was Inspector Sandport.

"Chief Superintendent Tibbett?"

"Speaking." Henry had heard distinct clicks on the telephone as other people in the house had lifted their bedside phones in response to the ring. Now, another series of clicks indicated that they were replacing them. But all of them . . . ? Henry could not be sure.

"Sandport here, sir. I've got some extraordinary news for you."

"Then don't discuss it over the telephone. Where are you?"

"At home. This report has just been phoned through to me. I'll be at police headquarters in Hindhurst in half an hour."

"I'll meet you there," said Henry.

The police station was bleak and chilly in the watery early-morning sunshine. Wisps of mist wreathed around the tall hollyhocks in the station garden, and spiders' webs trembled with dew crystals. Sandport was waiting for Henry. He came to the point at once.

"Here they are." He threw a sheaf of papers onto the desk. "Pathologist's report. Analyst's report. Nothing."

Henry said, "What do you mean—nothing?"

"Exactly what I say. Not a trace of parathion—or anything else, for that matter. No poison whatsoever in the body. Nothing in the champagne glass or bottle but champagne. Nothing in the cake but cake, cream, and marzipan No parathion spray on the roses. Not one single damn trace of anything."

"But . . . it's not possible. What was the cause of death, then?"

Sandport snorted. "They don't know. That's to say—the cause of death was . . ." He ruffled through one of the reports. "Acute respiratory and circulatory collapse . . . anaphylactic shock . . . and so on. These medicos and their jargon. The point is—the doctors have no idea what caused these symptoms. 'Possibility of a rare allergy,' it says somewhere here. Just means they don't know. The pathologist made a feeble joke about an oriental poison unknown to science. Meanwhile, he's simply put 'natural causes' on the death certificate. Nothing else he could do, when there are no unnatural causes. So there's no case. Which," Sandport added, "I don't mind admitting is a great relief to me. To you, too, I should think. Just 'natural causes.' "

Henry said, "There is a case, Inspector Sandport. And I shall investigate it."

"The chief constable will never——"

"I don't care what he does," said Henry. "There's a case, and I'd damn well better solve it, or I might as well retire and grow dahlias."

Leaving a surprised Inspector Sandport with his papers, Henry walked out of the police station into the growing warmth of another lovely day and drove off in the direction of Trimble Wells.

8

The assistant commissioner was more surprised than
pleased to find Henry Tibbett on his doorstep at eight
o'clock on a Sunday morning. He regarded his cottage at
Trimble Wells as the one sure haven to which he could retreat from the rough and tumble of work, a place where
he could wear old clothes and dig his garden and relax.

Henry's telephone call on Saturday evening had been distressing in more ways than one. For a start, although he had
never known Crystal Balaclava well, the A.C. felt a sharp
sense of personal loss on her death. The end of an era.
Then there was the question of Sir Basil and the Bishop
and all the other influential figures who loomed out of
Crystal's past. The assistant commissioner had—he admitted it freely to himself—been inclined to scoff at Crystal's
premonitions of disaster; nevertheless, he had agreed to
send Tibbett to Foxes' Trot for the weekend in order to
allay the fears of an elderly and imaginative woman. And
that woman was now dead, murdered—just as she had
predicted—right under Tibbett's nose. The A.C. knew that,
however unfair it might be, he would be blamed by Sir
Basil and the commissioner and all the rest of them.

As a consequence of these gloomy thoughts, he had
been rude to his wife the previous evening, which had
resulted in a domestic row. He had gone to bed early, and
failed to sleep. Now, standing on the doorstep at eight in
the morning, unshaven and slipperless and wrapped in an

ancient camel-hair dressing gown, he looked as disgruntled as he felt.

"Good God, Tibbett," he said. "What on earth are you doing here?"

"I'm sorry to disturb you, sir," said Henry. "I must talk to you."

"At this hour?"

"Yes. I've just come from Hindhurst police station. May I come in?"

"What? Oh, yes. Yes, of course. Forgive me. Not properly awake yet, I'm afraid. Can you make coffee?"

"Yes, sir."

"Then for God's sake, make some for both of us. Wife's still asleep. Kitchen's through there. You'll find all the fixings."

Ten minutes later Henry and the assistant commissioner were sitting one on each side of the dead embers of last night's fire, drinking strong, sweet coffee in the chintzy living room of the cottage. Henry related his call from Sandport, his visit to the police station, and the findings of the pathologist and the analyst. When he had finished, there was a moment of silence. The A.C. stirred his coffee, as if in a daze. At last he said, "It doesn't seem possible."

"Heaven knows what's possible and what isn't, sir," said Henry. "All I know is that I'm in an intolerable position."

"*You* are? What about me?"

"You, sir? But I'm the one who—"

"Sir Basil," said the A.C. gloomily. "The Bishop of Battersea. Admiral Lord Rochester. The commissioner himself, come to that. God damn it, I shall be a laughingstock. We all shall."

Henry nodded glumly. The A.C. went on, "It's bad enough the woman being murdered, actually in the presence of one of my senior officers. Now you want me to tell everybody that she died of natural causes, with all the symptoms of acute poisoning, and in a house fairly stuffed with toxic insecticide. It's just not possible." The A.C. looked up from his coffee, full into Henry's eyes. "What killed that woman, Tibbett?"

Henry shrugged. "An oriental poison unknown to science," he said. "As in all the best detective stories."

"Are you trying to be funny?"

"I'm quoting what the doctor said."

"Well, stop quoting and give me your opinion. Do you believe in these 'natural causes'?"

Henry considered. "I'm not a doctor," he said at last, "but I saw the wretched woman die, and if she died of natural causes, I'll eat my hat. My opinion, which is worthless, is that she was poisoned—but by a poison which leaves no trace."

"Poppycock. Such things don't exist outside the pages of fiction."

"Then you must accept the 'natural causes.' The doctors made every possible test. There was no poison."

"All right, all right. I take the point. What do the local police propose to do now?"

"There's not much they can do. Of course, there will be an inquest, and it'll be up to the inquest jury to decide. But Sandport is talking in terms of there being no case, and the less of a case there is, the happier he'll be. That goes for the chief constable, too, I imagine. My own view is that the police will soft-pedal at the inquest, the doctors will puff out a miasma of medical terminology, and the jury will accept the 'natural-causes' verdict. What else can they do? 'Murder by person or persons unknown, by poison or poisons unknown'? 'Misadventure due to unknown causes'? 'Natural causes induced by black magic'?"

"By what?" The A.C. looked up from his coffee cup. "What's that you said? Black magic?"

"Sorry. I forgot you didn't know about the table-turning, sir."

"Table-turning?"

"Well, not exactly. Tumbler-pushing, to be more exact." Henry recounted his brush with the late Baron Balaclava and the tooth mug. "So that's where she got the idea that somebody was planning to murder her. Whether she genuinely believed in the spirit's warning, or whether she rigged the whole thing herself, I don't know. What I do know is that you and I aren't the only people who know about her mysterious premonitions—"

"Of course we're not," interrupted the A.C. "Sir Basil, the commissioner—"

"I meant people in the village," said Henry. "The doctor, for instance. Dr. Griffiths, who by a strange coincidence has just gone on holiday. Miss Underwood-Threep—"

"Miss Who?"

"Dorothy Underwood-Threep. Lady Balaclava's companion."

"Good Lord. Dolly Underwood-Threep. I thought she'd been dead for years."

"You knew her, then, sir?"

"Not personally, but she was . . . well, she used to be something of a legend. Like Crystal. Who ever would have thought of them ending up together as Baroness Balaclava and her lady companion . . . ?" The assistant commissioner shook his head sadly. Then, becoming brisk again, he said, "This whole affair is extremely unfortunate, Tibbett. You know I spoke to the chief constable last night?"

"Yes, sir."

"Well, he agreed to call in the Yard and leave you in charge of the case. Now, if there's to be no case, where does that put us?"

Henry said, "We can't anticipate the inquest verdict, sir, but with the medical findings as they are, I don't see how the chief constable can do anything but drop the matter."

"Call Sandport off, you mean?"

"Exactly."

"And so—?"

"And so," said Henry, "with your permission, sir, I'd like to apply for leave."

"Leave?"

"Yes. Immediately. I'm planning to spend a week in the country with my wife. Make a nice break for us both."

"At Plumley Green, you mean?"

"At Foxes' Trot, if I can wangle an invitation. There's only one thing . . ."

"What's that?"

"The Swasheimers—that's the youngest daughter and her American husband—have firmly announced that they're leaving for Paris today. I don't see how anybody can stop them. Dr. Duval may be coming over from Geneva to be with his wife—that's the eldest daughter—and I guess he'll want to take her home right away. The middle daughter and her husband have a market garden to manage in Holland—and Mr. van der Hoven is anxious to get his wife home as soon as he can."

"There's no way of keeping these people here?" the A.C. asked.

"No way of compelling them. But I dare say that some of them may decide to stay for the reading of the will."

"Ah, yes. The will."

"After that—well, Emmy and I might just find ourselves taking part of our holiday on the Continent."

"I quite understand, Tibbett. It's very good of you to—"

"Nothing to do with being good of me," said Henry. He took a gulp of coffee. "I'm in an intolerable position. The classic detective's nightmare. Not only is murder committed in front of my eyes, but after I've been called in specifically to prevent it happening. And then it turns out to be another classic nightmare—the insoluble crime."

The A.C. grinned wryly. "The oriental poison unknown to science."

"Exactly. And since I don't believe in insoluble crimes or perfect murders or poisons unknown to science, I'm going to crack this one. I must. Otherwise, I'm finished."

"Now, Tibbett, I wouldn't—"

"You might not, but I would. With your permission, sir, I'm going to stay here and find out who and what killed Lady Balaclava. And if I fail, I shall resign."

"There's no need to be melodramatic, Tibbett."

"Isn't there? I'm not so sure."

"Of course, we can't help you officially—from the Yard, I mean. . . ."

"Just so long as you don't hinder me."

"No, no. Of course not."

"Then that's settled." Henry stood up. "Thanks for the coffee, sir. I'll get back to Plumley Green now."

Henry was back at Foxes' Trot soon after nine o'clock. The house seemed asleep in the sunshine. The windows, upstairs and down, were curtained, like blind eyes. The front door was shut. Nothing stirred, except the water that bubbled endlessly from the stone saxophone in the lily pond. In the drive, the old Bentley and the new Rolls stood side by side, like overgrown toys. Henry parked his car alongside them and walked around to the back of the house. In the quietness, his footsteps on the gravel sounded unnaturally loud.

The back of the house was considerably livelier and more cheerful than the front. The windows were uncurtained, the back door stood open, and somebody was moving about inside the kitchen. A glance through the window showed Henry that it was Emmy, wearing beige silk trousers and a white shirt, busy at the gas stove. A delicious smell of new-made coffee and toast floated out through the back door.

Emmy heard the footsteps, looked up, smiled, and waved. A couple of minutes later she and Henry were sitting at the kitchen table tucking in to boiled eggs and toast.

Emmy said, "Did you see Sandport, darling? Has the pathologist's report come in?"

"I have," said Henry. "And it has."

"Parathion poisoning," said Emmy, stating a fact.

"No."

"Was it in the cake, or—" Emmy suddenly stopped, butter knife in the air. "What did you say?"

"There's no poison. Nothing."

"Oh, don't be silly, Henry. What do you mean?"

"That there's not the remotest trace of anything poisonous, either in the body, or in the cake, the champagne, the rose—"

"Then why did she die?"

"Acute respiratory and circulatory collapse. Anaphylatic shock."

"What's that supposed to mean?"

"It means that Lady Balaclava's heart and lungs ceased to function, which naturally caused her to die. As to *why* they ceased to function . . ." Henry made a hopeless gesture. "The death certificate says 'natural causes.' That's the doctor's verdict."

"Then he must be mad," said Emmy decisively.

"What else could he put on the certificate? He probably doesn't believe it himself, but without a trace of poison anywhere . . . well, you see the point."

"I see more than that," said Emmy somberly. "I see you in one hell of a position. What are you going to do?"

Henry told her about his visit to the assistant commissioner, and his plan to stay on at Foxes' Trot and continue his investigation unofficially, Emmy nodded. "Yes, Yes, that's the best thing to do. Will Dolly agree to our staying on, do you think?"

"I'm not at all sure," said Henry, "that it will be up to Dolly. The next thing is to get the will read. Things may be a bit clearer then. Any sign of Dolly this morning, by the way?"

As if an answer to his question, the kitchen door opened and Dolly came in. Henry was shocked at her appearance. She seemed to have aged ten years since yesterday. Her powerful shoulders drooped under her old dressing gown, her gray hair straggled, her face under its heavy makeup seemed to have shriveled. For the first time Henry realized that Dolly was an old lady.

"Morning, chaps," she said with an attempt at breeziness. "Got yourselves something to eat, I see. Good show." She slumped into a chair. Emmy jumped up.

"Let me get you some breakfast, Dolly. How do you like your eggs? The coffee's made—just pour yourself a cup."

"Thanks, love," said Dolly with unusual meekness. "Four minutes in boiling water, and the toast well done." She paused and shook her head, as if in puzzlement. "Don't feel myself this morning. Couldn't wake up. Must be those infernal pills that woman gave me. Sorry."

Henry and Emmy murmured that she mustn't worry. With a touch of her old agressiveness Dolly said, "Not worry? Not worry? That's a joke. However, that's another story. For the moment . . . not like me at all . . ." Her voice trailed away.

Emmy said, "You've had a dreadful shock, Dolly. It's bound to take you a few days to get over it. Now, eat something and you'll feel better."

"You're a nice child," said Dolly. There was a moment of silence. Then Dolly said to Henry, "Well?"

"Well, what?"

"What are you trying to ask me?"

Henry smiled. "Is it so obvious?"

"I may be in a state of shock, but I'm not senile." Dolly seemed to be recovering a little. "Come on. Out with it."

"I was only wondering," said Henry, "if you knew the name of Lady Balaclava's solicitor."

"Of course I do. Why?"

"Because I think we should take steps to have the will read, as soon as possible."

There was a long silence. Emmy turned from the stove, spooning an egg from a small saucepan, and said, "Here we are, Dolly. Toast just coming up."

Dolly paid no attention. She sat brooding, contemplating the inside of her empty cup. Henry watched her. Emmy said, "There! Egg, toast, and butter!"—but in doing so she did not break the silence.

At long last Dolly said gruffly, "Yes."

Henry said, "I thought you knew what was in the will?"

"I—yes, I do."

"Then why are you frightened?"

"Frightened, me?"

"Yes."

Suddenly Dolly laughed. "Perceptive. That's what you're paid for, of course. All right, I'll tell you why I'm frightened. This house has been my home for a great many years. I don't want to be turned out."

"Who's going to turn you out?"

Dolly shrugged. "The girls. Everything goes to them, as

you know. They've always hated me—oh yes, they have. Don't think I don't know. I'm a coward, I suppose. It was too much to face all at once—losing Crys and my home. But you're right, of course." Dolly straightened her back. "Mr. Plunkett of Roberts, Roberts, Hightree, and Bunn, of Brown Street, Mayfair. Charlie's solicitors. Will you call him, or shall I?"

As it turned out, neither of them had to call him. Dolly had scarcely cracked the shell of her egg when the telephone rang.

"Damnation," said Dolly, putting down her spoon. "I suppose I'd better—"

"I'll answer it," said Henry. "It's probably the press, and I've some experience at handling them."

"You're very kind," said Dolly.

The voice on the other end of the line was dry and fussy. "Hello? Hello? Is that Lady Balaclava's house?"

"It is," said Henry.

"May I speak to Miss Underwood-Threep?"

"I'll see if she's available. Who wants her, please?"

"My name is Plunkett. Miss Underwood-Threep knows me well. I am Lady Balaclava's solicitor."

"Ah, good morning, Mr. Plunkett," said Henry. "We were just going to call you. You've heard the news, of course."

"Of course. Saw it in this morning's paper. Sad business. Very sad. May I ask to whom I have the honor—?"

"My name is Tibbett," said Henry. "I'm a house guest here for the weekend. It was Lady Balaclava's birthday yesterday, you see."

"Goodness gracious me. So it was. I had quite forgotten. So all the girls are there?"

"Yes."

"Well, well, well. That simplifies matters. The family is so dispersed, as a rule. I am Lady Balaclava's executor, you see, as well as being her solicitor. It will save a lot of tedious work to have the whole family together for the reading of the will." Plunkett cleared his throat. Then he said, "How is Miss Underwood-Threep?"

"She's very distressed," said Henry. "Naturally."

"Well, there's no need to bring her to the telephone. Just be a good fellow and tell her that, if it's convenient, I shall come down to Plumley Green tomorrow morning, with the will. Nothing to be done today, of course. Sunday. I shall arrive shortly before lunchtime." He paused hopefully. Henry said nothing. Plunkett went on, less hopefully, "I can always get a bite at the Hindhurst Arms. If it will be convenient for the family to assemble at Foxes' Trot at two-thirty—"

"Just hold on a moment, will you, Mr. Plunkett?" said Henry. "I'll have a word with Dolly."

"Don't tell me," said Dolly, as Henry came into the kitchen. She gave a sardonic, snorting laugh which sounded more like her old self. "Piggy Plunkett is planning to arrive at lunchtime, and will read the will at two-thirty. He can easily get himself a bite to eat at the Hindhurst Arms."

"You must be psychic," said Henry.

Dolly gave him a quick, suspicious look. Then she said, "Never once has that man visited this house without cadging a free meal. Oh, well—this'll be the last time. Pity to break the old tradition. Tell him he can lunch here."

"How extremely kind of her," said Mr. Plunkett primly, on receipt of Dolly's message. "Of course, I don't want to inconvenience her—or anybody else—at such a time. I can easily get a bite at—"

"She would like you to come to lunch," Henry repeated.

"Ah, well . . . in that case. Most kind. You will be there yourself, I trust? I shall consider it an honor to make your acquaintance, Mr. Tibbett."

"I trust I shall be here," said Henry.

Before Mr. Plunkett had concluded the lengthy formalities of farewell which he seemed to consider seemly, Henry was interested to hear three distinct clicks, as three extension telephones were gently replaced. Telling the girls, he decided, would be an unnecessary exercise. Nevertheless, he went through the formality of doing so when the van der Hovens came down in search of breakfast, closely followed by Primrose Duval and Chuck Swasheimer. Daffy, the latter explained, was still in bed. He planned to take a tray up to her, if Miss Dolly would allow it.

Primrose, Violet, and Piet all said at once that they would be available for the reading of the will. Only Chuck was doubtful.

"Gee, I'd be real sorry to miss a family occasion like that," he said, passing a large hand across his forehead, "but I just don't see how we can stay. We're all booked up on the night boat tonight, and I've several business appointments in Paris tomorrow that I just can't pass up. Daffy's got engagements, too—she was saying so only last evening. There's no legal obligation for all beneficiaries to be on hand when the will is read, is there?"

"No, no," said Henry. "Of course not."

"One never knows. Foreign countries have weird laws sometimes—begging your pardon, but you know what I mean." Chuck smiled rather shyly. "Well, I sure am sorry, but I guess this is one party we'll have to miss."

Emmy, who seemed to have been unanimously elected as standby cook, went on preparing eggs, toast, and coffee. Dolly ate morosely, planted firmly at the kitchen table. The others wandered off into the dining room, apparently taking it for granted that breakfast would be provided and that they would be waited upon.

Inspector Sandport arrived at half-past ten, looking excessively cheerful. He carried a small briefcase, from which he took a number of papers. These he spread out on a glass-topped table in the drawing room. Then he sat down, polished his spectacles, and asked Henry if it would be possible to assemble the entire household, as he had something to say to them.

The inmates of Foxes' Trot, not surprisingly, looked less cheerful than the inspector. Violet was white with the strain of tightly controlled emotion, Piet pathetically worried on her account; Primrose was highly nervous, continually consulting her wristwatch; Chuck was harassed, and Daffodil—who had appeared, reluctantly, in a silk chiffon negligee—angry and impatient. Dolly sat slumped in a chair, gazing morosely at her large feet.

Sandport looked around the assembled gathering with satisfaction and then said, "Well, ladies and gentlemen, I have some good news for you." Six pairs of eyes stared at him in surprise. "That may sound a heartless thing to say to a bereaved family," Sandport went on, "and I hope you'll forgive me. Nevertheless, I think you'll agree with me that it is good news to know that Lady Balaclava died from natural causes."

"But—she can't have." It was Primrose who put into words what all the others were thinking.

Sandport held up his hand. "I know, I know," he said soothingly. "It's hard to believe. You were all here, and saw the poor lady die—and nobody disputes that the symptoms were similar to those of acute poisoning. However—"

"What were these natural causes?" Chuck demanded. He sounded aggrieved rather than relieved. "I've never known natural causes to act *that* way."

"I have the pathologist's report here." Sandport held up an impressive document. "I won't read it to you, because it's in highly technical language—but any or all of you are entitled to a copy, if you wish. To summarize . . ." He adjusted his spectacles and picked up another sheaf of papers. "The doctor has put it into simple language for us. First of all, no trace of poison of any sort was found, either in Lady Balaclava's body, or in the various substances analyzed—that is, the champagne, the glass, the roses, and the cake." He said the last three words very deliberately, looking at Primrose, who began to cry quietly. "This rules out any possibility of poison, because there is no such thing as poison which leaves no trace. Is that clear?"

There was absolute silence in the room, broken only by a soft sob from Primrose. Piet van der Hoven nodded in earnest agreement with the inspector's words. Sandport went on, "As to the actual cause of death, that is more complicated. A complete collapse of the respiratory and circulatory system—that's what killed the lady. As to what caused these symptoms—the doctors can't be sure. There's the possibility of a very rare allergy . . . acute shock . . . serotonin . . . systemic anaphylaxy . . . I won't bore you with the medical terms . . . frankly, they mean nothing to me, and I'm sure they don't to you. What is clear is that Lady Balaclava died from natural causes. The fact that these natural causes produced symptoms resembling poisoning caused us all, very naturally, to jump to a false conclusion."

Sandport laid the papers down on the table and took off his glasses. "What I am saying, ladies and gentlemen, is that this lady was not poisoned. There will be an inquest, of course, and the medical evidence will be considered in detail—but there is no reason to suspect foul play. The police, therefore, have no further interest in the case; and I am sure it must be a relief to you all to know that there is not a murderer among you."

He paused. Once again the room was very quiet. Changing vocal gears into a more relaxed tone, Sandport said, "In the circumstances, therefore, there is no need to detain any of you here, unless of course you wish to stay. You will be notified of the inquest, and some of you may be asked to give evidence. Please don't be alarmed by this—you will simply be helping the doctors to establish the exact nature of Lady Balaclava's illness. And now, it only remains for me to offer my most sincere sympathy to you all in your bereavement, and to bid you good-bye."

Again, nobody moved or spoke. Briskly Sandport gathered up his papers, put them into his briefcase, and walked out into the hall. A moment later came the sound of the front door shutting, followed by the purr of a motor engine as the police car rolled away down the drive. It was only when the last sound of it had died away that Dolly broke the tension in the drawing room of Foxes' Trot. She lifted her grizzled head and said loudly, "Thank God for that."

9

The events of Sunday afternoon were unspectacular, but not uninteresting. First of all, Daffodil surprised everybody—not least her husband—by announcing at lunch that she intended to stay to hear the reading of the will. Chuck at once began to protest about car-ferry bookings, whereupon Daffy remarked in a voice of singular sweetness that if he was really so concerned to get back to Paris, he might go on his own; she could follow by air later on. Chuck, with an air of pardonable injury, pointed out that it was she, Daffy, who had been so anxious to get back to Paris. Of course, if she wanted to stay on at Foxes' Trot, then he would stay too; but it would mean canceling business appointments and altering the reservations, and . . . Daffy yawned and said, "I'll leave all of that to you, honey."

"I bet you will, you lazy little bitch," said Violet, shockingly, out of the silence of her grief. Piet immediately came blundering into the conversational breach, attempting to cover up for his wife's obviously intentional rudeness.

Primrose said to Dolly, "I don't think Daffy trusts the rest of us not to tamper with the will while her back's turned."

To which Dolly replied gruffly, "Well, she's got nothing to fear from me."

The awkward pause which followed this exchange was relieved by the ringing of the telephone. Primrose was out into the hall before any of the others had time to rise from their chairs. She returned in a matter of moments, flushed and triumphant.

"It was Edouard," she said. "He's at Hindhurst station. Chuck, I wonder if you'd—"

"*Edouard?*" said Daffodil, in exaggerated mock surprise. "How *very* unexpected. I thought he had a conference."

"He came because I asked him to." Primrose could not keep the satisfaction out of her voice. "I rang him yesterday, and naturally his first thought was to be at my side."

"How very touching," said Daffy acidly. "More likely, *he* doesn't trust the rest of us not to tamper—"

"How dare you say that!" Two bright spots of red had appeared on Primrose's pale face. Her voice rose in fury. "How dare you! Just because you—"

"Now, now, now, now, now," said Chuck pacifically. It sounded like a shower of rain on a tin roof. "I'm sure Daffy didn't mean—"

"I meant what I said."

"Well, now, why don't I go along and fetch poor Edouard from the railroad station?" Chuck's voice poured out, like oil, onto the stormy waters of the conversation; but it was ineffective.

Daffy almost screamed, "No! Why should you? I won't have you used like a bloody chauffeur! Let him make his own way, if he's so wife-besotted—"

Suddenly, with breathtaking authority, Dolly raised her head and spoke. "You girls will now kindly shut your traps," she said. "The will hasn't been read yet, which means that for the moment I am still in charge here, and I don't intend to tolerate vulgar squabbles at my table. You should all be ashamed of yourselves." She glared first at Violet, then at Daffy, and finally at Primrose. Nobody spoke. Dolly went on, addressing Henry, "Mr. Tibbett, I believe you have a car."

"I have," said Henry.

"Well, might I ask you to be so kind as to fetch Dr. Duval from the station? I'd go myself if the Bentley was operational."

"I'd be delighted," said Henry. He stood up.

"If I may suggest it," Dolly went on, "Emmy might go with you. There is a little family business to be discussed here, so if you don't mind—"

"Of course I don't," said Emmy.

Dolly smiled warmly. "Thank you, my dears," she said.

In the car, Emmy said to Henry, "That was a curious exhibition."

"They're all on edge." Henry spoke abstractedly, his eyes on the road, and at least half of his mind elsewhere. "You have to make allowances."

"Those sisters—they hate each other."

"Of course they do," said Henry. "Hadn't you realized?"

"Well—no, I hadn't. I suppose the awfulness of their mother's death has broken down the polite barriers—"

"No, no. The other way around."

"What d'you mean?"

"The disaster brought on a severe attack of family solidarity," said Henry. "Didn't you notice how nice they were all being to each other yesterday? No, it was today's news that cracked the artificial facade. Death from natural causes. Now they're all at each other's throats again."

"I wonder," said Emmy, "what Dr. Duval will be like?"

They soon found out. There was only one person waiting in the forecourt of the station—a dark, strongly built man, exuding efficiency. As Henry turned the car into the yard, Duval glanced quickly at his watch, as if checking on the timing of an important operation. From his expression, Henry gathered that things were not going in strict accordance with the doctor's timetable. However, as the car pulled up, Edouard Duval bent toward the driver's window and favored Henry with a wide smile. He removed his black homburg, picked up his briefcase, and said, "I am Edouard Duval. Am I correct to think that you are seeking me?" His English was excellent, if a little stilted, and his brown eyes twinkled behind his gold-rimmed spectacles.

Henry smiled back through the open window and said,

"You're quite right. My name is Tibbett, and this is my wife."

"Enchanted, Madame." Duval bowed even lower, pressing his hat to his bosom.

"Dolly is sorry she couldn't come herself," said Henry, "but the Bentley is out of action. Will you be all right in the back?" He reached back to open the rear door of the car.

"Perfectly, perfectly." Dr. Duval squeezed his solid body into the back seat. "You are most kind." Then, as Henry turned the car and headed back toward Foxes' Trot, he added, "This is a tragic business, is it not? Were you presently in the house when Lady Balaclava died?"

"Yes, we were," said Henry.

"Her death itself is not the worst," said Duval. "Primrose—my wife—tells me that poison is suspected. What a calamity!"

"Poison was suspected at first," said Henry.

"You mean—no longer?"

"The post mortem showed no signs whatsoever of poison, nor did the analysis of the various things Lady Balaclava had touched or eaten."

"The cake?" Duval rapped out the words.

"Absolutely harmless," said Henry. "A clean bill of health."

"Ah." The doctor managed to make the monosyllable sound at once satisfied and regretful. "So Primrose distressed herself for nothing. I may even say, it was not necessary for me to come. I have had to abandon an important conference, you see."

"I'm sure your wife will be very pleased that you're here, Dr. Duval," said Henry. "She has been very upset. Naturally."

Duval ignored this. He said, "What action will the police take?"

"None, as far as I can gather. They're not interested any longer."

"The pathologist's report. What was in the pathologist's report?"

"I can't tell you the medical details. Something about a rare allergy, I think."

"Pah!" said Dr. Duval. He seemed to class rare allergies with oriental poisons unknown to science. "Rare! The resort of the ignorant."

"That's as may be," said Henry. "Anyhow, the doctor has certified death from natural causes."

"Then I may take my Primrose home to Switzerland when I wish? Today, even?"

"Yes, as far as the police are concerned. But I rather think she wishes to stay for the reading of the will tomorrow afternoon."

"The reading of the will," repeated Dr. Duval thoughtfully. "Yes, of course. Primrose would not like to miss that."

As Dolly had intimated, order had been restored at Foxes' Trot. Lunch had been cleared away. Daffodil, Primrose, Chuck, and Dolly were in the drawing room drinking coffee. Violet was resting in her room, and Piet had gone for a walk. The atmosphere was relaxed, almost amiable. Henry wondered what Dolly had been up to in his absence.

Primrose greeted her husband with impeccable English offhandedness, not even setting down her coffee cup as she turned her cheek to receive his dutiful kiss. The conversation remained general, and Lady Balaclava's death was not even mentioned. However, after a few minutes Primrose remarked casually that Edouard would no doubt like to go up to their room for a wash after his journey, and that she would go with him to do his unpacking. Since Dr. Duval had arrived with only a briefcase, Primrose's services hardly seemed necessary; Henry realized that this was a transparent device for getting her husband to herself for a few moments of private conversation.

As soon as the Duvals had left the room, Daffodil announced her intention of going upstairs to lie down. Chuck offered to accompany her, but was snubbed. She was hoping, she said, to get a bit of sleep—not having slept a wink the night before, as Chuck very well knew, in spite of her new sleeping pills. How did he expect her to sleep if he was going to be on the telephone all the time?

"On the telephone?" Chuck echoed, looking like a bewildered bear. "Why on earth should I be on the telephone?"

"Because you are going to change the reservation back to Paris, honey, that's why. Or had you forgotten?"

"Land sakes." Chuck smiled ruefully, shaking his gray head. "I sure am all to pieces without my secretary. Sure, sure, I'll get onto it right away. Perhaps I could use the phone in the library, Miss Dolly? That way I won't get in anybody's hair."

"Of course you may, Chuck," said Dolly cordially. She shot a disapproving glance at Daffy and added, "And you'd better go and get your beauty sleep. You certainly need it."

Daffodil got up and walked to the door, remarking without heat, "There's no need to be bloody rude, Dolly."

"Isn't there?" Dolly laughed her rasping, unamused laugh. "My last chance, I should have thought."

Daffodil ignored this and followed her husband out of the room. Dolly turned to Henry and Emmy. "Well?" she said.

"Well, what?" Henry replied.

"So even the presence of the great Chief Superintendent Tibbett couldn't prevent Crys from dying of natural causes. The police are no longer interested. So—what do you two chaps intend to do now?"

"If you'll have us," said Henry, "we'd like to stay on here for a few days."

"If I'll have you? That's a laugh. It's hardly up to me."

"Until the will is read—" Emmy began.

"Oh, until the will is read. Yes, of course, by all means. Help yourselves. Be my guests. But don't blame me if the girls boot you out tomorrow afternoon. Personally, I'm going to pack tonight."

"You surely don't mean—?" Emmy was outraged.

"I certainly do." Dolly sounded grim. "I fully expect to

find myself without a roof over my head tomorrow evening."

"The solicitor would never allow it!"

"Old Piggy? He couldn't impose his will on a day-old kitten, let alone the three Codworthy girls in full cry. Besides, he knows which side of his bread is buttered."

"But they're all planning to leave England within a few days," Henry pointed out. "They surely wouldn't want to leave the house empty?"

"You mark my words," said Dolly gloomily. "They'll find some woman from the village to caretake. Anything to be rid of me." There was a little silence. Then Dolly, apparently feeling that further explanations were needed, said, "They've always hated me, you see. They've always resented my influence over Crys."

"But, Dolly," Emmy protested, "they're all married, they all live abroad—"

"Oh, this goes back a long way. Back to the beginning of the war, before Charlie was killed. Back to the time when Crys . . ." Dolly hesitated. "Crys went through a bad time, you see. She was . . . not at all well. Charlie was killed, and the girls had all been evacuated to Canada, so Crys . . . well, she turned to me, as it were, and I did what I could for her. When the war ended and the girls came home, they found me here, living with Crys. They tried to get me out then. Accused me of alienating their mother's affections, and a whole lot of similar trash. What they were really worried about was that I might get my hands on some of the cash that was due to them. Even when they heard about Charlie's will they didn't give up. 'Dolly is a bad influence on Mother.' 'Dolly shouldn't be allowed to run the house.' 'Mother should get rid of Dolly.'" Her imitation of Primrose was uncannily accurate. "They've been waiting for years for this moment. Wait and see what happens tomorrow, that's all. Just wait and see."

The silence that followed Dolly's lugubrious outburst was broken by the sound of the telephone ringing. It was answered almost at once—presumably by Chuck in the library. A few moments later Chuck himself came into the drawing room in a state of bordering on the distraught. There are few sights more affecting than that of a business tycoon, deprived of secretarial assistance, trying to cope unaided with the simpler problems of everyday life. It was Emmy who finally managed to unravel the tangled tale of Mr. Swasheimer's misfortunes.

It appeared that, after much difficulty, Chuck had succeeded in contacting the booking office of British Railways in order to change the reservation which he had made for himself, Daffy, and the car on the night boat from Dover to Dunkirk. Things had not been made easier by the fact that the London office was closed, it being Sunday, so that he had had to unearth the telephone number of the Dover dockside terminal, who informed him that nothing could be done without the approval of the London office. After a great deal of trouble, and conversation with various departments, he had persuaded Dover to cancel his reservation for that night. Hardly had he replaced the phone, however, when it had rung again—and this proved to be a telegram from his Paris office, urgently requesting his presence at a meeting at eleven A.M. the next day, Monday. This new development had proved too much for Charles Swasheimer, and he had come staggering to the drawing room in the blind belief that where there were women (women other than his wife, that is) there would surely be a secretary.

In this belief he was proved correct. Dolly left the room with a snort of disgust; Henry, aware of inadequacy, slipped out quietly after her; but Emmy remained, and Emmy coped.

First of all, she asked Chuck whether his presence at the Monday meeting was really essential. Brightening, Chuck replied that if his son, Warren, was back in Paris from Milan, he could surely fill the bill.

Emmy found the number of Warren C. Swasheimer's Paris apartment in Chuck's alligator-skin diary and called it. A grave English manservant answered, with the information that Mr. Swasheimer was still abroad, and was not expected back before the end of the week.

Chuck was despondent. In that case, he said, he would have to attend the meeting himself, and how the heck was he going to get that booking back again. . . . Emmy cut short the self-pitying monologue to ask crisply why Chuck didn't leave the Rolls here with Daffodil and take a plane himself. This idea appealed strongly to Swasheimer. Emmy guessed that his annual self-drive trip across England was something of a martyrdom.

By the time that she had organized him a seat on the evening plane to Paris, organized a chauffeur-driven car to meet him at Orly Airport, and confirmed with the Hotel Crillon that his usual suite, plus dinner, would be waiting him, Chuck was positively bursting with benevolence, and his briskly self-confident manner showed that the tycoon was once more in the saddle. He wilted a little, however, when Emmy suggested that he had better tell Daffodil about the change in arrangements. This, she felt, was no part of a secretary's duties. Glumly Chuck agreed and plodded upstairs.

Left alone, Emmy went in search of Henry. He was not in the Black Room, nor was he in the kitchen—which was as neat as a pin, Dolly having washed and cleared up. At last Emmy found her husband in the library. He was sitting at the late Lord Balaclava's desk, examining the contents of the drawers.

"Should you, Henry?" Emmy asked a little anxiously. "I mean, is it ethical?"

"I have Dolly's permission," said Henry, "and for the moment she's in charge. Tomorrow would certainly be too late." He went on sorting through the dusty papers.

"Anything interesting?"

"Not yet. Practically nothing except receipted bills, going back about fifty years. Tradesmen, doctors, tailors, and so on. All the documents relating to this house are here, for some reason—from the architect's first sketches to the final receipt for the glass ceiling in our bedroom and the saxophone fountain. Fascinating, really."

Henry pushed a fading blueprint of an architectural drawing across the desk to Emmy. It showed, as well as the ground plan, an "artist's impression" of what the completed house would look like, and it was certainly more impressive than the drab actuality. At the foot of the plan, in architect's impersonal script, was written *Foxes' Trot, Plumley Green, Surrey. An original design for Lady Balaclava, by David Arbuthnot-Jones and Partner.* There were also sketches of the *trompe l'oeil* chessboard and the stone saxophone, with *For Crystal's palace, from her Hubert* scribbled at the bottom in a faded Italian hand. All the bills were addressed to Lady Balaclava at the Barkman Square address. It was clear that Crystal had been the sole driving force behind the project; Charlie's role had merely been to pay the bills.

The only other items of possible interest were several books of press cuttings dating from the 1920's. A neat secretarial hand had clipped the newspaper columns and pictures, pasted them in chronological order into looseleaf albums, and added the name of the paper and the date in crabbed handwriting.

The earliest cuttings related to the doings of Charles Codworthy and his various business concerns, and were mostly reports of annual general meetings culled from the financial sections of the press. A few speeches were reported: *Mr. Charles Codworthy, head of the multimillion domestic-appliances empire, speaking at a Rotary dinner in Birmingham, today predicted the possibility of a serious slump on the American stock market and warned against undue reliance on "paper profits"*—so read a prophetic cutting from the year 1923. Codworthy's name also appeared, in small print, among the guest lists at various social functions.

In 1924, however, the picture changed abruptly. The pages were crammed with the announcement of the engagement of Miss Crystal Maltravers to Mr. Charles Codworthy. *Miss Maltravers is, of course* . . . began the blurb in nearly every case. There were photographs galore of Crystal, snipped from the pages of every magazine from

The Tatler to *Home Knitting,* of every newspaper from *The Times* to *The Bootle Echo*. Charlie Codworthy himself appeared only in the wedding pictures, although some editors—short of space, as usual—had even trimmed his likeness off these, rightly judging it to be irrelevant.

The thirties scrapbook was almost entirely devoted to gossip-column accounts of Crystal's own parties and of her appearance at other people's. The building of Foxes' Trot was chronicled. Charlie came in for a brief spell of glory on the occasion of his elevation to the peerage—but even here Crystal tended to elbow him out of the limelight. The outbreak of war in 1939 was the occasion for glamorized photographs of Lady Balaclava *(better known, perhaps, as the former Crystal Maltravers)* donning a chic uniform and signing on as parttime *chauffeuse* to Members of the Government. Then, unaccountably, came a gap of several years. There were, of course, other and more pressing matters occupying the press at that time; but Henry remembered that the war work of titled beauties had always been good for a line or two. He also remembered what Dolly had said.

There was no question of the scrapbooks having been neglected, for there were occasional references to Lord Balaclava, to his patriotism in switching the output of his factories to work of national importance (they were, in fact, making water closets for H.M. forces rather than for private buyers), to his championship of the National Savings Movement, and so forth. And then, in 1941, the brief obituary. *In his London home, as a result of enemy action . . .* Here the cuttings ended.

The desk contained nothing else, other than the piles of receipted bills, held together in bundles by perished rubber bands. Henry noticed that the drawer which contained the letter cards and tumbler was now empty. Dolly had evidently put a stop to *that,* once and for all.

Dinner was uneventful, notable only for the absence of Violet, Daffodil, and Chuck. Violet, Piet explained, was overtired and upset. She had great pain to her head, he explained earnestly, tripping over his English. She greatly sorrowed that she had spoken unkind to Daffodil. She would not say this if she were not sick. Daffodil had been so good and to understand. She had given Violet of her tablets, and now at last Violet could rest. Piet was leaving her to sleep.

Daffodil herself had taken the news of Chuck's imminent departure with perfect good humor. She had even volunteered to drive him to London Airport, and the two of them had left in the Rolls shortly before six, in a mood of affection bordering on high spirits. Daffy had told Dolly that she would have a meal at the airport, and might be late back. She might look up some friends in town. Nobody was to wait up for her. She would take a spare front-door key.

During dinner Piet and Dolly discussed horticultural matters—carefully avoiding the subjects of insecticides in general and Flyaway in particular. Dr. Duval probed discreetly in an endeavor to discover some facts about Henry—his profession, his connection with Lady Balaclava, the reason for his continued presence at Foxes' Trot. Henry replied blandly that he was a civil servant who worked in Westminster, that he had been introduced to Lady Balaclava through Sir Basil of the Home Office, that he and Emmy were staying on for a few days because Dolly had kindly asked them to do so. Edouard Duval looked neither convinced nor content with these explanations, but he had to make do with them. Primrose ate her dinner in silence and went up to bed soon afterward.

Before long, the rest of the party followed her example. It was shortly before four A.M. by Henry's watch when he was awakened by the sound of the front door opening and closing and a step on the staircase. Daffodil had come home.

Mr. Plunkett, of Roberts, Roberts, Hightree, and Bunn, arrived promptly at midday on Monday, carrying a small briefcase with rather more fuss and importance than most Chancellors of the Exchequer display when conveying that green dispatch case from Downing Street to the House of Commons.

The nickname of Piggy must, Henry decided, have arisen strictly on account of Mr. Plunkett's prodigious appetite, for there was nothing porcine in his appearance. He was a skinny little man with a small gray moustache and a scraggy neck on which even the smallest size of collar seemed too large. He looked as though he lived on air, mixed with a little dry dust and water—but Henry knew that appearances could be deceptive. Sure enough, Plunkett's first action on entering Foxes' Trot was to accept a large glass of sherry, and then to work his way through an entire plateful of Dolly's homemade cheese straws.

He accepted the presence of Henry and Emmy without comment, commiserated formally with the members of the family, and raised a faintly disapproving eyebrow when told of Chuck's inevitable absence. He then took another sherry and started on the second plate of cheese straws, making little legal jokes as his small teeth bit into the soft pastry.

Lunch was a superb meal. Immediately after breakfast Emmy had driven Dolly into Hindhurst to shop, and the pair of them had returned with bulging shopping bags and disappeared into the kitchen—from which Emmy was soon ejected, Dolly remarking that it was kind of her, but she got on quicker by herself, thanks. As Emmy remarked to Henry, Dolly was evidently determined to go with a bang and not a whimper.

The meal started with *coquilles St. Jacques au gratin,* followed by a most delicate clear soup which had not come out of a tin. The main course was fillet of beef, coated with homemade liver *pâté* and baked in an envelope of puff pastry, accompanied by green salad and young vegetables from the garden. Fresh sliced oranges steeped in blended liqueurs came next, and then a noble cheese board.

Piggy Plunkett, his eyes sparkling behind their rimless spectacles, did justice and more to the meal, cleaning the last drops of sauce from his plate with chunks of bread

("The French do it, and they are the greatest gourmets of all. It's a compliment to the sauce. You should be ashamed of yourself, Violet—you're wasting half yours"), and accepting second helpings whenever they were offered. He lavished praise on the food, but—as Henry noted with sympathy—did not remark upon the wine, which was an anonymous Entre Deux Mers followed by a highly suspect Beaujolais. Both had been purchased from the local grocer, who stocked—as Emmy had recounted to Henry—two sorts of wine, the red and the white.

When the last crumbs of cheese had been carefully swept onto biscuits and ingested, Mr. Plunkett sat back, wiped his moustache with his napkin, and said to Dolly, "I really must congratulate you, Miss Underwood-Threep. A most excellent luncheon."

"Thank you, Piggy," said Dolly. "Praise from you is praise indeed. Well, as I always say, no sense in hearing bad news on an empty stomach."

"Bad news? My dear lady—"

"Come off it, Piggy," said Dolly unceremoniously. She stood up. "If you'll all go into the drawing room, Piggy can get on with what he will certainly call the *res,* and I'll bring you all a cup of coffee with your legacies."

"I think it would be best," said Mr. Plunkett stiffly, "for us to drink our coffee first. Then we can proceed with the . . . ah . . . reading."

So coffee was served, and after an agonizingly long period of preparation, the sacred briefcase was opened, spectacles polished, papers sorted, and at last Plunkett was ready to begin.

He cleared his throat. "What I have to say will not, I think, come as a surprise to any of you. It concerns not only Lady Balaclava's will, but also that of her husband, the late Lord Balaclava. As you all know, he left the bulk of his fortune in trust for his three daughters, Primrose, Violet, and Daffodil, to be divided equally among them at the death of their mother." Plunkett paused and shuffled some documents. The crackling paper sounded unnaturally loud in the dead silence. The solicitor looked up and smiled dryly. "The sad death of Lady Balaclava has now, regrettably, taken place. Without going into technicalities—plenty of time for those later—I can now tell you that each of you three ladies, Mrs. Duval, Mrs. van der Hoven, and Mrs. Swasheimer, may expect to receive at least half a million pounds."

The room seemed to sigh with gently exhaled breath. Then Violet said shakily, "Half a million *each?*"

"That is correct, Mrs. van der Hoven."

"What about taxes and death duties?" Daffy spoke briskly. She, at least, was not impressed.

"All that has been taken into account," said Plunkett smugly. "The late Lord Balaclava took excellent legal advice, though I say it myself. I am speaking now of minimum tax-free amounts. Five hundred thousand pounds each." He rolled the words around his tongue. "And now," he continued in a different tone, "we come to Lady Balaclava's will."

The tension had gone out of the atmosphere. The three women relaxed, savoring the thought of riches. Plunkett fussed with his papers again, putting some away and unfolding others. At last, adjusting his glasses, he came up with the document he wanted.

"Lady Balaclava's last will and testament," he said, "is a very simple document. I will read it to you. "I, Crystal Margaret Balaclava, being of sound mind, et cetera, do hereby give and bequeath all moneys, property, securities, goods, and chattels of which I may be possessed at the time of my death, to my dear friend Dorothy Anne Underwood-Threep. Signed this twenty-fourth day of . . . et cetera, et cetera.' "

Mr. Plunkett took off his glasses and beamed at Dolly, who uttered her harsh laugh. "Thanks very much, Piggy," she said.

"But Miss Underwood-Threep, I don't think you understand—"

"Of course I understand. I inherit the clothes in Crys's wardrobe, which are too small for me, and a few kitchen implements, bought since Charlie's death. Oh, and the azaleas. I shall make a point of them."

"No, no, no, no, no." Plunkett sounded like an ineffective machine gun. "You are clearly not *au fait* with the true state of affairs. For a start, you inherit this house, with all its contents." The tension was back. Everybody was looking at Dolly. "Did you not know? Lord Balaclava had the foresight to put this house and its contents into his wife's name. Then there is her jewelry. That, too, she owned absolutely."

"But—" Dolly opened her mouth, but only a small sound emerged.

"You may be unaware of the fact, Miss Threep, but in a strongbox in the vaults of Lady Balaclava's London bank there is jewelry worth some fifty thousand pounds. There are also securities in Lady Balaclava's own name, whose market value should be around twenty thousand pounds. In fact, reckoning up the grand total—"

He was interrupted by a dull thud. Dolly had fainted.

10

After that, of course, there could be nothing but anticli-
max. Edouard Duval took professional charge of Dolly,
sending Daffodil winging in the Rolls to the local chemist
for sedatives, Primrose to the medicine cupboard for a
thermometer, and Violet to the kitchen to prepare a hot-
water bottle. Henry and Piggy Plunkett between them
helped Dolly up to her room—she had quickly recovered
consciousness, but seemed dazed and unwell and only too
willing to retire to bed.

Emmy, who went upstairs ahead to prepare the bed and
draw the curtains, was slightly shocked when she saw
Dolly's room. It had obviously been designed and furnished for a resident domestic help, and the contrast with
the Black Room, the Dali Room, and the Syrie Maugham
Room—not to mention Crystal's own luxurious suite—was
striking. Crystal Balaclava, Emmy decided, had been a
sharp-clawed, cruel little cat who had played with poor
Dolly—a pathetic, oversized mouse if ever there was one.
Crystal knew perfectly well that she owned the house and
valuable jewelry and securities, and she knew that she had
left them to Dolly; yet she had kept this knowledge to herself, allowing Dolly to believe that only Crystal's life stood
between her and poverty. She had used Dolly as a servant.
Emmy remembered the casual, drawling little voice saying,
"Just leave your cases in the hall. Dolly will take them up
later." In spite of herself, the thought came: supposing
Dolly had discovered the truth about her inheritance. . . .

As soon as Dolly had been ministered to, sympathized with, dosed, and tucked up in bed, the party at Foxes' Trot began a rapid process of dispersal. Daffy announced her intention of driving to London as soon as she had packed, and offered a lift to Violet and Piet, who had booked on the night ferry from Harwich and whose connecting train left Liverpool Street at eight. Piggy Plunkett packed away his papers, shaking his wizened head in amazement over the fact that Dolly should have been unaware of her legacy.

"I can only think it slipped Lady Balaclava's mind," he said earnestly to Violet. "She could hardly have *intended* to keep poor Miss Underwood-Threep in the dark. Dear me, how distressed the poor woman must have been these last days, not knowing that her friend had provided so comfortably for her. Although, of course, she must have known that you girls would see that she was well looked after."

Violet gave him a curious look. Then she said, "I don't think you need waste your sympathy on Dolly, Mr. Plunkett."

"No, no, no. Of course not. She is now a comparatively wealthy woman. Not in the same bracket as you and your sisters, of course"—Mr. Plunkett smirked—"but comfortable. Very comfortable. Well, now, I must be getting along. Is it perhaps possible to telephone for a cab to take me to the station?"

Henry at once offered to act as chauffeur, and soon his car was bowling along the now familiar road to Hindhurst, with Mr. Plunkett garrulously occupying the passenger seat. After reiterating his astonishment at Crystal's unaccountable lapse of memory, Plunkett added, "You'll be staying on for a few days at Foxes' Trot, I trust, Mr. Tibbett? You and your charming wife."

A little surprised, Henry said, "I hope so. Miss Underwood-Threep has kindly invited us."

"Good. Good. She's had a shock, poor lady—albeit a pleasant one, but she's not as young as she was, and I feel that she shouldn't be left alone. I shall keep in close touch.

I dare say she will need an advance of funds in order to carry on until probate is granted. That should be easily arranged. You may wonder why I don't suggest one of the girls tiding her over financially. Well, to be frank, Mr. Tibbett, I would rather not. You see, there has always been bad blood between Dolly and the girls. I still call them that, although of course they are mature women now. Yes, it's a great pity, but there it is—and that is why I am so glad that you will be staying on for a few days. Miss Underwood-Threep will need friends. Ah, here we are already. Most kind of you, Mr. Tibbett. No, no, I can manage the door quite well myself. Pray don't . . . there we are. Now, have I everything? Briefcase, gloves, hat, return ticket . . . all present and correct. Good-bye, Mr. Tibbett—or rather, *au revoir*. I shall be in touch. . . ."

Mr. Plunkett hurried into the station, his thin neck thrust forward, like a chicken with an urgent appointment to keep. Henry drove thoughtfully back to Foxes' Trot.

He was met in the hall by Primrose, who gave him a distinctly hostile look and said, "I have a telephone message for you, *Chief Superintendent* Tibbett."

"Oh, yes?"

Primrose consulted the pad beside the telephone. "Will you please ring Trimble Wells 482 when it is convenient for you?" She paused and then added, "So you are a policeman. From Scotland Yard. You were very secretive about it, I must say."

"I've always thought," said Henry blandly, "that people who talk about their jobs are extraordinarily boring."

Primrose ignored this. She said, "And Mother invited you for the weekend because you are a friend of her old beau, Basil."

"That's right," said Henry pleasantly.

"Well, I don't believe a word of it," said Primrose. "Dolly invited you here, because she was afraid—" She stopped.

"Afraid of what, Madame Duval?"

"Oh, well, it doesn't matter now." Primrose sounded exasperated. "There's nothing to be done, is there? Mother is dead, and the police are taking no further action, because she died from natural causes. I've never heard such rubbish in my life, and I can only say that the doctor's diagnosis was extremely fortunate for Dolly. After what we heard from Plunkett today, it's quite obvious—"

Henry said, "It's obvious, Madame Duval, that everybody in this house stood to gain by Lady Balaclava's death—except my wife and myself. Nevertheless, the fact remains that she was not poisoned. You heard what Inspector Sandport said. You can have copies of the postmortem report and the various analyses, if you wish."

"We've already asked for them. Edouard is a doctor, remember. He will soon find out what really happened to Mother."

"You will be staying on here, then?"

Primrose hesitated. "No, not here. We wouldn't want to impose on Dolly. We will stay at the Hindhurst Arms. I think I should warn you that Edouard is far from satisfied about Mother's death, and it's very probable that you haven't heard the last of the matter, Chief Superintendent." With a malicious, well-bred smile Primrose inclined her head slightly toward Henry and went into the drawing room, slamming the door behind her.

Henry looked again at the paper in his hand. Trimble Wells 482. The assistant commissioner. He must have decided to stay on in the country and commute to London. Please ring when convenient. Henry decided that it would not be convenient until Daffodil and the van der Hovens had left for London and the Duvals were installed at the Hindhurst Arms.

In the end, they all left together in the Rolls. Daffodil, the self-appointed chauffeur, seemed in high humor. Looking exquisite in a beige linen safari suit and the Paris equivalent of a bush hat, she astonished Emmy by carrying her own suitcases downstairs and helping to load them into the car.

Primrose appeared next, cool and neat in her inevitable cardigan and pearls. "I haven't been in to say good-bye to Dolly," she said to Henry. "I imagine the poor dear is resting, and in any case we shall be in Hindhurst. Just tell her, will you, that Edouard and I will be responsible for all the funeral arrangements? I have already spoken to Garbett's, the undertaker's. Mother is being taken to their Chapel of Rest in Hindhurst tomorrow, and the actual funeral will be on Wednesday. Yes, yes, Edouard will take care of the legal details with the police and the coroner. It's all quite in order. I suppose Dolly will insist on coming to the funeral." Primrose sighed impatiently. "Of course, she may not be well enough," she added, brightening. "You and Mrs. Tibbett will be back in London by then, of course." This was not so much a statement as a challenge. "I am sure that Mother would not have wished anybody outside the immediate family to attend the service. A funeral is such a very personal affair, don't you think?" This to Emmy, with an unfriendly smile. "Well, I think that's all for the time being. Don't hesitate to ring us at the Hindhurst Arms if there is anything we can do for Dolly. As for the inquest—Dolly has our address in Lausanne, but I really can't imagine that we'll be needed. Yes, Daffy, I'm coming. I was just telling Mrs. Tibbett where she could get in touch with me."

"I'll be at the Belgrave Towers Hotel tonight and maybe tomorrow, if you want me," said Daffodil. "Sorry about the funeral, but I really can't leave poor old Chuck on his own in Paris. I do think Vi and Piet might stay for it, though."

"Vi and Piet have to work for their living, unlike some people," said Primrose acidly. "It's lucky for the rest of you that Edouard and I are prepared to stay on and take all the responsibility. Edouard has had to give up an important conference, you know."

"You're a shocking old fraud, Prim," said Daffodil lazily and not unkindly. "You know you dragged him over here, telephoning in hysterics—"

"How do you know I telephoned?" Primrose was bristling. "You were eavesdropping, I suppose?"

"Of course I was, darling."

"Oh, were you? Well, two can play at that game, and it may interest you to know that I—"

"Hush, hush," said Daffodil reprovingly. "Here comes our wilting Violet, straight out from under that mossy stone, by the look of her."

Indeed, Violet did look uncommonly pale and tense, as she had done ever since her mother's death. She leaned heavily on Piet's arm, like a widow at a funeral depending on her eldest son. The difference in their ages was suddenly, grotesquely exaggerated. Violet whispered farewells to Henry and Emmy and then allowed herself to be helped into the Rolls by Dr. Duval, while Piet explained at unnecessary length that he himself would have made any sacrifice to attend his mother-in-law's funeral, but that he felt the strain would be too much for Violet. He ended by saying to Emmy, "You gave that to Miss Dolly? For her flowers?"

"I left it by her bed, Piet," said Emmy. "She's asleep at the moment."

"She will understand," said Piet. And again, "For her beautiful flowers."

It seemed very quiet in the house when the Rolls had driven off down the winding drive. Henry said to Emmy, "What was Piet going on about?"

"Oh, some sample he'd brought for Dolly to try in her greenhouse. He was too shy to take it into her room himself."

"How does Dolly seem?"

"She's sleeping like a baby. I saw Violet going in to say good-bye to her, but I don't suppose she heard a thing. Out like a light—and a good thing, too."

"Poor old Dolly," said Henry, and he went off into the library to telephone to the assistant commissioner.

The A.C. was, if anything, more embarrassed than ever. He had had, he told Henry frankly, one hell of a day. Lady Balaclava's death had caused a sensation, all right. Had it? Henry asked, mildly surprised. The press hadn't turned up at Foxes' Trot. Hadn't even telephoned. No, no, no, said the A.C. Not *that* sort of sensation. In fact, powerful influences were at work to prevent the press from latching onto the story. The sensation had been purely personal, among high-ranking individuals. Scotland Yard had come in for a lot of hard words, and its reputation was at a low ebb.

"I know that, sir," said Henry. "That's why I'm staying on here."

"Em . . . well . . . yes. I was coming to that, Tibbett. The general feeling among Lady Balaclava's friends is that, since this tragedy has happened, it would be better to leave well enough alone. Nothing can bring her back, and sooner than a public scandal . . . after all, the doctors have confirmed 'natural causes' . . . purely accidental. . . ."

"I don't believe, sir," said Henry, "that her death was either natural or accidental. That's why I'm staying here."

"I think, Tibbett, that it would be better if you returned to London."

"I am on leave, sir."

"In fact, I must categorically order you to return to London."

"I am on leave," said Henry again. "I am spending my leave in the country, staying with a lady who has kindly invited my wife and myself to spend a few days at her house—"

"If you mean poor old Dolly, it's not her house."

"It is. Lady Balaclava's will was read this afternoon. Miss Underwood-Threep inherits the house and a considerable amount of money to go with it."

There was dead silence from the other end of the line. Then the assistant commissioner said, "Well, I'll be damned." And then, "I can't prevent you from spending your leave where you like, Tibbett, but I beg you to use your discretion. Far better not to start raking up mud—"

Henry was intrigued. "You think there is mud to be raked, then?"

"I never said that. If any reporters should ring or call, let Dolly deal with them. You might be recognized, and I wouldn't want your presence broadcast."

"Nor would I," said Henry.

"Well . . . I'll be back in London as from tomorrow. Keep in touch. And . . . remember what I've said, Tibbett."

Dolly was asleep, but she stirred and opened her eyes as Emmy tiptoed into the darkened room.

"Whozzat? Crys . . ."

"It's me, Dolly. Emmy Tibbett."

"Tibbett? Who on earth . . . ? Oh, yes . . . remember now. . . ." Dolly gave a sort of groaning yawn and heaved herself up into a semi-sitting position. "Piggy Plunkett was here. Reading Crys's will. Where is everybody?"

"They're all gone, Dolly," said Emmy soothingly.

"Gone? Gone where?"

"Mrs. Swasheimer has gone to London. You remember, Mr. Swasheimer had to leave yesterday. Mr. and Mrs. van der Hoven are on their way back to Holland."

"Might have had the civility to say good-bye," said Dolly with a feeble resurgence of her usual spirit.

"Violet did, but you were asleep. The others sent their love. They didn't want to disturb you."

Dolly snorted. Then her eyes fell on the white packet beside her bed. "What's that? Medicine?"

"No, no," said Emmy. "Mr. van der Hoven left that for you. For your flowers. He said you'd understand. *That's* your medicine—the pills in the bottle with the chemist's label."

"Good old Piet," said Dolly. "Where are Prim and Edouard?"

"They're staying at the Hindhurst Arms," said Emmy. She moved the bottle of pills closer to Dolly's bedside and put Piet's offering on the far side of the table. "They asked me to tell you that they are making all the funeral arrangements, so you're not to worry about anything."

"Damned unsociable," Dolly grumbled. She groaned. "It'll be a double funeral if I go on feeling like this. What happened, anyway?"

"Nothing very much. You fainted, that's all. Dr. Duval thought you ought to keep quiet for a bit, so he gave you a sedative. You'll feel fine tomorrow."

"Fainted? What in hell's name would make me faint?" Emmy said nothing. Dolly wrinkled her brow for a moment, and then recollection came. She nodded slowly to herself. "Of course. The house."

"Dr. Duval said that you should have a light supper in bed, and then take another pill and have a good night's sleep," said Emmy. "Shall I bring you some soup and perhaps a poached egg? Then you can—"

"The house," said Dolly again.

"That's right. It's yours now," said Emmy encouragingly. "Mr. Plunkett is going to get in touch with you again soon about all the details."

"No, no." Dolly was struggling to sit upright. "I mean the house. Who's going to look after it and clean it and do the cooking, if I'm lying here eating poached eggs and sleeping pills? I'll have to get up—"

"No," said Emmy. Gently but firmly, she pushed Dolly back onto the pillows. "You're to stay where you are."

"But the bedrooms . . . sheets to be changed . . ."

"Now, don't worry," said Emmy. "I'll do all that."

Dolly lay back and closed her eyes. "All right. You're a good creature. You'll find clean linen in the cupboard next to Crystal's bathroom. Don't overcook my egg, will you, duckie?" There was another pause, and then Dolly said softly, "I must be getting bloody old. . . ."

It was after Dolly had had her supper, taken another pill, and was again sleeping that Emmy found time to do a quick round of the bedrooms, with the idea of stripping off the used sheets and leaving the beds to air until remade with fresh linen in the morning.

Predictably, the room which Primrose had occupied was clean and trim as a new pin: the sheets had already been taken off the bed and carefully folded. The van der Hoven's room was in the state in which any housewife expects to find a used guest room—somewhat tousled, the wastepaper basket and ashtrays full, but showing signs of a hasty effort having been made to leave the place reasonably tidy.

On the other hand, and equally predictably, the Syrie Maugham Room, which Daffy and Chuck had occupied, was a shambles. The pure white decor—in need of a repaint—was barely visible under the litter of lipstick-smeared tissues, empty cosmetics bottles, crumpled tissue paper, hairpins, and all the other discarded impedimenta of beauty. There were two empty whiskey bottles in the bathroom, with two dirty tooth mugs. The bathroom floor was swimming with the damp remains of a foam bath, in which soiled bath towels lay, limp and soggy. Most of the bedclothes were on the floor.

Emmy gave a little sigh of distaste and decided that she might as well begin, as intended, by stripping the bed and folding the sheets. It was while she was doing this that she heard the clatter of a small, hard object falling out from among the tangled bedding onto the floor. She stooped and picked up the diamond-and-emerald brooch which Daffodil had been wearing when her mother died.

For several seconds Emmy stood there holding the jewel in her hand. To her and Henry, it would represent, in value, the hard-earned savings of a lifetime; in beauty, something fantastic and precious, to be treasured forever. To Daffy and Chuck it was a trinket, a toy from a Christmas cracker. . . . Emmy pulled herself together. Even Daffodil would hardly relish the thought of losing such a possession. By now she must be at her London hotel, probably looking for the brooch and beginning to worry. There was a London directory as well as the local one beside the telephone. Emmy looked up the number of Belgrave Towers Hotel and dialed it.

"Belgrave Taws. Can I help yew?" The voice was young, female, and impossibly refined.

"I'd like to speak to Mrs. Swasheimer, please," said Emmy.

"Mrs. . . . can yew spell it?"

Emmy did so.

"Wan moment. Ah, yes, here we are. Mr. and Mrs.

Warren C. Swasheimer, Suite 208. Mr. Swasheimer booked in this morning, but Ai'm not sure if Mrs. Swasheimer has arrived yet."

"But—" Emmy began.

"Wan moment, please. I'll try to connect yew." The line was silent for a few seconds. Then, "Mrs. Swasheimer is on the line. Go ahead, please."

Daffy's voice said, "Hello. Who's that?"

Emmy said, "I'm sorry to bother you, Mrs. Swasheimer. It's Emmy Tibbett. I'm speaking from Foxes' Trot."

"Oh, God," said Daffy. "Not more trouble?"

"No. No trouble. It's just that I've found your emerald brooch. The one you were wearing on Saturday. I thought you'd like to know that it's safe."

"That's very kind of you." Daffy sounded almost cordial. "Actually, I hadn't noticed it was missing. Now, what's the best thing—?"

"Perhaps you could drive down and collect it," Emmy suggested. "I hardly like to put it in the post to Paris. The customs—"

"No, no." Daffy spoke briskly. "Pack it up carefully in a cardboard box with lots of cotton wool and send it to me here, registered, insured, and express."

"But—"

"I shall be here until Thursday, after all. There's plenty of time." In the background Emmy heard a masculine voice saying something indistinguishable. Daffy, her head turned away from the telephone, said faintly but audibly, "O.K., darling, I'm just coming. This funny old biddy from Foxes' Trot has found my brooch. Oh, just one Chuck gave me the other day." Then, into the telephone, "I'm so sorry, Mrs. Tibbett. I have a few friends in my suite, we're just off to the theater. Now, you understand? Pack up the brooch and send it to me here, at the hotel. Fine. Bye for now."

"Good-bye," said Emmy. She forbore to ask whether the package should be addressed to Mrs. Charles Z. Swasheimer or to Mrs. Warren C. Swasheimer, because the answer seemed obvious. Poor Chuck, she thought as she went downstairs. She considered telling Henry and then decided against it. Emmy hated gossip.

In any case, she would have had no chance to do so, because just as she reached the foot of the stairs the phone rang. Henry, who had been hanging about in the drawing room, hoping to be favored with something to eat, came out into the hall and answered it.

"Tibbett speaking."

"Superintendent! This is Sarah Massingham. I've just heard!" The doctor's voice fairly sizzled down the line.

"Heard what?" Henry asked.

"The—the verdict. That's not the right word. The diagnosis. 'Natural causes.' Fiddlesticks and bunkum!"

"Then you don't—?"

"If that woman died from natural causes, then pigs can fly and I'm a Dutchman and . . ." Dr. Massingham ran out of unlikelihoods.

"The police doctor—"

"Oh, I know. The police doctor has signed the death certificate and the police are no longer interested, and everybody is using their discretion madly." It jolted Henry a little to hear her using the A.C.'s very phrase. "Well, I'm not. And since you're still there, I think and hope and pray that you're not. By heaven, I'll crack this case if it's the last thing I do. Are you with me, Superintendent?"

"I certainly am."

"Then we must get together—as soon as possible."

"This evening?" said Henry. He found Sarah Massingham's enthusiasm infectious.

"Why not?"

"Will you come here, or shall I come to you?" Henry asked.

"You'd better come here. No inquisitive ears about. You know the address?"

"No."

"Then get a pencil. It's 24 Lion Street, Hindhurst. Turn left by the Hindhurst Arms, then first right, and it's on the left. . . . O.K.?"

"Fine," said Henry. "I'll have a bite to eat, and then I'll be right along."

As Henry put down the receiver, Emmy said, "Who was that?"

"The local doctor."

"Oh? New developments?"

"Not really. But very encouraging from my point of view."

"What does that mean?"

"That she doesn't believe it was a natural death, either. She's only just heard the police doctor's verdict, and she's hopping mad and full of fight. She'll be a marvelous ally. So hurry up and give me something to eat, love, because I've got a date in Hindhurst."

Emmy said, "You mean—it was Dr. Massingham? The pretty girl who was here—?"

"Of course. Who else should it be?"

"Oh. I don't know. I just thought Lady Balaclava's regular doctor might be back. Dr. Griffiths."

"No, thank God. Well, come on, woman—where's that food?"

11

Twenty-four Lion Street, Hindhurst, turned out to be a pretty red-brick Georgian townhouse situated on a narrow street behind the Victorian town hall. A neat brass plate beside the pilastered front door announced that Dr. A. Griffiths practiced at this address, and beneath it a less attractive sign in white lettering on black plastic gave details of surgery hours. Henry rang the bell.

Sarah Massingham answered the door herself. She was wearing a trouser suit of soft, silky material, patterned in dark blues, grays, and greens, and she looked more like a fashion model than a general practitioner. She greeted Henry warmly and invited him to follow her upstairs, explaining that the ground floor of the house was given over to the surgery, laboratory, and consulting room; indeed, the clinical atmosphere was apparent to both the eye and the nose, for the once-elegant hallway was painted in hospital green and cream and gave off a faint odor of disinfectant. A door at the bottom of the stairs separated this austere domain from Dr. Griffiths' living quarters.

Once past this door, there was an abrupt change. The staircase was softly carpeted in deep red, and eighteenth-century military prints decorated the pine-paneled walls. The first-floor drawing room was comfortably furnished with well-chosen antiques and a smattering of leather and parchment, adding up in Henry's mind to a luxury-bachelor style.

"It's a pretty house, isn't it?" said Sarah Massingham

"Sit down and I'll get you a drink. Will whiskey do? I'm afraid there isn't anything else except wine."

Henry said that whiskey would be fine. Sarah opened the doors of a beautiful Georgian tallboy, to reveal that the inside was fitted out as a bar, with racks for bottles and glasses.

"The bottom part is an icebox," she said. "The drawer fronts are false. Sacrilege, of course, but handy. Dr. Griffiths certainly does himself proud." She selected two glasses and began to pour. "You'll find all the papers on the sofa. I've been going through those reports with a fine-tooth comb."

"Any luck?" Henry asked.

"Depends what you mean by luck." Sarah put the drinks down on a low marble coffee table. "The police are thorough, I'll give them that. They don't seem to have overlooked a thing. Every test, every analysis you can think of. Every result negative."

"You mean," said Henry, "that they simply don't know what Lady Balaclava died of."

Sarah looked at him with a trace of impatience. "We all know what she died of. Anaphylactic shock."

"I don't suppose you could put that into language that a policeman of forty could understand?"

She smiled. "Not very easily, but it involves a complete collapse of the system—lungs, heart, the lot. The main symptoms one would expect after a massive dose of parathion."

"By which you mean Flyaway."

"Yes—or any other parathion insecticide. But there wasn't a trace of parathion, either in the body, or the cake, or the champagne—"

"Or even the roses, where one might expect to find it," said Henry.

"No, no." Sarah shook her head. "I mean—the roses might have been sprayed with a parathion solution, but that wouldn't have killed anyone who sniffed them. Accidental parathion poisonings happen to people who work with the stuff all the time, and gradually absorb it—either through the skin or by breathing it in. There have been cases, too, of children getting hold of so-called empty cans, which had enough of the stuff left in them to prove fatal. But to murder somebody with parathion, you'd need to administer a hefty dose, disguised in some way. Anyhow, that's all academic, because there wasn't any parathion."

"So where does that leave us?" Henry asked.

"With an allergy of some sort."

"That's what the police doctor's report said. 'Possibility of a rare allergy.' Dr. Duval didn't seem to think much of it. The resort of the ignorant, he called it."

"Doctor Which?"

"Duval. Swiss. Husband of Lady Balaclava's eldest daughter. He wasn't in the house when she died—he arrived yesterday, to hold his wife's hand."

"Well, if he thinks that a diagnosis of allergy is the resort of the ignorant, he hasn't been doing his homework," said Sarah. She sounded a little piqued. "Oh—I know what he means. People do tend to grab at an explanation like a rare allergy, because we know comparatively little about them. But it just so happens that I've been making a special study of allergic reactions and serum accidents. This p.m. report is absolutely typical. . . ." She ruffled through the pages of the report. ". . . acute emphysema of the lungs . . . dilation of the right ventricle . . . multiple small hemorrhages in the heart, lungs, kidneys, and adrenal glands. . . ."

"Typical of what?" Henry asked.

"Of anaphylactic shock or serum accident," Sarah explained patiently.

"Look," said Henry, "I'm only a poor ignorant detective. Do put it into plain language, there's a dear."

"I'm making it as plain as a pikestaff. Lady Balaclava died because she somehow absorbed a dose of some drug or other to which she was allergic, or if you prefer, to which she'd previously been sensitized. The rest of you were able to eat, drink, and be merry with exactly the same food, wine, and so on, because none of you happened to be sensitive to—whatever it was."

Henry considered this. Then he said, "That doesn't seem to get us much further. What you've described isn't most people's idea of allergy—I mean, I thought one came out in a rash, not dropped dead."

"Allergy can be very severe—but you're right, in a way. The very first sign is almost always a violent itching—"

"Wait a minute!" Henry was excited. "I remember now. The first thing she did was to rub at her face—"

"There you are!" cried Sarah triumphantly. "I wish you'd told me sooner—but of course you didn't realize it was important. That just about proves it was allergy—but to what? I've known violent reactions to penicillin, streptomycin, horse serum, phenytoin sodium—"

"There you go again," Henry complained. "Now, honestly, Dr. Massingham, you're not suggesting that there was horse serum or any of your other unpronounceables in the cake or the champagne, are you?"

"No." Sarah smiled. "If there had been, the analysis would have shown them up. Of course, some people are sensitive to flower pollen—"

"Pollen!" Henry sat up straight. "Now, that might be a lead."

"Or egg white."

"Now you're making fun of me."

"I'm not. People can be allergic to almost anything."

"I don't mean that."

"Then what do you mean?" Sarah asked.

"Just this. Lady Balaclava was in her own home, eating and drinking her routine food and drink. Even the birthday presents were traditional, which means that she's been drinking champagne and eating cake and smelling roses every year without the faintest ill effect. But this year, something was added. Either deliberately or by accident."

"You're very bright," said Sarah. She favored him with another smile. "Go on."

"You said," Henry said, thinking hard, "that she was allergic to something she had previously been sensitized to."

"I did, didn't I?"

"By minute doses of parathion over a long period, perhaps?"

"Sorry." Sarah shook her head emphatically. "It's a lovely theory, but it won't work. For one thing, parathion isn't something that you're allergic to or not. It's a perfectly straightforward and very dangerous poison. Second—to come back to our vicious circle—there wasn't any."

"What about penicillin?"

"That was the first thing I thought of," Sarah said. "It's the commonest of drug allergies. So I looked up Lady Balaclava's file among Dr. Griffiths' records. She has been treated with small doses of penicillin for minor ailments within the last year—and no sign of sensitivity. We can cross penicillin off the list, for what it's worth. Have another drink."

"It's all very well to keep shooting down my theories," said Henry, handing over his empty glass. "What about something positive? What's *your* theory?"

"I haven't got one yet," Sarah admitted. "Ice?"

"Please."

"Nothing you could really call a theory. Just a few ideas."

"Well, let's hear them."

"Say when. There. Hope I haven't drowned it. Now, where was I? Oh, yes. Ideas." Sarah sat down and stared at the empty fireplace. "First of all, we'd better dispose of the coincidence theory."

"Dispose of it?"

"When I recognized you at Foxes' Trot on Saturday evening, you told me that your presence there wasn't accidental." Henry said nothing. "You were expecting something to happen, weren't you?"

Henry considered for a moment. Then he said, "Yes and no. I went down to Foxes' Trot at Lady Balaclava's request, because she had a premonition that she was in danger."

"That she was going to be murdered?"

"Well . . . yes. She had somehow got the idea into her head."

"Where from, if one may ask?"

"I wish I knew," said Henry. "Ostensibly from the late Lord Balaclava, through the medium of a tooth mug. Don't laugh—it's true. At least, that was the act she put on for me, and she appeared to believe in it herself. It seems he had warned her."

"It also seems," said Sarah grimly, "that he was perfectly right."

"Anyhow," said Henry, "wherever the warning came from, Lady Balaclava took it seriously enough to pull all sorts of strings to get me down here for the weekend, under the guise of an ordinary house guest. And a fat lot of use I turned out to be," he added bitterly.

"Never mind about that," said Sarah crisply. "The point is that I think we're justified in assuming that an extra something—something Lady Balaclava was allergic to— was deliberately added to the festivities. In fact, that she was murdered—and in such a way as to leave no trace whatsoever. The question is—what was this something, and who supplied it? It comes down to deduction, my friend, and that's where you come in."

"I'm not a doctor," Henry protested.

"You don't need to be. You can leave the medical end of things to me. Your job is to find out facts. Who stood to gain by her death? Who knew her past medical history—that's very important. That's where we'll get our clue, with any luck. Who had the opportunity to—I seem to be giving you a lecture in your own job. Sorry."

"Don't be sorry," said Henry. "It's most stimulating. In fact, I feel more cheerful than I have done since Saturday. If we work together—"

"That's right. You bring me your deductions, and I'll work on the medical angles." Sarah was silent for a moment, and then she said, "Once you rule out coincidence, the picture is rather frightening, isn't it? I mean, somebody had really worked on this thing. Somebody who knew her really well and had a stupendous reason for wanting her dead. A very cool and ingenious person."

Henry nodded slowly. Then he rubbed the back of his neck with his left hand—always a sign that something was bothering him. He said, "It doesn't fit."

"What doesn't fit?"

"Everything you said just now is perfectly correct. A cool, calculating, ruthless murderer with an overwhelming motive. There simply isn't anybody like that in the family circle. Not on the face of it, anyhow."

"Local gossip has it," said Sarah, "that all the daughters have come into a lot of money."

"So they have. But if you consider them . . . Daffodil is married to a millionaire. Primrose was obviously fond of her mother, and she's very comfortably off as the wife of a Swiss doctor. Violet and her husband are probably the least well-off—or were, I should say—but they appear to be perfectly content. I expect Violet will enjoy buying some nice clothes and a new car—but she's hardly the sort of woman to murder her own mother for that. In any case, Lady Balaclava wouldn't have lived forever. The daughters all knew they'd inherit soon. It's just not a murder situation."

"What about the lady companion?" Sarah asked.

"Damned if I know," said Henry. "As it turns out, she's inherited a sizable bit too. But she didn't know she was going to—in fact, she was expecting to be thrown out into the cold world without a cent when Lady Balaclava died. If she was putting on an act at the reading of the will she deserves an Oscar."

"And there's nobody you can think of outside the family—?"

Henry shook his head. "Young Dr. Griffiths seems to have been the only outsider who visited the house regularly," he said. "Do you have his holiday address, by the way? I wouldn't mind having a word with him."

"Nor would I," said Sarah, "but all I have is the name of a *pensione* somewhere in southern Italy. You could write to him, I suppose. It's here somewhere." She went over to the eighteenth-century desk and opened a drawer. "Yes, here we are. Pensione del Sole, Santa Caterina, Calabria. He told me he was going to stay in the backwoods, miles from anywhere. They certainly don't have a telephone there. In any case, he'll be back at the end of the week."

Henry made a note of the address. Then he said, "You're really serious, aren't you?"

"Serious?" Her eyebrows went up, and she looked suspiciously frivolous.

"That it couldn't have been an accident, I mean."

"Of course it could have been an accident—if you're prepared to swallow a monumental coincidence. Taken in conjunction with these mysterious spirit messages, and the contents of the will . . . well, I don't believe in coincidences that big."

"You'd be surprised," said Henry, "at the coincidences that do happen in life. They make our work extremely difficult."

"Don't tell me you're backing out at this stage?"

"Of course not." Henry paused. Then he said, "I've told my superior officer that I'll resign if I can't solve this case." He felt a pang of guilt. He had not even told Emmy about this rash determination.

The eyebrows went up again. "A bit dramatic, surely?"

"I don't think so. I'm in one hell of a position. You must see that."

"You're in danger of looking like a fool," said Sarah Massingham. "I would have thought you could have endured that—especially as you are clearly not one. Still, it's academic, isn't it? We're going to solve this thing between us."

"You're very encouraging."

"You can do with a bit of encouragement. I'm not surprised. You need a doctor in your corner in a case like this. Now, your job is to find out what foreign substances were introduced into that house on Saturday—anything at all that wasn't on Lady Balaclava's regular order list. And dig into her past medical history, if you can. I'll put the two together, and at some point something will click. Once we know what killed her, from there to 'who' should be a short step. Agreed?"

"Agreed," said Henry.

"Good. Then let's have another drink on it."

Henry arrived back at Foxes' Trot just before eleven. He found Emmy alone in the drawing room drinking coffee and looking glum. She looked up when he came in and said, "Well?" in a flat voice.

"Well what?"

"How did you get on?"

"Famously. I really think we're getting somewhere." But Henry was aware of the glow of his enthusiasm dimming. "Sarah thinks—"

"Sarah?"

"Dr. Massingham. She thinks—in fact, she's sure—that Lady Balaclava died of anaphylactic shock."

"Oh, yes?"

"It resulted from an allergic reaction to some foreign substance to which she'd previously been sensitized, like horse serum—"

Emmy eyed her husband coldly. "I think," she said, "that you had better go to bed."

"I need a doctor in my corner, you see," Henry explained. "I shall compile a list of foreign substances and Lady Balaclava's previous history. Sarah will combine them—"

"Henry," said Emmy severely, "how many drinks have you had?"

"Drinks? Oh, one or two. Dr. Griffiths is in Calabria, you see, which is a great nuisance."

"I'm sure it is."

"How's Dolly?"

"She's . . ." Emmy hesitated. "She's asleep."

"Never mind. I'll talk to her in the morning."

"It would be better," said Emmy, "if you reserved all your talking for the morning." Henry, who had begun making notes on the back page of his pocket diary, looked up in surprise. Emmy went on. "Personally, I am going to bed." A little pause. "As a matter of fact, I'm worried about Dolly, and I was hoping to talk it over with you and ask your advice—but it's obvious you're in no condition to talk anything over. Good night."

Henry's sense of outraged innocence robbed him of speech for the few seconds that it took Emmy to reach the drawing-room door. Then he found his tongue. "You're making a very silly spectacle of yourself," he said with dignity. The fact that he had had three large whiskeys, and knew it, made him choose his words with especial care. "I had the foolish impression that you cared about my work, and wanted to help me. However, if you're going to fly into a jealous tantrum, just because Sarah Massingham happens to be an extremely attractive woman as well as a brilliant doctor—" He paused, partly for breath, and partly because he had become slightly confused as to the ultimate destination of his sentence.

"Oh, horse serum to you," said Emmy. She went out, slamming the door.

Henry at least had the rudimentary good sense not to follow too quickly upon her heels. He returned to his notebook and wrote down a list of names. Primrose and Edouard Duval. Violet and Piet van der Hoven. Daffodil and Chuck Swasheimer. Dolly Underwood-Threep. Anthony Griffiths. Then he considered them, one by one. First he drew a line through Primrose's name—a faint line which might possibly be erased later. Henry simply could not imagine Primrose murdering her mother for an inheritance which she would get in a few years anyhow. Against Edouard Duval's name went a question mark. The doctor himself gained nothing directly from Crystal's death. Or did he? Henry penciled in the words "Swiss law?"

Piet van der Hoven was also crossed out, although "Dutch law?" was marked against his name. Violet—a query. The arguments against Primrose's guilt went for her, too. Daffodil and Chuck Swaisheimer were eliminated without further ado. Dolly—a large query. Tony Griffiths—a query and the words "tooth mug."

Having completed this uninspired exercise, Henry glanced at his watch and decided that he might now safely go upstairs. Sure enough, although a light was still burning in the Black Room, Emmy was in bed and apparently sound asleep. The black silk sheets were drawn up tightly over her head, and she did not stir when the door opened. Henry undressed, took a fairly noisy shower in the black bathroom, and climbed into bed. For some minutes he read the novel by Michael Arlen which had been provided as bedside reading for Crystal's guests. Still Emmy did not move a muscle—which made it patently clear to Henry that she was wide awake.

He said, "Good night, darling. I hope you get off to sleep soon." And before she could react, he switched off the light.

12

The next morning Emmy was contrite. She got up before Henry was awake, went downstairs to the kitchen, and made two pots of tea. The first, laid out on the prettiest tray she could find, she carried up to Dolly's room. Getting no reply to her knock, she opened the door and went in quietly. Dolly was lying hunched up under the threadbare eiderdown, exactly as Emmy had left her the night before, breathing heavily and regularly.

"I've brought you a cup of tea, Dolly," said Emmy cheerfully. She set the tray down on the battered little bamboo table beside the bed and drew the curtains to let in the morning sunshine.

"Whazzat?" The woman in the bed stirred sluggishly.

"Tea," said Emmy.

A grunt from the bed was the only answer.

"Shall I bring you your breakfast later on, or will you come down?"

There was a pause, far from silent. From among the groans and yawns, Emmy thought she could distinguish the words "Come down."

"Good," she said brightly, feeling like a caricature of a hospital nurse. "I'm glad you're feeling better."

Dolly murmured something indistinct and rolled over, hiding her face in the pillow as if to escape from the daylight. Emmy sighed and went downstairs for the second tray.

This she brought up to the Black Room, where she had

more luck. Henry had awakened, and soon they were in the throes of that mutual self-recrimination which would be sickening to record verbatim, but which is such a satisfactory feature of a happy marriage.

At length Emmy said, for the umpteenth time, "No, it was *my* fault. I behaved like an idiot. But you see, darling, I really was worried about Dolly. I still am."

"What about her?"

"Well . . . I know the will was a shock to her, and I suppose one can't wonder at her fainting—though it did seem a bit out of character at the time, I must say."

"Dolly's not young," said Henry. "And you must remember that she's been under several sorts of nervous strain. Also . . ." He paused.

"What?"

"Well—Plunkett took it for granted that the shock of the will was a pleasant one."

"Wasn't it?"

"Not," said Henry, "if it made Dolly realize that she might be suspected of murder."

"I didn't think anybody was suspected of murder, officially."

"True. But Dolly was the only person in the house who knew who I was and why I had come here. Who knew about the glass-pushing and the spirit's warning. And who, up till that moment, had been completely in the clear because of a positive lack of motive. We all thought she stood to lose heavily by Crystal's death."

Emmy nodded. "I see what you mean," she said. "All right, let's take it that the fainting was understandable. But she recovered from that quite quickly—she was able to walk up to her room, with only a little help. Since then, she's . . . well, she's just not been with us."

"Dr. Duval gave her a sedative," Henry pointed out.

"I know. That was perfectly natural, too. I'd have expected her to sleep, or at least be drowsy, for a while and then to perk up again. But she hasn't. She just lies there as if she'd been drugged. I'm sure it isn't right."

Henry patted Emmy's hand comfortingly. "I think

you're worrying unnecessarily, love," he said. "I expect Dr. Duval gave her something pretty strong so that she'd have a good night's sleep. She'll be as right as rain this morning, you'll see."

"She isn't," said Emmy. "I've just taken her tea up. Oh, I don't mean that she's actually ill. She's just . . . blurred."

"Well," said Henry, "I want to talk to her anyway, so we'll see how she is after breakfast. If she's no better, I'll telephone Dr. Duval." He saw the doubt on Emmy's face. "What's wrong with that?"

"I don't suppose . . . couldn't Dr. Massingham see her?"

Henry sighed. "Heaven knows," he said. "We get all mixed up in questions of medical etiquette. Dr. Duval has started the treatment—"

"But Dolly's own doctor—"

"If Dr. Griffiths were here, it would be different. Sarah . . . Dr. Massingham . . . isn't Dolly's doctor."

"I still think an outsider should take a look at her," said Emmy stubbornly.

"I'll tell you what. If she doesn't seem better, I'll ring Dr. Duval and see what he says. After all, the Duvals are going back to Switzerland tomorrow after the funeral. That's it. I'll suggest to Duval that he get in touch with Sarah and tell her what he's been prescribing, so that she can continue the treatment if necessary."

Dolly did not appear downstairs for breakfast, so Emmy arranged another tray with eggs, toast, and coffee and carried it upstairs. She found Dolly a little brighter, sitting up in bed, but complaining of a bad headache.

"Decent of you chaps to rally around like this," she said. Her voice was slightly slurred, but stronger. "All the others gone, I suppose?"

Emmy explained again that Edouard and Primrose were at the Hindhurst Arms and were arranging the funeral. Dolly gave a ghost of her old, sardonic laugh. "Too proud to stay in the house now it's mine, I suppose. Typical. Still, at least they'll be here for the funeral. Poor Crys. Almost forgotten already. Makes you think." She poured coffee and hot milk into her cup with an unsteady hand and then said, "Oh. Reminds me. Better take another of those tablets Edouard gave me. Three times a day, he said. Pass them over, there's a love."

Emmy handed over the small bottle, and Dolly shook a white tablet from it. Then she poured milk shakily into her cup, spilling some on the bedclothes. Like a child she closed her eyes and screwed her face up in unpleasant anticipation, then quickly put the pill into her mouth and swallowed it, with a gulp of milk.

"There. Horrid things."

Emmy said, "Henry wondered if he could have a word with you after breakfast—that is, if it wouldn't tire you too much."

"Of course he can. Anytime."

"And now, why don't you let me make your bed up, and—"

"No, no, no. I'm perfectly fit, apart from my blasted head. I'll get up in a minute."

But by the time that Henry had finished his breakfast and made his way up to Dolly's room, he found her sluggish and sleepy again—evidently as the result of the fresh dose of sedative. Her headache was worse, not better—or so she said—and she was in no mood for conversation, especially when Henry brought up the subject of Crystal's "trouble" during the war.

Dolly, who had been leaning back on her pillows with her eyes closed, now opened one of them suspiciously. "What d'ja want to know about that for?"

"I'm interested," said Henry.

"None of your business."

"I'm just trying to get a complete picture—"

"See here, Tibbett. You know . . . damn and blast my bloody head . . . you know very well what the doctor said about Crys. Natural causes. If you come around trying to stir up trouble, you can't expect cooperation. Use your nut." As if the effort of so long a speech had exhausted her, she closed her eyes again, breathing heavily. Then she added, "In any case . . . promised Crys . . ."

"What did you promise, Dolly?"

"Never . . . never tell . . . never . . ." Dolly's voice trailed off into a soft moan, and a moment later she was asleep. Henry sighed, went downstairs, and telephoned to the Hindhurst Arms.

Dr. Duval did not appear pleased to receive Henry's call. He said impatiently that it was perfectly natural for Dolly to appear sleepy. He had decided that, in her state of shock, it would be beneficial to keep her under light sedation for a couple of days. That was why he had prescribed the tablets to be taken three times a day. The headache was a normal symptom, which the tablets would relieve.

When Henry mentioned Dr. Massingham, the telephone wire fairly crackled with medical etiquette, and the monstrosity of interfering laymen. Dr. Duval replied in a voice of ice that in the course of normal medical practice he had already, that morning, informed Dr. Massingham—in the absence of Dolly's usual medical adviser—of the treatment prescribed. Dr. Massingham was in complete agreement with the steps taken—and would, of course, take over the care of the patient if necessary. He, Dr. Duval, was, however, convinced that no further treatment would be needed. Dolly should take the tablets today and tomorrow, and be kept perfectly quiet. After that, she might resume her normal activities

As an afterthought, Dr. Duval mentioned almost in passing that there was, of course, no question of her attending Lady Balaclava's funeral the following day. In fact, said the doctor, he and his wife expected to be the only mourners, apart from Mr. Plunkett and possibly one or two of Lady Balaclava's old friends from London. If Henry and Emmy had been specifically forbidden to attend, the message could not have been clearer.

Next Henry attempted to ring Sarah Massingham, but was informed by a brisk female voice that the doctor was out on her rounds and would not be home before lunch.

He had only just replaced the receiver when the telephone rang.

"Ah, Mr. Tibbett? Plunkett here. How is everything? Miss Dolly quite recovered, I hope?"

Henry replied cautiously that Dolly was still keeping to her room, under doctor's orders.

"Ah, yes. Very wise, I am sure. I must say, it is a relief to know that she has friends with her. You and your wife, I mean. Primrose tells me that the other girls have left Plumley Green. I must say, I should have thought that Daffodil . . . Ah, well, she was always headstrong. The youngest, of course, and apt to be spoiled, I fear. Well, now, I trust I shall see you at the funeral tomorrow, with Miss Dolly."

"I'm afraid you won't," said Henry.

"But—?"

"Dr. Duval has forbidden Dolly to go—he thinks it would be too much for her. As for Emmy and myself—we were never close friends of Lady Balaclava's, you know, and the Duvals seem to want to keep the funeral a purely family affair."

"Oh." Plunkett sounded at a loss. "I'm sorry to hear that. I hope Primrose has not been . . . em . . . ungracious?"

"Not at all," said Henry. He himself did not feel that by missing Crystal's funeral he was being deprived of a rare treat.

Mr. Plunkett, however, seemed to think otherwise. "It strikes me as being somewhat inhospitable," he said primly. "However, Primrose has a will of her own. Very like her father in some ways. Perhaps she told you that I shall be coming down to Hindhurst for the—ah—sad occasion."

"Yes, she did."

"I shall see Primrose before lunch at the Hindhurst Arms. There are various financial matters to discuss. The funeral is at two-thirty and should be over by four at the latest. I would then like to come out to Foxes' Trot and have a word with Miss Underwood-Threep. I trust she will feel strong enough to see me."

"I'm sure she will," said Henry. "She's sleeping at the moment, but I'll tell her you're coming. We'll expect you about four." He hesitated and then said, "You've known the Codworthy family for a long time, haven't you, Mr. Plunkett?"

"Bless my soul, yes, indeed. Ever since I can remember. My father was Charlie's legal adviser all through the great years between the wars, when the business was really building up. I was only a youngster in those days, of course."

"But you knew them all well?"

"Everybody in London knew Crystal," said Plunkett reminiscently. "I can't pretend I was ever really in her crowd. I suppose I was never quite the type. A little bit too staid." Piggy Plunkett sighed, full of regret. "Then came 1939, and the war. I went off to do my bit in the Army. Those were stirring times."

"That's one way of putting it," said Henry sympathetically. He himself had fought in the desert, and then up through Italy. "Were you overseas?"

"Alas, no. I was attached to the legal department of the War Office. The vanguard of the Home Front."

"Yes, indeed. London in the Blitz can't have been any fun."

"We were evacuated to Dorchester, as a matter of fact," said Plunkett, and added, with no apparent sense of incongruity, "Yes, one had the feeling of participating in a great moment of history. I could never understand the fellows who shirked their duty. Reserved occupations, and all that. I was proud of my uniform."

Henry said, "When did you actually take over the Codworthys' affairs?"

"Oh, after the war. When my father died."

"After Lord Balaclava's death, in fact."

"Well . . . yes. You could put it that way."

"I see," said Henry. He was disappointed. He had supposed that the solicitor had been really intimate with the

family in the old days; now it appeared that in Lord Balaclava's lifetime Piggy Plunkett had been no more than a
callow youth, hanging around on the outskirts of his father's firm and of the Balaclava's social whirl. "Well, we'll
see you tomorrow afternoon, Mr. Plunkett," he said.
"Good-bye till then."

Henry rang off and after a moment of hesitation picked
up the telephone again and dialed a London number. A
few seconds later he was speaking to an old friend of his,
one Michael Barker, at the latter's Gray's Inn chambers.
For Mr. Barker was not only a barrister who had frequently been briefed to represent the police; he was also a
recognized authority on private international law. He
expressed delight at hearing from Henry, and readiness
not only to be consulted in his office that afternoon, but to
take luncheon first at Rule's.

Henry felt slightly guilty. It was not, strictly speaking,
necessary to make the trip to London in order to get the
information he wanted from Michael; but the atmosphere
at Foxes' Trot was beginning to oppress him with a sense
of failure. He saw no prospect of getting more information
out of Dolly until she had recovered sufficiently to respond
to rational argument. Without her help it would be difficult to act on Sarah Massingham's injunction to check on
"foreign substances" which had entered the house. Deliveries from local shops could perhaps be checked—but
Emmy was surely in a better position to do that. In plain
words, Henry wanted a break from Plumley Green. He
hoped that Emmy would understand.

He found her in the Black Room, engaged in wrapping
up a small box in brown paper. She showed no special
emotion when he told her he had to go to London to see
Michael Barker, but merely said, "Oh. Then you can be
an angel and post this for me. Registered, express, and
with all the insurance cover that the post office will give."

"What is it?"

"Daffodil's emerald brooch. She left it behind, and I
found it when I was clearing her room."

"Is it safe to post a valuable thing like that to Paris?"

"It's not going to Paris," said Emmy. She was busy addressing the package. "I phoned her last night. She's staying in London until Thursday."

"You mean, she's coming down for the funeral, after all?"

"I think that's highly unlikely," said Emmy. She drew a firm line under the words "London, W.1." "She's amusing herself with friends." She very nearly mentioned Warren C. Swasheimer at that moment, but decided against it.

"She's a tough little bitch," said Henry. "O.K. I'll post it in London. It should get there quicker." He took the small parcel, which was addressed simply to Mrs. Swasheimer at the Belgrave Towers Hotel, and slipped it into his pocket.

"When will you be back?" Emmy asked.

"Oh, not late. Certainly in time for supper. I'm lunching with Mike, and then we'll talk in his office afterward. Meanwhile, do you think you can find out from Dolly the names of the shops where she buys her household supplies?"

Emmy raised her eyebrows. "Of course, I know them already. She told me yesterday, so that I could put in the weekly order. Panton the grocer delivers on Wednesday and Friday. The butcher calls on Tuesday and Thursday. Baker and milk come every day, and Mrs. Spragg with the greengroceries drops in whenever she's passing this way in her van. You see, I really have taken over the running of the house."

"That's splendid," said Henry. "Then you might spend this afternoon getting in touch with all these people, and finding out exactly what they delivered here last week. Just a list from each of them. It may be important. And keep an eye on Dolly, of course."

"I certainly will, and if she seems worse, I shall ring Dr. Massingham," said Emmy firmly.

"You do that," said Henry. "But I'm sure she'll be better. It's just rest that she needs."

"I wish she'd let me do more for her," said Emmy. "She won't even let me make her bed or help her to wash. I'll return to the attack at lunchtime. Her bed must be terribly uncomfortable by now, but she keeps saying she doesn't want to give me any trouble."

Henry enjoyed his trip to London. The sun was shining, and the railway ran through wooded countryside and flower-banked cuttings before it hit the inevitable bleakness of the suburbs. Then London's river glinted and sparkled alongside the Gothic fantasy that was the Houses of Parliament, and Big Ben struck twelve as the train pulled into the shady cavern of Waterloo Station.

Henry posted Daffodil's brooch from the post office in the station and then took a bus to the City. Rule's was its usual crowded, hospitable self, and Michael Barker—small, slightly rotund, irrepressibly witty—was already sitting at a corner table, waiting for Henry.

During the excellent lunch, Mike and Henry spoke of old friends and new books, of trips abroad and families at home (Mike being the father of three teen-agers and an enthusiastic supporter of the new generation). Henry was regaled with the latest crop of stories currently circulating in the legal profession, and in return was able to satisfy Mike's curiosity as to some of the less-publicized aspects of a recent case involving some eminent international lawyers—because, as he explained to Henry, it's always funnier if you know the people.

In such pleasant company the problems and tensions of Foxes' Trot seemed remote, and it gave Henry a jolt when Mike suddenly said, "And now you can tell me the lowdown on poor old Crystal Balaclava."

"The lowdown?" Henry did his best to sound casual. "What do you mean? She's dead, that's all."

"My dear Henry, d'you mean to say you haven't heard?"

"Haven't heard what?"

"The rumors. London is buzzing with them. I thought you kept your ear to the ground. Where've you been?"

"You may well ask," said Henry. He added, "There's been practically nothing in the papers—"

"And that," said Mike triumphantly, "is the most interesting aspect of the whole matter. Somebody in high places is taking pains to hush the whole thing up. Well, since you've apparently been rusticating, I'll bring you up to date. Well-informed circles are convinced that somebody slipped a dose of something lethal into our Crystal's birthday cake. You know she died on her seventeenth birthday? In the bosom of her not-so-loving family, and under suspicious circumstances."

"What suspicious circumstances?" Henry demanded.

"My dear chap, I thought *you'd* be able to tell *me* that. All that rumor has been able to dig up is that her death was sudden, to say the least of it. The police were apparently called in, and all the boys of the dirt brigade were sharpening their pencils for a really juicy murder-in-high-society story, when—wham. The iron curtain came down. Police called off. Laconic announcement of death due to natural causes. Considering that the Codworthy millions are involved, speculation is naturally riding high. Frankly, I'm disappointed in you, Henry. I thought that if anybody could shed a bit of light, you could. And now I come to think of it," Mike added quizzically, "you're playing it just too innocent. I simply don't believe this is the first you've heard of it."

Henry smiled—but it was a small smile, drained by the weight of his sense of failure. "You're right, of course," he said.

"Ah," Mike sighed, satisfied.

"You're also right in thinking that if anybody could give you the true facts, I could. But unfortunately, I can't."

"Meaning that nobody can?"

"Meaning just that—for the moment, at any rate."

Mike said eagerly, "So you've spoken to people who were actually there?"

"I was there myself," said Henry.

"What?"

"I was there specifically to prevent anything from happening. And something happened. That's why I'm not exactly strewing roses from my hat or dancing hornpipes at the moment."

"But this is fascinating," said Mike with callous disregard for Henry's personal problems. "You must tell me all."

"Not here, I think," said Henry. "Let's save it for your office. In fact, it's what I wanted to talk to you about."

Half an hour later, from the comfortable depths of a leather armchair in Barker's chambers, Henry was outlining the events of the past few days at Foxes' Trot. When he had finished Mike said, "So it really was natural causes, after all?"

"The doctors haven't been able to find any evidence to the contrary."

"But you and the Massingham female are determined to fly in the faces of the experts and solve the mystery?"

"There's no need to make me sound like a starry-eyed amateur detective," said Henry. He was nettled by his friend's patronizing amusement. "Good God, I spend enough of my working life persuading people to stop romancing and accept hard facts, particularly about crime. But—"

"But in this case, you think you've come up against the perfect murder at last, and it has made you very cross. The more so because your personal reputation is involved."

Henry laughed. "All right. Put it like that if you want to. It's a fair summing up."

"That's better," said Mike with approval. "That's more like you. For a dreadful moment I thought you'd undergone a personality change."

"Meaning?"

"Lost your sense of humor," said Mike. He smiled. "Which would have been a pity."

"I'm sorry," said Henry. "I know I've been on edge lately. But when one is faced with a self-evident fact which is plain damned impossible—"

"It should," said Mike, "make you more sympathetic to other people, who come to you with self-evident damned impossible stories, and you brush them off by referring them to irrefutable expert evidence. You might remember it when you're prosecuting some of the poor devils."

Ignoring this, Henry said, "Well, at least I've now got some expert evidence in my corner. Sarah Massingham."

"She sounds to me," said Mike, "like an attractive, romantic, and headstrong girl, crazy about playing detectives."

"She's a doctor."

"The two things are not mutually exclusive."

"Well," said Henry stubbornly, "she was the first doctor to examine Lady Balaclava after her death, and she's the first and only doctor to come up with a viable theory about what might have happened."

"A rare allergy." Mike's disbelief was patent.

"My dear Mike," said Henry, "you know as well as I do that there are probably dozens of perfect murders committed every year. We've no idea how many, because they are undetected and virtually undetectable. It goes without saying that most of them are what you might call medical murders. You can't shoot a man or stick a knife into him and hope to get a verdict of death from natural causes; but a slight overdose, combined with an existing medical condition—"

"—will show up in a post-mortem examination," said Mike dryly. "I agree, if the murderer can make the death appear perfectly natural, so that there's no p.m., then he'll get away with it. But this case is the exact opposite, surely. The death appeared to be unnatural until it was thoroughly investigated, when it proved to be natural after all. Unusual, I agree. I'd take my hat off to your murderer, if there was one; but personally I'm inclined to think there isn't."

"And so is everyone else," said Henry.

"Except you and Sarah Massingham. Ah well, it makes a very pretty picture. What does Emmy think?"

Taken off his guard for a moment, Henry said defensively, "She thinks Sarah is a very efficient doctor and a very nice person."

Mike laughed. "Dear me. Has it gone that far? You misunderstood me, old man. I simply meant—what does

Emmy think about Lady Balaclava's death? I have a great respect for your wife's judgment, as you know."

"I walked right into that one, didn't I?" Henry remarked ruefully. "All right. To answer your question precisely—I really don't know. Now that I come to think of it, Emmy hasn't really expressed an opinion, one way or the other. She's been very busy, of course—virtually running the house. She seems more concerned about Dolly than she ever was about Crystal."

"The hysterical lady companion who inherits the house? What's the matter with her?"

"Well—nothing, really. She's being kept under mild sedation, and sleeps a lot, but otherwise she seems O.K. But for some reason, Emmy is worried about her. She wants Sarah to have a look at her."

"Then, my dear Henry, I would have Sarah take a look at her as soon as possible," said Mike.

"Oh, if it makes Emmy happy, I don't suppose it can do any harm."

"And perhaps might do the lady companion some good. After all," Mike pointed out, "you've just said that this is a medical murder—or nonmurder. Any doctor involved is automatically suspect."

"That's perfectly true," said Henry. "I'm trying to fit three separate aspects into a pattern that makes sense—rather like a jigsaw puzzle. The first piece is medical knowledge. The second is previous knowledge of Lady Balaclava—she had some sort of mysterious illness during the war. I haven't been able to get to the bottom of it yet, but I reckon that somebody has. And then, of course, there's the money angle—the inheritance of what you so rightly called the Codworthy millions. At least a million and a half, it seems, even after death duties. Which is why I came to see you."

"My dear chap, what can I tell you? The three daughters inherit equally, don't they? And the lady companion gets the house and Crystal's personal possessions. Nothing very complicated there."

"Not if the girls had married Englishmen and lived in

England," said Henry. "But they didn't. There's American, Swiss, and Dutch law involved." He leaned forward. "What I want to know from you, young Mike, is this. Just what rights do those three husbands have over their wives' inheritances?"

13

In the train which took him back to Hindhurst, Henry considered the information—largely unsatisfactory—which Michael Barker had given him. Of the three Codworthy daughters, it seemed that only Daffodil, with her American marriage, had an unqualified right to her own money; and this seemed hardly important, since Chuck had millions of his own. The other two cases were more complicated.

Dutch law, Mike had explained, contained several different regimes under which a marriage might take place. Property could be shared equally by both partners, or be completely separate, or be put in the husband's name alone. Each system had certain advantages and disadvantages, and it was up to each couple at the time of their wedding to decide which regime to adopt, after which they might not change their minds. Henry would have to find out which system Violet and Piet had chosen. It was at least possible that Violet had ensured an absolute right over her legacy.

The Swiss system—not surprisingly for a country in which some women still had no vote—was patriarchal. Everything belonged to the husband. Very definite and simple. But—for in Switzerland there is always a "but" in financial affairs—private arrangements might have been made. Marriage contracts might have been drawn up, legally binding on both parties, covering such special contingencies as expected inheritances. So Primrose and Edouard remained an enigma, and Henry could not imagine that they would tolerate any investigations into their private and personal affairs. In any case, Henry reflected gloomily, the Duvals were leaving for Switzerland after the funeral tomorrow, and he did not anticipate seeing them again unless he deliberately sought them out at the Hindhurst Arms.

In this supposition, however, he was wrong, for when he arrived back at Foxes' Trot, he found Primrose and Edouard in the drawing room with Emmy, drinking sherry. They both greeted him cordially, and Edouard explained that he had just dropped in to see how Dolly was.

"And how is she?" Henry asked. "We were a little worried, as you know."

"She is very good." Dr. Duval's English was not quite perfect. "She is exactly what she should be, with the tablets I gave her. After tomorrow, when the funeral is past, she may cease to take them, and she will quickly return to normality, much refreshed by her days of rest. It is because of the funeral, you understand, that I wish her to continue with the tablets for yet a day. She would certainly wish to assist it—"

"To attend it, Edouard," Primrose corrected. "You always make that mistake."

Dr. Duval smiled briefly at his wife. "Yes, my Primrose. Always I make the same mistake. As I said, Miss Dolly would wish to *attend* the funeral, and it would not be good to do so. Eventually she might—"

"Possibly, not eventually." This time Primrose's correction was sharper, but Dr. Duval chose to ignore it.

"—she might return to the state of shock and hysteria of yesterday."

"Supposing," said Emmy, "that she took too many of the pills?"

Edouard Duval beamed. "She will not take too many, I think. Miss Dolly does not enjoy to take medicine, as you may remark. But, Madame, even if she took too many, it would not be grave. She would sleep deeply, perhaps for twenty-four hours or more. And then she would wake, not the worse for wearing, as you say."

There was a little pause, and then Primrose said, "I have just been explaining to your wife, Mr. Tibbett, the arrangements I have made."

"Oh, yes?" said Henry with polite vagueness. Primrose's voice had an organizing edge to it. He wondered what she had been up to.

"You have been so very kind, both of you, staying on here and looking after Dolly so splendidly." Primrose was cooing now, but Henry had glimpsed the iron beneath the velvet. "We are tremendously grateful, but of course we can't presume on your generosity any longer."

"I was just saying to Madame Duval—" Emmy began a little desperately. Her eyes signaled plainly to Henry that Primrose was bent on dislodging them from Plumley Green and that she, Emmy, had been fighting a rearguard action and had not as yet capitulated. Henry replied with a reassuring smile intended to convey that her message had been received and understood, that she had done well, and that he would now take over.

"It's not a question of our generosity, but Dolly's," he said. "She has kindly invited us to stay for a few days in her house." He smiled at Primrose as he stressed the personal pronoun slightly.

Primrose was more than equal to this attack. "Poor dear Dolly," she said. "Yes, it must make her very happy to play the lady of the manor—but if she were feeling herself, she'd realize at once that she couldn't expect a busy and important police official to bury himself in the country and play nursemaid to her. I do hope you'll forgive her, Chief Superintendent. She has had several severe shocks, and she really isn't functioning normally at the moment. It's lucky that Edouard and I are here to make the arrangements that Dolly herself should be making."

"I am on a week's leave, Madame Duval," said Henry, "and I can't think of anywhere pleasanter to spend it."

Primrose ignored this diversion. She went on as though Henry had not spoken, "I have arranged with Mrs. Billing from Trimble Wells to come temporarily as cook-housekeeper. Fortunately, her husband is in Hindhurst Hospital having his appendix out, so she can move in here for a week or so—it is actually nearer for visiting the hospital than Trimble Wells. After that, Dolly should have quite recovered, and Mrs. Billing will come in for two hours every morning to do the heavy work. She is a very capable woman—my mother used to employ her when she wanted extra help in the house. We have been very fortunate to get her."

Primrose clearly implied, "*I* have been very clever to get her." She permitted herself a smile of self-congratulation, and then went on, "Mrs. Billing is arriving this evening, and she will take over the running of the house. She will also look after Dolly. So"—this time the smile was for Henry—"you and your wife must feel free to go back to London as soon as you like."

"How very kind," said Henry gravely. "We shall certainly feel quite free, and it's a relief to know that Dolly will be so well cared for. Once Mrs. Billing is installed, Emmy and I will be able to explore more of this lovely countryside. We are both very keen on walking," he added blandly.

Primrose glared at him. "I expect you'll be back in London before the funeral tomorrow," she said, abandoning subtlety.

"That's possible," said Henry. "As you so kindly pointed out, we can now feel quite free."

Wisely, Primrose decided not to press the point any further. She finished her sherry and stood up.

"Well, we must be off now. You'd be surprised how much organization is needed, even for such a quiet funeral. Of course, Mother was greatly loved. Ever since the anouncement in *The Times*, the undertakers have been inundated with flowers. And we expect a certain amount of trouble from the press. That is why we are keeping the detailed arrangements completely secret." She looked severely at Henry, as though he had been guilty of trying to probe these mysteries. In fact, Henry was profoundly uninterested in Lady Balaclava's funeral; what he wanted to know were the details of Dr. and Madame Duval's marriage contract, and it was obvious that he was not going to learn them here and now.

Primrose and Edouard left on foot, Primrose announcing their intention of walking to Plumley Green, whence they would catch the 5:40 bus to Hindhurst. Henry wondered if there was a clue there. A person who has just inherited half a million pounds could, if he or she wished, hire a car. And Edouard was patently less enthusiastic about the two-mile tramp and subsequent bus ride than was Primrose. Whose hand on the purse strings?

As soon as the Duvals had left, Emmy produced the fruits of her afternoon's investigations—lists of goods delivered to Foxes' Trot over the weekend by local tradesmen. She was not optimistic about their usefulness.

"Just the usual order, but rather more of everything because Lady Balaclava was expecting visitors. That was the answer everywhere. You can see for yourself—look, here's the grocer's book. Two pounds of sugar instead of one, a pound of bacon instead of a quarter, four dozen eggs instead of a dozen, and so on. But there's nothing that Dolly didn't order in smaller quantities every week of the year."

"Oh, well," said Henry. "It was worth a try. Thanks a lot, love. I'll go through the lists later, just to make sure. How's Dolly, by the way?"

Emmy shrugged. "You heard what Dr. Duval said. I suppose she's all right. Still very sleepy and still complaining of a headache—but Duval says that's normal, and he should know." Emmy glanced at her watch. "It's time for her evening pill. I'd better take her up some milk. And—oh, by the way, Henry—what are we going to do with this Billing woman?"

"What do you mean, do with her? She's coming to housekeep."

"Yes, I know," said Emmy, "but according to Primrose she's arriving this evening with bag and baggage to stay a week. Where's she going to sleep?"

"*I* don't know," said Henry. He was scanning the butcher's order book, comparing it with previous weeks. "I suppose there are some maid's rooms somewhere."

Emmy said tartly, "The only maid's room with any furniture in it is occupied by Dolly. I can't very well leave her in there and shove Mrs. Billing into the Syrie Maugham Room, now can I?"

"Oh, I should do whatever you like."

"Yes," said Emmy. And again, to herself, "Yes." She went upstairs.

It was about half an hour later, when Henry had come to the reluctant conclusion that Emmy had been right, and no "foreign substances" had been brought into the house, that the telephone rang. For some moments, Henry let it ring—hoping that Emmy might answer it from upstairs; but it continued to shrill impatiently, and so he went out into the hall and picked up the receiver.

"Plumley Green 384?" inquired an impersonal, silvertoned female. "Just one moment, please. I have a call for you from Paris." There followed the usual medley of clicks, buzzes, indecipherable snatches of distant conversation. Finally a male French voice said, "Oui. Hôtel Crillon." The buzzes and clicks broke out again in force, a French female rapped out the command, *"Parlez!"* and the Frenchman, now speaking in accented English, asked Henry if he was Plumley Green 384. Henry admitted that he was.

"An instant, Monsieur. Monsieur Swasheimer is calling you. I will connect you."

Chuck's voice came strongly and unmistakably down the wire.

"Hello? I'd like to speak with Mrs. Swasheimer, please. Mrs. Daffodil Swasheimer."

Henry said, "Tibbett here, Mr. Swasheimer. I'm afraid your wife isn't here."

"Oh, you mean she hasn't gotten back yet?"

"Back?"

"For the funeral. Surely you knew. She's coming back for the funeral tomorrow."

"It's the first I'd heard of it," said Henry. "As far as I know, she's in London, staying at the—"

To his surprise, Emmy's voice broke in, presumably

from one of the upstairs telephones. "Mr. Swasheimer? This is Emmy Tibbett. Do forgive me for interrupting. You see, I spoke to Daffodil on the telephone yesterday."

"And she told you she was coming back to Foxes' Trot?" demanded Chuck.

"No. I don't think she means to come back here."

"But she cabled me—"

"Dolly is still not at all well," said Emmy firmly. "She has to be kept very quiet. Dr. and Mrs. Duval are staying at the Hindhurst Arms until after the funeral, and I think you'll find that Mrs. Swasheimer will be there too."

"She never mentioned any Hindhurst Arms in the cable." Chuck was grumbling to himself. "What's the god-damn number of the place, anyhow? Had enough trouble getting through to you . . ."

"I don't know the number," said Emmy. "I'll have to look it up. Look, Mr. Swasheimer, why don't I contact Daffodil and ask her to telephone you in Paris?"

Chuck brightened at once. His high opinion of Emmy's efficiency rose yet another notch. "Say, that's a great idea, Mrs. Tibbett. You contact Daffy and have her call me here at the Crillon. I'll be in all evening. Thanks a lot. Oh, and I hope Miss Dolly will be better. Give her my regards. Well, so long."

Henry had just replaced the receiver when Emmy came down the stairs and into the hall. She said, "Sorry about that."

"Don't apologize," said Henry. "I'm intrigued. What's going on?"

"I didn't mean to tell anyone," said Emmy, "but I couldn't have Chuck ringing the Belgrave Towers."

"Why not, for heaven's sake?" Henry asked.

Emmy told him.

"Well, well, well," said Henry. "So—what do you propose to do?"

"Just what I told Chuck. I'll ring Daffy and tell her to call Chuck. I suppose she used the funeral as an excuse for staying on in England. And Warren is supposed to be in Milan. Well, she's got herself into this mess, and she can jolly well get herself out of it. All the same—I couldn't let Chuck ring the hotel, could I?" Emmy was almost pleading for justification.

Henry grinned. "The United League of Women in action again," he said. And before Emmy could protest, "All right, all right. I'd probably do as much for a fellow man. Here's the phone. You'd better contact Daffy."

"Belgrave Taws. Can I help yew?"

"I'd like to speak to Mrs. Swasheimer, please. Suite 208."

"Who is calling, please?"

This was a new development. Daffodil must be getting cautious. Emmy gave her name.

"One moment, please."

But it was, in fact, a couple of minutes before the same refined voice said, "I'm putting you through to Mrs. Swasheimer now."

There was a click, and then Daffy's voice said irritably, "What do you want this time, for heaven's sake? I was in the bath."

"I'm sorry," said Emmy, "but I think this may be urgent. Mr. Swasheimer has just telephoned here from Paris."

"Chuck? What on earth did he want?" The alarm was faint, but distinguishable.

"To speak to you," said Emmy. "He seemed to think you'd be here. He said you were coming back for the funeral."

"Oh, I'm so sorry you've been bothered like this." Daffy had recovered her momentarily jolted composure. "I'm afraid Chuck must have gotten the wrong end of the stick. I did mention the funeral when I called him yesterday, but I specifically said I wasn't going to it. Poor Chuck—he's getting just a bit deaf, although he won't admit it. What did you say to him?" The question was just too sharp. The edge of anxiety showed.

"I told him you weren't at Foxes' Trot," said Emmy carefully, "and that I imagined if you did decide to come for the funeral, you'd probably stay at the Hindhurst Arms, like Dr. and Mrs. Duval. To save Mr. Swasheimer the trouble of putting through a call from Paris on the off-chance, I said I'd contact you and ask you to call him back at the Crillon."

"Did you . . . did you mention the Belgrave Towers?"

"No. I didn't."

Daffy gave a little sigh of relief. "You've been very kind, Mrs. Tibbett. As a matter of fact, I think I may change my mind and come down for Mother's funeral, after all. I can be at the Hindhurst Arms in time for dinner." She hesitated. "If . . . if by any chance my husband calls again, will you tell him that I'm expected in Hindhurst this evening, around eight? I'll call him, of course," she added hastily, "but just in case I can't get through . . ."

"I'll tell him," Emmy promised, and she could not resist adding, "I'm glad you're coming for the funeral. I think you're very wise."

"How's Dolly?"

"Better, but still not well. Dr. Duval is keeping her under sedation for the time being. He thinks the funeral would upset her."

There was another short pause, and then Daffy said, "Thanks for the brooch."

"Oh, you've got it already? That was quick."

"You posted it in London." There was both a question and an accusation in Daffodil's voice.

"I didn't," said Emmy. "My husband had to go up to town on business, so he posted it."

"Ah, I see. Well, thanks again, Mrs. Tibbett. See you at the funeral tomorrow."

"I don't think so," said Emmy.

"You mean—you're leaving Foxes' Trot?"

"I didn't mean that exactly. Just that Mrs. Duval seems to want to keep the funeral a purely family affair. Mr. Plunkett will be the only outsider, I believe."

"Primmy would, wouldn't she?" Daffodil sounded amused. "It might be interesting to see old Plunkett, all the same. Well—good-bye."

Emmy found Henry in the drawing room trying to mix a White Lady. He sipped the resulting concoction, made a face, and said, "I can't understand it. It's only gin and Cointreau. I remember from my youth."

"Perhaps it's not cold enough?"

"No, it's not that. Hot or cold, this is revolting. Next time I see Dolly, I must ask her the secret."

"Which reminds me," said Emmy, "next time you see Dolly, she's in the Syrie Maugham Room—the white one, opposite ours."

"You persuaded her to move?"

Emmy smiled. "With no difficulty, I'm delighted to say. *And* I took the opportunity of making her up a new bed with clean sheets. That's why I was so long upstairs. Mrs. Billing will move into Dolly's old room."

"What about Dolly's things?"

"I've moved the obvious things, like sponge bags and hairbrushes, and cleared out the wardrobe. Not that it took long. Poor Dolly. Two pairs of corduroy trousers, a dinner jacket, and a couple of grisly crepe dresses. The other things can wait until tomorrow."

Mrs. Billing arrived a few minutes later, in the single ancient taxi which served the needs of Trimble Wells. She was a stout, motherly woman with gray hair drawn back into a neat bun, sensible shoes, a wide smile, and a battered suitcase. It was quickly apparent that she knew Foxes' Trot intimately from a domestic viewpoint—unlike Emmy, she was able to locate clean sheets, soap, and spare bags for the vacuum cleaner with no hesitation—but she admitted, in a confidential aside, that she had never before actually spent a night under Lady Balaclava's roof.

"I've been obliging Lady Balaclava, on and off, ever since I was a girl," she told Emmy as she carefully removed the long, black-headed pins from her straw hat in front of Dolly's bedroom mirror. "*Very* big parties they used to give in the old days, when the master was alive. Fifty and sixty people. I used to help in the kitchen, and with the serving. That was before I married Billing, of course. Yes, they were high-spirited, were Lady Balaclava's friends. Of course, most of them are very distinguished people now. Ministers and bishops and so on. I cut their pictures out of the papers whenever I see them. Well—it's nice, I mean, to remember them personal, whatever Billing may say. And how is Miss Threep?" she added with an abrupt swerve of topic. "Poor dear, such a shock—they were *very* close, Miss Threep and her ladyship. No wonder she's taken it hard."

Emmy reassured Mrs. Billing that Dolly was on the mend, while Mrs. Billing deftly removed her upper and outer garments, extracted a starched white apron from her suitcase, and tied it around her ample waist. Then Mrs. Billing said, "Well, now, I'll be getting a bite of dinner for you and Mr. Tibbett. And Miss Threep, of course. What do you fancy?"

Emmy said that she had been proposing to make an omelet. Mrs. Billing tut-tutted. She had nothing against omelets as such, she explained, but it was a great mistake to think you could make a meal out of one, like those French did. Miss Primrose, now, since she'd married that Frenchman—well, all right, Swiss, it's all the same, isn't it, dear?—Miss Primrose seemed to think you could serve an omelet as a main course. Well, she, Mrs. Billing, didn't hold with it, and she thought she'd just take a look in the larder and see what there was. . . . Emmy, delighted, urged her to make herself at home and to cook anything she felt like.

Downstairs Henry had experimented again, this time with disastrous effect, by adding a touch of bitters. The result was nauseous.

"Oh, well," said Henry. "It passes the time."

"Until what?" Emmy asked.

"Until—I don't know. Until the break comes, the light at the end of the tunnel. At least," Henry added, "we can add another name to the 'Motive' list."

"What do you mean? Whose name?"

"Daffodil Swasheimer."

"But she's—"

"Her husband," said Henry, "is a millionaire. His son, Warren, works for him—which means that Warren is dependent on Chuck for his high standard of living. From what you tell me, Daffodil has decided that she prefers Warren to his father. Now, I can't see our Daffy opting for love on a shoestring, and I dare say Mr. Swasheimer Junior feels the same way. If those two are ever going to cut loose, they'll need Daffy's money to do it. They could hardly expect Chuck to subsidize them."

Emmy nodded thoughtfully. "I see what you mean. Daffy actually needs the money more than either of the others."

"As far as we know. We know mighty little about Primrose or Violet so far, but we're going to have to find out."

At eight o'clock Mrs. Billing appeared in the drawing-room doorway, beaming. Dinner, she announced happily, was served. Just a scratch meal, but she hoped it would do. Cheese soufflé, roast chicken, and an apple pie to follow. What did Emmy think Miss Threep would like?

Emmy suggested that Mrs. Billing should take Dolly a small plate of chicken and vegetables after she had served the soufflé, and Mrs. Billing beamed agreement. The soufflé was excellent, and the Tibbetts were doing it full justice when the dining-room door burst open.

"Oh, madam!" Mrs. Billing was red-faced and terrified. "Oh, madam, you must come! I think she's dead!"

14

Dolly was not dead, but she was not far off it. An hour later, Sarah Massingham joined Henry and Emmy in the drawing room at Foxes' Trot. She had just returned from Hindhurst Hospital, whither she had accompanied Dolly in the ambulance. All was being done that could be done. Whether or not it would succeed was anybody's guess.

"She's still in a coma," said Sarah, "but her lungs and heart are almost back to normal. Her chances are about fifty-fifty." She sat down.

Henry said, "But what—?"

"Poison," said Sarah. "No doubt about it this time. Administered in small, cumulative doses, just a bit at a time."

"Those tablets of Dr. Duval's—" Emmy began.

"They'll be analyzed, of course," said Sarah, "but I'd be surprised if there's anything wrong with them. He prescribed pentobarbital tablets, each of one hundred mg.—which is precisely what I or any other doctor would have done. They were supplied by Trent's of Hindhurst, who are highly reputable chemists." She brought the little bottle of tablets out of her handbag. "He prescribed ten tablets—three a day for three days, with an extra one for luck. There are four left, as you can see, so there's no question of Dolly having helped herself to too many. Anyhow, even if she had, she wouldn't show symptoms of poisoning. She'd just be sound asleep."

"That's what Dr. Duval said," Henry put in.

"In any case," said Sarah, "it's very difficult to tamper with a tablet, unlike a powder."

"Supposing," said Henry, "that somebody had removed some genuine tablets and substituted poisoned ones?"

"Who?" said Emmy at once. "Daffy collected the pills from the chemist, but the bottle was still sealed when Dr. Duval gave Dolly the first tablet. I saw, I was in the room. After that, nobody saw Dolly again until I went up after they'd left . . . oh, no . . . Violet said she'd looked in to say good-bye. But you're surely not suggesting that she had some poisoned tablets with her which just happened to be the exact color, size, and shape of the ones from the chemist?"

"No," said Henry. "No, that would be ridiculous." To Sarah he added, "What poison is it? Do you know?"

She shook her head. "Not definitely. We'll be able to analyze it later on, I hope. A possible guess is one of these insecticides."

"Like Flyaway?"

"Just like that. Anyhow, she's being treated according to that hypothesis. In fact, what apparently killed Lady Balaclava may actually have poisoned Miss Underwood-Threep. She used Flyaway a lot, didn't she?"

"In the greenhouse," said Henry. "And she took tremendous precautions with it."

"All the same, she's probably been absorbing small doses of it for ages. It can have a cumulative effect, you see. If she's suddenly been subjected to a larger dose, it could have this effect of sending her into a coma."

Emmy said, "That stuff of Piet's . . ."

"What stuff of Piet's?" Henry asked.

"I told you. He left a packet of powder for Dolly. Something for her plants. I took it into her room myself."

"Piet told us he never used parathion insecticides."

"He may not use them himself, but he could have brought her a sample of something new from Holland."

Sarah Massingham, deeply interested, said, "You mean there was some sort of insecticide in her room all the time?"

"Just a little package," said Emmy. "Sealed up."

"Where is it now?"

"It must still be in Dolly's old room," said Emmy. "I didn't move it." She turned to Sarah in explanation. "I persuaded Dolly to move to a bigger bedroom this evening. The temporary housekeeper has her old room. I'll go up and see if I can find the powder."

Mrs. Billing was already in bed. In the soothing presence of doctors and ambulances she had soon recovered her equilibrium and become a tower of strength, dispensing coffee and biscuits and discussing Dolly's condition with gloomy relish. Once the ambulance had departed, she had announced her intention of retiring.

Emmy knocked tentatively at the bedroom door. There was a shuffling sound from inside, then the door was opened by Mrs. Billing, majestic in a red flannel dressing gown, and minus her teeth.

"Yes, madam? Is there something more I can do? Not bad news about poor Miss Threep, I hope?" she asked, lisping slightly.

Emmy explained. Mrs. Billing was all helpfulness. "Yes, I did come across some medicines and such. I put them all in this drawer, thinking they might be needed. I always say, you can't be too careful with medicines. I mean, they can be dangerous, can't they? What was written on the package, then, madam?"

"I don't think anything was written on it," said Emmy. "It's just a little upright cardboard box wrapped in white paper."

"Well, now, let's have a look." Mrs. Billing opened one of the dressing-table drawers. "This is just aspirin, or so it says. This one . . ." She peered and read out laboriously, "Der-mat-one . . . soothes away skin infections . . . that wouldn't be it, would it?"

"No," said Emmy. "Just a plain white package."

"Lax-o-pur . . . the laxative your system loves . . . that doesn't sound like it. Dr. Grotch's Syrup for tired throats . . . let's see . . . ah, this looks more like it. No writing at all." Triumphantly Mrs. Billing held up a small rectangular package wrapped in white paper.

"That's it," said Emmy at once. "May I have it, please? So sorry to have disturbed you, Mrs. Billing."

"Not at all, Madam. I was just having a bit of a read, and thinking. Funny, isn't it, Miss Threep ending up in the hospital with Billing? Well, not *with* him, of course, but as near as makes no matter. I do hope we'll have good news of her tomorrow. Oh, I never asked you what time you like your tea in the morning? And with milk or lemon?"

"With milk at half-past seven, if that's not too early."

"Not at all, Madam. I'll see to it. Good night, then."

Outside in the passage, Emmy examined the packet she carried. Then she went downstairs. Henry and Sarah Massingham were sitting close together on the sofa, poring over the tradesmen's order lists.

Suppressing a ripple of irritation, Emmy said, "Here it is. And it's been opened."

Sarah stood up and walked over to Emmy. "How do you know?" she asked.

"I happened to notice that the white paper wrapping was stuck down with a small piece of transparent tape," said Emmy. "That's been pulled off—look, you can see. And the paper has been refolded."

Henry joined the two women, saying, "Better let me have it. We don't want it covered with unnecessary fingerprints." He picked up the package delicately in a clean handkerchief, and laid it on the table. Then, with great caution, he removed the wrapping paper. Inside was a cardboard box with the name PESTKIL printed on it in large letters. In smaller print—in Dutch, French, and English—were instructions for mixing the contents with water in order to make an insecticide spray. Lower down, and smaller still, came the chemical formula, and right at the bottom an injunction that the powder should not be taken internally, and should be kept away from the eyes, the exposed skin, and all foodstuffs. Inside the cardboard box was a small plastic bag full of white powder. Or, strictly speaking, not quite full. Emmy was apparently right. It looked as though the packet had been opened and a small quantity of powder extracted.

Sarah was reading the formula. "It's another of the poisonous ones, all right," she said. "Even a tiny dose of this. . . . Could she have taken it by mistake, instead of her medicine?" And, answering her own question, "No, surely not. She may have been dopey, but one doesn't mistake a tablet for a powder. And if you do, you don't fasten the package up again carefully, so that it looks as though it hasn't been opened." She paused, looked at the formula again, and frowned.

Henry asked, "Are you thinking what I'm thinking?"

"What are you thinking?"

Henry said, "You told us that Dolly was being poisoned by small, persistent doses of something. Just now you said, 'Even a tiny dose of this—' Back to the hundred milligrams, or equivalent, of one small tablet, being instantly lethal. That's what I'm thinking."

Sarah smiled at him. "Bright as ever," she said.

"I'm logical," said Henry. "And I remember what people say. That's what I'm paid for."

"Certainly," said Sarah, "the theory that she took some of this by mistake for medicine is out. If she'd swallowed a quarter of a teaspoonful of this stuff she'd have been dead in a few minutes, with all the distressing symptoms that you saw in Lady Balaclava—when she died from natural causes." Sarah frowned again and shook her head. "I simply can't understand it. What it looks like . . ." She glanced apologetically at Emmy. ". . . it's ridiculous, of course . . . but it looks as if somebody had been giving her just a few grains with every meal."

"Me, you mean?" said Emmy.

"Of course not, but—"

"Well, I'm the only person who could possibly have done that."

There was an oppressive pause. Then Henry said, "We now come to the question of whether or not to call the police."

"The police?" Sarah's eyes opened wide. "You *are* the police."

"Not technically, I'm afraid. I'm quite unofficial. The usual procedure is for the doctor to take the decision, if he—or she—suspects any sort of dirty work. The police in this case would mean Inspector Sandport and his chief constable, who might—but probably wouldn't—decide to call me in. It's your problem, Sarah."

"Mine and Dr. Duval's," said Sarah quickly. "He treated her before I did, and prescribed the pentobarbital."

"Then I think you'd better call him at the Hindhurst Arms. Tell him what's happened and see what he says."

Sarah nodded briefly and went out into the hall. She was back in a very short time.

"I'm going down to the Hindhurst Arms to see him," she said. "He sounded very upset. I'll keep in touch." And she was gone.

An hour later, as Henry and Emmy were preparing for bed, Sarah telephoned. She sounded more relaxed. "I've had a long talk with Dr. Duval," she said, "and I've also been on to the hospital. They seem to think that Dolly will pull through, which is the main thing."

"Thank God for that," said Henry.

"She's still on the danger list, but her chances have gone up to . . . oh, about seven to three. That's one of the reasons Dr. Duval is against informing the police."

"Attempted murder—" Henry began.

"This is how we reasoned it out," said Sarah. "If we call Inspector Sandport, either he'll take us seriously or he won't. It's likely that he won't, because everybody knows that Dolly has been using Flyaway, and that small doses can be cumulative. As to the packet of Pestkil being open—well, there are a thousand accidental explanations for that."

"Are there?" said Henry. "I'd like to hear them."

"Well . . ." Sarah was embarrassed. "Mrs. Tibbett might so easily have . . ."

"I see," said Henry. "You mean that, accident or not, only Emmy could have opened that package."

"Well . . . it does look like it, doesn't it? Unless it was Dolly herself. Personally, I expect it was never properly sealed in the first place. There's no way of knowing whether any actual powder is missing."

"Are you telling me what you think, or what Dr. Duval said?" Henry asked gently.

"I'm telling you how I think the police will react," said Sarah. "Nobody had any motive for harming Dolly, and she's been handling dangerous insecticides and was in a state of lowered resistance. After the Lady Balaclava fiasco, I should think Sandport would just pat us on the head and tell us to run off home and play. But suppose he *did* take it seriously. Then policemen would go tramping all over the hospital, questioning Dolly and maybe retarding her recovery, or even causing a relapse. If they can't question her, there's nothing much they can do. Agreed?"

"I suppose so." Henry was dubious.

"So Dr. Duval and I think," Sarah went on, "that it's best to do nothing for the moment. If and when Dolly has quite recovered, as we hope she will, then you can question her, if you still think it's necessary. But I hope you won't. I'm sure she'd much rather not have a great fuss made. And besides . . ."

"And besides, Emmy would be involved. That's it, isn't it?" said Henry.

"Well . . . it wouldn't be very pleasant for her, would it? Anyhow," Sarah added crisply, "that's my decision."

Henry sighed. "Very well, Dr. Massingham. You're in charge. So be it."

"Good. Then we can concentrate on the case of Lady Balaclava. It's funny, isn't it?" said Sarah reflectively. "Lady Balaclava's death looked like poisoning, was analyzed as natural, and I'm certain it was deliberate. Dolly's illness looked natural at first, was analyzed as poison, and I'm certain it was accidental."

"You mean," said Henry, "that it's not easy to sort out the red herrings from the others. It never is, you know."

"Surely you generally know whether or not a murder has been committed?"

"The times when we don't," said Henry, "are the times when the murderer gets away with it."

"Anyhow," said Sarah, coming back to practicalities, "what about foreign substances? Anything unusual come into the house over the weekend?"

"Nothing, as far as we can make out."

"Oh, dear," Sarah was downcast. "So neither of us has had any luck."

"Neither of us? What have you been up to?"

"Nothing much. Just that when I was at the Hindhurst Arms, I tried to find out tactfully from Dr. Duval if he knew anything about Lady Balaclava's medical history—but no go. He had known the family before the war, he said—he actually met Primrose in 1938 when she was at finishing school in Lausanne—and he spent a holiday at Foxes' Trot just before war broke out. Then, of course, he didn't see any of them again until 1946. He'd been writing to Primrose all through the war years, and they met again and got married when she came back from Canada. But his impression was that Lady Balaclava was tremendously healthy. Full of energy, he said, like a dynamo. He obviously admired her a lot, even if he didn't like her much."

"Surely," said Henry, "there must be medical records somewhere?"

Sarah laughed wryly. "Somewhere is about right," she said. "Nowadays, with the National Health, registered patients have files which can be consulted. But before the war, private patients moved house and swapped doctors and it was all utterly disorganized. Anyhow, a country G.P. with no secretary never had time to keep proper records. *If* we knew every doctor that Lady Balaclava had consulted . . . *if* we could trace them . . . *if* they kept records . . . you see how many 'ifs' there are."

"Yes, I see."

"Still, we'll keep at it. This lawyer fellow tomorrow may be useful. He's an old family friend, isn't he? You'd better get him in a corner and third-degree him."

"I very much doubt," said Henry, "if I shall see him at all. He was coming here after the funeral to see Dolly, but now . . ."

"Well, you must talk to him," said Sarah. "Think of something."

"I'll try," Henry promised.

Emmy, creaming her face in the black bathroom, was indignant. "Of *course* I didn't open it by accident. It was sealed up with transparent tape when I took it into Dolly's room, and this evening the tape had been broken. No . . . nobody went in after I did—except Dr. Duval this afternoon, but I was there with him all the time. I know he didn't touch it. . . . Well, why on earth should Mrs. Billing open it? I'll ask her tomorrow, but . . . Well, if you put it like that, Violet. She was the only person who went in to say good-bye to Dolly."

"She was the only person who admitted going in," said Henry. "I reckon any of the others could have. We'll have to wait till we can talk to Dolly."

15

The luring of Piggy Plunkett turned out to be quite simple after all. At nine in the morning Henry rang the Hindhurst Arms and left a message requesting Mr. Plunkett—who was expected from London for Lady Balaclava's funeral—to telephone Foxes' Trot as a matter of some urgency. Henry knew that Plunkett was seeing Primrose before lunch; he also knew, by hearsay, that the cuisine of the Hindhurst Arms left something to be desired.

Plunkett rang at twelve. He was distressed to hear about Dolly, but cheered by the fact that the hospital authorities were hopeful. Out of the question to see her, of course. No visitors allowed. So, when he had talked to Primrose and Daffodil—had Henry heard that she'd decided to attend the funeral after all?—he, Plunkett, would just have a bite at the Hindhurst Arms before going to the funeral and . . .

No, no, Henry protested. He and Emmy would be most delighted if Mr. Plunkett would take lunch with them at Foxes' Trot. Mrs. Billing from Trimble Wells was installed as cook-housekeeper, and she and Emmy had spent the morning preparing a *navarin d'agneau printanier* which promised to be something rather special. All those delicious new summer vegetables from the garden were so tempting, weren't they?

Mr. Plunkett was easy to tempt. He had accepted even before Henry had finished talking about the petits pois. He had sampled Mrs. Billing's cooking before.

Over sherry, Mr. Plunkett pontificated. Emmy had mentioned the possibility of Dolly's illness being due to insecticide, whereupon she and Henry were treated to a ten-minute précis of the changes which, if Prime Minister, Mr. Plunkett would make in the laws concerning the sale of such lethal products. A plaintive obbligato reiterated the inconvenience caused by Dolly's nonavailability to sign certain urgent documents. Plunkett would have to make another journey from London. The affair would now drag on, and Mr. Plunkett liked to get things settled briskly. It was all most provoking.

Over lunch, however, the mood grew mellow. The *navarin* was as excellent as only young English lamb and garden vegetables could make it, and under its benign influence Mr. Plunkett slipped easily into the mood of reminiscence toward which Henry was busily nudging him. He recalled Charlie Codworthy with affection.

"A rough diamond, if you like, Mr. Tibbett—but of the first water, I can assure you. The best type of British businessman—upright, straight as a dye, his word was his bond . . . and yet, of course, extremely shrewd. Dear me, yes. You don't make a fortune in business unless you take infinite pains and never let a detail escape you. Why, I can remember times when he spotted a loophole in a contract which had escaped *me*." This was Mr. Plunkett's highest praise. "Tragic, him being killed like that. A comparatively young man. Never even had the joy of seeing his daughters married."

"He met Edouard Duval, though, didn't he?" Emmy said. "Before the war, I mean."

Plunkett chuckled. "He did indeed. He did indeed."

Henry raised inquiring eyebrows. Plunkett explained. "It wasn't that he didn't like Edouard. No, no. He took quite a fancy to the young man, as a matter of fact. He hoped that he and Primrose . . . no, what I meant was that it was meeting Edouard which first brought home to Charlie the fact that his daughters would marry someday—possibly sooner rather than later."

"Why shouldn't they marry?" Henry asked.

"Oh, no reason, no reason at all. Thank you, Mrs. Tibbett . . . just a little more . . . a few beans, if you please . . . most delicious. . . . As I was saying, Charlie had already drawn up his will with immense care. I helped my father to work on it. Charlie's idea was that Crystal should be well provided for as long as she lived, but she should never have the chance to squander the family fortune. Crystal was inclined to be . . . well . . ." Mr. Plunkett made an extravagant gesture. "I'm sure you understand me. Charlie intended to bring up his daughters to understand and value money in a way which their mother did not, and to give them ultimate control of his fortune. And then he met Edouard Duval, who was obviously making advances to Primrose, and it made him think."

"Because Edouard was Swiss?" Henry asked.

Plunkett beamed at him. "You are quick on the uptake, Mr. Tibbett. Yes, because Edouard was Swiss. Up till then it had never occurred to Charlie that his daughters might marry foreigners. Here in Britain, of course, they would have the protection of the Married Women's Property Act, and no scoundrel of a husband could lay hands on the Balaclava fortune. But if they married foreigners . . . Charlie was in quite a stew. I remember it well. He came to my father's office and talked for a couple of hours, nonstop. Something had to be done. The will had to be so phrased that *nobody* who married one of the girls could ever claim her inheritance. My father had to tell him that what he wanted was impossible."

"That can't have pleased him," said Henry.

"Ah, but we were able to offer an alternative solution." Plunkett paused to insert a large forkful of *navarin* into his mouth. "We told Lord Balaclava that, while there was no possibility of drawing up such a will as he suggested, we could and would make it our business to see that each of the girls was protected in law at the time of her marriage."

"You did?" Henry tried not to sound too interested, but time was running short. "How?"

Plunkett seemed unaware that he was being pumped for

information. He was on his hobbyhorse, and enjoying the ride. "In Primrose's case, we had a marriage settlement drawn up. We worked in collaboration with a firm of Swiss lawyers, of course. Edouard signed it most willingly, I am glad to say. He renounced any rights that he might have had over Primrose's money under Swiss law. She, for her part, agreed to provide for him up to a reasonable sum per annum, once she had inherited, if his own income fell below a certain figure—which it has not, of course, and never will—but it was an equitable clause. The provision would continue to operate should she leave him, or should he divorce her for some matrimonial offense. On the other hand, should he desert her, or give her grounds for divorce, then the clause is automatically annulled. A very good settlement, though I say it myself. Edouard has no claim whatsoever on Primrose's money, but so long as he behaves himself he can be assured of a most reasonable income, as of right." Plunkett leaned back in his chair and wiped his lips with his napkin.

"And the others?" prompted Henry.

"Very little trouble," said Plunkett complacently. "The Dutch have several different matrimonial regimes, so of course we made sure that Violet and Piet were married under the arrangement which gave her control of her own property. I confess that I was a little . . . what shall I say? . . . apprehensive in Violet's case. After all, growing roses is hardly a profession which *leads* anywhere. . . . I suppose you could call it more of a vocation, a labor of love. Not at all satisfactory financially. Piet might as well have been an author or an artist. He knew that Violet was an heiress, and . . . well, I was uneasy. We knew nothing about him. They met in the Rijksmuseum in Amsterdam on a rainy Sunday—hardly a propitious start to a marriage, I would have said. Also he is younger than she. However, it seems that my fears were groundless. Piet agreed instantly to the marriage contract which we proposed. He also appears to be extremely fond of his wife." Plunkett spoke with faint but unmistakable surprise.

"And Daffodil was easy, of course," said Emmy.

Plunkett beamed. "Daffodil's marriage would have made Charlie very, very happy," he said. "I can't help feeling that there is something quite poetic about the fact that Mr. Swasheimer's name is also Charles and that he manufactures sanitary equipment. An ideal match."

"He's a lot older than she is," said Emmy.

"An ideal match," repeated Plunkett firmly. Then he glanced at his watch. "Gracious me. How time does fly. If I might just have a small piece of Mrs. Billing's apple pie—yes, a little cream, thank you so much—and then I must be off."

"Lady Balaclava wasn't consulted about these arrangements, I suppose?" said Henry.

Plunkett raised his eyes briefly from his apple pie. "Crystal? Certainly not. Why should she have been? She wouldn't have understood the first thing about the matter."

"And, of course, she was ill," Henry added.

"Ill? Ill?" Another gulp, and the pie was finished. "Crystal ill? When?"

"During the war," said Henry. "Or so I heard."

"I can't think where you heard *that*," said Plunkett. "Crystal always had the energy of a horse. Always darting off here and there, all over Europe . . . then back to England, throwing six parties at once. . . . Crystal is *never* ill . . . that is, I should say . . ." Deeply embarrassed, and perhaps even genuinely affected, Plunkett attempted to cover up his gaffe. "Poor Crystal . . . one simply can't take in the fact that she's—gone. Always such a vital person . . . and now . . ." Plunkett was saved by the front-door bell. "Ah! That must be the taxi I ordered. Sorry I must rush away . . . sad duty to perform . . . my thanks for an excellent lunch, Mrs. Tibbett, and my best wishes to Miss Dolly. . . ."

As they watched the ramshackle cab weaving its way slowly down the drive, Henry said to Emmy, "It certainly looks like one of the girls."

"Or Dolly."

"Or Dolly," Henry agreed.

"Supposing," said Emmy, "that one of the husbands had persuaded his wife to agree to—"

Henry said, "Chuck doesn't need the money, Piet doesn't want it, and Edouard wouldn't have a hope of getting a sixpence out of Primrose, if I'm any judge of character. Dolly and Daffodil had the strongest motives. Violet and Primrose may have their ordinary share of human greed—but it takes a monster to murder an aging mother for the sake of a fortune which they know they'll soon get anyway."

"And what about Dolly being poisoned?" Emmy asked. There was a slight cutting edge to her voice.

"Well, you know—quite honestly, darling, I think it must have been an accident."

"You mean, I'm lying?"

"Now, don't get worked up, love. Of course that's not what I mean. But anybody can make a mistake."

"I see." Emmy's chin went up. "And of course Dr. Duval and Dr. Massingham both agree with you. I wish," she added with some bitterness, "that I had a doctor in *my* corner."

"Do you? Why?"

"It would be pleasant to be believed."

Remembering what Sarah Massingham had said, Henry remarked, "You might not find it so pleasant, you know. Your doctor might present a bill."

Indignation toppled Emmy from her high horse. "Henry!" She wheeled to face him. "Henry, you don't think that I tampered with that powder?"

"Of course I don't, darling. But it might look that way to—to an outsider." Henry sighed. "And, now," he said, "I suppose we'd better go and pack."

"Pack?"

"That's what I said. I shall ring the assistant commissioner and tell him that I'm finished here."

"Oh, Henry." Emmy's anger melted in the warmth of her solicitude. "You don't mean you're giving up?"

He smiled, but it was a tired smile. "Not entirely, I hope. But we really can't stay here. I hope I succeeded in bluffing Primrose, but the fact is that our position is impossible. Dolly's in hospital, and can't even be visited. Mrs. Billing is in charge of the house. While Dolly was here, we had some excuse for staying on as guests, but whoever heard of guests without a hostess? And even if we did stay, there's nothing more to be got out of this house."

But Henry was wrong. Foxes' Trot still had a couple of aces up its sleeve.

The first appeared as a result of the most domestic of interludes. While Henry went to telephone the A.C., Emmy explained to Mrs. Billing in the kitchen that she and her husband were going back to London that evening. Mrs. Billing expressed polite regret, but it was clear that she approved. None too soon, if you asked her, was her unspoken comment.

"In that case, madam," she said, "you won't mind if I strip down your bed now and make up the laundry. Then perhaps you'd be kind enough to drop it in at the Snow White in Hindhurst, if you're passing that way in the car. They only call Mondays, so otherwise I'd have missed them for a week, and there's a lot to go."

Emmy agreed and then took herself for a gloomy walk in the garden. It was three o'clock, and she found herself dwelling morbidly on the thought of the heavy brown earth thudding down on Crystal's coffin, and of the group at the graveside—Piggy Plunkett, full of hollow solemnity; Daffodil, her beautiful little face hard and angry at being cheated of another day with her lover; Edouard Duval, glancing at his watch, anxious to be off and away; Primrose . . . Emmy wondered. Primrose, perhaps, might be the only genuine mourner.

These meditations were interrupted by Mrs. Billing, who opened an upstairs window, leaned out, and called penetratingly, "Madam!"

Emmy looked up. "Yes, Mrs. Billing! What is it?"

"I'm sorry to bother you, madam, but I can't find the dirty linen. It's not in the usual place," added Mrs. Billing censuriously.

"Oh, I'm sorry." Emmy dragged her thoughts back to

the mundane world of dirty linen. "I didn't know where
the usual place was. I'll come and show you."

Emmy had, in fact, folded up the used sheets and pil-
lowcases and laid them in the bottom of the clothes cupboard in each of the bedrooms, intending to ask Dolly
later what should be done with them. Pair by pair, she extracted the sheets to add to Mrs. Billing's growing pile.
Last of all she remembered the sheets which she had
hastily stripped from Dolly's bed before making it up for
Mrs. Billing. They were in a cupboard in the housekeeper's room.

Kneeling down, Emmy pulled out the soiled and
crumpled sheets. "Here we are," she said. "This is the last
lot. The ones that were on . . ." Her voice trailed away to
silence. For as she moved the sheets, a small cloud of
white powder rose from them, like snowy dust; and there
was a trace of it on the cupboard floor where the linen
had been lying.

Emmy stood up. "I don't think we'll send these sheets to
the laundry after all, Mrs. Billing."

"Eh? They look grubby enough to me."

"Just leave them where they are. And don't touch them.
I'm going to find my husband."

Sarah Massingham, infuriatingly, was out on a round of
visits. Henry could do no more than leave a message with
the receptionist at the surgery. A baffled and disapproving
Mrs. Billing was told that the Tibbetts would be staying
till the next day, after all. Emmy's offer to make up their
bed again herself was refused with a put-upon sniff. Some
people couldn't make up their own minds, never mind the
trouble others were put to. All that fuss about a pair of
dirty sheets. . . .

It was after five when Sarah arrived, deeply interested.
She carefully transferred a small quantity of the powder
into a clean envelope. "I'll get it analyzed at once," she
said, "but I'm certain it's the same stuff. Funny, I did
think about absorption through the skin, but of course by
the time I saw Dolly she had clean bedclothes."

"I should have noticed when I stripped the bed," Emmy reproached herself.

"You did very well to notice this time," said Sarah briskly. "If those sheets had been allowed to go to the laundry . . . One thing puzzles me, though. There's still a lot in the packet, isn't there? I'm surprised that this small amount could produce such drastic results, even in someone who'd been in regular contact with parathion." She frowned. "Unless, of course, Dolly suffered from some sort of skin infection."

"Dermatone!" exclaimed Emmy.

"What?"

"When we were looking for the insecticide powder, Mrs. Billing found some medicines that Dolly had presumably been using. One of them was called Dermatone, for soothing away skin infections . . . look, here's the tube."

"That would account for all that thick makeup," said Henry.

"And for her keeping under the bedclothes and refusing to let me make up her bed or wash her," said Emmy. "I suppose she didn't want anybody to know."

Sarah Massingham nodded. "I'll check with the hospital," she said, "but it certainly fits. Someone who knew Dolly had been handling Flyaway thought they could rely on Pestkil powder in her sheets to combine with the sedative and keep her feeling headachy and mildly ill. This somebody can't have known that she suffered from dermatitis, which increases the toxic effect of absorption enormously."

"Or did know, and intended to kill her," said Henry.

"That's your problem," said Sarah. "I'm just the medical bod. Well, I'll be off now. Powder sample to the labs, and a word with the hospital. I'll be in touch."

"And when, if I may ask, do you intend to eat?" Henry asked.

"Oh, I'll get something at the hospital canteen. Unappetizing but nourishing. Better lock up those sheets—they may be evidence."

"You're an angel," said Henry.

"Not at all. Just an inquisitive female who happens to be a doctor."

"Which reminds me," Henry added, as Sarah clattered downstairs toward the front door, "don't forget to send in your bill for all this!"

"You bet I won't forget!" A smile, a wave, and Sarah had gone.

But Emmy was standing quite still at the top of the stairs, thinking. Suddenly she said, "Doctors' bills!"

"If there's a prosecution, the police will pay," said Henry. "If not, I certainly don't intend to let Sarah do all this work for—"

"No, no. Don't be silly, Henry. Doctors' bills!"

"That's what I was—"

"In the library. Lord Balaclava's desk. All those receipts. Some of them were doctors' bills!"

So Foxes' Trot yielded its second trump card of the evening. Both Tibbetts hurried downstairs and dashed for the library in an undignified scramble, nearly upending Mrs. Billing, who was making a stately progress from kitchen to dining room with a tray of cold meats.

It did not take them long to sort out the doctors' bills from the others. In the 1930's the Balaclavas patronized a certain Dr. Palmer of Barkman Mews, W.1.—presumably a G.P., and conveniently situated for Barkman Square. His bills were presented and paid quarterly, and represented modest fees for consultations and occasional visits— the usual incidence of flu and stomach upsets which would be normal in any family. Three separate accounts from a Harley Street gynecologist required no explanation. Early in 1940, however, a new element crept in. Lady Balaclava went for consultations to a Dr. Powers-Thompson, also of Harley Street, whose fees—for those days—were enormous. Later in the same year she apparently spent some time in a private nursing home in Westmorland. And then came 1941, and a total blank. Charles Codworthy, that meticulous keeper of receipted bills, had—in Crystal's phrase—gone to join the morning stars, assisted on his way by a Nazi bomb. All that Henry could do was note the addresses and telephone numbers of Dr. Powers-Thompson and the Sunnyside Private Nursing Home, together with the relevant dates.

The final event of the evening was a late telephone call from Sarah Massingham. The white powder from the sheets corresponded with the chemical formula of Pestkil, and the hospital doctor confirmed that Dolly was suffering from chronic eczema, mild on her face but more severe on her back. Sarah had told him that some Pestkil had been accidentally spilled on Dolly's bed.

"Accidentally?" said Henry.

After a tiny pause Sarah said, "For the moment. I thought it was better to put it like that. The doctor was delighted."

"He was, was he?"

"What I mean is, he had been puzzling himself silly about just what *was* the matter with Dolly. Now, of course, it's all explained and he's gone home to bed with a load off his mind. Incidentally, the patient continues to progress, although she's not off the danger list yet."

"That's good news. And we've made some headway this end, too." Henry told Sarah about the medical bills. "So we'll be leaving here tomorrow. I'll give you our London address and phone number, and let you know if we plan going elsewhere."

"Elsewhere?"

"Like Paris," Henry explained. "Or Lausanne. Or even Holland."

16

The Sunnyside Private Nursing Home in Monkswich, Westmorland, had long ago ceased to exist. The establishment which Henry contacted, when he rang its number the next day from his London home, announced itself in over-refined accents as Monkswich Manor College for Young Ladies. Henry was eventually connected with the headmistress, a majestic-sounding lady who informed him that the manor had, indeed, been a private nursing home at one stage in its history, many years ago.

"Before I took over," she announced, as if speaking of the Dark Ages. "I believe it was turned into a convalescent home for the wounded during the war. Officers, of course. Then, in 1945, when the military had no further use of it, it was put up for sale. That was when Miss Birchington, our first principal, bought it and founded the college. The Army Medical Corps might be able to help you," she added, with a crispness intended to disguise the patent idiocy of the idea. Henry could imagine her dicta to her girls: "Always make a positive, constructive suggestion; flabby speaking means flabby thinking," and so on. "And now I'm afraid I must ring off, Mr. Er. I am a very busy woman, you know. Best of luck in your quest. Good-bye." And the telephone receiver was replaced with a positive, constructive click.

As a last resort, Henry did, in fact, contact a friend at the Ministry of Defense, who agreed with no enthusiasm to turn up some old files. His report—which Henry received too late to have any relevance to the case—stated that the Sunnyside Nursing Home had indeed become the Monkswich Convalescent Center for Other Ranks in 1942. It had been purchased—obviously a dying concern financially—from its owner, a Dr. Blair, who had been over seventy at the time, and so might reasonably be assumed to be dead now. No records of any sort existed from its nursing-home days. As for the appellation "manor," that must have been a figment of Miss Birchington's vivid imagination. The building was in fact a Victorian red-brick structure of surpassing ugliness—or so reported a member of the department who had had the experience of a short stay there after being wounded in Italy. To the Other Ranks who patronized it, it had been known as Monk's Bitch.

Dr. Powers-Thompson proved almost equally elusive, due to the fact that he had returned in 1958. His Harley Street consulting rooms were now occupied by a thoroughly legal abortionist—a charming but busy man whose two Rolls-Royces were a familiar sight in London's top medical quarter. In spite of the pressure of work, however, he found time to instruct one of his secretaries to look up some details of his predecessor for Henry.

The secretary soon returned with the information neatly typed on dye-stamped writing paper. Dr. Powers-Thompson had been a lung specialist. The address which he had given to his successor on retiring had been the Old Manse, Langfleet, Somerset. Whether he still lived there—or, indeed, anywhere—the secretary could not say. They had had no correspondence with Dr. Powers-Thompson for more than ten years.

"I thought so!" said Sarah Massingham triumphantly when Henry telephoned her. "T.B., of course. I didn't like to jump to conclusions, but you told me that people remarked on her frenetic energy, her almost transparent complexion—"

"And her visits to Switzerland," Henry put in. "I didn't tell you that. Old Plunkett remarked at lunch that she was continually rushing off to Europe—to Switzerland, among other places. Not entirely for pleasure, perhaps."

"Now, wait a minute." For once Sarah did not take up his idea with gusto. "If you mean she might have been taking sanatorium treatment in the mountains—no, it won't do. You didn't simply rush off to a sanatorium for a week or so, as if it was a health farm, to set you up for another season of hectic parties. People stayed for months, if not years—and many never came out at all. Besides, as far as we know, she didn't contract the disease until the war had started. No, I think you'll find the Swiss visits were purely social."

"Then how was she cured? Because she was cured, wasn't she?"

"That," said Sarah Massingham, "is what is so interesting. You'd better get on the Powers-Thompson trail."

"Easy," said Henry. "I've got his address and phone number."

It was not easy, of course. Things seldom are. The telephone was answered by a charming, elderly gentleman who introduced himself as Colonel Wycroft. Oh, dear, he was very sorry, but Henry had missed the doctor by a matter of five years. He, Wycroft, and his wife had bought the Old Manse from Powers-Thompson after the sad death of the doctor's wife. The doctor had felt that the house was really too large for a man on his own. Where had he moved to? Can't tell you, I'm afraid, sir. That is to say, he moved temporarily into the local hotel, the Langfleet Arms, and there he had stayed during all the negotiations over the Old Manse. As to where he was now, the colonel had no idea. "So sorry, my dear sir. Afraid I can't help you. The Langfleet Arms is the last address we had for him."

And so Henry rang the Langfleet Arms. After agonizingly long negotiations, costing a small fortune in telephone charges, the hotel register of five years back was found. Dr. Powers-Thompson had given his address as care of the National Conservative Club, Pall Mall. The National Conservative Club reported that Dr. Powers-

Thompson was no longer a member and that the last address they had for him was the Old Manse, Langfleet. The vicious circle seemed complete.

Near despair, Henry suddenly, wildly grasped at a last straw. Something that Primrose had said. It was the slimmest of chances, but it just might turn up trumps. Crystal Balaclava had been a popular person, especially in the old days.

First he telephoned Plunkett. Surprised, Plunkett answered Henry's question. "You didn't know? Why, the Hindhurst Crematorium. A couple of miles outside the town, on the Petersfield road."

I didn't even know she'd been cremated, Henry thought. I wonder whose idea that was. Nothing to stop it, of course, with the post mortem over, and "natural causes" on the death certificate.

So, for the second time in a week, Henry and Emmy took the road out of London and onto the Kingston bypass, and eventually through green and dappled countryside to Hindhurst. This time, however, they ignored the signpost to Plumley Green and followed the main road toward Petersfield. Sure enough, after a couple of miles a notice, wrought-iron gates, and a sweeping driveway informed them that they had arrived at Hindhurst Crematorium.

It was a beautiful and surprisingly cheerful place. The gardens were superb—grassy meadows rather than formal flowerbeds, shaded by magnificent trees and radiant with the flowers and shrubs which many families donated instead of cold marble to commemorate their cherished dead. The chapel was quiet, simple, and full of flowers, and the cleansing furnaces screened—but in no shamefaced manner—by flowering trees. Near the chapel a roofed colonnade was used as a display stand for flowers and wreaths received for recent funerals, and Henry and Emmy were not the only people admiring them and inspecting the attached cards.

The central apse of this colonnade had been reserved

for Lady Balaclava's flowers, and it was instantly obvious that Primrose had not been exaggerating when she described the undertakers as having been inundated. It was a magnificent display, and it took a long time to look at all the cards. Many notable names were represented. Sir Basil, of course, and also several cabinet ministers. The admiral who had smuggled Crystal to the Mediterranean. Two bishops. Many actors and actresses. An enormous, overpoweringly scented wreath from the chairman and board of the Codworthy Corporation. A tiny bunch of violets inscribed *All our love, darling Crystal, Davy and Hubert,* in a crabbed, old-maidish hand. A wreath from each of Crystal's daughters and their husbands, correct but unostentatious. And, of course, a mass of wreaths and vases of cut flowers from names which meant nothing either to Henry personally or to the world at large. At last, hardly daring to believe in his good luck, Henry found what he was looking for. A small sheaf of red roses, with a handwritten card—*Charles and Elizabeth Powers-Thompson, Appletree Cottage, Cheriston, Kent.*

After that, it really was easy. Dr. Powers-Thompson was contacted by telephone and said that he and his sister—with whom he now lived—would be only too pleased to see Chief Superintendent and Mrs. Tibbett the following day. Would they be able to stay to luncheon? Splendid. Lady Balaclava? He had admired her greatly. A woman of extraordinary courage. He had been saddened by her death, and would be only too pleased to help in any way he could. Might he ask . . . ? No, no. Of course, he must not. Let it wait until tomorrow. Now, when you get to Cheriston Church, turn right down Chestnut Lane, and then take the first left. We're the third house on the right. Can't miss it. He sounded vigorous and youthful, for all his decade of retirement.

Thanks to the doctor's excellent instructions, Henry and Emmy arrived at Appletree Cottage without mishap shortly after half-past twelve on the next day, Friday. Cheriston turned out to be a picture-book village set in a fold of the downs near Canterbury, and Appletree Cottage lived up to its name—a neat, pleasing modern house, single-storied and white-painted, its red-tiled roof almost hidden among laden branches of a small apple orchard. The elderly gardener in threadbare gray flannels and battered panama hat was Dr. Powers-Thompson himself.

He greeted Henry and Emmy warmly and handed out glasses of excellent sherry. Then Miss Powers-Thompson appeared—a handsome, energetic woman in her late sixties whose slightly formidable aspect melted magically when she smiled. The lunch which followed proved her to be a most competent cook as well as an entertaining and informed hostess.

In the course of the conversation it emerged that she, like her brother, had devoted her life to medicine. In her case, her vocation had been nursing, and she had ended her distinguished career as matron in chief at a renowned hospital. It struck Henry as being sad, and wasteful in human terms, that while her brother had naturally married and raised a family while pursuing his career, her chosen profession had virtually ruled out the possibility of marriage. Miss Powers-Thompson herself, however, showed no sign of frustration or deprivation, and in fact the meal was so enjoyable that Emmy, at least, almost forgot the errand which had brought her to Cheriston.

When coffee had been served, however, Miss Powers-Thompson said, "And now, you must be wanting to talk to Charles about Crystal. Do forgive me if I leave you—I have a parish council meeting at three."

When she had gone, Dr. Powers-Thompson said, "Most tragic, Crystal Balaclava's death. So very sudden. Elizabeth was really upset, even though they hadn't met for years."

"Your sister was a personal friend of Lady Balaclava's?" Henry asked.

"Oh, yes, indeed. Crystal Maltravers and Elizabeth were at school together. Complete opposites, of course—but it's odd, isn't it, how the most unlikely friendships often turn out to be the most lasting ones? Elizabeth always had her heart set on nursing, while Crystal . . . well, all the world knows how Crystal spent her youth. All the world *knew*, I should say. I suppose she died forgotten, poor dear."

"I wouldn't say that," said Henry. "You should have seen the flowers."

Powers-Thompson looked pleased. "That's heartening," he said. "Sometimes one feels that nobody is remembered. In any case, different as their lives were, Crystal and Elizabeth kept in touch. That's why Crystal came to Elizabeth for help when . . ." Powers-Thompson paused, filling his pipe. "You know, I suppose, that she contracted tuberculosis."

"So I have gathered," said Henry. "But I understand she made a secret of it. Didn't want anybody to know."

"That's quite correct. Crystal couldn't bear to be ill. She was such a very vital person. When she got to the point where she couldn't ignore the symptoms anymore, she went to Elizabeth. Elizabeth naturally referred her to me, as lung diseases happened to be my specialty. That must have been in . . . let me see . . ." Dr. Powers-Thompson frowned in an effort of memory.

Henry said, "Nineteen-forty. March, 1940."

"That's right. How did you know?"

"Lord Balaclava was meticulous about keeping receipted bills."

Powers-Thompson smiled. "Of course, of course. That must be how you got on to me. Yes, it was the spring of 1940. The war was on, of course—no question of sanatorium treatment in Switzerland. The best I could do was to send her up to a nursing home in the Lake District—but she wouldn't stay there. Something Bitch, she used to call it. Can't remember now what its real name was. At any rate, it did her a bit of good, and as soon as she felt better she discharged herself and came back to Foxes' Trot. As you say, she refused to tell anyone about her illness. Her husband knew, of course, and Elizabeth and myself—but apart from that, I think there was only one other person in on the secret. A third old school friend. A rather curious woman called . . . what was it . . . ?"

"Underwood-Threep," said Henry.

"That's right. Dotty, or something, they called her. She went to live at Foxes' Trot to look after Crystal. Then Lord Balaclava was killed in the blitz."

"Exactly," said Henry. "And what happened then? My available records end there, you see."

Powers-Thompson hesitated, "Forgive me," he said, "but you are an officer of the CID, are you not?"

"I am."

"Then—am I to understand that there was something unnatural about Crystal's death? It was announced as very sudden, the result of an illness . . . and she has been cremated, has she not? I hope you don't think me inquisitive, but—"

"I think," said Henry, "that you are one of the least inquisitive people I've had the good fortune to meet, Doctor. The answer to your question is quite simple. Lady Balaclava appeared to die from acute poisoning. I know, I was there. But the autopsy showed no trace of poison of any sort, and the doctors certified 'natural causes.' I wasn't satisfied, and neither was the local doctor who was called in at the time—but we weren't in a position to contradict the official police pathologist. I must emphasize that I was at Foxes' Trot as a private person. I was not in charge of the police investigation which followed Lady Balaclava's death. Now I'm trying to locate this poison which was not a poison, and to find out just what did kill Lady Balaclava; but I'm doing it unofficially." He glanced at Powers-Thompson. The doctor was interested. More than interested. Henry went on, "I assume her death couldn't have been due to T.B. After all, she was cured, wasn't she?"

"Yes. She was cured."

"Completely?"

"Completely."

"How? By some miracle?"

"The miracle," said Powers-Thompson, "is how she survived the war years. Sheer determination not to die—there's no other explanation. That, and the devoted care of the Dotty woman, plus the fact that the air at Foxes' Trot is exceptionally pure. Anyhow, miracle or not, Crystal Balaclava was still alive in 1945, when Waksman isolated streptomycin. The very early experiments made it clear that it was a wonder drug for the treatment of tuberculosis. It was quickly developed in the States—patients were being treated with it as early as 1946. We heard about it over here, of course, but we couldn't lay hands on it. Then, in 1947, I managed to get some—rather ahead of most people in this country."

"How?" Henry asked, but he was so sure that he knew the answer that he went on, "Through Switzerland? Through a clinic in Lausanne? Through a young doctor who was engaged to Lady Balaclava's daughter?"

Powers-Thompson leaned back in his chair and laughed, "I really don't know why you bothered to come and see me, young man," he said. "You know as much as I do, and remember it better. You'll have to tell me the name of the Swiss doctor, because I've certainly forgotten it these twenty years, although I believe Elizabeth kept in touch for some time. . . ."

"Edouard Duval."

"I'm sure you are right. The name means nothing to me now. At any rate, I got hold of the streptomycin, I treated Lady Balaclava with it, and the miracle drug worked. She was cured. Completely, as I said." Another pause. "Of course, we don't use it in that way anymore."

"Why isn't it used now, if it's so marvelous?" It was Emmy who put the question.

Powers-Thompson sighed and smiled at the same time. "All of us these days . . . all scientists and doctors, I should say . . . are taking greater and greater liberties with nature. We are forcing her to give up her secrets, and when we know them, we tend to use them recklessly. But nature has her own methods for getting back at us. Every advance brings new complications and new dangers. Unfortunately, the dangers only become apparent after the advances—inevitably."

"You mean, side effects?" said Henry.

"Side effects, gradual immunization, the evolution of

strains of bacteria resistant to the new drug—all those things. In the case of streptomycin, the tuberculosis cures looked really miraculous—but we had to use massive doses to get results. The side effects only became apparent gradually. Deafness. Vertigo. Sometimes allergy to the drug itself—"

"Allergy?" Henry pounced on the word.

"Yes, all those things. A small price to pay for a T.B. cure, you might think—but fortunately other drugs have now been developed. Streptomycin is still used, of course, but in smaller doses, combined with these other drugs. No doctor today would administer the massive doses which cured Crystal Balaclava in 1947."

"You mentioned allergy," Henry persisted.

"Yes. That is one of the side effects which is difficult to trace, because it may not appear for some years after the original treatment, and it is less common than with some other drugs."

"And Lady Balaclava suffered from these side effects?"

The doctor looked surprised. "No, no. I hope I did not give that impression. No, most fortunately Crystal appeared to reap nothing but benefit from the treatment. Of course, she may have developed an extreme sensitivity to streptomycin later on; but there would be only one way to find out."

"And what would that be?"

"Why to give her another dose of streptomycin some years later. Had she developed this sensitivity, even a minute amount could . . . but then, of course, no doctor would give a streptomycin injection without inquiring into the patient's past history. If he heard that he—or she—had been treated with massive doses in the past, then he would experiment with a minuscule amount. If there was any adverse reaction, he would prescribe some other treatment." Powers-Thompson paused. "You say you were there when Crystal died?"

"Yes. Emmy and I were both there."

"And the symptoms apparently indicated poison, but the autopsy revealed nothing."

"That's right."

"Was any particular type of poison suspected?"

"Yes," said Henry. "It looked like a clear case of poisoning by a parathion insecticide—especially as there were cans of the stuff in the house. But none was found in the post mortem."

"Describe the symptoms to me, will you?" asked Powers-Thompson. "In as much detail as you can."

Unwillingly, because the memory of it was distressing in the extreme, Henry and Emmy told as much as they could of the exact circumstances of Crystal's death. When they had finished, there was a long silence. Then Dr. Powers-Thompson said, "No. I'm afraid it won't do."

"What won't do?"

"I thought I had solved your mystery for you—but it's impossible."

"What is?"

"Well—from all you tell me, and knowing Lady Balaclava's medical history, I'd have said that she had become sensitized to streptomycin as a result of her treatment in the forties, and that her collapse and death were the result of taking another dose of the stuff. Everything fits—the symptoms of anaphylactic shock, which are very similar to those of parathion poisoning—the absence of any poison in the body—"

"The absence of any streptomycin, too," said Henry.

"Oh, that does not necessarily follow. For one thing, streptomycin disappears very quickly. Twenty-four hours or so after an injection, there would be no trace."

"But the post mortem was done within five or six hours," said Henry.

"In that case, there might have been slight traces of streptomycin in the urine—which could have been detected, if they had been looked for."

"You mean—?"

"I mean that streptomycin is far from being a poison, and there'd have been no earthly reason why the pathologist should have made the necessary tests. No, no, it wouldn't necessarily have shown up in the body. But you tell me that she had done no more than eat a piece of birthday cake and sip a glass of champagne before she died."

"And smell a bunch of roses," said Henry.

Powers-Thompson ignored this. "The cake and champagne were chemically analyzed?"

"Of course. Nothing was found."

"Streptomycin would have shown up there. In any case, a violent reaction such as you describe would only occur if, a very short time before, she had received an injection of streptomycin, or at least handled a syringe containing it. You're sure there was no streptomycin in the house?"

"As sure as I can be."

"None of the family or servants were receiving any such treatment?"

Henry smiled. "There were no servants," he said. "All the daughters and their husbands seemed perfectly well— and in any case, you say that Lady Balaclava would have had to have handled the drug herself?"

"Oh, indeed. If she had been giving one of them an injection—"

"I think we can rule that out," said Henry. "As far as I know, Lady Balaclava didn't even go into any of her daughters' bedrooms. It was Dolly—"

"That's right! It was Dolly, not Dotty. You mean, she was still living there with Crystal, after all these years?"

"She was. She has also inherited Foxes' Trot and quite a bit of money—if she lives to enjoy it."

"If she lives—?" Powers-Thompson raised his eyebrows.

"By a strange coincidence," Henry explained, "Dolly Underwood-Threep is at the moment in Hindhurst Hospital recovering—or so we hope—from an accidental dose of parathion poisoning."

"How very remarkable."

"It's more than remarkable," said Henry. "It stinks to high heaven, and yet I can't make sense of it. So—you rule out streptomycin allergy as the cause of Lady Balaclava's death?"

"Now don't misunderstand me," said Powers-Thompson.

"I'm not ruling out allergy. On the contrary, everything points to it, including the sudden itching on the face. But unless you can show me where the streptomycin was, and how she absorbed it . . . yes, I must rule out *streptomycin* allergy."

"At least," said Henry, "you've reassured me in one way."

"Reassured you?"

Henry grinned. "Yes. I was beginning to believe in the existence of an oriental poison unknown to science, as described in the best penny-dreadfuls. Now you tell me that it is medically possible for a person to be poisoned—"

"Not poisoned. No, no. An extreme sensitivity or allergy—"

"I should say," Henry amended, "it's possible for a person to be murdered, exhibiting all the symptoms of poisoning, when in fact they have not taken poison at all. When the post mortem reveals nothing, when the analysis of the food and drink reveals nothing—"

Powers-Thompson, smiling, held up his hand. "Wait a minute, wait a minute. Not so fast. I have described to you what would happen to one of the rare people in this world who is supersensitive to streptomycin, should that person come into contact with a sizable dose of the drug. As to your suggestion of murder, that borders on fantasy. The murderer would have to select his victim from the tiny group of people suffering from this sensitivity. He would have to know the victim's medical history and to have satisfied himself that the person in question suffered from this allergy. Not all people who have been treated with streptomycin would react in this way. Far from it. It's a very rare condition. So you see, Chief Superintendent, I don't think you need worry about a wave of apparently insoluble mass murders."

"I'm only worrying about one murder at the moment," said Henry.

"If you are referring to Crystal Balaclava," said the doctor, "it certainly couldn't have been murder—for the reasons I've just outlined. And it couldn't have been an accident with streptomycin, because there wasn't any."

"I suppose you're right. It's a pity. It was such a nice theory."

"Ah," said Powers-Thompson, "if only all our nice theories would hold water . . . but there it is. I am so sorry I haven't been able to help you. And now, let's take a turn in the garden before tea. Elizabeth will be back soon. She will be most interested to hear all about Crystal. Most interested."

"It has to be streptomycin," said Sarah Massingham. "It simply has to be."

"And yet it isn't," said Emmy. "There wasn't any."

"It's the only explanation that covers the facts," said Sarah.

It was Monday, just before noon. Henry, Emmy, and Sarah were sitting in the midday sunshine in the small paved garden at the back of the Tibbetts' Chelsea flat. The white-painted metal garden table was strewn with papers.

The day before, Dr. Tony Griffiths had arrived back from his Italian holiday, deeply tanned and disgustingly fit. Sarah reported that he had seemed genuinely upset to hear of Lady Balaclava's death—news of which had not penetrated to his remote *pensione*. He had unhesitatingly confirmed that neither Crystal nor Dolly had received any sort of streptomycin treatment since they came under his care. Dolly had consulted him about her dermatitis, and he had prescribed the soothing ointment. Crystal had always been in the best of health. He had no idea that she had once suffered from T.B.

On the subject of Crystal's spiritualistic experiments with the cards and toothmug, he had been equally emphatic. Yes, he knew about it. No, he had never taken part. Crystal had tried to persuade him, but he had always refused. As far as he knew, her partner had always been Dolly. He considered it to be a fairly harmless lark indulged in by two bored old women, more of a joke than a menace. The trouble was that you never knew where such things might end—hence his refusal to participate.

As Dolly's regular doctor, he had visited her in hospital. She was better, and would almost certainly survive, but it would be several days before she was allowed visitors—and then, he had added warningly, the visits were to be brief and purely social. Nobody was to badger her with questions, nor to mention Lady Balaclava's death or Flyaway or any other subject which might distress her. In plain terms, Dolly was still incommunicado. All this was set out in a letter to Henry, which now lay on the garden table.

With it was the pathologist's report, together with a supplementary note supplied at Henry's request. It could not have been clearer. Streptomycin had not been looked for in the viscera. Even if it had been, the very tiny quantity of the allergen ("That's whatever the person happens to be allergic to," Sarah explained) needed to provoke fatal results might have escaped identification. The pathologist agreed that the likeliest cause of death had been an acute allergic reaction, but it was quite impossible to say what the allergen had been. The fact that the lady had once been treated with streptomycin was no valid reason for jumping to the conclusion that she had become hypersensitive to it. The allergen could as well have been flower pollen, a wasp sting, egg white, shellfish, or a hundred other things. The mystery would remain a mystery, but the one clear fact was that the death had been accidental, due to natural causes.

"So we're back where we started," said Emmy. "She was allergic to something, and accidentally got a dose of it on her birthday."

"But she didn't." Henry was stubborn. "We know for a fact that she wasn't allergic to flower pollen or egg white or shellfish, because she was in contact with all those things while we were there, with no ill effects. She certainly wasn't stung by a wasp—"

"But those are just some of the more usual things," said

Emmy. "It says here that people can be allergic to almost anything."

"What Henry means, surely," said Sarah, "is that Lady Balaclava didn't come into contact just before she died with anything that she wasn't in the habit of eating, drinking, or touching. The symptoms would appear in a matter of seconds—"

"Which means," said Henry, "that Emmy and I—not to mention the members of the Codworthy clan—must actually have seen her ingesting, if that's the word, whatever it was that killed her."

"The champagne, the cake, and the roses," said Emmy. "But there was nothing unusual about any of them. We know that."

"There were the other presents," said Henry suddenly.

"What other presents?" Sarah asked.

"Our box of chocolates and Dolly's card game. They were both wrapped up and lying on the table in front of Crystal. If one of them had been dusted with streptomycin—"

Sarah laughed. "Now you're getting fanciful," she said. "For a start, streptomycin is a liquid."

"Sprayed, then."

"All right. Be as fanciful as you like. Supposing somebody got hold of some streptomycin—which isn't available to the public, I can assure—and soaked one of those packages in it. I can't believe that nobody would have noticed."

"It would have dried again," said Henry.

"Very well. And left a deposit on the paper. Even so, that wouldn't have hurt Lady Balaclava unless she had handled the parcel, and you say she didn't."

"Edouard Duval," said Henry doggedly, "is a doctor. He could have come by streptomycin easily enough. He and Dolly were the only two people there who knew about Crystal's previous illness and treatment . . . and he lied about it. Said she'd never been ill."

"Because Crystal had made him promise never to tell," Emmy pointed out. "In any case, Henry darling, Dr. Duval couldn't have tampered with any of the things at

Foxes' Trot, because he wasn't even in England, if you remember. Primrose collected the cake from the shop on her way to the airport. Are you suggesting that Edouard visited the shop first, asked to see the cake, and . . . but in any case, it was analyzed, wasn't it? Strictly nothing but marzipan, sponge cake, and sugar icing."

"If Duval knew about the T.B.," said Sarah, "it's a fair bet his wife knew too. And she had a lot to gain financially." She turned to Henry. "Do you think that—?"

Henry had been looking very thoughtful. Now he smiled suddenly and said, "I think that we should all have a drink before Emmy goes to pack."

"To pack? Why should I pack?"

"Because," said Henry, "we are going to Switzerland."

17

The Tibbetts were lucky. It was a Monday, and just slightly early in the year for the big holiday rush; they were able to get a reservation for that same night on the Dover-Dunkirk car ferry. By six o'clock the next morning their small but sprightly saloon car was bowling southward down the flat, straight, poplar-lined roads of northern France.

Leaving Paris well to the west, by midmorning they had left the industrial north behind and were enjoying the rolling countryside around Reims. In Joinville they stopped for a quick lunch beside the River Marne, and soon afterward found themselves among the woods and hills of the Haute-Saône. At Besançon the hills grew into mountains, and the car's average speed inevitably dropped as it snaked upward into the Jura. Twilight was beginning to fall by the time they reached Pontarlier, and at the Swiss frontier it was already growing rather too dark to appreciate the fir-clad landscape. Then, down through meadow-lined roads to Vallorbe, a final pull uphill through Cossonay, and at last—over the top. There below them lay the great dark shape of Lake Geneva, with the blazing lights of Lausanne facing the elegant glitter of Evian across the water.

They checked in at a lakeside hotel at Lutry, a few kilometers outside Lausanne itself, at half-past nine—and their tiredness fell away miraculously under the benign influence of a huge dish of *filets de perche meunière* and a flask of Fendant.

On the face of it, they were just another couple of English holiday-makers taking a well-earned break, relaxing under the vines on the terrace, beside the little port with its necklace of fairy lights strung above the old gray harbor wall; and Henry seemed to be in a holiday mood, infused with the lightness of heart that seems to come to the English south of Dijon. But Emmy knew that this was not a holiday and Henry's threat of resignation—which he had admitted to her on the boat the night before—had not been made lightly. Crystal Balaclava's death and Dolly's mysterious illness had put Henry's professional reputation at stake, and—whatever the official verdict might be—what really mattered were those rumors and innuendos which Michael Barker and his like were bandying so lightheartedly around their pubs and clubs. Of all the investigations in which he had been involved, this case which was not a case at all was probably the most vital of Henry's career.

But all that Emmy said was, "Just look at the moonlight on the water . . . it's like *Swan Lake*. . . ." And, as if on cue, two majestic swans, shepherding their brood of cygnets, cruised gracefully across the harbor mouth and down the silver lane of moonlight. It was all a long way from the cubist saxophone fountain and the stained concrete of Foxes' Trot.

The next morning they went to call on Dr. and Madame Duval in the sunny apartment overlooking Ouchy and the lake—having found the address by the simple expedient of looking it up in the telephone directory.

Emmy was frankly nervous and longed to get the visit over and done with. She had found both the Duvals somewhat formidable, and was reasonably sure that she and Henry would be unwelcome. Outside the blue-painted front door, on the sixth floor of the tall apartment block, she had to fight down the impulse to escape into the lift again and leave Henry to cope on his own. But Henry's finger was firmly on the bell-push, and within seconds Primrose opened the door.

There was no doubt about her surprise at seeing her visitors, but to Emmy's relief she was neither alarmed nor angry; if anything, she seemed distrait. She invited the Tibbetts in, accepted without comment Henry's explanation that they were on a motoring holiday, and asked for news of Dolly.

"She's better, I'm glad to say," said Henry. "The doctors seem to think she'll pull through."

Primrose shrugged. "She was always as strong as a horse," she remarked. "It would take more than a packet of weedkiller to finish her off."

"Insecticide," Henry corrected her.

"Oh well, it comes to the same thing."

"As a matter of interest, Madame Duval," Henry said, "did you go into Miss Underwood-Threep's bedroom to say good-bye to her before you all went off in the Rolls?"

"Me? Certainly not. Why should I? Edouard and I were only going as far as Hindhurst."

"You didn't go into her room at all?"

"Of course I didn't. What's the point of all this?" Primrose was becoming either nervous or irritated.

"Did you know that Dolly suffers from dermatitis?"

"What extraordinary questions you ask, Mr. Tibbett. Does she?"

"Yes, she does. Did you know?"

"Of course not." Primrose's mouth snapped shut in a hard line.

There was a little pause, then Henry said, "You knew, of course, that your mother had tuberculosis during the war?"

For a long moment Primrose stared at Henry. Then she said, "How did you find out?"

"I was interested," said Henry. "Did you know?"

"Yes. Edouard and I both knew—in the end."

"What do you mean by 'in the end'?"

"Well." Primrose lit a cigarette and blew out a thin line of smoke. "I mean that none of us knew anything about it while we were in Canada—or when we came back, for that matter. Edouard told me in 1947—we were engaged then—because Mother's doctor had approached him to get some special drug which wasn't obtainable in England."

"And yet," said Henry, "Dr. Duval has said he knew nothing about your mother's medical history."

Primrose smiled, a little grimly. "He was sworn to secrecy," she said. "He wasn't even supposed to tell me, and Mother never knew that I knew. Neither of my sisters has ever had the slightest inkling. Heaven knows why she should have made such a secret of it, but she was a vain and selfish woman in many ways."

"I should have thought," said Henry, "that your husband might have remembered her previous illness when—when she died so suddenly."

"Why should he have? The two things can't have any possible connection. She was cured of her T.B. years ago."

Henry did not pursue the subject, but said, "When was the last time Lady Balaclava visited you here?"

"She never—" Primrose began, but checked herself. "No, that's not true. She's been here exactly once, for a couple of hours. She had a longish wait between planes at Geneva, and so she came to lunch. It must have been about ten years ago. It was a miserable occasion."

"Miserable? Why?"

"Oh, well—Mother and Edouard never got on well. I can't remember what they argued about that day, or who started it—but it got really vicious. Fortunately, Mother had the tact to throw a fainting fit before they actually came to blows."

"A fainting fit?" Henry was enormously interested. "How do you mean?"

"Oh, she pretended to feel dizzy, and said she must go and lie down. There was nothing the matter with her, of course—she just wanted to put an end to an unpleasant situation. We had other friends here, you see. It was all extremely awkward. I told Edouard afterward that he should have been grateful to her for being so tactful. He didn't agree, of course."

"He thought she really was ill, did he?"

Primrose laughed shortly. "Goodness me, no. He maintained that she had resorted to the typically feminine device—when defeated in logical argument, swoon. He used to accuse me of doing the same thing."

"This could be very interesting, Madame Duval," said Henry. "Can you remember what you had to eat that day?"

"My dear man—can *you* remember what you ate on a particular day ten years ago? I haven't the remotest idea. Now that you mention it, though, I *can* tell you what we had to drink."

"Really?" Henry was intrigued.

"Yes—that's how the row started. We're wine-drinkers, of course, and Mother always wanted gin. Edouard hates the stuff, and refused to have any in the house. When Mother refused wine, Edouard simply gave her a glass of fruit juice. She was absolutely livid." She glanced at Henry, sharp and worried. "Why are you asking me all these questions."

"Before you left England," Henry said, "you told me that your husband wasn't happy about Lady Balaclava's death, and intended to investigate it further—"

"Oh, that . . ." Primrose was vague to the point of distraction. "Well . . . I think he's changed his mind. . . ."

"In any case," said Henry, "*I'm* interested in finding out the truth, and I'd like to have a word with Dr. Duval."

"With Edouard? But he's not here."

"Obviously. But if you can tell me what time he's expected home—"

"You don't understand. He's not in Switzerland."

Emmy said, "That conference that he was supposed to address—?"

"No, no. Not that. He's . . . he's in Paris." Primrose was suddenly speaking fast, more firmly. "He's in Paris seeing some people at the Institute of Immunology. Edouard is very keen to set up a research unit of his own, and he needs financial backing. I really don't know how long he'll be away."

"That's disappointing for me," said Henry; but Emmy thought that he sounded oddly cheerful. He added, "It's none of my business, of course, but now that you've inherited your father's money, I suppose you could finance the project if you wanted to."

A curtain came down on Primrose's face—the same look of locked-in hostility which Emmy had noticed at Foxes' Trot. She stood up. "I would never," she said, "give Edouard money. Never." For a tiny moment Primrose closed her eyes, as if to shut out a painful sight. Then she opened them and said briskly, "And now, you must forgive me if I seem inhospitable, but I shall have to ask you to go. I am expecting . . . somebody. My lawyer, as a matter of fact."

"Of course," said Henry, "your mother's death and your father's will must be causing legal complications."

"Oh, yes. Yes, there's that, too. Well, good-bye, Mrs. Tibbett . . . Chief Superintendent . . . I hope you enjoy your holiday. . . ."

Around the corner from the Duvals' apartment there was a post office. From it Henry called the second number listed under the name of Dr. Edouard Duval—his professional number. This was answered by a languorous young woman who announced herself as the Clinique du Lac.

"Dr. Edouard Duval, please."

"An instant, Monsieur."

A series of clicks and buzzes was followed by a brisk female voice. "*Le cabinet du Docteur Duval* . . . no, I am sorry, Monsieur, the doctor is away on holiday . . . Doctor Rey is looking after his patients. If I might have your name, Monsieur . . . no, I am not sure when Dr. Duval will return . . . he is touring in Spain, I believe. If I might have your name, Monsieur . . ."

Henry rang off.

Maison Bonnet was a delectable establishment. Its dark-paneled interior and exuberant brass-and-plush decor had not changed since the early days of the century—nor had the delicious sugar-and-spice smell of cakes and coffee which pervaded it. Beyond the massive mahogany counter with its tempting array of goodies, there was a small tea room, where bejeweled ladies met for coffee, gossip, and wicked cream cakes. Henry and Emmy made their way to a small table which had just been vacated by two women in mink coats and a miniature poodle in a diamond-studded collar. They sat down on the gilt and brocade chairs and ordered coffee from an elderly waitress.

Emmy said, "So where is Dr. Duval?"

"He may be in Paris."

"But the woman at the clinic said—"

"It's possible," said Henry, "that he doesn't want the clinic to know what he's up to. What's your guess?"

Emmy said, "I couldn't make Primrose out at first. She seemed worried and—"

"Frightened?"

Emmy shook her head. "No. Not frightened. Sort of vague . . . and angry at the same time. But not with us. And then, when she started talking about her husband, I suddenly realized."

"You suddenly realized what?"

"That he's left her," said Emmy simply.

"What?"

"Isn't that what you thought?"

"No, I can't say I imagined anything so drastic," said Henry. "It seemed that she was doing some hasty improvisation about Edouard's present whereabouts, certainly."

"And yet, all that stuff about the something-or-other institute in Paris sounded pretty authentic."

"I'm sure it was. I dare say Dr. Duval has made just such a trip recently. Didn't you notice how the details came pouring out, as soon as Primrose thought of using it as a cover story?"

"So," said Emmy, "you think she knows where he is, and she's just not telling?"

"That's what I did think," said Henry, "but you've opened up another line of country. I'm a great believer in feminine instinct," he added with a grin, "especially when applied to other women. So you think Edouard Duval has walked out on his wife?"

Emmy nodded vigorously, her mouth full of one of the chocolate and almond cakes which an unscrupulous management had placed, unasked, on the table, and which Emmy had sworn to ignore. "I think they had a row about money. I think he's been waiting all these years for her to inherit, so that he could get the money for his research center, or whatever it is. Now that Lady Balaclava is dead, and Primrose still won't unbelt—well, I think he's simply pushed off. Why d'you think she's seeing her lawyer, anyhow?"

"Divorce, you mean?"

"I can't imagine Primrose relishing that idea," Emmy admitted. "What I am sure of is that she'll be putting the final touches to the knots that tie up her own money." She paused. "Poor Edouard."

"What do you mean, poor Edouard?"

"Well . . . if he did . . ." She hesitated. "If he had anything to do with Crystal's death, it hasn't done him much good, has it?"

"Do you think he had anything to do with it?"

Emmy made a small, deprecatory gesture. "Honestly," she said, "you're the detective, not me."

They were interrupted by the gray-haired waitress, who arrived with two cups of coffee on a pretty tray. Indicating the depleted cake plate, Henry said, "You see, my wife couldn't resist your cakes, after all."

The waitress beamed. "All the ladies love our *pâtisseries,*" she said, adding untruthfully, "and Madame is lucky, she doesn't need to worry about her figure. Not like some. I had an American lady in here yesterday—a *very* plump lady—and she ate a whole plateful, and then ordered a big *gâteau* to take back to Washington with her. Of course, our cakes go all over the world."

"I know," said Henry. "We were enjoying one in England only last week."

"In England? Now isn't that interesting?" The tea room was emptying as noon approached, and the waitress was in no hurry. "Of course, we had a lot of English clients in the old days, but now they just don't have the money, poor dears."

"This was a very special cake," said Henry. "A birthday cake."

The waitress's face lit up. "Madame Duval's cake? For her mother, *Madame la Duchesse?*"

"That's right," said Henry. He did not feel equal to setting the waitress right as to Crystal's precise titular status. "You make one for her every year, I believe?"

"Yes, indeed, Monsieur. Our chef takes great pride in it. I packed it up myself this year, and carried it out to the taxi for Madame Duval. She was in a hurry to get to the airport."

"It was a beautiful cake," said Emmy.

"You are too kind, Madame."

"Dr. Duval also admired it very much, I believe." Henry poised the remark delicately, just short of a question.

The waitress looked puzzled. "Dr. Duval? Madame said he would not be able to attend the celebration—"

"Yes, but when he came in to see the cake—"

The waitress was not bewildered now; she was definite. "But he did not, Monsieur. He did not."

"Perhaps you were off duty at the time."

"No, no, Monsieur. I happen to know, because there was a small . . . a very small *crise* in the kitchen that day. One of the pastry cooks was taken ill, and there was a little doubt if the cake would be ready on time. When Madame Duval arrived, I went into the kitchen and found Chef himself just putting the finishing touches to the icing—so we were saved by the peel of our teeth, as you say in England. No, no—nobody else saw the cake until it arrived in England. I trust *Madame la Duchesse* enjoyed it?"

Henry was relieved that the waitress was called away to serve another table at that moment, thus saving him from the embarrassment of answering her question. When she had gone, he said to Emmy, "So you would cast Edouard Duval as the villain of the piece, would you?"

"Well—it seems obvious, doesn't it? He's a doctor. He knew about Crystal's previous treatment with streptomycin. Now we hear that she had a dizzy spell on the only occasion when she visited the Duvals. Surely that could mean that he was experimenting with a minute dose to see if she was allergic—just like Dr. Powers-Thompson said? You see—everything fits."

Henry sighed. "It doesn't, you know."

"What doesn't?"

"First, it's perfectly obvious that he couldn't have tampered with the cake; and anyway, the chemical analysis would have shown up any trace of streptomycin in it."

"He's a doctor," said Emmy again stubbornly. "He could have brought the streptomycin over with him and—oh, I see what you mean. He wasn't even there."

"Exactly."

"If he and Primrose planned it together—"

"Apart from that being the most unlikely thing I can think of," said Henry, "she would hardly have given herself away by telling us about the fainting fit. And that's another weak point in the case against Duval. If he was really experimenting to see if Crystal was allergic, and found she was, why wait ten years to kill her?"

"I still think he's the obvious suspect," said Emmy.

"A bit too obvious, perhaps," said Henry. "I must say I wish I knew where he was at this moment. Oh, well, I suppose we'd better start off with a process of elimination."

"How?"

"First, by checking with the Institute of Immunology. There's no more to be done here, and I'd like a chat with the Swasheimers anyhow. Daffy has become . . . well, let's say that her situation is interesting."

So, with regret, Henry and Emmy packed their suitcases and said *au revoir* to the lakeside hotel, promising the smiling proprietress to return as soon as they could. Then they climbed into the little saloon car again and headed its nose toward the Jura Mountains, the frontier at St. Cergue, and Paris.

18

The hotel in Paris could hardly have been a greater contrast to the one in Lutry. It was small and ugly and tucked away in a side street in Montmartre. Instead of a vista of lake and mountain, the Tibbetts' room commanded a view of gray rooftops and peeling shutters. However, the room itself was prettily tricked out in flowered chintz, the plumbing worked, the morning coffee was good, and the price was reasonable. Henry and Emmy checked in at eight o'clock in the evening. Tired after their drive, they bathed, took a quick but delicious dinner at the nearby café Chez Marcel, and went to bed.

In the morning Emmy went off to the Rue de Rivoli. Although, with her slender packet of travelers' checks, she could do no more than lick the windows of the shops—as the French put it so vividly—still she was adamant that this was an admirable way to spend a couple of hours. "I don't need to buy anything," she explained to Henry. "I just *look*. It gives me a whole new feeling about fashion. As Virginia Woolf said, it refreshes the eye."

"Sooner you than me," said Henry, whose idea of hell was shopping for clothes. The thought of spending the best part of a morning looking at shop windows appalled him. It was with relief that he made his way to the Institute of Immunology.

This august body was housed in premises which did not quite live up to the resounding title on the brass plaque. It was, in fact, a thin gray house in the neighborhood of the

Madeleine, and it suggested to Henry the headquarters of a gently unsuccessful family business. However, there was a pretty brunette presiding over the small office marked *Réception,* and she was friendliness itself.

"Dr. Duval? Oh, I'm so sorry, Monsieur. You have just missed him."

"Just? You mean, he's in Paris?"

"I really couldn't say, Monsieur. I understood he was going back to Switzerland. But he *was* here, only a matter of . . . let me see . . . it must be about two weeks ago. I can give you his address in Lausanne if you . . . oh. Oh, I see. No, he certainly hasn't been back to see us again since then. . . . Conference? Which conference?"

"I understand," said Henry, "that Dr. Duval was about to address a conference of your Institute in Switzerland last week, when he was suddenly called away to England."

The brunette looked puzzled. "No, no Monsieur. You must have been misinformed. We hold only one conference annually, each February, here in Paris. Of course, Dr. Duval may be a member of several medical bodies. It must have been some other conference."

"So," said Henry to Emmy later as they drank coffee under the trees on the Champs Elysées, "Duval isn't in Paris. As I thought, he did visit the Institute a few weeks ago, and Primrose simply substituted details of that visit—either to hide the truth or to cover up her ignorance. As for the conference that stopped him from coming to Foxes' Trot—well, it looks very much as if that was a diplomatic fiction, an excuse to miss the birthday party."

"An excuse which Primrose believed was true, though," said Emmy. "Judging from that telephone conversation you overheard, when she was begging him to come over."

"Of course," Henry went on, following his own train of thought, "we know that Edouard didn't get on with his mother-in-law. There needn't have been anything more sinister than that in it. He simply didn't want to come to England."

"There you go again. Making excuses for him."

"I'm not making excuses. But I'm also trying to avoid

putting the worst possible construction on facts which may be quite innocent."

"If you're implying that *I*—"

"I'm implying," said Henry, "that you should finish your coffee and rub that smut off your nose. We are about to move into high society."

The Place de la Concorde was vast, sunny, windy, and crawling with solid masses of traffic. Stepping from its roar into the hushed luxury of the Hotel Crillon was rather like passing from a fairground into a cathedral. In the lofty marble hall, uniformed porters carried pigskin cases around with reverence, while behind the massive altar of the reception desk, lordly, black-garbed gentlemen made slow, solemn entries in leatherbound volumes, as weighty as the chronicles of the recording angel. Henry and Emmy approached this sanctum with some trepidation and asked for Mr. and Mrs. Swasheimer.

The high priest, or chief concierge, regarded Henry with benign saintliness for a moment and then remarked, more in sorrow than in anger, that it was useless to seek communion with Mr. Swasheimer at this hour of the day. Between ten and twelve o'clock Mr. Swasheimer was invariably at his office. As for Mrs. Swasheimer . . . the high priest sighed, implying that there were mysteries beyond the range of mortal comprehension. He would, he said, inquire. If Henry would divulge his name . . .

Henry did so, and the chief concierge slowly lifted the black telephone at his elbow and whispered into it that he desired to be connected with Suite 103. He then half-turned his back on Henry and Emmy and leaned on the counter in such a way as to prevent them from seeing his mouth, had they wished to lip-read his conversation.

He could not, however, disguise the fact that the telephone was answered in Suite 103, and Henry distinctly heard his own name mentioned. A pause of several minutes ensued. Then the telephone was replaced, and the high priest informed them, sorrowfully, that Mrs. Swasheimer was not at home. He had no idea of when she would return, and could make no suggestion as to the best means of contacting her. He did not actually add that all flesh is as grass, but he implied it strongly. If Henry would care to leave a written message, he would have it sent up to the suite. Emmy had a vision of the message ascending like incense, impelled heavenward by faith rather than by science.

Henry said briskly, "No, I won't bother, thank you. Come along, darling." He took Emmy's arm, and—to her surprise—led her not toward the street door, but into the interior of the hotel. The high priest watched them go, gravely. It did cross his mind to telephone again to Mrs. Swasheimer, but then, with a gentle sigh of relief, he decided that it was not his business.

Meanwhile, Henry and Emmy had installed themselves at a table in the elegant foyer, under the imposing marble statue of Crillon himself, engraved with the curiously lukewarm tribute taken from a letter of Henry IV: ". . . *brave Crillon, nous avons combattu à Arques et tu n'y étais pas . . .*" Whoever may or may not have been fighting at Arques in the sixteenth century, however, plenty of rich and leisured citizens, of both sexes and many nationalities, had decided to while away the midmorning by taking a cup of the Crillon's excellent coffee. Henry, trying not to think about what it would cost, ordered a pot for Emmy and himself.

When the waiter had gone, Emmy said, "You think Daffy's here?"

"I'm certain of it."

"It might have been a maid who answered the phone."

"I'm sure it was," said Henry. "That's why she had to go and consult Daffy. If Daffy had really been out, either there'd have been no reply or the maid would have said so at once. Daffodil is obviously at home to some people and not at home to others—and we're among the others."

"So we waylay her, do we?" Emmy sounded unenthusiastic.

"If and when she comes out, it will either be down those stairs or from one of those lifts. So drink up your coffee and keep your eyes skinned."

For ten minutes or so nothing happened except the usual subdued bustle of the great hotel. Then Emmy noticed a young man who had just arrived through the big revolving door from the street. He was dark and strikingly handsome, and there was something familiar about his face. Clearly he was looking for somebody. His eyes flickered around the coffee tables, scanning the faces and not finding the one he wanted. He glanced impatiently at his watch and then sat down at a small table near the foot of the stairs.

Emmy leaned forward toward Henry and said quietly, "Don't look now, but I *think* the young man at the table behind you may be Warren Swasheimer. He looks a lot like Chuck, anyhow. If it is him, he's waiting for Daffy."

"No longer," said Henry.

"What—?" Emmy began; but Henry was on his feet, as was the dark young man. Emmy looked over her shoulder. Daffodil Swasheimer was coming out of one of the lifts, looking ravishingly beautiful and extremely bad-tempered. The young man and Henry dead-heated to the lift door, but Henry, in a photo finish, got in his, "Ah, Mrs. Swasheimer, I was hoping to see you—" just ahead of the young man's "Daffy!"

Daffodil looked at Henry in a way which made it perfectly clear that the hope had not been mutual, but she was trapped. Heads were beginning to turn in her direction, and the last thing she wanted was a scene—word of which might get back to Chuck. So she managed a frosty smile and said, "Well, well, Mr. Tibbett. What a surprise."

"Daffy—" said the young man again with a sort of anguish.

"I must introduce you," said Daffy with distaste. "Warren Swasheimer, my . . . my stepson. Chief Superintendent Tibbett of Scotland Yard."

"Scotland Yard," repeated Warren. He had gone very pale.

"You remember, I told you that we met the chief superintendent in England." Daffodil gave Henry another icy smile. "So nice to see you again. Now, I am afraid that Warren and I have a—"

"Emmy and I," said Henry firmly, "would be so pleased if you would join us for a drink."

"I am so sorry," Daffodil was equally firm.

"So am I," said Henry, "but I'm afraid I must insist. Not here, I think. Mr. Swasheimer Senior will be coming back to lunch soon."

Daffodil hesitated. It was clear that she was deciding whether or not she dared to refuse. Then she said, "Very well. We have a few minutes to spare."

"Good." Henry grinned at her. "I'll just settle my bill and collect Emmy."

Ten minutes later all four of them were sitting at a table in a more modest establishment a few blocks away, drinking aperitifs. The café was extremely large and extremely crowded, which made it possible to hold a private conversation with no fear of being overheard. As soon as the waiter had gone Henry said, "I'm sorry about this, Mrs. Swasheimer, but it has to be done. You probably knew that I'm investigating the death of your mother, and the attempted murder of Miss Underwood-Threep."

"The . . . what?" Daffodil's pose of icy boredom cracked a little.

"I'll explain in due course. Now, the first thing I want to make clear is that personally I don't give a damn what you do with your private life."

"Really, I don't—" Daffy began on a note of high indignation, but Henry stopped her.

"Please don't let's waste time. You haven't been very discreet, you know. The Belgrave Towers Hotel—"

Daffodil turned on Emmy, furious. "You snide bitch," she said. "If you've told—"

"I've told nobody."

"Your husband seems very well informed."

"But yours isn't," said Emmy. "I had to tell Henry, to prevent him from having Chuck ring the Belgrave Towers."

"Oh. I see." Daffodil was distinctly subdued. She turned back to Henry. "Well?"

"As I was saying," said Henry, "your private life is your own business. Nevertheless, you must see that this state of affairs gives you a very strong motive for—for wishing to inherit your father's money."

"Just what are you implying?"

"Nothing. I'm stating facts and asking questions. I'm sorry if they sound impertinent. First of all, do you intend to leave your husband and marry his son?"

"Daffy . . ." said Warren again. His contribution to the conversation was becoming somewhat monotonous.

"Shut up, Warren," said Daffodil shortly. Then, to Henry, "Yes. As soon as the money is actually in my bank account."

"What," said Henry, "would you have done if your mother had lived for another twenty years?"

Daffodil looked at him steadily. "The question doesn't arise, does it? Mother is dead."

"I'm still asking."

Warren Swasheimer found his tongue at last. In a quick, nervous rush he said, "Daffy and I would have gotten married anyhow. The money isn't important."

Henry raised his eyebrows. To Daffy he said, "Isn't it?"

"I'm not exactly a pauper, you know," Warren added. "I manage the whole European end of the business."

"Your father's business," Henry pointed out. "You don't really think you'll keep that job when—"

"I can get another. The money doesn't matter, I tell you." Warren was obviously frightened.

"In that case," said Henry, "why all this secrecy until, as Mrs. Swasheimer has said, the money is actually in her bank account?"

Daffy and Warren exchanged a quick glance, and then Daffy shrugged and said, "Since Mother *is* dead, it seemed only sensible to wait for the will to be proved, before—"

"I see," said Henry. "Now, another question. When did you find out that your mother suffered from tuberculosis during the war?"

"From—*what?*" Either Daffodil was an excellent actress, or her astonishment was real. "Don't be silly. Mother is . . . was . . . never ill."

"You maintain that you didn't know?"

"I maintain you are talking rubbish. It's true, come to think of it, that Mother kept us all away from Foxes' Trot after we came back from Canada—but I've always assumed that she didn't want a gang of giggling schoolgirls around the place. I'd have done the same in her place. But as for T.B.—I simply don't believe it."

"Your sister Primrose knew about it," said Henry. "Lady Balaclava's doctor managed to get hold of streptomycin in 1947 through Edouard Duval. It cured her."

"Well, I'm damned," said Daffodil.

Warren Swasheimer, who had been looking progressively more unhappy and bewildered, broke in, "What's all this about, for God's sake, Daffy?"

"You'd better ask the chief superintendent. I haven't the faintest idea."

Henry said, "What about the champagne?"

"What about it?"

"Where did it come from? Who delivered it, and when?"

Daffodil looked and sounded bored. "Chuck forgot to order it," she said. "I had to remind him. Then, as far as I know, he had his secretary arrange for the case to be waiting for us at Dover. And so it was. We loaded it into the car and drove it to Foxes' Trot."

"It was sealed up?"

"Of course."

"Nobody could have tampered with it?"

"Oh, don't be foolish," said Daffodil impatiently. "Just try tampering with a bottle of champagne."

"Did you," Henry asked, "go in to say good-bye to Dolly before you left Foxes' Trot?"

"No. I was told she was asleep."

"Who told you?"

"Primrose, I think. No, Violet. I met her coming out of Dolly's room, looking tragic and mumbling something about poor, poor Dolly. Vi's a great one for tragedy. I said I was going in to say good-bye, and Vi went into a Victorian melodrama scene—you know, the hand on my arm, the break in the voice . . . 'No, no Daffodil . . . let the poor soul rest . . . she's sleeping like a little child. . . .' Nauseating. Still, I was glad enough of the excuse, so I just went on down to the car."

Henry thought for a moment. Then he said suddenly, "And where is Edouard Duval now?"

Daffodil's eyebrows went up. "I *beg* your pardon?"

"Edouard Duval. Where is he?"

"How on earth should I know? Lausanne, I presume."

"No."

"Then you'd better ask Primrose, hadn't you?"

"I've already asked her."

"Really?" Daffodil was interested. "You mean she's lost him?"

"She told me," said Henry, "that he was visiting a medical institute here. But they know nothing of it, and haven't seen him for several weeks."

"How fascinating," said Daffodil. She did, indeed, sound fascinated. "I'm only sorry I can't help you. Imagine old Edouard kicking over the traces. I suppose he's shacked up with some little broad somewhere."

"You think that's likely?"

"It's the unlikeliest thing I ever heard—but then, just imagine what life with Primrose must be like." Daffodil smiled languorously at Warren. How different, said the smile, would be life with Daffodil.

Warren, evidently feeling that his part in the proceedings had been less than heroic, now became truculent. "And now, Mister Superintendent," he said, "perhaps we may be allowed to ask a few questions for a change. What do you mean by—?"

Henry stood up. "I mean nothing," he said. "I wanted certain information, and I got it. You and your stepmother may now get on with whatever it was that you were about to do when we interrupted you. Come along, Emmy."

As they left the café, Emmy could sense, although she

could not see, the openmouthed, outraged expression on Warren Swasheimer's face. For Daffy's reaction, however, she could rely on the evidence of her senses. Daffy was laughing.

In the street Henry hailed a cab, and remained silent all the way back to the Montmartre hotel. There, in the chintzy bedroom, he lay down on his back on the bed, lit a cigarette, and stared at the ceiling.

After ten minutes of silence Emmy said, "D'you want any lunch? It's half-past one."

Henry said, "No. No lunch. Sorry, love, but I'm thinking. You go and get yourself something at the place on the corner." After a moment he added, "It all fits, except that it's just bloody impossible, that's all."

Emmy, who had many years' experience of remarks of this kind, did not reply. She took herself off to Chez Marcel, where for a modest sum she ate onion soup made with real onions and home-baked bread, and a beautifully dressed salad which tasted of real lettuce and chives— compensations for a thin, tough steak and tinned peas. The excellent cheese board nicely balanced the awful *coupe Jacques.* If it's true, Emmy reflected, that English food would be delicious if one had three breakfasts a day, then by the same token cheap French meals could be improved by omitting the main dishes and concentrating on the incidentals.

She arrived back at the hotel to find Henry no longer horizontal and brooding, but vertical and energetic. He was, in fact, packing. He was also whistling tunelessly to himself, and looked almost cheerful.

"Well?" said Emmy. "Where now?"

"Holland. We can be over the border by seven, if we hurry."

"Oh. All right."

Henry looked up from the pajamas he was folding. "You sound disappointed," he said. "Don't you like Holland?"

"You know I love it," said Emmy. "It's only that . . . well . . ."

"Well, what?"

"You seemed so . . . I don't know . . . as if you'd got the answer. I thought we were off somewhere totally unexpected, to solve the mystery. But it seems we're just carrying out the routine we planned. First Primrose, then Daffodil, now Violet."

"That's right."

"And after that?"

"We go back to England—what else?"

The drive from Paris to Holland can hardly be called a scenic delight. After a dismal crawl through the suburbs, poplar-lined roads with excruciating surfaces lead the traveler across the plains of the industrial north, and into the grimy red-brick towns over the Belgian border—for the possession of which hundreds of thousands of young men died in two world wars. Brussels would have been interesting if the traffic had not been quite so intense and apparently suicidal. Beyond the city a promising-looking motorway degenerated into a bumpy double-track road. This eventually led to the confusion of Antwerp, where Henry lost his way twice.

By the time that the dogged little car had finally steered clear of the city and set its nose on the road to Breda and the Netherlands, both its occupants were feeling dirty, tired, and in need of a long, cool drink. And, almost at once, a sort of miracle occurred. The road began to run through flat, wooded country. The houses spruced themselves up, put on neatly thatched roofs, and settled themselves among trim, colorful gardens. The countryside pulled itself together, scrubbed its cattle clean of mud, cropped its grass into tailored green fields. Another few minutes, and there was the frontier—and beyond it, a spruce café with carpets on the tables, a plate of savory *bitterballen*, and two tall glasses of Dutch lager, misting on the outside and icy to the touch.

"Oh, Henry," said Emmy, "I *am* glad to be back."

After that it was plain sailing, up the smooth motorway to Rotterdam, over the wide Maas waterway by the grace-

ful Brienenoord Bridge, past Gouda, and then northwest-
ward across the rolling green of the Rhineland, until at
dusk they came to Aalsmeer. Aalsmeer, the town afloat on
a thousand tiny islands, each of them a nursery garden;
Aalsmeer, the town of the Dutch auction, the biggest
flower market in the world; Aalsmeer, the town of roses.

19

The little hotel was spotlessly clean and very comfortable. The interior decor was inclined to be lumpish, but was relieved by a profusion of indoor plants which gave Emmy the impression of living in a conservatory. Breakfast was enormous, consisting of slices of cheese and cold sausage as well as copious coffee and bread and butter—the latter served, if desired, sprinkled with chocolate flakes. Afterward Henry and Emmy set out for the flower market, where a special visit had been arranged for them.

The outside was not inspiring—a vast, industrial-looking mass of red brick, a collection of warehouses crossed with a barracks. The inside took the breath away. One after another, great hangarlike buildings were literally filled with flowers. The color and the perfume dazzled the senses. Pink, white, red, and yellow carnations; tawny lilies; exotic orchids—purple, mauve, green, and yellow; deep blue, velvety African daisies; indoor plants in every shade of green from silver-gray to polished laurel; and above all, the roses. There were halls and galleries and vistas of roses— lanes and avenues of red and pink and white and orange and yellow. Porters, barely visible behind their fragrant loads, pushed huge trolleys piled high with blossoms.

Among the riot of color and the seeming confusion, men in dark suits moved quietly, shrewdly examining, assessing, making decisions. These were the wholesale florists who had come to buy—men who knew to the last centime the market value of every bloom, whose expertise extended not only to appraising the quality of the flowers, but who took account of the fact that white carnations fetched high prices in England in late March because of the beat-the-tax weddings, that certain saints' days in France produced a demand for certain flowers, that springtime first communions pushed up the sale of white blooms of all sorts. Above all, these men were expert in the frighteningly difficult technique of the Dutch auction.

Inside one of the auction rooms, silent except for the continuous and unintelligible spiel of the auctioneer, the guide explained the system. The room was like an amphitheater, with semicircular tiers of numbered seats. Each of these seats was allocated to a particular buyer—without a seat, it was impossible to take part in the auction. Beside each seat was a small electric button.

The "acting area" of the amphitheater was occupied by a trolley of flowers, representing a sample of the lot currently under the hammer. On the wall above it, facing the tiers of seats, was the heart of the auction—the huge, white-faced clock. At the start of bidding for each lot, the clock—whose figures represented sums of money—had its single hand set to a figure obviously too high for the value of the flowers being sold. Then, at incredible speed, the hand spun around, showing a lower and lower price. The first buyer to press his electric button automatically stopped the clock. His number was electrically recorded, and the flowers were his, at the price shown on the clock when it stopped. The nicety of judgment needed to press the button at the right time made Henry's head spin—especially when the guide pointed out that the auctioneers were able to dispose of up to four hundred lots in a single hour.

And once the flowers had been sold? Henry and Emmy were guided through the cool, shaded rooms where the precious blooms were packed in damp moss and porous plastic, carefully arranged in long, perforated cardboard boxes. From these packing rooms the flowers were rushed to the airport, to be flown thousands of miles and still arrive in perfect condition.

"And these flowers from Aalsmeer find their way all over the world." The guide was in full spate. "Every possible precaution is taken to make sure that they arrive in perfect condition. At the nurseries, the blooms are sprayed with penicillin, aureomycin, or streptomycin to preserve them from bacterial decay. Here in the auction sheds, they are kept in cool, moist—"

"Streptomycin!" hissed Emmy into Henry's ear.

"—in the packing rooms, each individual orchid is carefully wrapped in . . ."

"Let's get out of here," said Henry.

The commisionaire on the gate was friendly, but unable to be very helpful. Glancing at his watch, he remarked that it was eleven o'clock already and that the growers would all be away by now. They brought in their flowers before seven in the morning. Most of them just waited long enough to see the consignment safely delivered and then went back to their glasshouses. Oh, a few might stay around to see how much their produce fetched at the auction—but even they would be gone by now. Why, the selling must be nearly over for the day. Mijnheer van der Hoven? Oh, yes, the commissionaire knew him well. Him and his father before him. He had been in early with his van, bringing a load of roses, but he'd gone long since. Left about eight o'clock. He'll be at his nursery garden, no doubt, if you want to talk to him. . . .

It did not take Henry and Emmy long to find their way to the neat little house on the green island, with its trim garden and rustic signboard. They pulled the car in to the side of the road and walked over the little white bridge and up to the front door.

The house seemed deserted. Twice Henry rang the bell, and twice its echoes died away into silence. Then, unexpectedly, Piet himself came around the corner from the back of the house, beaming welcome.

"Mr. Tibbett . . . Mrs. Emmy . . . what a good surprise! Forgive me, I am in working togs, as you can see. I was in the greenhouse over there. I saw you come, and feared to miss you. There is nobody at home, you see. Do please come in. You are on holiday?"

Piet led the way indoors. The house was like a newly polished pin, small and scrubbed and immaculate. It was also far from luxurious. The furniture and carpets, although scrupulously polished and swept, were not new and had never been expensive. An effective but ugly paraffin stove took the place of more sophisticated central heating. The rooms were tiny, and there were not many of them. It was in every particular the house of an honest, hard-working Dutchman in the lower-middle income bracket. The contrast with the Hotel Crillon and the Lausanne apartment was very marked.

Piet was saying, "You are just in time for a cup of coffee and a cookie. I always have one at this hour. You will join me? What is the news of Miss Dolly? Good, I hope. She is a strong lady and will get better." He carried a tray of coffee cups from the kitchen into the tiny sitting room, where Henry and Emmy were installed. "Now, tell me what you do here in Aalsmeer?"

"We were hoping," said Henry, "to see your wife."

"Violet? Oh, I am sorry. She is just now away. She have a telephone from this Mister—what is the name? The thin man who dines so well. The lawyer. She must go to London about this money. I don't understand all this." Piet disappeared into the kitchen again. They could hear him fumbling about, dropping something on the floor. Through the open door he added, "All this makes a great bother for my poor Violet. She and I, we are alike, we live simple. So much money brings only nuisances, and it will not grow better roses." He came in, carrying a steaming coffee pot and a plate of biscuits.

Sipping the delicious sweet coffee, Henry said, "So you're not thinking of giving up your market gardening?"

"Giving up?" Piet's hand, which had been conveying his cup to his lips, stopped in midair. He looked at Henry in shocked surprise. "You mean, leave my roses? No, no, naturally not. My father and his father . . . we are a family of rose-growers, Mr. Tibbett. This is my work, and here is my home. No, no, no . . ." And Piet laughed, shaking his head as if to brush away the ridiculous idea.

"In any case," Henry remarked, "the money is your wife's."

"Yes, yes, of course. Entirely hers. We married under a divided-property regime, you see. But what does it matter? The money will make no difference here. Some new dresses for Violet . . . a new carpet . . . such little things. Poor Violet. She has been so sad since the death of her mother. She would rather have the good Lady Balaclava alive again than all the money in the world, I assure you, sir. We are not people of ambition—not like Primrose and Edouard. We make our garden grow, and are content."

There was a little pause, while Piet drank deeply, tilting the thick earthenware cup so that it hid his broad nose. Henry said, "That packet of insecticide you left for Dolly . . ."

The cup was lowered, the candid blue eyes turned inquiringly to Henry. "What of it? It is a new preparation from America, which Miss Dolly was anxious to try. Another parathion solution. Bad. Very bad."

"Ineffective, you mean?"

"No, no. Very effective, but dangerous. I would never use such a thing in my greenhouses. I told you that in England."

"I know you did. Where did you get the Pestkil?"

"Why, here in Aalsmeer. It is freely available. Many growers use it." Piet looked hard at Henry. "Why do you ask all this? Is Miss Dolly's illness connected with this Pestkil, is that your meaning?"

"It may be," said Henry. "She has a sensitive skin condition, and it seems that the powder came into contact with—"

"You see?" roared Piet triumphantly. "You see how it is dangerous!"

"But presumably you use something—some sort of insecticide?"

"There are other preparations which are not so dangerous," said Piet, slightly on the defensive.

"And then, of course, you use preservatives on the blooms themselves to keep them in good condition," said Henry.

"Of course. Every grower does that."

"Streptomycin, I suppose."

Piet showed no surprise. He simply shook his head. "No, I don't use it myself. Many people do, especially for roses. Kaes van Steen swears by it . . . my next-door neighbor." Piet jerked his head toward the window, indicating the adjoining island. "Why do you ask?"

"You mean that the roses you brought to Lady Balaclava couldn't have been sprayed with streptomycin?"

Piet had finished his coffee and was now lighting a stubby cigar. "They could have been, of course—but they were not, because I never use the stuff. Does it make a difference?"

"It makes a great deal of difference," said Henry. After a pause he went on, "You knew very well, didn't you, that it would be fatal for Lady Balaclava to inhale streptomycin?"

"I knew . . . what is this, please?" Piet made no indignant denial, no shocked rebuttal. He simply did not understand. "You must suppose me very stupid, Mr. Tibbett, but . . . what can this streptomycin have to do with my poor mamma-in-law?"

For a long moment the two men looked at each other. Then Henry said, "If you don't know, Mr. van der Hoven, then there is no point in my telling you. When do you expect Violet back?"

Piet shrugged. "Who knows? She will telephone. Tomorrow perhaps, perhaps the day after. Now, while you are here, will you not see my roses? It will be my great pleasure to show you."

So Henry and Emmy went on a tour of the acres of glasshouses which extended behind the house, from small island to small island, linked by little footbridges, almost as far as the lake known as the Westeinder Plas. In some of the greenhouses men were tending, clipping, and spraying the plants—although, as Piet pointed out with pride, modern methods of automation had eliminated much of the need for human labor. At one moment, while Emmy encouraged Piet to explain the process of grafting, Henry managed to have a quiet word in Dutch with one of the young workmen. The man confirmed precisely what Piet had said. No parathion insecticide and no streptomycin were ever used in the van der Hoven nurseries. Mr. Piet wouldn't have them in the place.

Back at the hotel Henry put through a telephone call to Sarah Massingham's London flat. She listened carefully to what he had to say, and then exclaimed, "But of course! It must have been the roses!"

"It would be possible, then?" asked Henry. "I mean, being sensitive to streptomycin, Lady Balaclava could have been killed just by smelling a bunch of flowers?"

"Why not? If she was highly sensitive, even a few molecules left on the flowers would have been enough—provided she took a good hard sniff at them. What's more, anybody else in the room could have smelled them with no ill effects at all."

"As we all did," said Henry.

"Of course . . ." Sarah hesitated, her first fine flush of enthusiasm a little dimmed. "Of course, the person who arranged it all must have known that she was allergic . . ."

"And must have had access both to streptomycin and to the roses," Henry pointed out.

"Edouard Duval is a doctor," said Sarah. "He knew she'd had streptomycin treatment. And your story of the dizzy fit in Lausanne . . . streptomycin is highly soluble in water, and fruit juice would hide its slightly bitter taste. That could have been the test—"

"It could also have been a perfectly ordinary glass of fruit juice—and anyhow it was ten years ago. The point is that Edouard Duval could not possibly have got at the roses."

"And yet he did," said Sarah stubbornly.

"I wonder very much," said Henry. "How's Dolly?"

There was a little pause, then Sarah said, "I can't tell

you. Dr. Griffiths has taken over the case. I haven't been down to Hindhurst since—"

"Well, I wish you'd go," said Henry. "Are you busy just now?"

"No. I start another locum job next week, but—"

"Then do me a favor, Sarah. Go down to Hindhurst, and stick to Dolly closer than the paper on the wall. Keep all visitors away from her, especially members of the Codworthy family."

"But how on earth can I—?"

"You'll have to think of a way. You're a doctor—that gives you a head start. I'll get back as soon as I can, but there are still things to be done here. Ring me at this hotel if there are any developments. O.K.?"

"I suppose so." Sarah sounded doubtful. "I only undertook to cope with the medical end, remember. I really don't like this—"

"Rubbish," said Henry. "You're enjoying every moment of it."

He was rewarded by a warm, chuckling laugh. "All right. Perhaps I am. I'll be at the Hindhurst Arms, if I can get a room."

"You're an angel, and I adore you," said Henry. It was not entirely fortunate that Emmy chose that moment to come back into the room. Henry added, "Well, good-bye, Sarah. Emmy sends her love." He rang off.

Emmy raised her eyebrows and made an effort to look cold and haughty; but, as so often, it failed. She caught Henry's eye, said, "Honestly, Henry, you're a *monster* . . ." and began to laugh.

"Not at all," said Henry. "I'm just an expert at getting cooperation by a tactful personal approach."

"Tactful!" said Emmy. "Ye gods. Anyhow, I've got the phone number you wanted, Kaes van Steen, rose-grower. Aalsmeer 817."

Mijnheer van Steen was surprised to receive a telephone call from an unknown Englishman who wanted to visit his nurseries; but as a Dutchman, he was far too polite not to extend a cordial welcome to the stranger—and besides, who knew, Henry might turn out to be a possible client. An appointment was fixed for the same afternoon.

Outwardly, the van Steen establishment was very similar to Piet van der Hoven's; but Henry could sense at once that the underlying spirit was quite different. Van Steen was a keen, brisk young man in an impeccably pressed suit who operated from a modern office which seemed incongruous among the glasshouses. The walls were covered with graphs and charts, there were three telephones on the large, shiny desk, and a mini-skirted typist tapped busily among the filing cabinets in an adjoining office. The contrast with Piet van der Hoven, ambling around his greenhouses in clogs and shirtsleeves, could not have been more marked. To Piet, roses were more than a business: they were a heritage, a way of life, a trust for which no amount of work and loving care could be too much. To Kaes van Steen, roses were figures on a chart and money in the bank. Roses were a part of Holland's economic miracle, and, properly automated, could be big business.

Henry, who had been deliberately vague on the telephone, took in Mr. van Steen, his office, his charts, and his typist in one swift glance—and introduced himself as a free-lance writer who was hoping to write an article about the Dutch cut-flower industry. He judged that van Steen was not the man to turn down free publicity, even if this were presented as no more than a faint possibility.

The Tibbetts were taken on a grand tour of the nurseries, were treated to a blow-by-blow explanation of the growth and efficiency charts, were given a scientific analysis of the modern electrical and chemical aids which enabled something as delicate as a rose to be turned out by mass-production methods.

Parathion insecticides? Van Steen was briefly appreciative of the fact that a mere writer had even heard of them. Done his homework, evidently. Yes, of course, they were used extensively. Dangerous? Not at all, so long as elementary safety precautions were observed. Possible long-term effects? My dear sir, I am not a scientist. I am a businessman, and concerned with the short term. If long-term effects prove harmful, then the research scientists will tell us so. What do we pay them for, after all? Streptomycin? Naturally. The van Steen establishment employed various antibiotics as preservatives. Penicillin and aureomycin had proved excellent for carnations and other varieties, but in his—van Steen's—opinion, there was nothing like streptomycin for preserving roses in prime condition. To take an example, roses from his greenhouses were regularly flown to New York—a journey which at the quickest involved twelve hours from door to door . . . and to take another case, a consignment specially ordered for North Africa . . .

Henry interrupted to say that he understood there were various schools of thought on the subject of antibiotic sprays. Van Steen stopped in mid-spate. Schools of thought? What did Henry mean? Why, it was an acknowledged fact that—

Henry said, "I only meant that some growers don't use them. I was talking earlier on to Mr. van der Hoven—"

An expression of intense disdain creased Mr. van Steen's immaculate countenance. "I hope you did not waste your time in *that* establishment, Mr. Tibbett," he said in his perfect English. "Piet van der Hoven is the kind of grower who gets the whole industry a bad name. He is old-fashioned, inefficient, and prejudiced."

"He grows beautiful roses," said Henry.

"Pah! Beautiful roses, I grant you, but in uneconomic quantities and with undesirable commercial properties. The Netherlands can no longer afford such . . . such village industry . . . such charming but unpractical . . . what is it you say? . . . arty-craftiness. Yes, that is the English phrase. Piet van der Hoven should be a private gardener working for some milord, producing six perfect roses each day for his master, to lay on the breakfast table along with the delicious thin-skinned tomatoes which will travel to the next village, the luscious peaches which will bruise at a touch, the thin-stemmed carnations which will wither by evening . . ." His indignation was sincere, and, Henry had to admit, made sense.

"Nevertheless," Henry said, "he obviously believes in what he's doing."

"You think so?" Van Steen leaned toward Henry with the satisfied expression of one about to produce a trump card. "Then I will tell you otherwise. For only a few days ago Piet van der Hoven came to me to ask for the loan of some streptomycin spray."

"He did?" Henry hardly dared to breathe.

"And why? Because he was taking a special consignment of roses to England, and it was necessary for them to remain in perfect condition for at least twenty-four hours after being cut. Does that show you the humbug of van der Hoven's attitude, Mr. Tibbett, or does it not?"

"So you lent him streptomycin spray for this particular bunch of roses? The ones he took to England?"

"That's right. For his mother's birthday, or some such occasion."

"And did you also give him a sample of a parathion insecticide called Pestkil?"

"I did. He had some story of a friend who wished to experiment with it. Do you know what I think, Mr. Tibbett? I think he wanted it for himself. I think Mr. van der Hoven is at last beginning to realize that we are living in the twentieth century, that in this day and age his methods are old hat. But he will not admit it. So I hope that when you come to write your article, you will not glorify the boys of the old brigade." Van Steen's English was embarrassingly idiomatic. "Now, if you will study this graph, it will show you that by concentrating on disease-resistant strains, we have been able to boost our output over the past four years . . ."

Back at the hotel, Emmy said to Henry, "So it was Piet van der Hoven, all the time. But why? In heaven's name, why?"

"He's very fond of his wife," said Henry. He sat down on the bed and rubbed the back of his neck with his hand.

"You mean—she talked him into it?"

"I don't know just what I mean."

"But it must have been Piet."

"Yes," said Henry. "Yes, it must have been."

It was then that the telephone rang. "Henry? Oh, thank goodness. I've been trying to get you all afternoon. This is Sarah."

"What's happened, Sarah? Where are you?"

Henry could hear Sarah taking a deep breath. Then she said, "I'm at the Hindhurst Arms. I arrived before lunch. I got on to the hospital right away. Dolly Underwood-Threep is better, and she's being discharged from hospital tomorrow morning."

"That's good news," said Henry.

"Is it? You haven't heard anything yet. You said to stick by her, and to keep the family away."

"That's right."

"Well, I don't see how I can."

"What do you mean?" Henry asked sharply.

"I asked the doctor if he was sure she was fit to go home, with only Mrs. What's-her-name to look after her. And he said that it was perfectly all right, because Lady Balaclava's daughter and son-in-law were in England and were going to stay with Dolly at Foxes' Trot. Dr. and Mrs. Duval."

"Good God."

"They arrive tonight, and they're going to pick Dolly up from the hospital at nine o'clock tomorrow morning. What on earth am I to do, Henry?"

"There's nothing for it, darling," said Henry. "We'll have to split up. One of us stays here and the other goes to England."

"I don't like it one little bit," said Emmy. She was sitting on the edge of the bed in the little Dutch hotel, hugging her knees. "It's perfectly obvious that Piet van der Hoven killed Crystal Balaclava—"

"Piet and/or Violet."

"All right. Piet and/or Violet. So I don't see how it can possibly matter whether or not Edouard and Primrose decide to spend a few days with Dolly. This is where the action is—here in Aalsmeer."

"Violet is in England," Henry pointed out.

"On business, seeing the Plunkett man. I suppose that's why Primrose has had to go over—he must want to see them all. Honestly, Henry, I can't see that it's important. The only thing that matters now is to *prove* how Piet van der Hoven—"

"Just a minute." Henry stood up and began pacing up and down the little room. "You've given me an idea."

"I have?"

"Yes. Yes, everything fits at last. Why didn't I see it sooner?"

"Henry, what are you talking about? What did I say?"

"Never mind." Henry sat down at the inadequate dressing table and began to scribble in his notebook. "Be an angel, and ask the switchboard for some telephone calls."

"Calls to where?"

"First to Mr. van Steen. Second, to the Hotel Crillon. Third, to Appletree Cottage, Cheriston. I want to talk to Miss Elizabeth Powers-Thompson.

Mr. van Steen, surprised, said, "What a very odd question. Let me see . . . now that you come to mention it . . . yes, that's right . . . so it was . . . I suppose he was busy at the time . . ."

Daffy, bored, said, "You again! My God . . . No. No, of course not. Not a word."

Miss Elizabeth Powers-Thompson placidly said, "Mr. Tibbett! What a very pleasant surprise. We did so enjoy meeting you and your wife. . . . Did I what? Now, how could you have known that, I wonder? Yes, as a matter of fact, I did. For old times' sake, I suppose . . . and because

I was . . . well, I was a little bothered by what my brother told me. I do hope I didn't cause any trouble. . . ."

Henry said, "And now we'd better ring Cook's. We're both going to England."

20

Again they were lucky. There was room for the car and two passengers on the night boat to Harwich. By half-past seven the Tibbetts were on the road again, heading southward toward London and Hindhurst. At eight Henry pulled up outside a transport café and suggested a stop for breakfast.

"I thought we were in too much of a hurry?" Emmy said.

Henry shook his head. "We've no hope of getting to Hindhurst Hospital by nine," he said. "What we need is a telephone. We may as well have something to eat at the same time."

The café was large and clean, if not elaborate, and produced an excellent fry-up and tea with the brisk efficiency demanded by its regular clientele of long-distance lorry drivers. There was also a telephone, and after some delay Henry succeeded in making contact with the Hindhurst Arms Hotel—if contact is the right word to describe a highly unsatisfactory conversation with an adenoidal girl whose vocabulary seemed confined to the single monosyllable "Wot?" In the end, however, she was persuaded to go in search of the proprietress. A long silence ensued, twice broken by the operator asking Henry if he had finished, and—when he said he had not—if he had begun. At last an angry female voice said, "Hello! Well, what do you want and who are you?"

"My name is Tibbett," said Henry apologetically. "I'd like to book a double room for tonight."

"Just the one night?" snapped the voice.

"I'm not sure. It might be longer."

"I could let you have number eight for the one night," said the voice grudgingly. "But if it was for longer, you'd have to move to number twelve. So long as you realize that."

"Perhaps we could start off in number twelve?" Henry suggested.

"Oh, no. No, I don't think you'd like number twelve. All those stairs. If you'd let me know sooner, I could have put you in number ten."

"Look," said Henry, "just keep us a couple of beds for tonight, will you?"

"There's no need to take that tone, I'm sure. I'm only trying to do you a favor."

"I'm sorry," said Henry, "but I'm rather in a hurry."

"So I should think, ringing at this hour." The proprietress sniffed. "What was the name again? Tipper?"

"Tibbett," said Henry.

"Mr. and Mrs.?"

"Of course."

"You could," said the voice scornfully, "have been two gentlemen."

"Well, I'm not," said Henry. "And now, may I speak to Dr. Massingham?"

"To who?"

"Dr. Massingham. One of your hotel guests."

"We've got no doctor staying here," said the voice with some indignation.

"You have, you know."

"You'll pardon me, Mr. Tipper, I think I may be allowed to know who is stopping in my hotel. Apart from regular guests, there's just one lady on her own."

"That's right. Dr. Sarah Massingham. May I please speak to her?"

"A *lady* doctor?" The proprietress sounded outraged.

"Well, she never told me, that's all I can say. She's in number seven."

"If I might speak to her—"

"All right, all right. Hold on." There was a clatter, followed by weird and echoing calls to someone by the name of Annie to fetch the lady from number seven.

After some minutes had passed, Henry was relieved to hear Sarah's voice, "Dr. Massingham speaking."

"Thank God. This is Henry."

"Henry! Where are you?"

"Somewhere in Essex. On our way to Hindhurst, but we haven't a hope of getting there before about eleven. Are you up?"

"Of course I'm up," said Sarah. "That's why the half-witted girl took such an age to find me. She was looking in my room, and all the time I was having breakfast a couple of feet away from the telephone. Now, what's all this?"

"I want you to listen carefully," said Henry. "First of all, ring Hindhurst Hospital and make sure that . . ." He spoke quickly and earnestly for a few minutes and then went back to the table, to find his eggs and bacon congealed and his tea cold. Another few minutes, and the Tibbetts were off again.

They skirted the worst of London, using the North Circular Road—and at times wondered if it might not have been quicker to go through the center of the city. Although it was Saturday, the lemming rush was in full spate, the suburbs pouring their millions in bus, tube, train, and car into the central sea. Making one's way across the wheel-spoke streams of traffic was rather like fording a river in full spate. It was ten o'clock when Henry thankfully steered the car clear of Putney and Roehampton and onto the comparatively tranquil Portsmouth Road; and well after eleven before he parked it in the yard of the Hindhurst Arms. There was no sign of Sarah's little red Triumph.

The owner of the telephone voice proved to be Mrs. Creely, the hotel proprietress. She was a handsome, authoritative woman who contrived to give the impression that her clients were a great nuisance, interrupting the real work of running the hotel. However, she showed Henry and Emmy into number eight—a pleasant room overlooking the garden—with a stern warning that if they wished to stay for more than one night they must brave the rigors of number twelve, which apparently was a back attic. About Dr. Massingham, Mrs. Creely was unhelpful.

"Miss Massingham? She's out, I think. I saw her driving off in that little car. No, indeed, Mr. Tipper, she left no message for you—of that I *am* sure. And now, if you've all you need . . . I'm very busy this morning."

Henry was puzzled. He had expected to find Sarah herself at the hotel; or, at the very least, a message. It was galling to have wrestled with London traffic and flogged his engine on motorways, in order to find—nothing. He hardly knew whether to be worried or exasperated.

In fact, he had misjudged Sarah. The first thing he saw on the reception desk was an envelope addressed to him in Sarah's bold hand. He pointed this out to Mrs. Creely, who was arranging flowers in the residents' lounge.

"A letter? I'm sure I knew nothing of it. On the reception desk? Oh, well, I suppose we had better go and look." Reluctantly abandoning her flowers, Mrs. Creely accompanied Henry to the desk. She put on her glasses, held the letter at arm's length for several seconds, and then said, "But this is addressed to a Mr. Tibbett."

"That's right," said Henry patiently. "That's me."

"Tipper, you said on the telephone. Distinctly. I wrote it down."

"My name is Tibbett." Henry's patience was wearing thin. "Do you want to see my passport?"

"Certainly not! What a suggestion! You should be capable of knowing what your own name is, I should hope. Well, you'd better take the letter." Mrs. Creely handed it to Henry with distaste.

Henry . . . Great haste. Phoned hospital as you said, but Dolly had already left. Seems a car came for her at eight o'clock. Chauffeur-driven, no sign of Duvals. Ward sister told me D. didn't know Duvals were here—they wanted it to be a surprise for her. In view of yr. instructions, have gone to Foxes' Trot myself. . . . Sarah.

The two cars nearly collided. Henry was just turning into the gateway of Foxes' Trot as the red Triumph drove out, with a worried-looking Sarah at the wheel. Her face broke into a relieved smile as she saw Henry and Emmy. She leaned out of the window and said, "Welcome. And I mean that."

"How are things?"

"I . . . I don't know. Where can we talk?"

"Is Dolly O.K.?"

Sarah hesitated. "I think so."

"Right," said Henry. "Drive on toward Plumley Green and pull off the road where you can. We'll follow you."

A few minutes later both cars were parked on the grassy verge, and Henry, Emmy, and Sarah were sitting on the ground under a clump of tall pine trees on a small hillock.

Sarah was talking. "They were both absolutely charming—the Duvals, I mean. I explained that as I had treated Dolly, I was naturally interested in the case, and so, as I happened to have another patient in Hindhurst Hospital, I'd inquired after Dolly and been told she'd been discharged. I thought she might be on her own, I said, so I'd looked in to see if there was anything I could do to help. It sounded pretty unconvincing to me, but they seemed to swallow it with no questions asked. Madame Duval asked me in and made coffee."

"Primrose did?"

"With her own fair hands."

"No—I mean, you're sure it was Primrose? You recognized her?"

"Of course I did."

"Oh, God," said Henry. "Then I'm all wrong."

"What do you mean?"

"Just that I had a perfectly lovely theory, and you've exploded it. Now I'll have to start again, damn it. So Primrose made coffee. Why not Mrs. Billing?"

Sarah frowned. "There was no sign of her at all. I think they've sent her away. I couldn't ask outright, of course, but I did my best—I said how lucky it was for Dolly that the Duvals were there, but what would happen when they left? To which Madame Duval said that they'd arranged for a woman from the village to come and live in after they'd gone. Then Dr. Duval came in, and he couldn't have been friendlier. Finally I asked if I could see Dolly. Of course, of course, he said—but that she was asleep. She was still very weak, and the trip from the hospital had tired her. Then he took me upstairs and into Dolly's room."

"Her old room?"

"No. She's in a different one now—a curious affair, all black."

"The one we had," said Emmy. "It's grim, isn't it?"

"I didn't get much of a look at it," said Sarah. "The curtains were drawn, and with that black wallpaper it was as dark as the grave. Dolly was lying in the bed, asleep. Her breathing sounded all right, and she didn't look too bad—one wouldn't expect her to be a picture of health. But whether she's sleeping naturally, or . . . I just don't know. It was so awkward. I couldn't start carrying out a clinical examination. Dr. Duval whispered that we'd better not wake her, and we all tiptoed out. After that there seemed no possible excuse for my staying any longer."

"Sarah," said Henry suddenly, "you've met Madame Duval before, haven't you?"

"Of course. That's to say—I saw her in the passage upstairs on the day Lady Balaclava died, when I was taking that sedative to Dolly. I didn't know which of the sisters she was at the time, of course."

"But later on, when you went to the Hindhurst Arms to discuss Dolly's case with Dr. Duval—you must have met her there."

Sarah shook her head. "No, she didn't appear. He said she'd gone to bed early because of a headache."

"By God," said Henry, "perhaps I wasn't wrong after all. Sarah, will you describe Primrose Duval to me?"

Sarah looked surprised. "I thought you knew her well?"

"Just describe her."

"Well—late thirties, I should think. Small and slim and very neat, with black hair and—"

"Violet!" Emmy cried.

"What?" Sarah's face was a mask of astonishment.

Henry said, "Precisely. The woman at Foxes' Trot is not Primrose Duval. She is Violet van der Hoven. I've been convinced of that ever since yesterday."

"But how on earth . . . what on earth . . . ?" Emmy began.

"That's the link, you see," said Henry.

"I simply don't understand," said Sarah.

"Then don't try," said Henry. "There's no time for explanations. The first thing, Sarah, is to get you away. You must not just go, you must be seen to go."

"Where to?"

"Anywhere. As far as possible." Henry thought for a moment. "Go back to the hotel, pack your things, and check out. Then ring Foxes' Trot and ask the Duvals to say good-bye to Dolly for you. Explain that you've just had a letter confirming the immediate offer of a job in . . . oh, it doesn't matter. Canada, Africa, Pakistan. Say that you're off to London now, and leaving the country next week. Then scram."

"Where to?"

Henry considered. Then he said, "Yes. Yes, of course. Thank God it's Saturday."

"What," said Sarah, "is that supposed to mean?"

"It means," said Henry, "that my assistant commissioner will be at his country cottage in Trimble Wells instead of behind his desk at Scotland Yard." He began to write rapidly in his notebook. When he had covered two pages, he tore them out, folded them up, and gave them to Sarah. "Take these to the A.C. Here's the address. You can't miss his cottage—turn right at the church, and it's the second house on the left, the one with the thatched roof. He'll know what to do."

"Suppose he's not there?"

"If he's somewhere around the village, find him. If by some ghastly chance he's not in Trimble Wells at all, you'll have to go to the Hindhurst police. Get Sandport—you remember him. Give him my note. The important thing after that is for you to stay put—either in the A.C.'s house or the Hindhurst police station. Don't put your nose outside until I come for you, and try not to be alone. You'd also better find a parking place where your car can't be seen from the road. No sense in advertising your presence."

"Honestly," said Sarah, "this is all a bit melodramatic, isn't it? I mean, there I was in Foxes' Trot a few minutes ago, quite alone and vulnerable, and all they did was to give me coffee."

"A few minutes ago," said Henry, "you weren't a menace to a murderer. At least, the murderer didn't think so. Very shortly, however, the murderer will realize just how dangerous you are. Now, hurry. I'll give you just half an hour to check out of the hotel and phone Dr. Duval. Then—"

"What are you going to do?" Sarah asked.

It was Emmy who answered. "We're going to Foxes' Trot," she said, "to prevent another murder. If we're not too late." She looked at Henry, "Right, darling?"

"Right."

21

The gardens of Foxes' Trot looked as serene and well tended as ever, the house was shabby and ludicrous. It seemed to Emmy incredible that it was only two weeks ago, to the day, that she and Henry had awakened in the Black Room, had met the Codworthy daughters and their husbands, had drunk White Ladies with Crystal Balaclava, and then watched her die in her own drawing room. It seemed even more incredible that a sinister shadow should lie over this peaceful, sunny place.

The saxophone fountain bubbled contentedly, throwing its lazy jet of water in a gentle curve, to fall back into the shallow pool. The azaleas and rhododendrons were making an even braver show than a fortnight ago, blazing with purple and gold and scarlet. Across the lawn, a slim, dark-haired woman was cutting roses and laying them in a trug basket. It was a typically English summer scene, the epitome of peace and graceful living. With a sense of utter unreality Emmy got out of the car.

Violet—for she was the rose-gatherer—had straightened and turned at the sound of wheels on the gravel. Now she came across the lawn, her expression a mixture of surprise and anxiety. However, she broke into a smile as she recognized them.

"Why, Mr. and Mrs. Tibbett! What a pleasant surprise! We—we weren't expecting visitors—and now you are our second callers of the day. That nice young woman doctor dropped in earlier on to ask after Dolly." Violet sounded perfectly composed and self-possessed.

"It's an unexpected pleasure for us to see you, Mrs. van der Hoven," said Henry as he took her outstretched hand. "They told us at the Hindhurst Arms that Dr. and Madame Duval were here, but not you."

Violet smiled again, steadily. "And now I suppose there will be a great scandal," she said. "Country people are terrible, aren't they?"

"You mean, Madame Duval isn't here?"

"No, no. Primmy is in Switzerland. It's all very simple. I had to come over to see Plunkett, the lawyer, and so it seemed only reasonable to come down and give Dolly a hand until she's up and about again. Edouard had a medical conference in London, and had the same charitable idea—so we shall both be here for a few days. Edouard has to get back to Switzerland on Tuesday, but I shall probably stay as long as Dolly needs me. Now, do come indoors and let me get you a drink."

It was smoothly done and entirely convincing. Emmy had to prevent herself from glancing at Henry to see his reaction. Henry said rather grimly, "Yes, Mrs. van der Hoven. I think we should go in and have a talk."

"I've been cutting a few roses to put in Dolly's room," said Violet as she led the way into the house. "She does so love flowers, poor old thing."

Before Henry or Emmy could reply, Edouard Duval came out of the drawing room to greet them. "Well, well, well. So you have discovered the guilty secret?" He laughed, enjoying the joke. "I saw your car arriving, but I was speaking on the telephone so I had to leave it to Violet to welcome you. You have explained to the chief superintendent, Violet, how we both happen to be here?" Was it Emmy's imagination, or did she detect a faint note of warning.

"Yes, indeed, Edouard," said Violet. "I've told them about your conference, and my meeting with Plunkett. I think I've convinced them that we're not a pair of middle-aged elopers."

"Good, good. Now, come in. By the way, my dear," Duval added as he stood back to let Emmy precede him into the drawing room, "that was Dr. Massingham on the telephone."

"Really? What did she want?"

"Just to say good-bye. It seems she is leaving us for good. She has been offered a job in Canada, and is off in a few days."

"How extraordinary," said Violet mildly. "She never mentioned it this morning. What will you drink, Mrs. Tibbett? Gin? Sherry?"

Emmy shook her head, and Henry said, "I think I should explain, Mrs. van der Hoven. This isn't a social call, I'm afraid."

Violet and Edouard exchanged a quick, alarmed glance. Henry went on, "You know who I am, of course. But as a matter of form, here's my official card. You'll doubtless think it strange that I have brought my wife along, but she is here as a chaperon, in the official sense. There was no policewoman available at Plumley Green."

Violet, who had gone as white as a sheet, instinctively moved closer to Edouard. The doctor stood facing Henry, stocky and immobile. Henry went on easily, "As you will have guessed, I have come to interview Miss Underwood-Threep."

"Dolly?" said Violet. It was a whisper.

"Yes." Henry turned to Edouard Duval. "I'm glad you are here to act as medical adviser, Doctor. You see, I shall have to ask the lady to accompany me to the police station to . . . to help us in our inquiries."

"She is too ill to be moved," said Dr. Duval without hesitation.

"She was discharged from hospital this morning," Henry pointed out.

"Traveling to her own home in a chauffeur-driven car is not the same thing as being arrested," said Duval. "I could not allow it."

"I didn't say I was going to arrest her," said Henry. He added, "At this stage."

It seemed to Emmy that the tension relaxed slightly. Henry went on, "I think that I owe you both an explanation. You are friends of Miss Underwood-Threep's, and you are here in her house. More important, you are both related to the late Lady Balaclava. When you have heard what I have to say, I think that you will agree to let me interview Miss Underwood-Threep. Shall we sit down? Cigarette?"

Edouard and Violet both shook their heads. They sat down, tense as coiled springs. Henry lit a cigarette slowly, leaned back in his armchair, took a long pull, and blew out a cloud of smoke. Violet watched it, fascinated, as it writhed toward the ceiling.

Henry said, "It's a long story, I'm afraid, and it goes back a long way. It starts, in fact, during Lady Balaclava's schooldays, when she made two great friends among her fellow pupils. Dolly Underwood-Threep and Elizabeth Powers-Thompson."

"Elizabeth Who?" Violet looked bewildered.

"Dr. Duval knows the lady," said Henry. "Don't you, Doctor? In fact, I believe she has been in touch with you quite recently—on the occasion of Lady Balaclava's death."

Edouard, expressionless, said, "I knew her at one time, yes."

"The three girls," Henry went on, "kept in touch after they left school, in spite of the fact that they were such different people. Elizabeth became a nurse, and never married. Dolly became a . . . a distinctive character. Both acted as foils for Crystal, the brilliant butterfly. So it was to them that she turned when, during the war, she contracted tuberculosis."

There was absolute silence in the room. The sunshine flickered on the pink glass of the cocktail cabinet. In the distance an aircraft droned. Henry said, "You knew this, of course?" The question was directed at both Violet and Edouard.

Violet bent her head slightly forward, so that she was looking down at her own tightly clasped hands. She said nothing. Edouard said, "Since you know already, Monsieur Superintendent, I will confirm that I knew of this illness. Not at the time, of course. Later, after the war." He glanced at Violet. "All this will come as new to you, Violet. Well . . . not quite all. You knew that I had encountered my Primrose when she was at the school for young ladies in Lausanne before the war. You knew I had visited your family in England. Then came the war, and all was separated. Primrose and her sisters went across the Atlantic for safety. We wrote letters to each other. I completed my medical studies and joined the staff of the clinic where I still work. It must have been in 1947 that I received a letter from this Dr. Powers-Thompson. He told me he was a lung specialist—this, of course, I knew already. His name was internationally famous in that field. He said that he was treating Lady Balaclava, who had been suffering from tuberculosis for several years, and whose condition was grave. He had heard of the so-called wonder drug streptomycin, which had been used so successfully in the States and was now available in Switzerland but not in England. He thought that it might save her life, and he asked me if I could procure it."

There was a short silence, and then Henry said, "And you did?"

"Yes. I arranged to visit England—Primrose and I were engaged by then—and I brought a supply with me. After that, I came over frequently, bringing streptomycin each time. Lady Balaclava recovered. Primrose and I became married."

"And it was on these visits that you met Elizabeth Powers-Thompson?" said Henry.

"That is correct. Lady Balaclava had a horror of being ill, of being an object of sympathy, and so she insisted on keeping all knowledge of her disease from her family. Violet is now hearing of it for the first time—is that not so, Violet?"

Violet nodded. She said, almost in a whisper, "When we came home from Canada, she wouldn't see us. I thought . . . I thought it was because she hated us. She had sent us away, which was bad enough—and then, when we came back, she made us live in a rented flat in London. She wouldn't have us down here. She wouldn't have anybody . . . except Dolly." The last two words came out as a sort of hiss.

Edouard Duval shrugged and smiled at Henry. "Oh, to be a psychiatrist," he said, his voice edged with wry humor. "You see how Violet developed a complex because she thought her mother had rejected her, while all the time Lady Balaclava's only thought was to spare her daughters the worry and pain of her illness. Crystal—forgive me, I always called her so—Crystal tried to stop me from telling Primrose, even. Of course I did so, but Crystal never knew that. The only people in the secret were Dolly, who lived here to nurse Crystal. Powers-Thompson, her doctor, and his sister, Elizabeth, who was a qualified nurse and who also spent a lot of time here. And, of course, myself. That is how I came to know Miss Elizabeth."

Henry nodded. "And then?"

"And then—what? Nothing. The miracle happened—she was cured. Primrose and I married. The Powers-Thompsons disappeared from our lives. Nothing is left but one permanent psychological scar." Edouard Duval looked steadily at Violet, who put one white hand briefly to her eyes and then back to her lap. "I think, Superintendent," said Edouard, "that it is for you to take up the story now."

"Yes," said Henry. "As you say—nothing happened. But another scar was left—another invisible scar. Owing to the intensive treatment she had been given, Crystal Balaclava developed a hypersensitivity to streptomycin. As you must know, Doctor, this allergy develops slowly after the intensive treatment ceases. For some time now, even a minute amount of streptomycin would have been enough to cause definite symptoms in Lady Balaclava, and the small quantity known medically as a massive dose would undoubtedly kill her."

Edouard Duval had gone very pale. He stroked his chin and said, "Indeed. Most interesting. We have heard of these rare cases, although they do not fall precisely within my province."

"Let us now turn," said Henry blandly, "to the question of Lady Balaclava's will. You both know its provisions too well for me to go over them again. Four people stood to benefit. Mrs. Swasheimer—who is amply provided for in any case. Madame Duval, to whom the same applies— does it not, Doctor?"

Edouard Duval raised a feeble smile. "Of course," he said.

"And Mrs. van der Hoven, who is clearly a lady to whom extravagant living is not important."

Violet bent her head even lower and said nothing.

Henry went on. "The husbands of these ladies, we can disregard, as precautions had been taken legally to prevent them from acquiring their wives' fortunes. In any case, Lady Balaclava would not live forever. Sooner or later her daughters would benefit, and they knew it. Meanwhile, they visited their mother exactly once a year, on her birthday. All were living comfortably. Now, I am a policeman, and I have to deal in possibilities and probabilities. The idea that any of Lady Balaclava's daughters or sons-in-law might decide to murder her was clearly ludicrous. I ruled it out at once."

There was no doubt now about the relaxation in tension. Even Violet raised her eyes and unclasped her hands. Edouard leaned back and lit a small cigar.

"So—?" he said.

"We are left with the fourth beneficiary," said Henry. "Miss Underwood-Threep. Unlike the others, an unsuspected beneficiary. Unlike the others, she lived with Lady Balaclava, day in, day out. She had to endure the uncertainties of her friend's capricious temperament. She was treated somewhere between a pet dog and a servant. She was given a miserable bedroom and expected to do all the work of the house and garden. She got no thanks for all the years of patient nursing during Crystal's illness. All this she endured, uncomplainingly . . . because, as she thought, she had no alternative. She had no money of her own, and would inherit none. In a very real sense, Lady Balaclava's life was her life. She knew that she was disliked by Crystal's daughters"—Violet's eyes went down to her lap again—"and she would be turned out of this house when her mistress died. She, of all people in the world, had reason to wish long life to Crystal Balaclava." Henry paused. "Until, of course, she found out."

"Found out?" echoed Duval.

"About the provision of the will. That Crystal had been playing a cruel game with her all these years. That, in fact, she stood to inherit not only this house, but money and jewelry as well. That she would gain immensely by Lady Balaclava's death."

Edouard Duval leaned forward in his chair. "You think she found this out?"

"I am sure of it."

"How?"

"I have to use a little guesswork here. Certainly not from Plunkett. But there is an important link which we must now inspect. The link between Dolly Underwood-Threep and Dr. Anthony Griffiths."

"Griffiths? Who is this Griffiths?"

"Lady Balaclava's regular physician. A young doctor who recently set up in general practice in Hindhurst. He was a frequent visitor to this house and struck up close friendships with both Lady Balaclava and Miss Underwood-Threep. He gained the confidence of both women, and both told him secrets. I think my wife will agree with me that when we saw all three of them here, the day before Lady Balaclava died, it was quite plain that the two elderly ladies were competing for Dr. Griffiths' attention. Each, I am sure, tried to make herself more interesting by producing tidbits of information. Miss Underwood-Threep told him the secret of Lady Balaclava's tuberculosis and its treatment. Lady Balaclava told him the secret of her unsuspected legacy to Dolly.

"As for Griffiths himself, he must have summed them up accurately. Crystal Balaclava, the eternal coquette, was as hard as nails and would never part with a brass farthing. Dolly, the apparent amazon, was soft under the surface. Once let her inherit, and he would be on to a very good thing indeed."

"If this is true," said Duval, "then you should be arresting this Griffiths, not poor Dolly."

Henry shook his head. "Moral judgments are one thing," he said. "Facts are another. Griffiths, we must presume, told Dolly about the will. He carried out an unobtrusive test with streptomycin to prove that Lady Balaclava was sensitive to it. He then told Dolly quite casually, that the smallest whiff of it would kill Crystal, leaving no detectable trace. He then made it simple for her to help herself to the stuff in his surgery. He may be morally guilty, but he committed no crime—and he carefully arranged to be out of the country at the moment when he was reasonably sure the murder attempt would be made. There is nothing we can charge him with. Miss Underwood-Threep, on the other hand—"

Violet spoke for the first time. "Dolly fainted when she heard about her legacy," she said.

Henry looked at Edouard Duval and raised his eyebrows slightly. "She *appeared* to faint," he said. "Dr. Duval, you attended her. Was that a genuine faint?"

Edouard Duval hesitated. "She was in a state of shock," he said at last. "Understandable, in the circumstances . . . poor Dolly. I don't like to tell tales out of school."

"You mean, you knew all along that she was bluffing?"

Duval sighed. "You have said it, Superintendent. Not I. But—"

"Her recent illness was no bluff," said Violet quite sharply.

"No, no. That was parathion poisoning, brought on by exposing her skin, which was affected by dermatitis, to contact with a parathion insecticide. The insecticide which you brought from Holland, Mrs. van der Hoven."

Violet's hand went to her mouth. "Oh, *no!*"

"Which you brought," Henry pointed out, "at Dolly's own request. She engineered this illness herself, so as to avoid awkward questioning."

"She very nearly killed herself," said Duval thoughtfully.

"Yes." Henry paused. "Perhaps she would not have minded greatly if she had died. She killed Lady Balaclava out of emotional spite, I think, and not really for the sake of the inheritance. Afterward . . . well, one must feel a little sorry for her. She may even have wished to commit suicide, but she failed. The doctors at Hindhurst Hospital were too good for her. And now I am here, and the real unpleasantness will start for the poor creature." He stood up. "I think and hope I have made it clear, Dr. Duval, that I must see her at once, and take her away from here for questioning."

Duval stood up. "As a doctor," he said, "I cannot allow it."

"As a policeman," said Henry, "I must insist."

Edouard Duval sighed. He said, "I see there is nothing for it. I fear I have not been entirely frank with you, Superintendent."

"You haven't?"

"No. I understand now, of course, why the poor woman did it. Before, I imagined it was accidental."

"What are you talking about?" asked Henry sharply.

"This morning, Dolly attempted to take her own life."

"She's not dead?"

"No." Duval paused. "Perhaps, in view of what you have told us, it would be better if she was. I have been using all my skill to save her."

"How did she make this suicide attempt?"

"The most usual way. An overdose of sleeping pills. I found her, soon after she had arrived from the hospital and been put to bed here. She was in a coma, with the empty bottle of pills beside her. Naturally, I took immediate steps. She was still in a deep sleep when Dr. Massingham arrived. I said nothing of the matter. I did not wish to cause trouble for the poor creature." He paused again. "She is, I think, still sleeping now. You may, if you wish, come up and see for yourself. She is in no condition to answer your questions."

"I should like to see her," said Henry.

Duval led the way out of the drawing room. Emmy, Violet, and Henry followed him. On the stairs Duval stopped and said to Violet, "But we are forgetting that it is Saturday."

"Saturday?" Violet repeated vaguely.

"All this is most distressing," said Dr. Duval, "but we really do not need you in the sickroom, Violet, and the business of living must go on. You were about to go to the village, were you not, to make the shopping for the weekend? Tomorrow, all shops will be closed. I think you should go now. Take my car."

"Very well, Edouard," said Violet.

"You might look in at the Hindhurst Arms and say good-bye to Dr. Massingham, if she has not already left."

"Yes, Edouard." Like a slim, dark ghost, Violet turned and walked down the stairs and out of the front door. The other three went up to the Black Room. At the door, Dr. Duval paused for a moment, apparently fiddling with the handle. Then he led the way in.

It was just as Sarah had described it—as dark as a tomb, with stray streaks of sunshine struggling through the gaps between the curtains, to make fingers of patterned light on the black walls. Between the black sheets, Dolly lay like an effigy. Henry could see that she was breathing strongly. He stepped up to the bed and picked up one of the big, work-roughened hands. It was very cold. Dolly did not stir.

Henry said loudly, "Poor woman. I see what you mean. However, you say that she is out of danger."

Edouard Duval shrugged. "For the moment. If she continues to receive expert care. But who can say? Normally, she is a strong, healthy woman—but her constitution has been weakened by her recent illness. No, Superintendent, on reflection I cannot say that she is out of danger."

"If she should die, Dr. Duval—would not your position be a little awkward?"

"I think not. Of course, I would inform the coroner of

what I told you just now—that she took her own life. Violet will confirm this."

"But," Henry pointed out, "you would be asked why you did not inform a doctor."

Duval smiled. "My dear sir, I am a doctor. I have done all possible."

"As much as a hospital could have done?"

"Certainly."

In the pause that followed, Henry heard the sound of wheels in the drive outside. He went to the window, pulled back the curtain, and looked out. Then, turning back to face the doctor, he said, "Ah, well, we must all hope for her recovery, mustn't we? In any case, Dr. Duval, you will not need to concern yourself with Dolly any longer."

"What do you mean, Superintendent?"

"Just that the ambulance is here," said Henry. "Since she had been so ill, I naturally ordered an ambulance so that she could be moved to hospital under police guard after I had questioned her. I didn't anticipate, of course, that she would be unconscious, but I thought it a wise precaution. And so it has turned out to be." Downstairs, the front-door bell rang its grisly chime. "Perhaps you'd be kind enough to let the ambulance men in, doctor. And tell them they'll need a stretcher."

Edouard Duval said, "I really cannot allow my patient to be moved."

Henry stood quite still. With his eyes on Duval he said, "Emmy, darling, go down and open the front door, will you?"

Emmy did not answer, but slipped quietly and quickly out of the room, shutting the door behind her. Dr. Duval glanced after her. Then he said with a smile, "Very well, Superintendent. Against my medical conscience, I shall bow to bureaucracy. I shall write a statement."

"A statement?"

"Which I shall require you to sign. Stating that Miss Underwood-Threep is being moved against my advice, and entirely on your responsibility."

"I shall be pleased to sign it," said Henry.

"I shall also give the poor lady an injection, which will help her to survive the journey. You have no objection?"

"None," said Henry. "You travel with a full medical kit, do you?"

"A full kit, no. But certain basic requirements—in case of emergencies . . ." Duval had gone into the black bathroom, and spoke over his shoulder. Henry saw that he had opened a large, flat briefcase, fitted out inside with medical impedimenta. As he spoke, the doctor broke a plastic ampul and transferred its contents into a hypodermic syringe. "There. That should make things a little easier for her. As I have already said, I cannot approve of your conduct, Superintendent, but . . ."

Henry moved a step closer to the bed. He could hear the sound of feet coming up the stairs. Edouard Duval came out of the bathroom, syringe in hand.

"Now—if you would just step aside, Superintendent—"

"No," said Henry.

"I beg your pardon?"

"I said no," Henry remarked equably. The door handle rattled from the outside. Raising his voice, Henry called, "Come in!"

Duval said, "I am afraid they cannot, Superintendent. Not until the door is opened from the inside. Did you not realize? It was a whim of my late mother-in-law's. I dare say the catch was fixed in the open position when you stayed here, but normally these doors open only from the inside without a key—like hotel rooms, you know. As soon as I have given the injection—"

With a gentle smile, Duval stepped up to the bedside. Henry shouted, with all the decibels at his disposal, "Break down the door!" Then he launched himself at Duval. The doctor was surprisingly strong and agile—nor did he seem surprised at the attack. As the sounds of hammering increased outside the bedroom door, inside the struggle went on in grim silence.

To Henry's surprise, Duval did not make any attempt to get at Dolly. On the contrary, he fell back at once under Henry's onslaught, taking the latter off his balance. Then

Henry realized what he was trying to do. He was trying to pin Henry down, so that he could administer to him the contents of the syringe prepared for Dolly.

Outside, men shouted and banged ineffectually. Duval had Henry's right arm now, gripped in one strong hand. The other held the syringe, which Henry was desperately trying to ward off with his left arm. As the two men swayed together, locked in nightmare combat, Duval called out in a remarkably steady voice, "I'm just coming. I fear the superintendent is unwell—"

Henry, his left arm near breaking point, kicked out with his right foot, trying to shake Duval's balance. But it was useless. As Henry's grip gradually weakened, the needle of the syringe, like a snake's tongue, crept nearer and nearer to his exposed right wrist. Another few millimeters, and it would touch his skin. He couldn't hold it off any longer. And then . . .

And then there was a shattering of glass behind Duval, and a large man in the uniform of an ambulance attendant leaped through the broken window and pinioned Edouard Duval expertly from behind. Another man followed, and another. Wildly, Duval pressed the plunger of the syringe, but the liquid shot haphazardly out onto the carpet.

Henry stood still for a moment, rubbing his wrist where the syringe would have penetrated it, where he could almost feel its sharp, pricking sting. Then he walked over to the door and opened it. Emmy, who was still belaboring the door with her shoe to divert attention from the attack through the window, caught him a neat blow across the nose before she fell into his arms.

22

It was two days later. Dolly had been moved from the
Black Room, with its gaping, glassless window, into the
white shell of the Syrie Maugham Room, where she now
sat up in bed looking remarkably cheerful, with a glass of
champagne in her hand. Henry and Emmy sat on one side
of the bed, Doctors Sarah Massingham and Tony Griffiths
on the other, and each held a full glass—which accounted
neatly for the first bottle. A second stood in an ice bucket
on the bedside table.

"Your very good health, Miss Underwood-Threep," said
Henry. "And here's to a quick recovery."

"Dolly to you. And I'm as right as rain. No need to stay
in bed."

Sarah and Tony began a simultaneous protest. "Oh, all
right, all right," Dolly conceded, taking a good swig from
her glass. "But you chaps don't half fuss. Not that I'm not
grateful," she added gruffly. "Wouldn't be here at all, by
all accounts, if it hadn't been for you."

"If it hadn't been for Henry," said Sarah.

"And for Sarah and for Emmy," said Henry. "Sarah did
the medical sleuthwork. I'd never have begun to suspect
the truth without her. And as for Emmy"—he squeezed
her hand—"if she hadn't got out of that death trap of a
Black Room and let the police in, neither Dolly nor I
would have lived to tell the tale."

"Talking of telling the tale," remarked Tony Griffiths,
"I wish somebody would tell *me* what's been going on on

my own doorstep. Seems I can't even take a week's holiday without all hell breaking loose. Sarah's told me the outline—about the streptomycin allergy and all that—but there seem to be a lot of loose ends. How did you know it was Duval and Violet who killed Crystal?"

Henry said, "Yes, there are some gaps to fill in. Some I don't even know myself. Dolly will have to supply the missing pieces of the jigsaw."

"Me? Why me?"

"For a start," said Henry, "how and when did you find out about Edouard Duval and Violet?"

"What makes you think I found out?" demanded Dolly, red-faced.

"Because it's the only explanation for what happened later."

"Well, you're right, of course. It was last year, on Crys's birthday. The usual family gathering. Primrose had gone into Hindhurst to shop, and Piet was helping me in the greenhouse. Edouard had announced that he was going for a stroll in the garden, and Violet was supposed to be lying down indoors. Well, I found I was out of garden twine, so I left Piet in the greenhouse and went to the kitchen to get some. As I was coming back, I heard them—Vi and Edouard—on the other side of the rose-garden hedge. I didn't overhear much, but it was enough." Dolly snorted. "Enough to tell me they were lovers. That didn't surprise me."

"It didn't?" Emmy asked.

"Certainly not. Nor you, Tibbett, I imagine," Dolly added.

"No," Henry agreed. "Anybody could see that Violet was bored to death by Piet, and by her provincial life in Holland. Anybody could see that Primrose was a cold fish but had her fist tightly fastened on the purse strings. A great disappointment to Edouard, who had probably married her for her money—or at least, her eventual inheritance. Duval was a passionate man—and not only over women. His work, too. When he realized once and for all that he would never get a penny out of Primrose for his research center, or anything else, he looked around for another heiress—and found Violet. She was utterly infatuated by him and would have happily handed all her money over to him. Her husband couldn't lay hands on it—but her lover might have. Charlie Codworthy never thought of that. The trouble was that Lady Balaclava showed no signs of dying."

"Edouard's very words, that day last year," said Dolly. "Violet said something, half-joking, about pushing her under a bus. It was then that Edouard said, very quietly, 'No, no. Nothing so crude.' Then he laughed and said, 'I have been planning to kill your mother for some time.' Vi said, 'Oh, don't be silly, Edouard'—and he said, 'I am not being silly, I assure you. I would have done it some time ago, but—' And then he stopped."

"Meaning," said Henry, "that he had discovered it wouldn't do him any good. Primrose wasn't going to part with a sou."

"Exactly. Then he went off onto a new line with Violet . . . how they must be patient, how they could do nothing about the situation while Crys was alive, and so on. It was perfectly obvious," Dolly added, "that he was working her up to the idea of killing Crys."

"He didn't go into details?"

"No, no. It was all vague—almost joking, as I told you. But I was scared. I knew Edouard wouldn't stop at murder, if it suited him. But what could I do? Crys would have laughed at me, and called me a silly old—well, she could be unkind, you know. Edouard and Violet would simply have laughed it off. The police would have written me off as a cranky old woman—wouldn't they?" she added accusingly, looking straight at Henry.

Henry grinned. "I expect so."

"So what could I do?"

"What you did," said Henry. "You knew Crystal very well indeed. She'd have laughed at a warning from you, but she was impressed by a spirit message purporting to come from her late husband. You got her interested in table-turning and did a little judicious pushing of the tooth mug. Why did you go to such lengths to deny that you had anything to do with it?"

Dolly reddened. "I don't like to admit it," she said, "but I was frightened of Duval. I wanted to warn Crys, but I didn't want anybody to know that the warning came from me. I knew he'd stop at nothing."

"You were perfectly right," said Henry grimly. "So you warned Crystal, and she was impressed, as you hoped. She sent for me. And a fat lot of use I was."

"Nobody could have stopped it," Sarah broke in. "It was the perfect murder. The miracle is that you solved it in the end."

"You're very kind," said Henry, "but that didn't help Crystal. However, to get on. Dolly was quite right—Duval did get Violet to help him. Whether or not she knew at the beginning that she was conniving at murder, we shall never know. You heard about Violet?"

Dolly nodded. "Crashed the car," she said. "Killed outright. Was it deliberate?"

"Who knows? Either it was deliberate, or she was in such a wrought-up state that she simply missed the corner. Anyhow, what Edouard Duval asked her to do was quite simple and not at all illegal. She was to get hold of some streptomycin spray—which Piet never uses—and spray her mother's birthday roses with it. Mr. van Steen, Piet's neighbor and another market gardener, confirmed to me that it was Violet and not Piet who borrowed the spray. Since Violet didn't know about her mother's illness, and many Dutch growers use streptomycin as a preservative for roses, I think we must give her the benefit of the doubt and assume that she didn't know what she was doing. Later, of course, she found out. That was why she was so upset when Lady Balaclava died. And why she dared not disobey Duval in anything."

"Duval himself kept out of the way on Crystal's birthday," said Emmy. "Why did he come over afterward?"

"Primrose telephoned him, as we know. She told him we were here, and that worried him. He liked to have everything exactly calculated, and we were no part of his plan. Violet could not be relied upon—she might break down and talk. So he came, and found a situation far from his liking. I was poking my nose in where it wasn't wanted, and he began to get definite suspicions about Dolly. He didn't know, of course, that she had overheard his year-old conversation with Violet; but he did know that Dolly was in on the secret of Crystal's streptomycin treatment, and he knew she was an old friend of the Powers-Thompsons. They sent a wreath to the funeral, and it was likely they'd get in touch with Dolly. Between them, they might add up two and two, and make four.

"Edouard Duval decided that Dolly should be put out of the way—not permanently, just until the fuss had died down. He knew that she was using parathion spray in her greenhouse, and, as a doctor, that her dermatitis would make it very dangerous if it came in contact with her skin. It was a piece of luck for him that Piet had brought over—at Dolly's own request—a sample of a similar but even more deadly insecticide."

"What about the Flyaway tin we found in the kitchen?" Emmy asked.

"That must have been planted by Violet, at Edouard's request, to throw suspicion on to Dolly, should any awkward questions be asked."

"Didn't I say so?" Dolly demanded indignantly.

"Anyhow, Duval gave Dolly a strong sedative—a perfectly reasonable thing to do, as Sarah pointed out—and then instructed Violet to sprinkle a little of the insecticide powder over the bed while Dolly was sleeping, when she went in to say good-bye. His plan worked beautifully. Dolly became more and more ill, and eventually was taken off to hospital, where she couldn't be questioned. Emmy and I went back to London. The police doctors had certified 'natural causes.' All was serene."

"So what went wrong?" asked Tony Griffiths.

"Elizabeth Powers-Thompson," said Henry. "I tracked her down—that's to say, I tracked down her brother, and I met Elizabeth. Talk about old times, and Crystal's recent death, quite naturally prompted her to get in touch with

Dolly again. She found that she couldn't, because Dolly was in hospital. So instead, she wrote to Edouard Duval, whom she had known well after the war, and who was still working at the same clinic in Lausanne. In her letter she mentioned that Emmy and I had been to see her brother and that I was investigating Lady Balaclava's death.

"This was serious news for Duval. It meant that I was on the trail, and I must not be allowed to speak to Dolly—ever. So Dolly had to go. I think he had arranged his assignation with Violet previously—they had to meet privately to discuss future plans. Duval invented a conference in Paris, and Violet invented a call from Plunkett—both of which fictions were quite easily exploded. The institute in Paris knew nothing of Duval's visit, and Daffodil had received no summons from Plunkett. Nor had Primrose. There'd be no reason for him to confer with one sister and not the others.

"Once in England, however, Duval's purpose turned to sterner matters—the elimination of Dolly. He was in a tricky position. He and Violet could establish themselves here. They could fetch Dolly from hospital. Duval could kill her at his leisure—except that he must produce a watertight explanation for her death. Dolly, of course, didn't know they were here—"

"I'll say I didn't," said Dolly. "By God, d'you think I'd have come back here with that precious pair in residence, if I'd known? When I found they were here, I nearly died—" She gave a bark of laughter. "No pun intended. I really did nearly die. Edouard gave me some pernicious injection. I fought him—but Violet helped him, and he's very strong. I thought I was done for then. But Henry says it was only a sleeping draft."

"Yes. He kept Dolly under heavy sedation while he decided how to finish her off—probably by a series of small overdoses. I had guessed all this—but I couldn't act officially, and I had nothing that looked like real proof. So I had to smoke him out."

"You certainly succeeded," said Sarah. "But how, exactly?"

"First, I sent you off to the assistant commissioner with a letter," said Henry. "That letter explained the position, and asked him to send an ambulance to Foxes' Trot, with a strong-arm squad disguised as ambulance men, so that at least I could get Dolly away and out of danger. Then Emmy and I walked in here with a preposterous story about having come to arrest Dolly for Crystal's murder."

"You did *what*?" Dolly exploded. "Of all the bloody-cheek—!"

"I'm sorry," said Henry. "It was the only way. I also took your name in vain, Dr. Griffiths, for which I apologize. The whole fiction was pretty weak, but Duval fell for it, as I knew he would."

"How could you know?" asked Griffiths.

"I gave him exactly the letout he was praying for. I hinted that Dolly, in a fit of remorse, might be contemplating suicide. An overdose. Perfect, from his point of view. He agreed enthusiastically. We both decided that Dolly's original fainting fit was a fraud—"

"That's a damned lie," Dolly remarked.

"Of course. But Duval leaped at the bait. I gave him a dream setup—the suicide which he had tried to prevent, but alas . . . and perhaps for the best, after all . . . If he had been a little more perceptive and a little less keen on neat arrangements, he might have smelled a rat—but he didn't. He sent Violet away, because he doubted if she would stand by and watch him inject Dolly with poison—that is, with a gross overdose on top of the sedatives she'd been having. The ambulance arrived in the nick of time, and Emmy went down to meet it, thank God. I didn't know, of course, about the one-way lock on the door.

"Duval, of course, couldn't afford to let Dolly out of the house alive. When he realized that I was going to stop him from injecting her, he changed his tactics, in a last desperate effort. If he could have put me out of action—even temporarily—he could have finished Dolly off before he let the ambulance men into the room. He'd have had some sort of medical explanation to account for my unconsciousness—and when I eventually came to, who would ever believe me? Without Dolly's testimony, and with the coroner's verdict on Crystal—well, you can see for yourselves. As it was, I was able to force him into the sort of violent action which would condemn him. And to save Dolly."

"Your priorities," said Dolly, "seem dubious to me. Well, come on, chaps. You, young Griffiths. Let go of Sarah's hand, and open up the second bottle. And someone had better put a couple more on ice."

EPILOGUE

Chief Superintendent and Mrs. Henry Tibbett thank Miss Dorothy Underwood-Threep for her kind invitation to a pajama party in a captive spacecraft in the grounds of Foxes' Trot, Plumley Green, on September 9, on the occasion of the engagement of Dr. Anthony Griffiths to Dr. Sarah Massingham. They have much pleasure in accepting, and will bring no flowers, by request.

AFTERWORD

Acknowledgments are usually made at the beginning of a book; but obviously I could not record my enormous debt to Dr. Pierre Dorolle, and his colleagues at the World Health Organization, without giving away the whole plot of this book. So they have had to wait until now to receive my most sincere thanks.

Needless to say, all the characters in this book are pure fiction—but the medical facts are true. The real-life case occurred some years ago in Italy, where a middle-aged lady fell suddenly and mysteriously ill with symptoms of asphyxia, circulatory collapse, and other manifestations of acute poisoning. I am glad to say that, in her case, medical aid was immediately to hand, and her life was saved.

Italian law, however, required this case of apparent poisoning to be reported to the police, and Professor Penso, the director of the Department of Microbiology of the Istituto Superiore di Sanità, was appointed to carry out the investigation.

What followed was a fascinating piece of real-life medical detection. No trace of poison of any sort could be found—and I am assured by my medical friends that, had the unfortunate lady died, a post-mortem examination would have revealed precisely nothing. Professor Penso, however, refused to accept defeat. He traced back the lady's medical history and discovered that she had at one time suffered from tuberculosis and been treated twice with streptomycin, the second series, having been interrupt-

ed after an "accident." Although sensitivity to streptomycin is rare, Penso was convinced that he had found the
clue. He began to search for evidence of streptomycin in
the house at the time of the lady's collapse. Was anybody
in the house ill at the time and being treated with the
drug?

The lady herself emphatically asserted that everybody
had been perfectly well. She remembered this, she said, because it had been her birthday, and the whole family had
been celebrating it with her when her husband arrived
with a large bunch of roses for her. It was just after smelling them that she had collapsed.

This led the professor to suspect sensitivity to rose pollen; but the lady assured him that she frequently had roses
in the house, with no ill effects. So, with considerable difficulty, Professor Penso traced the history of this particular
bunch of flowers. They had been bought from a most exclusive shop in Rome, and the shop was able to identify
the suppliers. Professor Penso contacted this firm and was
astonished to her that their roses were routinely sprayed
with streptomycin to prevent bacterial decay. Tests proved
that the lady was, in fact, suffering from an allergy to
streptomycin, and had undergone severe anaphylactic
shock due to the minute quantity of streptomycin which
she inhaled when smelling the roses. In her case, of course,
the whole affair was purely accidental.

This was the story told to me by Dr. Pierre Dorolle, the
deputy director general of the World Health Organization
and my very good neighbor in Switzerland. Since then he
and his colleagues have shown endless patience with my
clumsy lack of expertise, putting me right on all medical
matters and taking endless trouble to find authentic medical facts which would fit into the fiction of my plot.
Merely to thank them is quite inadequate. For once, it is
perfectly true to say that without Dr. Dorolle and his colleagues, this book could not possibly have been written.

P.M.

AN OCCULT NOVEL OF UNSURPASSED TERROR

EFFIGIES

BY **William K. Wells**

Holland County was an oasis of peace and beauty . . .
until beautiful Nicole Bannister got a horrible package that triggered a nightmare,
until little Leslie Bannister's invisible playmate vanished and Elvida took her place,
until Estelle Dixon's Ouija board spelled out the message: I AM COMING—SOON.

A menacing pall settled over the gracious houses and rank decay took hold of the lush woodlands. Hell had come to Holland County —to stay.

A Dell Book $2.95 (12245-7)

Dell Bestsellers